two novels by

I. Compton-Burnett

A Family and a Fortune

and

More Women than Men

(previously unpublished in this country)

SIMON AND SCHUSTER
NEW YORK   1965

A Family
and a Fortune

"JUSTINE, I have told you that I do not like the coffee touched until I come down. How can I remember who has had it, and manage about the second cups, if it is taken out of my hands? I don't know how many times I have asked you to leave it alone."

"A good many, Mother dear, but you tend to be rather a laggard. When the poor boys sit in thirsty patience it quite goes to my heart."

"It would not hurt them to wait a few minutes. Your father and your uncle are not down yet. There is no such hurry."

Mrs. Gaveston dealt with the coffee with small, pale, stiff hands, looking with querulous affection at her children and signing in a somewhat strained manner to the servant to take the cups. She had rather uncertain movements and made one or two mistakes, which she rectified with a sort of distracted precision. She lifted her face for her children's greetings with an air of forgetting the observance as each one passed, and of being reminded of it by the next. She was a rather tall, very pale woman of about sixty, who somehow gave the impression of being small, and whose spareness of build was without the wiriness supposed to accompany it. She had wavy, grey hair, a long, narrow chin, long, narrow, dark eyes in a stiff, narrow, handsome face, and a permanent air of being held from her normal interest by some passing strain or distraction.

Her only daughter and eldest child was shorter and stronger in build, with clear, light eyes, a fuller face, pleasant features which seemed to be without a plan, and a likeness to her mother which was seen at once to overlie a great difference. She looked as much less than her thirty years as her mother looked more than her double number. Strangers often took Blanche for her children's grandmother, a fact which she had not suspected and would not have believed. She considered that she looked young for her age, or rather assumed that she did so, as she also took it for granted that she was successful, intelligent and admired, an attitude which came from a sort of natural buoyancy and had little meaning. She really gave little thought to herself and could almost be said to live for others. Her children had for her a lively, if not the deepest affection, and she was more than satisfied with it. She would hardly have recognised the deepest feeling, as she had never experienced or inspired it.

The three sons kissed their mother and returned to their seats. The eldest was a short, solid young man of twenty-eight, with large, grey eyes, the dark, curly hair his mother had had in her youth, a broader, blunter but perhaps more attractive face, and an air of being reasonably at peace with himself and his world. The second, Clement, was taller and thinner, with straight hair and darker skin, and looked the same age as Mark, although two years younger. He had cold, dark eyes, a cold, aloof expression, and a definite resemblance in feature to his mother. He seemed to look what he was, and neither to require nor repay observation. Aubrey, the youngest by eleven years, was a boy of fifteen, small and plain to the point of being odd and undersized, with a one-sided smile which often called for the abused term of grin, an indefinable lack of balance in movement, and a reputed backwardness which did not actually extend beyond his books. They had all been named after godparents from whom their mother had vague expectations for them. The expectations had not materialised, but Blanche had been too indefinite about them to resent it, or even actually to imagine their doing so, and felt less disappointment than vague appreciation that they had been possible.

Justine and Mark conversed with goodwill and ate with an ordinary appetite; Clement did not converse and showed an excellent one; Blanche watched her children's plates and made as good a meal as she could without giving her attention to it; and Aubrey sat and swung his feet and did not speak or eat.

"Are you not enjoying your breakfast, my dear?" said Blanche, in a faintly outraged and incredulous manner, which was possibly due to surprise that this should happen again after so many times.

Aubrey gave her a smile, or gave a smile in her direction. The smile seemed to relate to his own thoughts, and did so.

"Wake up, little boy," said Justine, leaning across to tap his shoulder.

Her brother gave a smile of another kind, intended to show that he was at ease under this treatment.

"If I have some toast, perhaps I shall grow tall enough to go to school."

Aubrey's life at home with a tutor was a source of mingled embarrassment and content, and the hope that he would eventually go to Eton like his brothers was held by everyone but himself. Everyone knew his age of fifteen, but he alone realised it, and knew that the likelihood of a normal school life was getting less. Blanche regarded him as a young child, Justine as a slightly older one, Mark as an innocently ludicrous exception to a normal family, and Clement as a natural object of uneasiness and distaste. Aubrey saw his family as they were, having had full opportunity to know them, and made his own use of it.

"This omelette is surely a breach with tradition," said Clement.

"It is not," said Blanche, instantly and without looking at it or following the words beyond recognising a criticism. "It is very good and very wholesome."

"Clement speaks from experience," said Aubrey, glancing at his brother's plate.

"Why do you eat it, if you don't like it?" said Mark, with no sting in his tone.

"I am hungry; I must eat something."

"There is ham," said Justine.

"Clement will eat the flesh of the pig," said Aubrey.

"It is certainly odd that civilised people should have it on their tables," said his brother.

"Do uncivilised people have things on tables?"

"Now, little boy, don't try to be clever," said Justine, in automatic reproof, beginning to cut the ham.

"Justine understands Clement," said Aubrey.

"Well, I know you all in and out. After all, I ought, having practically brought you all up."

"Well, hardly that, dear," said Blanche, looking at her daughter with the contraction of her eyes which marked her disagreement. "You were only two when Mark was born. It is I who have brought up the four of you, as is natural."

"Well, well, have it your own way, little Mother."

"It is not only Mother's way. It is the way of the world," said Mark.

"Would some ham make me grow?" said Aubrey. "I am afraid my size is really worrying for Clement."

"What does it matter on what scale Aubrey is?" said the latter.

"I should always be your little brother. So you do not mind."

"Always Mother's little boy," said Blanche, taking Aubrey's hand.

"Mother's hand looks lily-white in my brown, boyish one."

"Don't let us sit bickering all through breakfast," said Justine, in an absent tone.

"We are surely not doing that, dear," said Blanche, her eyes again contracting. "We are only having some conversation. We can't all think alike about everything."

"But you do all agree that I am hardly up to my age," said Aubrey. "Not that there is anything to take hold of."

"I thought the conversation was tending to a bickering note."

"I don't think it was, dear. I do not know what you mean."

"Well, then, neither do I, little Mother. I was only talking at random."

"Suppose Justine's voice was to be stilled!" said Aubrey. "What should we feel about it then?"

"Don't say such things," said his mother, turning on him sharply.

"I am not so very late," said a voice at the door. "You will be able to feel that you had me in the first hour of your day."

"Well, Uncle dear," said Justine, accepting the normal entrance of a member of the house.

"Good morning, good morning," said another voice. "Good morning, Blanche; good morning, Justine; good morning, my sons. Good morning."

"Good morning, Father dear," said Justine, leaning forward to adjust the cups for her mother.

The two brothers who entered were tall, lean men in the earlier fifties, the elder being the squire of the neighbourhood, or rather the descendant of men who had held this title together with a larger estate. He had thick, straight, speckled hair, speckled, hazel eyes, vaguely speckled clothes, a long solid nose and chin, a look of having more bone and less flesh than other men, a face and hands which would have been called bronzed, if there had been anything in the English climate of his home to have this effect on them, and a suggestion of utter honesty which he had transmitted to his daughter. The younger brother, Dudley, was of the same height and lighter build, and was said to be a caricature of the elder, and was so in the sense that his face was cast in a similar mould and had its own deviations from it. His nose was less straight; his eyes were not entirely on a line, and had a hint of his youngest nephew's; and his skin was rather pale than bronzed, though the pair had lived in the same place, even in the same house, all their lives. It was a question in the neighbourhood which brother looked the more distinguished, and it was thought a subtle judgement to decide for Dudley. The truth was that Dudley looked the more distinguished when he was seen with his brother, and Edgar by himself, Dudley being dependent on Edgar's setting of the type, and Edgar affording the less reward to a real comparison. The butler who followed them into the room, bearing a dish to replace the cold one, was a round-featured, high-coloured man about thirty, of the same height as his masters but in other respects very different.

"Good morning, sir; good morning, sir," he said with a slight, separate bow to each.

"Good morning," said Dudley.

"Good morning, good morning," said Edgar, taking no longer over the words.

Blanche looked up in a daily disapproval of Jellamy's initiative in speech, which had never been definite enough to be expressed.

"It is a very unsettled day, sir."

"Yes, it appears to be," said Edgar; "yes, it is unsettled."

"The atmosphere is humid, sir."

"Yes, humid; yes, it seems to be damp."

Edgar seldom made a definite statement. It was as if he feared to commit himself to something that was not the utter truth.

"I love a conversation between Father and Jellamy," said Justine, in an undertone.

Blanche looked up with an expression which merely said that she did not share the feeling.

"The plaster is peeling off the walls in the hall, sir."

"I will come some time and see. I will try to remember to come and look at it."

"I meant the servants' hall, sir," said Jellamy, as if his master would hardly penetrate to this point.

"That room you all use to sit in? The one that used to have a sink in it?"

"The sink has been removed, sir. It is now put to the individual purpose."

"That will do, Jellamy, thank you," said Blanche, who disliked the presence of servants at meals. "If we want you again we will ring."

"It would be a good plan to remove all sinks and make all rooms into halls," said Dudley. "It would send up the standard of things."

"In this poor old world," said Aubrey.

"How did you sleep, Father?" said Justine.

"Very well, my dear; I think I can say well. I slept for some hours. I hope you have a good account to give."

"Oh, don't ask about the sleep of a healthy young woman, Father. Trust you to worry about the sleep of your only daughter!" Edgar flinched in proportion to his doubt how far this confidence was justified. "It is your sleep that matters, and I am not half satisfied about it."

"The young need sleep, my dear."

"Oh, I am not as young as all that. A ripe thirty, and all my years lived to the full! I would not have missed out one of them. I don't rank myself with the callow young any longer."

"Always Father's little girl," murmured Aubrey.

"What, my son?" said Edgar.

"I still rank myself with the young," said Aubrey, as if repeating what he had said. "I think I had better until I go to school. Anything else would make me look silly, and Clement would not like me to look that."

"Get on with your breakfast, little boy," said Justine. "Straight on and not another word until you have finished."

"I was making my little effort to keep the ball of conversation rolling. Every little counts."

"So it does, dear, and with all our hearts we acknowledge it."

Blanche smiled from her eldest to her youngest child in appreciation of their feeling.

"Aubrey meets with continual success," said Mark. "He is indeed a kind of success in himself."

"What kind?" said Clement.

"Too simple, Clement," said Justine, shaking her head. "How did you sleep, Uncle?"

"Very well until I was awakened by the rain. Then I went to the window and stood looking out into the night. I see now that people really do that."

"They really shut out the air," said Clement.

"Is Clement a soured young man?" said Aubrey.

"I had a very bad night," said Blanche, in a mild, conversational tone, without complaint that no enquiry had been made of her. "I have almost forgotten what it is to have a good one."

"Poor little Mother! But you sleep in the afternoon," said Justine.

"I never do. I have my rest, of course; I could not get on without it. But I never sleep. I may close my eyes to ease them, but I am always awake."

"You were snoring yesterday, Mother," said Justine, with the insistence upon people's sleeping and giving this sign which seems to be a human characteristic.

"No, I was not," said Blanche, with the annoyance at the course, which is unfortunately another. "I never snore even at night, so I certainly do not when I am just resting in the day."

"Mother, I tiptoed in and you did not give a sign."

"If you made no sound, and I was resting my eyes, I may not have heard you, of course."

"Anyhow a few minutes in the day do not make up for a bad night," said Mark.

"But I do not sleep in the day, even for a few minutes," said his mother in a shriller tone. "I don't know what to say to make you all understand."

"I don't know why people mind admitting to a few

minutes' sleep in the day," said Dudley, "when we all acknowledge hours at night and indeed require compassion if we do not have them."

"Who has acknowledged them?" said Clement. "It will appear that as a family we do without sleep."

"But I do not mind admitting to them," said Blanche. "What I mean is that it is not the truth. There is no point in not speaking the truth even about a trivial matter."

"I do not describe insomnia in that way," said Mark.

"Dear boy, you do understand," said Blanche, holding out her hand with an almost wild air. "You do prevent my feeling quite alone."

"Come, come, Mother, I was tactless, I admit," said Justine. "I know people hate confessing that they sleep in the day. I ought to have remembered it."

"Justine now shows tact," murmured Aubrey.

"It is possible—it seems to be possible," said Edgar, "to be resting with closed eyes and give the impression of sleep."

"You forget the snoring, Father," said Justine, in a voice so low and light as to escape her mother's ears.

"If you don't forget it too, I don't know what we are to do," said Mark, in the same manner.

"Snoring is not proof of being asleep," said Dudley.

"But I was not snoring," said Blanche, in the easier tone of one losing grasp of a situation. "I should have known it myself. It would not be possible to be awake and make a noise and not hear it."

Justine gave an arch look at anyone who would receive it. Edgar did so as a duty and rapidly withdrew his eyes as another.

"Why do we not learn that no one ever snores under any circumstances?" said Clement.

"I wonder how the idea of snoring arose," said Mark.

"Mother, are you going to eat no more than that?" said Justine. "You are not ashamed of eating as well as of sleeping, I hope."

"There has been no question of sleeping. And I am not ashamed of either. I always eat very well and I always sleep very badly. There is no connection between them."

"You seem to be making an exception in the first matter to-day," said her husband.

"Well, it upsets me to be contradicted, Edgar, and told that I do things when I don't do them, and when I know quite well what I do, myself," said Blanche, almost flouncing in her chair.

"It certainly does, Mother dear. So we will leave it at that; that you know quite well what you do yourself."

"It seems a reasonable conclusion," said Mark.

"I believe people always know that best," said Dudley. "If we could see ourselves as others see us, we should be much more misled, though people always talk as if we ought to try to do it."

"They want us to be misled and cruelly," said his nephew.

"I don't know," said Justine. "We might often meet a good, sound, impartial judgement."

"And we know, when we have one described like that, what a dreadful judgement it is," said her uncle.

"Half the truth, the blackest of lies," said Mark.

"The whitest of lies really," said Clement. "Or there is no such thing as a white lie."

"Well, there is not," said his sister. "Truth is truth and a lie is a lie."

"What is Truth?" said Aubrey. "Has Justine told us?"

"Truth is whatever happens to be true under the circumstances," said his sister, doing so at the moment. "We ought not to mind a searchlight being turned on our inner selves, if we are honest about them."

"That is our reason," said Mark. " 'Know thyself' is a most superfluous direction. We can't avoid it."

"We can only hope that no one else knows," said Dudley.

"Uncle, what nonsense!" said Justine. "You are the

most transparent and genuine person, the very last to say that."

"What do you all really mean?" said Edgar, speaking rather hurriedly, as if to check any further personal description.

"I think I only mean," said his brother, "that human beings ought always to be judged very tenderly, and that no one will be as tender as themselves. 'Remember what you owe to yourself' is another piece of superfluous advice."

"But better than most advice," said Aubrey, lowering his voice as he ended. "More tender."

"Now, little boy, hurry up with your breakfast," said Justine. "Mr. Penrose will be here in a few minutes."

"To pursue his life work of improving Aubrey," said Clement.

"Clement ought to have ended with a sigh," said Aubrey. "But I daresay the work has its own unexpected rewards."

"I forget what I learned at Eton," said his uncle.

"Yes, so do I; yes, so to a great extent do I," said Edgar. "Yes, I believe I forgot the greater part of it."

"You can't really have lost it, Father," said Justine. "An education in the greatest school in the world must have left its trace. It must have contributed to your forming."

"It does not seem to matter that I can't go to school," said Aubrey. "It will be a shorter cut to the same end."

"Now, little boy, don't take that obvious line. And remember that self-education is the greatest school of all."

"And education by Penrose? What is that?"

"Say Mr. Penrose. And get on with your breakfast."

"He has only had one piece of toast," said Blanche, in a tone which suggested that it would be one of despair if the situation were not familiar. "And he is a growing boy."

"I should not describe him in those terms," said Mark.

21

"I should be at a loss to describe him," said Clement.

"Don't be silly," said their mother at once. "You are both of you just as difficult to describe."

"Some people defy description," said Aubrey. "Uncle and I are among them."

"There is something in it," said Justine, looking round.

"Perhaps we should not—it may be as well not to discuss people who are present," said Edgar.

"Right as usual, Father. I wish the boys would emulate you."

"Oh, I think they do, dear," said Blanche, in an automatic tone. "I see a great likeness in them both to their father. It gets more striking."

"And does no one think poor Uncle a worthy object of emulation? He is as experienced and polished a person as Father."

Edgar looked up at this swift disregard of accepted advice.

"I am a changeling," said Dudley. "Aubrey and I are very hard to get hold of."

"And you can't send a person you can't put your finger on to school," said his nephew.

"You can see that he does the next best thing," said Justine. "Off with you at once. There is Mr. Penrose on the steps. Don't keep the poor little man waiting."

"Justine refers to every other person as poor," said Clement.

"Well, I am not quite without the bowels of human compassion. The ups and downs of the world do strike me, I confess."

"Chiefly the downs."

"Well, there are more of them."

"Poor little man," murmured Aubrey, leaving his seat. "Whose little man is he? I am Justine's little boy."

"It seems—is it not rather soon after breakfast to work?" said Edgar.

"They go for a walk first, as you know, Father. It is

good for Aubrey to have a little adult conversation apart from his family. I asked Mr. Penrose to make the talk educational."

"Did you, dear?" said Blanche, contracting her eyes. "I think you should leave that kind of thing to Father or me."

"Indeed I should not, Mother. And not have it done at all? That would be a nice alternative. I should do all I can for you all, as it comes into my head, as I always have and always shall. Don't try to prevent what is useful and right."

Blanche subsided under this reasonable direction.

"Now off with you both! Off to your occupations," said Justine, waving her hand towards her brothers. "I hope you have some. I have, and they will not wait."

"I am glad I have none," said Dudley. "I could not bear to have regular employment."

"Do you know what I have discovered?" said his niece. "I have discovered a likeness between our little boy and you, Uncle. A real, incontrovertible and bona fide likeness. It is no good for you all to open your eyes. I have made my discovery and will stick to it."

"I have always thought they were alike," said Blanche.

"Oh, now, Mother, that is not at all on the line. You know it has only occurred to you at this moment."

"No, I am bound to say," said Edgar, definite in the interests of justice, "that I have heard your mother point our a resemblance."

"Then dear little Mother, she has got in first, and I am the last person to grudge her the credit. So you see it, Mother? Because I am certain of it, certain. I should almost have thought that Uncle would see it himself."

"We can hardly expect him to call attention to it," said Clement.

"I am aware of it," said Dudley, "and I invite the attention of you all."

"Then I am a laggard and see things last instead of

first. But I am none the less interested in them. My interest does not depend upon personal triumph. It is a much more genuine and independent thing."

"Mine is feebler, I admit," said Mark.

"Now, Mother, you will have a rest this morning to make up for your poor night. And I will drive the house on its course. You can be quite at ease."

Justine put her hand against her mother's cheek, and Blanche lifted her own hand and held it for a moment, smiling at her daughter.

"What a dear, good girl she is!" she said, as the latter left them. "What should we do without her?"

"What we do now," said Clement.

"Indeed we should not," said his mother, rounding on him at once. "We should find everything entirely different, as you know quite well."

"Indeed, indeed," said Edgar in a deliberate voice. "Indeed."

Edgar and Blanche had fallen in love thirty-one years before, in the year eighteen hundred and seventy, when Edgar was twenty-four and Blanche thirty; and now that the feeling was a memory, and a rare and even embarrassing one, Blanche regarded her husband with trust and pride, and Edgar his wife with compassionate affection. It meant little that neither was ever disloyal to the other, for neither was capable of disloyalty. They had come to be rather shy of each other and were little together by day or night. It was hard to imagine how their shyness had ever been enough in abeyance to allow of their courtship and marriage, and they found it especially the case. They could only remember, and this they did as seldom as they could. Blanche seemed to wander aloof through her life, finding enough to live for in the members of her family and in her sense of pride and possession in each. It was typical of her that she regarded Dudley as a brother, and had no jealousy of her husband's relation with him.

Edgar's life was largely in his brother and the friendship which dated from their infancy. Mark helped his father in his halting and efficient management of the estate, and as the eldest son had been given no profession. Clement had gained a fellowship at Cambridge with a view to being a scholar and a don. Each brother had a faint compassion and contempt for the other's employment and prospect.

"Mother dear," said Justine, returning to the room, "here is a letter which came for you last night and which you have not opened. There is a way to discharge your duties! I suggest that you remedy the omission."

Blanche held the letter at arm's length to read the address, while she felt for her glasses.

"It is from your grandfather," she said, adjusting the glasses and looking at her daughter over them. "It is from my father, Edgar. It is so seldom that he writes himself. Of course, he is getting an old man. He must soon begin to feel his age."

"Probably fairly soon, as he is eighty-seven," said Clement.

"Too obvious once again, Clement," said Justine. "Open the letter, Mother. You should have read it last night."

Blanche proceeded to do so at the reminder, and Edgar gave a glance of disapproval at his son, which seemed to be late as the result of his weighing its justice.

His wife's voice came suddenly and with unusual expression.

"Oh, he wants to know if the lodge is still to let. And if it is, he thinks of taking it! He would come with Matty to live here. Oh, it would be nice to have them. What a difference it would make! They want to know the lowest rent we can take, and we could not charge much to my family. I wish we could let them have it for nothing, but I suppose we must not afford that?"

There was a pause.

"We certainly should not do so," said Mark. "Things are paying badly as it is."

"It opens up quite a different life," said Justine.

"Are we qualified for it?" said her brother.

"I don't see why we should not ask a normal rent," said Clement. "They would not expect help from us in any other way, and they do not need it."

"They are not well off, dear," said Blanche, again looking over her glasses. "They have lost a good deal of their money and will have to take great care. And it would be such an advantage to have them. We must think of that."

"They think of it evidently, and intend to charge us for it. I wonder at what they value themselves."

"They ought to pay us for our presence too," said Mark. "I suppose it is worth an equal price."

"I believe I am more companionable than either of them," said Dudley.

"Oh, we ought not to talk like that even in joke," said Blanche, taking the most hopeful view of the conversation. "We ought to think what we can do to help them. They have had to give up their home, and this seems such a good solution. With my father getting old and my sister so lame, they ought to be near their relations."

"Do you consider, Mother dear, how you and Aunt Matty are likely to conduct yourselves when you are within a stone's throw?" said Justine, with deliberate dryness. "On the occasions when you have stayed with each other, rumours have come from her house, which have been confirmed in ours. Do remember that discretion is the better part of many another quality."

"Whatever do you mean? We have our own ways with each other, of course, just as all of you have, and your uncle and your father; as brothers and sisters must. But it has been nothing more."

"Edgar and I have not any," said Dudley. "I don't know how you can say so. I have a great dislike for ways;

I think few things are worse. And I don't think you and your sister ought to live near to each other, if you have them."

"What an absurd way to talk! Matty and I have never disagreed. There is no need for us to treat each other as if we were strangers."

"Now remember, Mother dear," said Justine, lifting a finger, "that there is need for just that. Treat each other as strangers and I will ask no more. I shall be utterly satisfied."

"What a way to talk!" repeated Blanche, her tone showing her really rancourless nature. "Do let us stop talking like this and think of the pleasure they will be to us."

"If they bring any happiness to you, little Mother, we welcome them from our hearts. But we are afraid that it will not be without alloy."

"I think—I have been considering," said Edgar, "I think we might suggest the rent which we should ask from a stranger, and then see what their not being strangers must cost us." He gave his deliberate smile, which did not alter his face, while his brother's, which followed it, seemed to irradiate light. "We must hope it will not be much, as we have not much to spare."

"I suppose the sums involved are small," said Justine.

"We are running things close," said Mark. "And why should they put a price on themselves when other people do not?"

"Oh, my old father and my invalid sister!" said Blanche. "And the house has been empty for such a long time, and the rents in this county are so low."

"We shall take all that into account," said Edgar, in the tone he used to his wife, gentler and slower than to other people, as if he wished to make things clear and easy for her. "And it will tend to lower the rent."

"Then why not just ask them very little and think no more about it? I don't know why we have this kind of talk. It will be so nice to have them, and now we have made it into a subject which will always bring argument and acrimoniousness. It is a great shame." Blanche shook her shoulders and looked down with tears in her eyes.

"They want us to write at once, if Mother does not mind my looking at the letter," said Justine, assuming that this was the case. "Dear Grandpa! His writing begins to quaver. They have their plans to make."

"If his writing quavers, his rent must be low, of course," said Mark. "We are not brutes and oppressors."

Blanche looked up with a clearing face, as reason and feeling asserted themselves in her son.

"Yes, yes, we must let them know," said Edgar. "And of course it will be an advantage to have them—any benefit which comes from them will be ours. We cannot dispute it."

"We do not want to," said his daughter, "or to dispute anything else. This foretaste of such things is enough. Let us make our little sacrifice, if it must be made. We ought not to jib at it so much."

"Let us leave this aspect of the matter and turn to the others," said Mark, keeping his face grave. "Do you suppose they really know about Aubrey?"

"I don't see how they can," said Clement. "He was too young the last time they were here for it to be recognised."

"I don't know what you mean," said Blanche, who fell into every trap. "They will be devoted to him, as people always are."

"Yes, Aubrey will be a great success, I will wager," said Justine. "We shall all of us pale beside him. You wait and see."

"I shall have the same sort of triumph," said Dudley. "They will begin by noticing my brother and find their attention gradually drawn to me."

"And then it will be all up with everyone else," said Justine, sighing. "Oh, dreadful Uncle, we all know how it can be."

"And then they will think—I will not say what. It will be for them to say it."

"Well, poor Uncle, you can't always play second fiddle."

"Yes, I can," said Dudley, his eyes on Edgar. "It is a great art and I have mastered it."

Edgar rose as though hearing a signal and went to the door, resting his arm in his brother's, and a minute later the pair appeared on the path outside the house.

"Those two tall figures!" said Justine. "It is a sight of which I can never tire. If I live to be a hundred I do not wish to see one more satisfying."

Blanche looked up and followed her daughter's eyes in proper support of her.

Mark took Clement's arm and walked up and down before his sister.

"No, away with you!" she said with a gesture. "I don't want an imitation; I don't want anything spurious. I have the real thing before my eyes."

"I like to see them walking together like that," said Blanche.

"Well, I do not, Mother. It is a mockery of something better and I see nothing about it to like."

"I am sure they are very good friends. We need not call it a mockery. It illustrates a genuine feeling, even if the action itself was a joke."

"Genuine feeling, yes, Mother, but nothing like the feeling between Father and Uncle. We must face it. You have not produced that in your family. It has skipped that generation."

Blanche looked on in an impotent way, as her daughter left the room, but appreciation replaced any other feeling on her face. She had the unusual quality of loving all her children equally, or of believing that she did. If Mark and Aubrey held the chief place in her heart, the place was available for the others when they needed it, so that she was justified in feeling that she gave it to them all.

Neither she nor Clement suspected that she cared for Clement the least, and if Dudley and Aubrey knew it, it was part of that knowledge in them which was their own. Edgar would not have been surprised to hear that her second son was her favourite.

Jellamy came into the room as his mistress left it, and carried some silver to the sideboard.

"So we are to have Mr. Seaton and Miss Seaton at the lodge, sir?"

"How did you know?" said Mark. "We have only just heard."

"The same applies to me, sir," said Jellamy, speaking with truth, as he had heard at the same moment. "Miss Seaton will be a companion for the mistress, sir. The master and Mr. Dudley being so much together leaves the mistress rather by herself." Jellamy's eyes protruded over a subject which was rife in the kitchen, and had never presented itself to Blanche.

"She is never by herself," said Clement. "We all live in a chattering crowd, each of us waiting for a chance to be heard."

Luncheon found the family rather as Clement described it. Edgar sat at the head of the table, Blanche at the foot; Dudley and Justine sat on either side of the former, Mark and Clement of the latter; and Aubrey and his tutor faced each other in the middle of the board. Mr. Penrose was treated with friendliness and supplied with the best of fare, and found the family luncheon the trial of his day. He sat in a conscious rigour, which he hardly helped by starting when he was addressed, and gazing at various objects in the room with deep concentration. He was a blue-eyed, bearded little man of forty-five, of the order known as self-made, who spoke of himself to his wife as at the top of the tree, and accepted her support when she added that he was in this position in the truest sense. He had a sharp nose, supporting misty spectacles, and neat clothes which had a good deal of black about them. He was pleasant and patient with Aubrey, and made as much progress with him as was possible in view of this circumstance, and had a great admiration for Edgar, whom he occasionally addressed. Edgar and Dudley treated him with ordinary simplicity and never referred to him in any other spirit. Justine spoke of him with compassion, Mark with humour, Blanche with respect for his learning. Clement did not speak of him, and Aubrey saw him with the adult dryness of boys towards their teachers.

"Well, Mr. Penrose, a good morning's work?" said Justine.

"Probably on Mr. Penrose's part," said Clement.

"Yes, I am glad to say it was on the whole satisfactory, Miss Gaveston. I have no complaint to make."

"I wish we could sometimes hear some positive praise of our little boy."

"He is before you," said Mark. "Consider what you ask."

"Don't talk nonsense," said Blanche. "None of you was perfect at his age. If you tease him, I shall be very much annoyed. Have you done well yourself this morning, Clement?"

"Well enough, thank you, Mother."

"We hear some positive praise of Clement," said Aubrey.

"Clement ought to have a mediocre future before him," said Dudley, "and Aubrey a great one."

"I don't agree with this theory that early failure tends to ultimate success," said Justine. "Do you, Mr. Penrose?"

"Well, Miss Gaveston, that has undoubtedly been the sequence in some cases. But the one may not lead to the other. There may be no connection and I think it is probable that there is not."

"Dear little Aubrey!" said Blanche, looking into space. "What will he become in time?"

Mr. Penrose rested his eyes on her, and then dropped them as if to cover an answer to this question.

"That is the best of an early lack of bent," said Clement. "It leaves an open future."

"The child is father of the man," said Mark. "It is no good to shut our eyes to it."

"I cannot grow into anything," said Aubrey, "until I begin to grow. I am not big enough to be my own son yet."

Edgar laughed, and Blanche glanced from him to his son with a mild glow in her face.

"We were talking of the growth of the mind, little boy," said Justine.

"I am sure he is much taller," said Blanche.

"Mother dear, his head comes to exactly the same place on the wall. We have not moved it for a year."

"I moved it yesterday," said Aubrey, looking aside. "I have grown an inch."

"I knew he had!" said Blanche, with a triumph which did not strike anyone as disproportionate.

"If we indicate Aubrey on the wall," said Clement, "have we not dealt sufficiently with him?"

"Why do you talk about him like that? Why are you any better than he is?"

"We must now hear some more positive praise of Clement," said Aubrey.

"It need not amount to that," said his brother.

"I don't want to have him just like everyone else," said Blanche, causing Aubrey's face to change at the inexplicable attitude. "I like a little individuality. It is a definite advantage."

"A good mother likes the ugly duckling best," said Justine, coming to her mother's aid in her support of her son, and with apparent success, as the latter smiled to himself. "How do you really think he is getting along, Mr. Penrose?"

"Mr. Penrose has given us one account of him," said Edgar. "I think we will not—perhaps we will not ask him for another."

"But I think we will, Father. The account was not very definite. Unless you really want to leave the subject, in which case your only daughter will not go against you. That would not be at all to your mind. Well, have you heard, Mr. Penrose, that we are to have a family of relations at the lodge?"

"No, I have not, Miss Gaveston. I have hardly had the opportunity."

"Grandpa and Aunt Matty and Miss Griffin," said Aubrey.

"How do you know, little boy? We had the news when you had gone."

"Jellamy told me when he was setting the luncheon."

"Father, do you like Aubrey to make a companion of Jellamy?"

"Well, my dear, I think so; I do not think—I see no objection."

"Then there is none. Your word on such a matter is enough. I shall like to see poor Miss Griffin again. I wonder how she is getting on."

"Do I understand, Mr. Gaveston, that it is Mrs. Gaveston's family who is coming to the vicinity?" said Mr. Penrose.

"Yes, Mr. Penrose," said Justine, clearly. "My mother's father and sister, and the sister's companion, who has become a friend."

"My father is an old man now," said Blanche.

"Well, Mother dear, he can hardly be anything else, with you—well, I will leave you the option in the matter of your own age—with a granddaughter thirty. Mr. Penrose hardly needed that information."

"And my sister is a little older than I am," continued Blanche, not looking at her daughter, though with no thought of venting annoyance. "She is an invalid from an accident, but very well in herself. I am so much looking forward to having her."

"Poor little Mother! It sounds as if you suffered from

33

a lack of companionship. But we can't skip a generation and become your contemporaries."

"I do not want you to. I like to have my children at their stage and my sister at hers. I shall be a very rich woman."

"Well, you will, Mother dear. What a good thing you realise it! So many people do not until it is too late."

"Then they are not rich," said Clement.

"People seem very good at so many things," said Dudley, "except for not being quite in time. It seems hard that that should count so much."

"Mother will be rich in Aunt Matty," said Aubrey.

"I shall," said Blanche.

"Really, you boys contribute very tame little speeches," said Justine. "You are indifferent conversationalists."

"If you wish us to be anything else," said Clement, "you must allow us some practice."

"Do you mean that I am always talking myself? What a very ungallant speech! I will put it to the vote. Father, do you think that I talk too much?"

"No, my dear—well, it is natural for young people to talk."

"So you do. Well, I must sit down under it. But I know who will cure me; Aunt Matty. She is the person to prevent anyone from indulging in excess of talk. And I don't mean to say anything against her; I love her flow of words. But she does pour them out; there is no doubt of that."

"We all have our little idiosyncrasies," said Blanche. "We should not be human without them."

"It is a pity we have to be human," said Dudley. "Human failings, human vanity, human weakness! We don't hear the word applied to anything good. Even human nature seems a derogatory term. It is simply an excuse for everything."

"Human charity, human kindness," said Justine. "I think that gives us to think, Uncle."

"There are great examples of human nobility and sacrifice," said Blanche. "Mr. Penrose must know many of them."

"People are always so pleased about people's sacrifice," said Dudley; "I mean other people's. It is not very nice of them. I suppose it is only human."

"They are not. They can admire it without being pleased."

"So I am to write—you wish me to write to your father, my dear," said Edgar, "and say that he is welcome as a tenant at a sacrifice to be determined?"

"Yes, of course. But you need not mention the sacrifice. And I am sure we do not feel it to be that. Just say how much we want to have them."

"Father dear, I don't think we need bring out our little family problems before Mr. Penrose," said Justine. "They concern us but they do not—can hardly interest him."

"Oh, I don't think that mattered, dear," said Blanche. "Mr. Penrose will forgive us. He was kind enough to be interested."

"Yes, indeed, Mrs. Gaveston. It is a most interesting piece of news," said Mr. Penrose, relinquishing a spoon he was examining, as if to liberate his attention, which had certainly been occupied. "I must remember to tell Mrs. Penrose. She is always interested in any little piece of information about the family—in the neighbourhood. Not that this particular piece merits the term, little. From your point of view quite the contrary."

"We shall have to do up the lodge," said Blanche to her husband. "It is fortunate that it is such a good size. Matty must have remembered it. The back room will make a library for my father, and Matty will have the front one as a drawing-room. And the third room on that floor can be her bedroom, to save her the stairs. I can quite see it in my mind's eye."

"Drawing room and library are rather grandiloquent terms for those little rooms," said Justine.

"Well, call them anything you like, dear. Sitting room and study. It makes no difference."

"No, it makes none, Mother, but that is what we will call them."

"We need not decide," said Clement. "Aunt Matty will do that."

"Aunt Matty would never use exaggerated terms for anything to do with herself."

"There are other ways of exaggerating," said Mark.

"Mrs. Gaveston," said Mr. Penrose, balancing the spoon on his finger, to show that his words were not very serious to him, "it may interest you to hear how Mrs. Penrose and I arranged rooms on a somewhat similar scale, as I gather, as those you mention."

"Yes, we should like to hear indeed."

"Thank you very much, Mr. Penrose," said Justine, warmly, sitting forward with her eyes on Mr. Penrose's face.

"We selected large patterns for the carpets, to give an impression of space, though it might hardly be thought that the choice would have that result. And we kept the walls plain with the same purpose."

"We can have the walls plain," said Justine, "but we must use the carpets at our disposal, Mr. Penrose. We are not as fortunate as you were."

"We shall not be able to write in time for them to hear by the first post," said Blanche. "I hope it won't seem that we are in any doubt about it."

"About the sacrifice," said Dudley. "I hope not. I said that people were pleased by other people's sacrifice. They would not like them to have any hesitation in making it."

"It would be an unwilling sacrifice," said Aubrey.

"Another point to be made," continued Mr. Penrose——

"Yes, Mr. Penrose, one moment," said Justine, leaning to her father and laying a hand on his arm, while glan-

cing back at the tutor. "It is very kind and we are so interested, but one moment. Would it not be better,
Father, to send the letter into the town to catch the
afternoon post? Things always get to Grandpa in the
morning if we do that."

"It might be—it probably would be better, I will write
directly after luncheon, or as soon as we have decided
what to say. What is Mr. Penrose telling us?"

"It does not matter, Mr. Gaveston. I was only mentioning that in the experience of Mrs. Penrose and myself—
it is of no consequence," said Mr. Penrose, observing that
Justine had turned to her mother, and resuming the
spoon.

"Indeed it is of consequence," almost called Justine,
leaning towards Blanche over Aubrey and giving another
backward glance.

"You have one of our seventeenth-century spoons?"
said Edgar.

"Yes, Mr. Gaveston, I was wondering if it was one of
them. I see it is not," said Mr. Penrose, laying down a
spoon which his scrutiny had enabled him to assign to
his own day. "You have some very beautiful ones, have
you not?"

"They are all put away, Mr. Penrose," called Justine,
in a voice which seemed to encourage Mr. Penrose with
the admission of economy. "We are not allowed to use
them any more. They only come out on special occasions."

"Do go and write the letter, Edgar," said Blanche.
"Poor Father, let him have his luncheon in peace."

"He has finished, dear. He is only playing with that
fruit and wasting it."

"Waste not, want not, Father," said Justine, in a warning tone which seemed to be directed to Mr. Penrose's
ears.

Edgar rose and left the room with his brother, and
Justine's eyes followed them.

"Are they not a perfect pair, Mr. Penrose?"

"Yes, indeed, Miss Gaveston. It appears to be a most conspicuous friendship."

"What are you doing?" said Blanche, suddenly, as she perceived her elder sons amusedly regarding the youngest, whose expression of set jauntiness told her that he was nearly in tears. "You are teasing him again! I will not have it. It is mean and unmanly to torment your little brother. I am thoroughly ashamed of you both. Justine, I wonder you allow it."

"I merely did not observe it, Mother. I was talking to you and Father. Now I certainly will not countenance it. Boys, I have a word to say."

"It is unworthy to torment someone who cannot retaliate," said Blanche, giving her daughter the basis of her homily.

"I have managed to get my own back," said Aubrey, in an easy drawl, depriving her of it.

"We were only wondering how to keep Aubrey out of Grandpa's sight and Aunt Matty's," said Mark. "A shock is bad for old and invalid people."

"You are silly boys. Why do you not keep out of their sight yourselves?" said his mother.

"That might be the best way to cover up the truth," said Mark, looking at his brother as if weighing this idea. "It would avoid any normal comparison."

"Suppose either should come upon him unawares! They have not seen him since we could hope it was a passing phase."

"A phase of what?" said Blanche. "I do not know what you mean and neither do you."

"We thought a postscript might be added to the letter," said Mark. "So that they might be a little prepared."

"Prepared for what?"

"Just something such as: 'If you see Aubrey, you will understand.'"

"Understand what?" almost screamed his mother.

"You don't understand, yourselves, so naturally they would not."

"Mother, Mother dear," said Justine, laughing gently, "you are pandering to them by falling into their hands like that. Take no notice of them and they will desist. They are only trying to attract attention to themselves."

"Well, that is natural at their stage," said Aubrey.

"We did take no notice and they had reduced poor Aubrey nearly to tears," said Blanche, too lost in her partisanship of her son to observe its effect upon him.

"They are naughty boys, or, what is worse, they are malicious young men, and I am very much annoyed with them. I did not mean that I was not."

"Then speak to them about it," said Blanche, standing back and looking with expectance born of experience from her daughter to her sons.

"Boys, boys," said Justine gravely, "this will not do, you know. Take example from that." She pointed to the garden, where Edgar and Dudley were walking arm-in-arm. "There is a spectacle of brotherhood. Look at it and take a lesson."

"So your father has not written the letter!" said Blanche.

"If you will excuse us, Mrs. Gaveston, Aubrey and I should be thinking of our walk," said Mr. Penrose, who had been uncertain whether the family had forgotten his presence.

"Yes, of course, Mr. Penrose, please do as you like," said Blanche, who had forgotten it, and even now did not completely recall it. "If he does not write it soon, it will have no chance of the post."

Aubrey went up to his brothers and linked their arms, and taking a step backwards with a jeering face, took his tutor's arm himself and walked from the room.

"Dear, dear, what a little boy!" said Justine. "I think Mr. Penrose carried that off very well."

"Edgar!" called Blanche from the window. "You

are not writing that letter! And it has to go in an hour."

"We are deciding upon the terms—we are discussing the wording, my dear," said her husband, pausing and maintaining the courtesy of his voice, though he had to open his mouth to raise it. "It needs to be expressed with a certain care."

"Indeed," said Mark. "There is no need to employ any crudeness in telling Grandpa that we can't do him too much charity."

"Oh, that is all right then," said Blanche, turning from the window. "There is no question of charity. That is not the way to speak of your grandfather. It is the coachman's day out. Who had better drive the trap into the town? I have seen Jellamy drive. Would your father mind his driving the mare? I wish you would some of you listen to me, and not leave me to settle everything by myself."

"Mother, come and have your rest," said Justine, taking Blanche's arm. "I will take the trap myself. You need have no fear. I also have seen Jellamy drive, and if Father does not grudge him the particular indulgence, I do."

Blanche walked compliantly out of the room, relaxing her face and her thoughts together, and her husband and his brother passed to the library.

"I think that will express it," said Dudley. "You are to drop a sum every year and not refer to it, and feel guilty that you take money from your wife's relations for giving them a bare roof."

"I think it should be good for Blanche to have them. I hope we may think it should. I fear there may be—I fear——"

"I fear all sorts of things; I am sick with fear. But we must think what Blanche is facing. I always think that women's courage is hard on men. It seems absurd for men and women to share the same life. I simply don't know how we are to share Blanche's life in future."

"I am never sure how to address my father-in-law."

"When we speak to him, we say 'sir'. I like saying 'sir' to people. It makes me feel young and well-behaved, and I can't think of two better things, or more in tune with my personality. What a good thing that Blanche will not ask to see the letter! I have a great respect for her lack of curiosity. It is a thing I could never attain."

Dudley drafted and dictated the letter, and Edgar wrote it and submitted it for his inspection, and then suggested a game of chess. When Justine came for the letter, the brothers were sitting silent over the board. They played chess often, Dudley playing the better, but Edgar playing for the sake of the game, careless and almost unconscious of success. Justine tiptoed from the room, mutely kissing her hand towards the table.

II

"IS this a house or a hutch? It is meant, I suppose, for human habitation," said Blanche's father, walking about his new home. "It is well that I shall soon be gone and leave you alone in it. For it is better for one than for two, as I cannot but see."

"Come, Father, pluck up heart. You are an able-bodied man and not a crippled woman. I must not be given any more to bear. You must remember your poor invalid, though I never remind you that I am that."

"If that was not a reminder, I need not take it as one. I grant that that fall made a poor thing of you, but you want a chair to sit upon, all the more. And I don't see where we are to put one, on a first sight."

"There are plenty of chairs, Father. Let us sit down in two of them. Come, I think they have done their best. It only needed a little best for such a little home, but such as it had to be, I think it is done. And we must be as grateful as they will expect us to be." Blanche's sister put back her head and went into mirth. "This room is quite a pretty little place. So we must try to feel at home in it. We are not peopple to fail in courage."

Matilda Seaton was two years older than Blanche, of the same height as her sister, but of the suppler, stronger build of her niece, Justine. She had hair less grey than her sister's, a darker skin less lined, and the same narrow, dark eyes looking out with a sharper, deeper gaze. A fall from a horse had rendered her an invalid, or rather obliged her to walk with a stick, but her energy seemed to accumulate, and to work itself out at the cost of some havoc within her. Her voice was deeper than her sister's and had some sweeter tones. She appeared handsomer, though she also looked her age and her features were of the same mould. Her father admired her the more, and believed her maidenhood to be due to her invalid state, though her accident had not happened until she was middle-aged. It had done him a service in a way, as he had been at a loss to account for the position. The truth was that Matty had had many chances to marry and had not accepted them. She had never met a man whom she saw as her equal, as her conception of herself was above any human standard. She may also have had some feeling that a family would take her attention and that of others from herself. The idea that anyone could pity her found no place in her mind; there was no place there for such a feeling. Even her lameness she saw as giving a touch of tragic interest to an already remarkable impression. Oliver knew of her offers, or rather had been told of them, as his daughter kept nothing which seemed to exalt her to herself, but he thought it normal self-respect in a woman to invent proposals if they were not forthcoming. Matty did not guess that she had not justice from her father, as he thought it wise to keep his doubt to himself, indeed knew it was. The father and daughter were less alike than they had been, for Oliver's face, once the original type, was fallen and shrunk from age. His figure was of the same size for a man as his elder daughter's for a woman, and had a touch of the awkwardness of the younger's which was something apart from the stiffness of the old. When he was seen with Blanche and her youngest son, this lack of balance became a family trait. His wife had been some years his senior and had herself lived to an advanced age, and at her death he had been old enough to accept his daughter in her place.

"Yes, I am sure they have done what they can," said Matty, still looking round. "It is a funny little pattern on the paper. Suitable for the funny little room, I suppose. We are not to forget how we are placed. They thought it was better for us to take the plunge at once. Well, I daresay they are right. We will try to think they are. That is a lesson we shall have to learn."

"You seem to be failing at the moment," said Oliver, as Matty wiped her eyes. "I can't see that the scrawl on the paper makes much odds. And the room seems to hold two people, which is what we want of it. What are you crying about? Aren't you thankful to have a home?"

"I am not so very at the moment. I can't help thinking of the one we have left. Perhaps it shows the feeling I had for that," said Matty, putting her handkerchief away with a courageously final movement. "I shall soon be able to be myself, but it is rather a sudden difference, the little paper and all." She put her hand to her mouth in her sudden laughter. "Well, shall we say that we appreciated our old home so much? I think we may say that without being unthankful."

Oliver was silent. He had suffered from leaving his home as well as his daughter, almost feeling that he left his youth and his prime and his married life behind in it, but the lessening grasp of his age had saved him the worst. He had lived all his life on private means, and his capital had dwindled, partly in the natural course—his investments suffering from age like himself, and even in some cases succumbing like his wife—and partly because he had annually spent a portion of it. The eventual result struck him as a sudden misfortune, and his daughter faced their retrenchment in this spirit.

"Is that commotion to continue?" he said, as sounds of adjusting furniture came from the hall. "No one would guess that we left our possessions behind. I should not have thought that the place was large enough to allow of it."

"We must have a few necessities even in a little home. But there is less to be done than if we were to have what we have always had. That is one bright side to it."

"And you see it, do you? When did you get your glimpse?"

"Things will soon be done, and you can have your dinner," said Matty, retaliating on her father by explaining his mood. "Miss Griffin will come and tell us."

"You will eat as well as I, I suppose, and so will she. Will she be able to put up with the corner in which she finds herself?"

"It is the only home we can give her. We have to be content with it."

"I meant what I said, her corner of it," said Oliver, with a grin which recalled his youngest grandson. "I still mean what I say."

"We cannot help having had to leave our house for this one. It is not a pleasure for us."

"No, my dear, you give no sign that it is. I grant it to you. Well, Miss Griffin is a good woman not to leave us. She has indeed been a remarkable person not to do that. I cannot say what she gets out of serving us."

"Of course you can. It is quite clear. We give her a home when she has no other."

"Sell it to her for herself, I should say. I would not congratulate her on her bargain."

"It is better to stay with people who are fond of her, than to start again with strangers."

44

"Strangers would treat her as a stranger. That was rather in my mind. And fond of her! You may be that; I am myself. But I shouldn't be proud of your way of showing it. Indeed I am not proud of it."

"It would take her a long time to get to the same stage with another family."

"Why, that is what I meant; this stage could not come at once. But I suppose women understand each other. I can only hope it. I don't see what I can do more. But it doesn't seem enough to keep a human being at my beck and call."

"They have not come down to see us," said Matty, glancing at the time. "They have not run across from their big house to see how we are faring on our first evening in our small one. Well, I suppose they have many other claims: we must think they have." She looked again at the clock and tapped her knee with her hand, making a simultaneous movement with her foot, as if she would have tapped the ground if she had been able.

"Well, I cannot tell. But we have not been in the house above two hours."

"They are long hours when you have to sit still and hear other people about and doing, and feel how much better you could do it all, if you were as they are. They have been long ones."

"Why, so they have, child, for me as well as for you."

"Well, we must be still and go on a little longer."

"Why, so we must, and for how much longer we cannot say. But it will not help us for you to cry about it. And what is your reason? You have a home and a bed and a woman to wait on you, haven't you?"

"Yes, I have, and I am going to feel it. I have more than many people. But it did seem to me for a moment that people who have more still—and we must say much more—might spare a thought to us in our first isolation. It was just for the moment."

45

"Then it doesn't seem to you so any longer."

"No, it must not," said Matty, again concealing her handkerchief. "There shall be nothing in our minds but bright and thankful thoughts."

"Well, that will make a difference. And here is someone in the hall. So if you want to hide your handkerchief, find a place that serves your purpose. It is well that you are what you say in time."

"Well, Matty dear, well, Father dear!" said Blanche's voice, the unconscious order of the names telling its tale. "Well, here is a red-letter day for us all!"

"Red-letter day, when we have left our home and all we have, behind!" said Matty in a rapid aside to her father, pressing her handkerchief to her face in another spirit.

Blanche entered with outstretched arms and stumbled slightly over nothing apparent, as she hurried forward.

"Well, how do you like coming here amongst us? We like to have you so much. How are you both after your journey? I could not wait another minute to come and see."

Blanche gave her father and sister a long embrace, stooping to the latter, as she remained in her seat, and then stood back to receive her response.

"Well, how do you feel about coming to share our life?" she said, as something more was needed to produce it.

"We shall be happy in it, dear. We shall," promised Matty, rapidly using her handkerchief and hiding it. "We see that now. We did not feel quite amongst you until this moment. But we do now indeed." She took her sister's hand and lifted it to her face, as Blanche often did her daughter's.

"Sit down, my dear, sit down," said Oliver. "You give us a welcome and we do the same for you. I think there is a chair; I think there is room for three."

"Of course there is. It is a very nice little room," said Blanche, sitting down and looking round. "How do you

like the little paper? Don't you think it is just the thing?
It is the one the boys have in their study."

"Yes, dear, is it? Yes, it would be nice for that," said
Matty, following her sister's eyes. "Just the thing, as you
say. For this room in my house, and for a little, odd room
in yours. It is the suitable choice."

"Don't you like it in this room, dear?" said Blanche,
evidently accustomed to answering her sister's meaning
rather than her words.

"Yes, yes, I do. It is best to realise that we are in a little
room, and not in a big one any longer. Best to leap the
gulf and have a paper like the one in the boys' study."
Matty began to laugh but checked herself at once. "Far
better not to try to make it like the room at home, as we
might have done by ourselves. We might have tried and
failed, and it is so much wiser not to do that. Yes, it was
best for people to deal with it who saw it from outside
and not from within. And it was so good of you to do it
for us, and it is kindly and wisely done."

"I thought you would like it so much; I did not know
that you would want it like the drawing-room at home.
That was so much larger that I thought it would be better
to start afresh."

"So it was, dear; that is what I said."

"No, you said other things, child," said Oliver.

"That is what we are doing, starting afresh, and finding
rather a task at the moment," said Matty, not looking at
her father. "But we shall manage it. It is only hard at
first, and we can't help it that you find us in the first
stage." She touched her eyes and this time retained the
handkerchief.

"Keep it, my dear," said Oliver, offering her another.
"It is more convenient to you at hand."

Matty held up the handkerchief to her sister with a
smile for its size, and went on as if she had not paused.

"We shall make a success of it, as you have done with
the room."

"The room serves its purpose, my dear," said Oliver to Blanche. "The paper covers the walls and the plaster would not look as well without it, and what more should be done? You have managed well for us, and so we should tell you, and I do so for us both."

"Yes, if we have seemed ungrateful, we are not," said Matty, not explaining the impression. "We both thank you from our hearts. So Edgar did not come with you to see us?"

"He came with me to the door and left me. He thought we should like our first meeting by ourselves."

"He is always so thoughtful, and we have liked it indeed. And we shall like one with him as well the next time he is at our door. We have come to a place where we hope there will be so many meetings."

"Blanche is enough for us," said Oliver. "We do not want her man. Why not say that you want the whole family? You almost did say it."

"Well, I did have a thought that they might all come running down to greet the old aunt on her first night. I had almost imagined myself the centre of a family circle."

"You imagined yourself the centre! So that is what is wrong. No wonder you wanted a room like the one at home. I don't know where you would have put them."

"They could have got in quite well," said Blanche. "No doubt they will often do so. But to-night we thought you would want to be spared." She paused and seemed to yield to another impulse. "I am glad that you are so little depressed by the goodbye to the old home. We thought you might be rather upset by it." Her way of speaking with a sting seemed an echo of her sister's in a lighter medium.

"We are too affected by that to show it on the surface," said Matty. "That is not where the feeling would appear. Is that where you would look for it?"

"Then what can we see there?" said Oliver. "Your

48

sister can find something, and does so. If that isn't where it ought to be, put it in its place."

"Edgar is coming to fetch me in an hour," said Blanche, resuming her normal manner. "You will see him then, and he will see you. He is looking forward to it."

"You are only staying an hour, dear? I thought that you might have dinner with us, or we with you, on our first night."

"Why pack so much into it?" said Oliver. "There are other nights and others after those. And your sister is right that we are not fit for it. You were certainly not, when you were crying into a rag. And why did you order dinner here, if you wanted to eat it somewhere else?"

"We had to have it somewhere, Father, and we did not hear."

"Oh, we thought you would be tired," said Blanche. "And there are so many of us. It would not be restful for you. And we are not prepared for you to-night. We shall be so delighted to see you when it is arranged, and we hope that will be very often."

"I did not make anything of extra guests, when I ran a large house," said Matty, with a simple wonder which was not entirely assumed, as her housekeeping had played its part in her father's debts.

"And that may be partly why you are now running a small one," said the latter, with a guess rather than a glimpse at the truth.

"We are hoping to see you constantly," said Blanche. "We can't quite manage our home so that people can come without notice, but we hope to plan so many things and to carry them out."

"We can't run in and out, as if we were of the same family? We felt we were that when we came. That indeed is why we are here. You can do so in this little house. You will remember and tell the children?"

"I hope she will not retain any of this talk," said Oliver, looking at his elder daughter, nevertheless, with

49

his own admiration. "I will ask her to forget it. Well, Miss Griffin, have you done enough of putting away what we have, in a space that cannot hold it?"

"We shall have to get rid of some furniture, dear," said Matty to her sister, with a vague note of reproach.

"My dear, you have not brought all the furniture of that big house?"

"No, no, we remembered the size of this one, and only brought the things we knew and loved. I daresay you would not remember some of them. But we did not realise that it was quite such a cot. I expect our thoughts of it were tinged with memories of you and your large one, as that is how we have seen the life here. Never mind, we shall call it our cottage home, and be quite happy in it."

"Then pray begin to be so," said Oliver. "Happiness is too good a thing to put off. And I am not at the age for doing that with anything."

"How do you do, Miss Griffin?" said Blanche, shaking hands with her sister's attendant and companion. "I hope you are not too tired with all your efforts?"

"How do you do, Mrs. Gaveston? No, I am not so very tired," said Miss Griffin, a short, thin woman of fifty, with a long, sallow face, large, hazel eyes, features which might have been anyone's except for their lines of sufferance and kindness, hands which were more developed than her body, and a look of being very tired indeed. "It is very good of you to come to welcome us."

"Mrs. Gaveston came in to see her father and sister, of course," said Matty, in a tone which said so much more than her words, that it brought a silence.

"Yes, indeed, dear," said her sister. "And when you want me to go and leave you to your dinner, you must tell me."

"The dinner is not—the dinner will not be ready yet," said Miss Griffin, in a stumbling tone, glancing at Matty and away. "The maid does not know where anything is yet. She is quite new."

"Of course she is, as we did not bring her with us,"
said Matty, with her little laugh. "Couldn't you show her
where the things are, as you have just unpacked them?"

"She put everything together—I put it all together—we
have not sorted them yet. She is just finding what she
can."

"I should have put all the things in their places as I
took them out. I should not have thought of any other
way."

"We couldn't do that. The men were waiting to take
the cases. We had to put them all down anywhere."

"I should have known where anywhere was. I often
wish I were able-bodied, for everyone's sake."

"We wish you were, child, but for your own," said
Oliver.

"I think Miss Griffin has managed wonders from the
look of the house," said Blanche.

"We have all done that to-day," said her sister. "I
almost think I have managed the most, in keeping still
through all the stir and turmoil. I hope we shall never
have such a day again. I can't help hoping it."

"I know I shall not," said her father.

"I remember so well the day when you came to us,
Miss Griffin," said Blanche. "It was thirty-one years ago,
a few days before my wedding. And you were so kind in
helping me to pack and put the last touches to my
clothes. I wish I was taking you with me."

"I remember thinking that you were using my companion as your own," said Matty, smiling from one to
the other.

Miss Griffin turned her face aside, finding it unsteadied
by ordinary kindness.

"Sit down, Miss Griffin, and rest until dinner," said
Matty. "There is no need to stand more than you must,
though I often wish I could do a little of it. That may
make me think other people more fortunate than they
are."

Miss Griffin sat down in the sudden, limp way of someone who would soon have had to do so.

"There is Edgar," said Blanche. "He will come in and
say a word, and then we will leave you all to rest."

"Why, Edgar, this is nice," said Matty, rising from her
seat as she had not done for her sister, and showing that
she stood tall and straight, in spite of disabled lower
limbs. "I did not think you would forget us on our first
night. We had not forgotten you. No, you have been in
our minds and on our lips. Now what do you say to our
settling at your very gates?"

"That it is—that I hope it is the best place for you to
be," said Edgar, putting out all his effort and accordingly
unable to say more.

"And your brother! I am never quite sure what to call
him," said Matty, putting round her head to look at
Dudley. "Come in and let us hear your voice. We have
been cheered by it so many times."

"I am glad you have. I have always meant you to be.
I am in my element in a chat. My strong point is those
little things which are more important than big ones,
because they make up life. It seems that big ones do not
do that, and I daresay it is fortunate."

"Yes, it is indeed. We have been involved in the latter
to-day, and we see that we could not manage too many.
Now it is so good to hear you talk again. We see we have
not given up our home for nothing."

"Indeed you have not. You have left it to make a new
one with all of us," said Blanche, relieved by the turn of
the talk and not disturbed that she had been unable to
produce it.

"Such a lot of happiness, such a lot of affection and
kindness," said Matty, in a tone charged with sweetness
and excitement. "It is so good to know that we are welcome."

"It is indeed," said Oliver; "for a moment since I
should have thought that we could not be."

"How are you, sir?" said Edgar and Dudley, speaking at one moment but obliged to shake hands in turn.

"I am well, I thank you, and I hope that both of you are better by thirty odd years, as you should be."

Oliver put a chair for his son-in-law and settled down to talk. He gave his feeling to his daughters but he liked to talk with men.

"How are you, Miss Griffin?" said Dudley, turning from the pair. "I hope you are not hiding feelings of your own on the occasion."

"No, I am not; it all makes a change," said Miss Griffin, admitting more feeling than she knew into the last word. "And we did not want that large house for so few people. It is better to be in a little one, where there is less work and more comfort. And I don't mind the small rooms. I rather like to be snug and compact."

"Now I would not claim that that is just my taste. I confess to a certain disposition towards the opposite," said Matty, in a clear tone. "It is not of my own will that I have changed my scale of life. I admit that I felt more at home with the other. It is all a matter of what fits our different personalities, I suppose."

"I hope I do not make cosy corners wherever I go," said Dudley. "I don't want too many merely lovable qualities. They are better for other people than for oneself."

"Well, there will always be such a corner for you here. I shall be grateful if you will help me to make one, as it is rather outside my experience and scope. But once made, it will be always hospitable and always ready. If we can't have one thing we will have another, or anyhow I will. I am not a person to give up because I can't have just what I should choose, just what fits me, shall we say?"

"I don't know why we should say it, child," said Oliver. "And anyhow you should not."

"I wish my parents were not dead," said Dudley. "I

should like to be called 'child' by someone. It would prove that there were people about who were a generation older than me, and it will soon want proof."

"Welcome, welcome to your new home!" said Justine's voice. "Welcome to your new life. I know I am one too many; I know you are tired out; I know your room is full. I know it all. But I simply had to come to wish you happiness, and to say to you, Welcome, well come."

"So you had, dear, and it gives us such pleasure to hear it," said Matty, raising her face from her chair. "I did hope that some of you would feel that and come to tell us so. It seemed to me that you would, and I see I was not wrong. One, two, three, four dear faces! Only three left at home. It is such a help to us in starting again, and it is a thing which does need help. You don't know that yet, and may it be long before you do."

"Well, I judged it, Aunt Matty, and that is why I am here. Of course, you must need courage. You can't start again without a good deal of looking back. That must be part of it. And I did feel a wish to say a word to help you to look forward."

Blanche looked at her daughter in simple appreciation; Edgar threw her a glance and withdrew it; and Oliver surveyed the scene as if it were not his concern.

"You help us, dear, indeed," said Matty. "It was a kind and loving wish, and as such we accept it and will try to let it do its work."

"I know you will, Aunt Matty dear; I know your inexhaustible fund of courage. You know, I am of those who remember you of old, straight and tall and proud, as you appeared to my childish eyes. My feeling for you has its ineradicable root in the past."

The words brought a silence, and Justine, fair in all her dealings, broke it herself.

"How are you, Miss Griffin?" she said, shaking hands with great cordiality, and then sitting down and seeming to render the room at once completely full. "Now this is a snug little cottage parlour. Now, how do you take to it, Aunt Matty?"

"We shall be content in it, dear. We mean to be. And where there is a will there is a way. And it should not be difficult to come to like it, our little cottage parlour. Those are good and pretty words for it. They give the idea without any adding to it or taking away."

"It is not a cottage, dear," said Blanche, looking at her daughter.

"Isn't it, Mother? Well, no, we know it strictly is not. But it gives all the idea of one somehow. And I mean nothing disparaging; I like a roomy cottage. When I am a middle-aged woman and Mark is supreme in the home, I shall like nothing better than to have perhaps this very little place, and reign in it, and do all I can for people outside. Now does not that strike you all as an alluring prospect?"

"Yes, it sounds very nice," said Miss Griffin, who thought that it did, and who was perhaps the natural person to reply, as the arrangement involved the death of most of the other people present.

"I don't think it gives the idea of a cottage at all," said Blanche, looking round with contracting eyes. "The rooms are so high and the windows so broad. One could almost imagine oneself anywhere."

"But not quite," said her sister, bending her head and looking up at the men from under it. "We can't, for example, imagine ourselves where we used to be."

"Well, no, not there, dear. We must both of us leave that. It was my old home too, as you seem to forget."

"No, dear. You do at times, I think. That is natural. You have put too much over it. Other things have overlaid the memory. I chose to keep it clear and by itself. There is the difference."

"Well, it *is* natural, Aunt Matty," said Justine. "I don't think Mother must be blamed for it. There *is* a difference."

"Yes, dear, and so you will not blame her. I have said that I do not. And is the old aunt already making herself tiresome? She must be so bright and easy as an invalid in a strange place?"

"Come, Aunt Matty, invalid is not the word. You are disabled, we know, and we do not underrate the handicap, but your invalidism begins and ends there. Now I am not going to countenance any repining. You are in your virtual prime; you have health and looks and brains; and we are going to expect a good deal from you."

"My dear, did Aunt Matty ask you to sum up her position?" said Blanche, a faint note of triumphant pride underlying her reproof.

"No, Mother, you know she did not, so why put the question? I did not wait to be asked; it is rather my way not to. You need not put on a disapproving face. I have to be taken as I am. I do not regret what I said, and Aunt Matty will not when she thinks it over."

"Or forgets it," said her aunt. "Yes, I think that is what Aunt Matty had better do. She has not the will or the energy to think it over at this juncture of her life. And forgetting it will be better, so that is the effort she must make."

"Now I am in disgrace, but I do not regard it. I have had my say and I always find that enough," said Justine, who was wise in this attitude, as she would seldom have been advised to go further.

"How very unlike Edgar and Justine are, dear!" said Matty to her sister. "They have not a touch of each other, and they say that daughters are like their fathers. They are both indeed themselves."

"Well, that is as well," said Justine. "Father would not like me to be a copy of him. He would not feel the attraction of opposites."

"Opposite. Yes, that is almost the word," said her aunt.

Miss Griffin gave the sudden, sharp breath of someone

awaking from a minute's sleep, and looked about with bewildered eyes.

"Poor Miss Griffin, you are tired out," said Blanche.

"I am so glad you got off for a minute, Miss Griffin," said Justine.

"I did not know where I was; I must have dropped off with all the voices round me," said Miss Griffin, with a view of the talk which she would hardly have taken if she had heard it. "I don't know why I did, I am sure."

"Being overtired is quite enough reason," said Justine.

"So Miss Griffin is the first of us to make it one," said Matty, in an easy tone.

"It is a stronger reason in her case."

"Is it, dear?" said Matty, so lightly that she hardly seemed to enunciate the words.

"Why, Aunt Matty, she must have done twice as much as you—as anyone else. You know that."

"Twice as much as I have, dear? Many times as much, I daresay; I have been able to do hardly anything. And of course I know it." Matty gave her little laugh. "But what we have mostly done to-day, is sitting in the train, and we have done it together."

"Yes, but the preparations before and the unpacking afterwards! It must have been overwhelming. The time in the train must have been quite a respite."

"Yes, that is what I meant, dear."

"But it was only one day, only part of one. The work must have begun directly you reached this house. I can see how much has been achieved. You can't possibly grasp it, sitting in a chair."

"So sitting in a chair has become an advantage, has it?"

"Poor, dear Aunt Matty!" said Justine, sitting on the arm of the chair, as if to share for the moment her aunt's lot. "But it cannot contribute to the actual weariness, you know. That is a thing by itself."

"So there is only one kind of weariness," said Matty,

putting her hand on her niece's and speaking in a tone of gentle tolerance towards her unknowing youth.

"Dear Aunt Matty! There must be times when to be hustled and driven seems the most enviable thing in the world. You are more unfortunate than anyone," said Justine, indicating and accepting her aunt's lot and Miss Griffin's.

Miss Griffin rose and went to the door with an explanatory look at Matty. Dudley opened it and followed her.

"How do people feel on a first night in a new place? I have never had the experience. I have lived in the same house all my life."

Miss Griffin lifted her eyes with a look he had not expected, almost of consternation.

"It does make you feel uncertain about things. But I expect you soon get used to it. I was in the last house thirty-one years. Miss Seaton had never lived in any other."

"And are you sorry to come away from it?"

"No, not very. It makes a change. We shall see different people. And it will be nice for Miss Seaton to have her sister and her family. It was the wisest plan."

"The best plan, not the wisest. It was very unwise. But a great many of the best things are that."

Miss Griffin looked at him with a hint of a smile.

"You agree with me, do you not?"

Miss Griffin checked her smile and looked aside.

"You and I must be very much alike. We both live in other people's houses; we are both very kind; and I am very good at playing second fiddle, and I believe you are too."

"Oh, I never mind doing that," said Miss Griffin in a full tone.

"I have minded in my weaker moments, but I have conquered my worse self. You have no worse self, have you?"

"No," said Miss Griffin, speaking the truth before she thought. "Well, I don't know. Perhaps everyone has."

"You have to think of other people's. So I see that you have not. And as I have suppressed mine, it is another point we have in common."

Miss Griffin stood with a cheered expression.

"Has Miss Seaton a better self?" said Dudley.

Miss Griffin gave him a half smile which turned to a look of reproach.

"Yes, of course she has. Everyone has."

"So it was her worse self we saw this evening?"

"I did not mean that she had a worse self. You know I did not. She was very tired. It must be so dreadful not to be able to get about." Miss Griffin's voice died away on a note of pure pity."

"Well, good night, Miss Griffin; we shall often meet."

"Good night, Mr. Dudley," said Miss Griffin, turning towards the kitchen with a lighter step.

Dudley returned to the parlour to find the family dispersing. Matty was on her feet, talking with the lively affection which followed her difficult moods, and which she believed to efface their memory.

"Goodbye, dearest; goodbye, my Justine; you will often come in to see the cross old aunt who loves you. Goodbye, Dudley; where have you been wandering? It was clever to find enough space to lose yourself. Goodbye, Edgar; my father has so enjoyed his masculine talk. It is a thing that does him so much good."

"And how have you enjoyed your feminine one?" said Oliver, who had caught snatches of this dialogue. "Upon my word, I daresay a good deal. You look the better for it."

"Goodbye, Aunt Matty dear," said Justine. "I have seemed a brute, but I have meant it for your good, and you are large enough to take it as it was meant."

"Goodbye," said Edgar at once. "We shall often meet; I hope we shall meet very often."

"Well, of course, people are only human," said Dudley to his brother, as they walked to the house behind the women. "But it really does not seem much for them to be."

"Yes, we must do what we can in our new life," said Edgar, as if in reply. "I think we may call it that. It may be a better life for Blanche. I think—I trust it may."

"Is her present life so bad?"

"She may be lonely without knowing it. I fear it may have been the case. I feel—I fear I have little to be proud of in my family life."

"It is I who have the cause for pride. It is wonderful, the way in which I have put myself aside and kept your affection and won your wife's. But I think the things we suffer without knowing are the best, as we are born to suffer. It is not as if Blanche had suspected her loneliness. And she can't be with her sister and be unconscious of it."

"Neither can any of us," said Edgar, with the short, broken laugh which was chiefly heard by his brother. "I could see—I saw that she realised it to-day."

"I saw that Justine did too. The sight became too much for me and I had to escape."

"What were you doing all that time?"

"Why do people say that they do not like having to account for their every action? I do like it. I like telling everything about myself and feeling that people take an interest. I was saying a kind word to Miss Griffin. They say that a kind word may work wonders; and I saw that something had to work wonders for her; and so I said the word and it did."

"Poor Miss Griffin! I mean that we cannot judge of other people's lives."

"Of course we can. We all have lives and know about them. No one will have it said that he has no knowledge of life; and it could not be true."

"She has been with Matty and her father for a long time. I am not sure how long."

"I am. She told me. But there are things which cannot pass my lips."

"It must be over thirty years."

"You are a tougher creature than I am. I wonder if people know that you are."

"It is difficult to form a picture of all those years."

"Edgar, you do sometimes say the most dreadful things. You should remember my shrinking nature. I shall have to see a great deal of Miss Griffin. Will seeing her take away that picture before my eyes?"

"Come along, you two," called Justine, turning with beckoning hand. "If you wait every minute to argue, we shall never get up the drive. Mother does not like to keep stopping."

That was true of Blanche, and therefore she had not stopped, but was proceeding towards the house, with her short, unequal steps carrying her rapidly over the ground. When she came to the porch she paused, as if waiting there affected her differently.

"There is that little brick house beyond the trees," said Justine, turning to look back as they all met.

"Your eyes do not deceive you," said her father, with a smile.

"Now don't try to snub me, Father; that is not like your dealings. There it is, and it is good to think of Grandpa and Aunt Matty snugly sheltered in it. I shall call up the picture to-night when I am in bed."

"At night," murmured Dudley, "and in bed! In those hours when things rise up before us out of their true proportion!"

"What are you murmuring about to yourself, Uncle?"

"About the picture which you will call up in the night."

"You like to share it with me? It is a pretty picture, isn't it? Dear Grandpa, with his white hair and fine old face; and Aunt Matty, handsome in the firelight, vivacious and fluent, and no more querulous than one can forgive in her helpless state; and dear, patient Miss Griffin, thinking of everyone but herself. It is a satisfying sight."

"Perhaps it is healthier to bring it out into the light."

"You were the one who did not forgive your aunt," said Edgar, smiling again at his daughter.

"Now, Father, don't think that your naughty little thrusts are atoned for by your especial smile for me, dear to me though it is." Edgar's expression wavered as he heard it defined. "Aunt Matty and I are the firmest friends and very good for one another. We never mind looking at ourselves through each other's eyes and getting useful light on our personalities. I do not believe in putting disabled people on one side and denying them their share in healthy human life. It seems to me a wrong thing to do, and in the end bad for everyone. So I sound my bracing note and snap my fingers at the consequences." Justine illustrated what she said.

The scene in the lodge was as she saw it, except that Matty's querulousness was missing. The latter was sitting at dinner, talking with a great liveliness, as if her audience were larger than it was, almost as if in practice for greater occasions. She often threw herself into the entertainment of her father and her companion, with or without thought of imaginary listeners.

"And then those funny, little, country shoes! Dear Blanche, still full of her quaint, little, old touches! I had to laugh to myself when I saw her come tripping and stumbling in, such a dear, familiar figure!"

"No one would have known you had," said Oliver. "It might have been better to give some sign. It seemed the last thing to expect of you."

Matty was indifferent to her father's criticism and knew that her talk diverted him.

"And then her own little, charitable ways, a mixture of daughter and sister and lady bountiful! So full of affection and kindness and yet with her own little sharpness, just our old Blanche! And her dear Justine"—Matty put

62

her hand to her lips and fell into mirth—"so sure of her right to improve us all and so satisfied with it! So pleased with her effort to influence her aunt, who has faced so much more than she could conceive! Dear child, may she never even have to attempt it. Well, we are not all alike and perhaps it is as well. Perhaps it is good that we are all on our different steps in the human scale. And there are good things on each level. In some ways we might take a leaf out of her book."

"We might, but I do not think of it, and I do not ask it of you."

"It is naughty to say it, but does she remind you of that church worker at home? Someone so good and useful that everyone loved her and no one admired her? Now how unkind and malicious! I am quite ashamed."

"Have I met a person of that kind?"

"You must remember poor Miss Dunn at home."

"Why should I single her out of all that I remember? And how could I guess her employment?"

"The coat and the collar and the shoes," said Matty, again in mirth.

"They both wear such things, I grant you. I do the same and shall do it still for a short time."

"Poor Miss Griffin, you were the target. You might have been a little dark slave or a wee beastie in a trap, from the way she spoke. We do not move every day, do we? It has only been once in thirty years."

Miss Griffin felt that there was some reproach in the rareness of the step, though she would willingly have taken it oftener.

"She meant to be very kind, I am sure."

"She meant to be a little stern with me, just a tiny bit severe. But I did not mind. She is my dear, good niece and wants to improve the world and the people in it, Aunt Matty into the bargain."

"They might be the better for it," said Oliver, "but it is not her business."

"She feels it is, and so we must let her do it. We must take it up as a funny little cross and carry it with us."

"Why do that? Why not close her mouth upon things which are not her concern? That is a thing you can do. I have observed it."

"Edgar is a handsome man," said Matty in another tone. "He was very tall and distinguished in this little room. Oh, wasn't it funny, the way they kept talking about it? Calling it snug and cosy. We might be cottagers."

"That is what we are, though your sister did not allow it."

"And Justine said that she was glad we were safe in it. We had no other refuge, had we?"

"I cannot tell you of one. So we have our cause for thankfulness. But it is not for her to point it out. She seems to me to have greater cause."

"Mr. Gaveston and Mr. Dudley are not so much alike when you get to know them," said Miss Griffin.

"They are of the same type, but Mr. Gaveston is the better example," said Matty, who maintained the full formal distance between herself and her companion, in spite of her habit of frankness before her.

"I like Mr. Dudley's face better."

"Do you? It is not the better face. It has not the line or the symmetry. It is a thought out of drawing. But they are a fine pair of brothers."

"There is something in Mr. Dudley's face that makes it quite different from Mr. Gaveston's. I hardly know how to say what I mean."

"That might be said of any two people. They are not just alike, of course."

"Mr. Dudley's face has a different kind of attraction."

"There is only one kind, of the one we were talking of," said Matty in a tone which closed the subject.

"Miss Griffin has found another," said Oliver, "or has fancied it. But why talk of the fellows' looks? They are not women. And both of you are, so it is wise to leave the matter."

"Was Mr. Dudley talking to you outside?" said Matty in a sudden, different tone to Miss Griffin.

"No—yes—he just said a word, and then went out to look at the night, into the porch," said Miss Grffin, who told a falsehood when she could see no other course.

Oliver had heard the voices in the hall, but he did not speak. He never crossed the barrier into the women's world. If he had done so, he would have had to protect Miss Griffin and anger his daughter; and he felt unequal to either of these things, which would have tried the strength of a younger man.

"Did you notice the way they set off home?" said Matty, with a return of mirth. "I saw them from the window. My eyes are still alert for what they can see, though I am tied to my chair. Blanche leading the way, and Justine trying to keep up and to keep step, and failing in both in spite of her youth and her strength! And the two men walking behind, as tranquil as if they were unconscious of the feminine creatures in front! Blanche leading a group is one of my earliest memories. Her stiff, little legs marching on, how they come back to me! And they are so little different, the active, determined, little legs. How much of her height is in her body! Well, my legs are not so much to boast of now. I have not my old advantage. Dear, dear, it is a funny thing, a family. I can't help feeling glad sometimes that I have had no part in making one."

"Why try to help it? It is well to be glad of anything, and you do not too often seem so. Though some people might not choose just that reason."

"Well, mine is not a lot which calls for much gladness. It needs some courage to find any cause for it."

"So courage is the word for your talk of your sister. We could find others."

"Blanche and I are the closest friends. I am going to rejoice in being the elder sister again. You and she are the only people who see me as I was, and not as I am, the poor, baffled, helpless creature who has to get her outlet somehow. Yes, I was bright and young once. Even Miss Griffin remembers part of that time."

"Yes, indeed I do; indeed you were," said Miss Griffin.

"Miss Griffin was even younger," said Oliver, bringing a new idea to both his hearers as he rose to leave them.

"Yes, I was a naughty, sprightly person," continued Matty after a moment's pause, during which the idea left her. "Always looking for something on which to work my wits. Something or someone; I fear it did not matter as long as my penetration had its exercise. Well, we can't choose the pattern on which we are made. And perhaps I would not alter mine. Perhaps there is no need to meddle with it, eh, Miss Griffin?"

Miss Griffin was standing with her hand on her chair, thinking of the next step in her day. She gave a faint start as she realised her plight and saw the look on Matty's face. The next moment she heard her voice.

"Don't go dragging away from the table like that. Either move about and get something done, or don't pretend to do anything. Just posing as being a weary drudge will not get us anywhere."

"Perhaps the things which have made me that, have got us somewhere," said Miss Griffin, in an even, oddly hopeless tone, with little idea that the words on her lips marked a turning point in her life.

"You need not answer like that. That is not going to begin, so you need not think it is. I do not expect to have my words taken up as if I were a woman on the common line. I am a very exceptional person and in a tragic position, and you will have to grasp it, or you are no good to me. And going off in that way, pretending not to hear, taking advantage of my helplessness! That is a thing of such a dreadful meanness that no one would speak to

you if he knew it; no one would go near you; you would
be shunned and spat upon!"

Matty's voice rose to a scream, as her words did nothing
and Miss Griffin passed out of hearing. She rocked herself to and fro and muttered to herself, with her hands
clenched and her jaw thrust forward in a manner which
would have made a piece of acting and really had something of this in it, as she did not lose sight of herself.

Miss Griffin went along the passage and paused at the
end where the wall made a support, and looked to see
that Matty had not followed.

"It is all I have. Just this. I have nothing else. I have
no home, no friends. I go on, year after year, never have
any pleasure, never have any change. She feels nothing
for me after I have been with her for thirty years. All the
best years of my life. And it gets worse with every year.
I thought this move might make a change, but it is going
to be the same. And my life is going; I may never have
anything else; and no one ought to have only that." She
shed some tears, scanty through fear and furtiveness, and
lightening her face and throwing off a part of her burden, went into the kitchen to the maid, glad of this
degree of human fellowship.

Matty, left to herself, relaxed her body and her mind
and hoped that her father had not heard her voice, or
rather recalled that he would behave as if he had not
done so. When Oliver came from his study to bid her a
good night, she rose to meet him, hiding what she could
of her lameness, and led him to a chair, amending both
his and her own conception of herself.

"I come to take my leave of you, my dear, in case I do
not see you again. My end may come at any time and
why not to-night? The strength ebbs after dark and I
have used too much of mine to-day. So good night and
more, if that is to be."

"Come, Father, you are overtired and depressed by
being in this funny little place. Cosy we are to call it, and

we will do our best. We have to try to do so many things
and in time we shall succeed. We are not people who
fail. We will not be."

"I am almost glad that your mother is not here to-
night, Matty. This would not have been a home for her.
It will do for you and me."

"I don't know why we should be so easily satisfied,"
said Matty, unable to accept this view of herself in any
mood. "But we shall have another outlook to-morrow and
it will seem a different place, and we shall wish Mother
back with us, as I have wished her many times to-day."
Her father must pay for using such words of his daughter. "But we can't do anything more to-night. We have
striven to our limit and beyond. It is no wonder if we
fail a little. I daresay we have all had our lapses from our
level."

Oliver, who was in no doubt of it, left her and mounted
the stairs, bringing his feet together on each. In his room
above the step became stronger, and Matty listened and
put him from her mind. She understood her father. A
good deal of him had come down to her.

Miss Griffin came in later with a tray, to find Matty
in an attitude of drooping weariness, with a pallor which
was real after her stress of feeling.

"Will you have something hot to drink?" she said
in a tone which seemed to beseech something besides
what it said. "It will do you good before you go to bed."

"It will do us both good. It was a sensible thought. If
you will bring up that little table and move that chair"
—Matty indicated with vivacious hand this further effort
for Miss Griffin—"we will have a cosy time together and
feel that we are doing what we should, as cosy is what we
are supposed to be."

"It really is rather cosy in here," said Miss Griffin, looking round with a faint air of surprise.

"Yes, it is foolish to fret for the might-have-beens. Or
for the have-beens in this case."

Miss Griffin did not fret for these.

"Now do not shirk drinking your share," said Matty, replenishing the cups. "You need it as much as I do. Being up and doing is as tiring as sitting still, however much one may envy it. Mr. Seaton has gone to bed. He was overtired and sorry for himself, but I did not take much notice. It was wiser not to sympathise."

"Oh, I expect he was very tired," said Miss Griffin, sitting up as if to put her full energy into her compassion.

"He begins to feel his age, but he is very well and strong. And we are all tired."

"Yes," said Miss Griffin, speaking in a mechanical tone and suddenly enlivening it. "But it is a healthy tiredness." She had been so often told of the beneficial effects of weariness on the human frame, that she felt she should know them.

"It has gone a little beyond that to-day. But it is only once in a lifetime. We must not complain."

Miss Griffin was not going to do this, but her nod had something besides agreement.

"Come, come now, we must go to bed," said Matty, keeping her eyes from the other as if in fear of what might meet them. "We shall be a couple of sleepy old maids in the morning, if we do not take care."

Miss Griffin's eyes opened wide and held themselves on Matty's face.

"We owe it to ourselves and to other people not to sink to that. We must not quite lose our self-respect. This is a matter in which considering ourselves is best for everyone. Has Emma gone to bed?"

"Yes, hours ago," said Miss Griffin, only realising her implication when she had spoken.

Matty did not comment on it, possibly for the reason that Emma had only been half a day in her service and had not yet learned the benefits of exhaustion.

"Well, then she can be up bright and early to wait upon us," she said with an effort which did not say nothing for her will. "We will not be down until ten o'clock. We have had a nice little chat. Good night, and mind you sleep."

Matty went to her room, feeling that she had made her companion ample amends, and the latter, waiting to turn out the lamps, wondered that she did not feel the same, as she had felt it so many times. This was the reason for her not feeling it again.

III

"I AM ready for Aunt Matty," said Aubrey.

"Are you, little boy? And very nice and trim you look. I wish I could feel the same. I am done with village dressmakers. I am not much of a woman for personal adornment, but there are stages beyond even me. I ought to think of my family; it was selfish and lazy of me. I certainly can't expect to rejoice their eyes." Justine sighed over her conclusion.

"Won't smoothing it make it better?"

"No, it will not, impertinent child. It will leave it as it is." Justine aimed a blow in her brother's direction without moving towards him.

"Mark, are you ready for your aunt?" said Aubrey.

"As far as the outward man can count. But her eyes may pierce the surface and pounce on what is beneath."

"Now I won't have Aunt Matty laughed at for her penetration," said Justine. "It is a valuable quality and one which deserves to be reckoned with."

"And is more than any other."

"She has none," said Clement. "She attributes motives to people, whether they are there or not. That gets us further from the truth than anything. Mother has really a sounder penetration."

70

"Dear little Mother," said Justine, giving a pitying tenderness to the same quality in Blanche.

"Clement, are you ready for your aunt?"

"Nothing would prepare me for the manners, the morals and the methods of such a woman. She is at once super and sub-human. I always wonder if she is goddess or beast."

"Clement, Clement, that is neither gallant nor kind," said Justine. "A man does not speak of a woman like that, you know. And can't you brush the collar of your coat? Not that I have any right to speak."

"But I think both the boys look very nice, Justine," said Aubrey.

"How does Justine appear?" said Clement. "I will hear the accepted view before I express my own."

"Oh, you are right; it is hopeless. It deserves anything you like to say. You need not be afraid that I shall rise up in its defence like a mother with her young."

"You might help to smooth it, Clement," said Aubrey. "It is all that can be done now."

"Why don't you change it?" said Mark. "What about that one you generally wear?"

"No, I will stick to it now. I will remain in it and face the music. Mother is expecting to see me in something different, and I daresay she will like it. I won't take refuge in some old one which does not catch the eye. It will teach me a lesson that I deserve."

"It is not a matter of such mighty import," said Clement.

"Indeed it is! It should be a point of great interest to you all, how your only sister looks. I will not have it in any other way. I have no patience with that kind of high-and-mightiness. It is the last thing that exalts anyone."

"Clement, are you listening to Justine?" said Aubrey.

"He does not know how true quality is shown," said Mark. "That is a thing which cannot be taught."

"All Clement's learning will stand him in but poor stead."

"Here are the guests! And Father and Mother are not down!" said Justine, in a tone of consternation.

"They are remedying the position," said Clement, showing that he did not recommend the feeling.

Blanche led the way into the room, in an old-fashioned gown of heavy material and indifferent cut, which had been altered to show successfully how it should have been made, and which in its countrified quality and stiffness became her well.

"Well, dear ones, how nice you look! Justice, it is a very pretty colour. I do want Aunt Matty to see you all at your best. And dear Grandpa has seen so little of you for so long." Blanche spoke to her children of their relations either from their point of view or her own.

"Mr. and Mrs. Middleton," said Jellamy.

"How are you, Mrs. Middleton? It is kind of you to adapt yourselves to our early hours," said Blanche, who observed the formalities with guests with sincerity and goodwill. "My father and sister will be here in a moment. It is a long time since you have met."

"Whose idea was it that they should come to live here?"

"It was their own. But we welcomed it with great delight. My sister and I have missed each other for so many years."

"Isn't the lodge rather small after their old home?"

Sarah Middleton's questions seemed to come in spite of herself, as if her curiosity were stronger than her will.

"Yes, it has to be that. They have lost money lately and are obliged to live on a small scale. And it is a nice little house."

"Very nice indeed," said Sarah, with the full cordiality of relief from pain, which was the state produced in her by a satisfied urge to know.

Sarah Middleton was a tall, upright woman of seventy,

strong and young for her age, with a fair, rather empty face and an expression at once eager and soured and kind. Her grey hair was done in some way which seemed to belong to a world where men and women were more different, and her cap had been assumed in her prime in tribute to matronhood, though to Justine and her brothers it was a simple emblem of age. She looked about as she talked, as if she feared to miss enlightenment on any matter, a thing which tried her beyond her strength and which happily seldom occurred. Her husband, who was ten years younger and in the same physical stage, was a tall, spare, stooping man, with a good head, pale, weak eyes, a surprisingly classic nose, and an air of depression and an excellence of deportment which seemed to depend on each other, as though he felt that the sadness of life entitled people to courtesy and consideration. He had wanted to write, and had been a schoolmaster because of the periods of leisure, but had found that the demands of the other periods exhausted his energy. After his marriage to a woman of means he was still prevented, though he did not give the reason, indeed did not know it. Neither did he state what he wished to write, and this was natural, as he had not yet decided. Sarah felt that the desire gave him enough occupation, and he almost seemed to feel the same.

"Yes, say what you like, Uncle," said Justine, standing before Dudley and holding out her skirts. "It merits it all and more. I have not a word to say. This will teach me not to waste my time and energy on going backwards and forwards to poor Miss Spurr. She has not an ounce of skill in her composition."

Blanche looked at the dress with mild, and Sarah with eager attention.

"It could be made into a dressing-gown," said Dudley, taking a sudden step forward. "I see just how it could be done."

"My dear, that beautiful material!" said Sarah, holding up her hands and turning her eyes on Justine to indicate the direction of her address.

"I am sure it is a very pretty colour," said Blanche, implying and indeed feeling that this was a great part of the matter.

"I knew I could count on a word of encouragement from you, little Mother."

"Dressing gowns are always the best colours," said Aubrey. "I go in and look at them sometimes."

"You little scamp," said Justine. "You are happy in being young enough for that sort of thing."

"Dear boy!" said Sarah.

"What is the matter with the dress?" said Edgar, with careful interest. "Do you mean that it ought to be better made?"

"Yes, Father, I do mean that. Everyone means it. We all mean it. Don't go unerringly to the point like that, as if it were almost too obvious to call for comment."

"I don't think it calls for so much comment," said Clement.

"Well, I daresay it does not. Let us leave it now. After all, we all look ourselves in whatever we wear," said Justine, deriving open satisfaction from this conclusion, and taking Aubrey's chin in her hand. "What are you meditating upon, little boy?"

"I was expecting Aunt Matty," said Aubrey, reluctant to explain that he had been imagining future daughters for himself and deciding the colours of their dressing gowns.

"Well, dear ones all," said Matty, almost standing still on the threshold, partly in her natural slowness and partly to be seen. "Well, here is a happy, handsome"—she rapidly substituted another word—"healthy family. So much health and happiness is so good to see. It is just what I want, isn't it?"

Blanche looked up with narrowing eyes at the change of word, though she knew that it was prompted by the sight of more and not less handsomeness than her sister had expected.

"Is not Father coming?" she said in a cool tone, putting down her embroidery before she rose.

Sarah looked from sister to sister with full comprehension and the urbanity which accompanied it.

"Yes, dear, he will not be a moment. He is only rather slow. I came on to get a start of him, as I am even slower." Matty kissed Blanche with more than her usual affection in tacit atonement for what had passed, but seemed to feel rather soon that atonement had been made. "It seems that I know him better in these days and have to tell you about him. Perhaps he has always belonged to me a little the most. Why, Mrs. Middleton, how are you both? So we are to be neighbours as well as friends."

"It did not take you long to make up your mind to the change," said Sarah, her tone leading up to further information.

"No, I am a person of rapid decision. Fleet of foot, fleet of thought and fleet of action I used to be called in the old days." Blanche looked up as if in an effort of memory. "And I have retained as much of my fleetness as I can. So I made my resolve and straightway acted upon it."

"My dear, you have retained so much of what you had," said Sarah, shaking her head.

"Mr. Seaton," said Jellamy.

"Now I can barely walk forward to greet you," said Oliver, pushing his feet along the ground, "but I am glad to find myself welcome as I am. There have come moments when I thought that we might not meet again. So, Middleton, I am pleased to see you once more on this side of the grave."

Thomas shook hands with an air which accepted and rejected these words in the right measure.

"Why are people proud of expecting to die soon?" said Dudley to Mark. "I think it is humiliating to have so little life left."

"They are triumphant at having made sure of more life than other people. And they don't really think they will die."

"No, of course, they have got into the way of living. I see it is a lifelong habit."

"Have we no relations who can enter a room in the usual way?" said Clement.

"None in the neighbourhood," said his brother.

"Now, Grandpa, that is naughty talk," said Justine, leading Oliver forward by the arm as if no one else would think of the office. "Now which chair would you like?"

"Any one will serve my purpose; I ask but to sit in it."

"Dear Grandpa!" said Justine, keeping her hands on his arms as he sat down, as if she were lowering him into it.

"That is a fine gown, my dear," he said, as he let go the chair and sank back.

"It is the most fearful thing, Grandpa; I forbid you to look at it. It will be my shame all the evening."

"You know why you put it on, I suppose. I should have thought it was intended to catch the eye, as it has caught mine."

"I think it is such a nice colour," said Blanche.

"Beautiful," said Sarah, shaking her head again.

"Why, so it is, my dear," said Oliver, relaxing his limbs. "Your girl looks well in it, and what more would you have?"

"But the shape of it, Grandpa!" said Justine, withdrawing her strictures upon his looking to the extent of disposing herself that he might the better do so. "The cut, the hang, the balance, the fit!"

"Well, I do not see any of those, my dear; I do not know if you are trying to show them to me."

"I am trying to show you the lack of them."

"Then you do so, child; I see it," said Oliver, lifting one leg over the other.

"Well, if anyone received a snub!" said Justine, looking about her at the success of her effort.

"What is the colour?" said Matty, her easy tone revealing her opinion that enough had been said on the matter. "Magenta?"

"No, dear," said Blanche. "It is a kind of old rose."

"Is it, dear?" said Matty, contracting her eyes on the dress and looking almost exactly like her sister for the moment. "A new sort of old rose then." She smiled at her niece, taking her disparagement of the dress at its literal value.

"Oh, come, Aunt Matty, there is nothing wrong with the colour. It is the one redeeming point."

"Yes, dear?" said Matty, in questioning agreement, her eyes again on the dress.

"Oh dear, this garment! Is it destined to be a bone of contention in addition to its other disadvantages?"

"I tremble to think about its destiny," said Clement, "as its history up to date is what it is."

"Why is magenta an offensive term?" said Mark. "It seems to be."

"It is odd how colours seem to owe their names to some quality in them," said his aunt.

"Their names come about in quite a different way."

"Now we don't want a philological lecture," said Matty, showing her awareness of this.

"Magenta can be a beautiful colour," said Sarah, in a tone of considerable feeling. "I remember a dress I once had of a kind of brocade which we do not see now. Oh, it would have suited you, Mrs. Gaveston."

"Those old, thick brocades were very becoming," said Matty.

"Aunt Matty does not restrict the application of her words," said Aubrey, seeming to speak to himself, as he often did when he adopted adult phrase.

"I can imagine you looking regal in one of them, Aunt

Matty," said Justine, in a tone of saying something that was expected.

"Dinner is ready, ma'am," said Jellamy.

"And not too soon," said Clement. "I hope that food will be a better subject for our attention than clothes."

Edgar gave his arm to Sarah and led the way in conventional talk, which he maintained at whatever happened to be the cost to himself. Dudley adapted his step to Matty's with an exactness which involved his almost standing still, and kept up a flow of conversation at no personal expense at all. Matty was known to prefer Dudley to a son of the house, and her nephews supported her choice. Blanche and her father walked together, as the result of his suggestion that it might be their last opportunity, which was proffered to Thomas as an excuse and duly repudiated and accepted. They were assisted by Justine to link their arms and take their first steps—and indeed there might have been a less perilous association —and checked by her serious hand from a too precipitate advance. Justine herself went with Thomas, placing her free arm in Mark's.

"Now I do not require four partners, but I may as well use up one superfluous young man. Follow on, you other two. Aubrey can be the lady."

"I place my delicate hand on Clement's arm and lean on his strength."

Thomas gave a laugh and Clement shook off the hand and walked on alone.

"What a really beautiful room, dear!" said Matty to her sister, with appreciation brought to birth by the lights and wine and the presence of Dudley and Edgar. "It is like a little glimpse of home, or if I may not say that, it is like itself and satisfying indeed to my fastidious eye. And my own little room seems to gain, not lose by the comparison. This one seems to show how beauty is everywhere itself. I quite feel that I have taken a lesson from it."

"And one which was needed, from what I hear," said Mark.

"Is that how happiness does not depend on surroundings?" said Aubrey.

Mark and Aubrey often talked aside to each other. Clement would join them when inclined to talk, Justine when inclined to talk aside. Aubrey also talked aside to himself.

"Naughty boys, making fun of the poor old aunt!" said Matty, shaking her finger at them without interest in what they said.

"What was it, Mark?" said Edgar, with a hint in his tone that his eldest son should speak for the ears of the table.

"I was agreeing with Aunt Matty, sir."

"Yes, yes, we may praise our own home, may we not, when it is as good as this?" said his aunt.

"I was doing the same, Father—the same, sir," said Aubrey, who had lately followed his brothers in this mode of address.

"Dear boy!" said Sarah, moved by the step towards maturity.

Edgar had come as near to reproof as he ever did. His hints were always heeded, and if it was not true that they were followed more than if he had raised his voice or resorted to violence, it was as true as it ever is. To Justine he never hinted a reproof, partly because of her sex and partly because he might have had to hint too much. Edgar did not love his children, though he believed or rather assumed that he did, and meted out kindness and interest in fair measure. He had a concerned affection for his wife, a great love for his brother and less than the usual feeling for himself. Dudley spent his emotion on his brother, and gave any feeling which arose in him to anyone else. Justine believed that she was her father's darling, and Edgar, viewing the belief with an outsider's eye, welcomed it, feeling that it ought to be a true one, and made intermittent effort to give it support. Other people accordingly accepted it, with the exception of Dudley and Aubrey, who saw the truth. Clement would have seen it if he had regarded the matter, and Blanche liked the belief and accordingly cherished it.

"Does Jellamy manage by himself in this room now?" said Matty to her sister. "It seems rather much for one person."

"Yes, he has to, dear. It makes us slower, of course, but it cannot be helped. We have to be very economical."

Matty glanced about the room with a faintly derisive smile.

"No, indeed, Aunt Matty," said Justine, answering the look, "you are quite wrong. Mother is speaking the simple truth: Strict economy is necessary. There is no pose about it."

Matty lifted her brows in light enquiry.

"Now, Aunt Matty, you made the comment in all good faith, as clearly as you could have made it in words, intending it to be so taken. And that being the case, it must be so answered. And my answer is that economy is essential, and that Jellamy works single-handed for that reason."

"Is it, dear? Such a lot of answer for such a little question."

"It was not the question. It was the comment upon the reply."

"No one is to make a comment but you, dear?"

"Justine does make them," murmured Aubrey.

"Now, little boy, how much did you follow of it?"

"Upon my word, I do not follow any of it," said Oliver.

Sarah leaned back almost in exhaustion, having followed it all. Her husband had kept his eyes down in order not to do so.

"Well, we mustn't get too subtle," said Justine. "They say that that is a woman's fault, so I must beware."

Aubrey gave a crow of laughter, checked it and suffered a choke which exceeded the bounds of convention.

"Aubrey darling!" said Blanche, as if to a little child.

"Now, little boy, now, little boy," said Aubrey, looking at his sister with inflamed cheeks and starting eyes.

"Now, little boy, indeed," she said in a grave tone.

"Poor child!" said Sarah.

"What shall I do when there is no one to call me little boy?" said Aubrey, looking round to meet the general eye, but discovering that it was not on him, and returning to his dinner.

"Aubrey has a look of Father, Blanche," said Matty.

"I believe you are right, Aunt Matty," said Justine, with more than the usual expression. "I often see different likenesses going across his face. It has a more elusive quality than any of our faces."

"I mean something quite definite, dear. It was unmistakable for the moment."

"Yes, for the moment. But the moment after there is nothing there. It is a face which one has to watch for its fleeting moods and expressions. Would not you say so, Father?"

Edgar raised his eyes.

"Father has to watch," said Aubrey, awaiting the proceeding with a grin.

"What a gallant smile!" said Clement, unaware that this was the truth.

"There, Uncle's smile!" said Justine.

The quality of the grin changed.

"And now Grandpa's! Don't you see it, Aunt Matty?"

"I spoke of it, dear. Yes."

"And don't you, Father? You have to look for a moment."

Edgar again fixed his eyes on his son.

"There, it has gone! The moment has passed. I knew it would."

Aubrey had not shared the knowledge, the moment having seemed to him interminable.

"Father need not watch any longer," he said, and would have grinned, if he had dared to grin.

"The process does not seem to be attended by adequate reward," said Mark.

Clement raised his eyes and drew a breath and dropped his eyes again.

"Clement need not watch any longer either," said Aubrey.

"Now, little boy, you pass out of the common eye."

Oliver turned his eyes on his grandson.

"The lad is getting older," he said.

"Now that is indubitably true, Grandpa," said Justine. "It might be said of all of us. And it is true of him in another sense; he has developed a lot lately. But do take your eyes off him and let him forget himself. This is all so bad for him."

"He could not help it, dear," said Blanche, expressing the thought of her son.

"Now are our little affairs of any interest to you?" said Matty, who had been waiting to interpose and at once arrested Sarah's eyes. "If they are, we have our own little piece of news. We are to have a guest, who is to spend quite a while with us. I am looking forward to it, as I have a good deal of time to myself in my new life. There are many people whom I miss from the old one, though I have others to do their part indeed. And this is one of the first, and one whose place it would be difficult to fill."

"We have found a corner for her," said Oliver, "though you might not think it."

"She will have the spare room, of course, Father," said Blanche. "It is quite a good little room."

"Yes, Mother, of course it is," said Justine, in a low, suddenly exasperated tone. "But it is to be like that. The house is to be a hut and the room a corner, and there is

82

an end of it. Let us leave it as they prefer it. People can't do more than have what they would choose."

Matty looked at the two heads inclined to each other, but did not strain her ears to catch the words. Sarah did so and controlled a smile as she caught them.

"Well, are you going to let me share this advantage with you?" went on Matty. "It is to be a great pleasure in my life, and I hope it will count in yours. There is no great change of companionship round about."

"Well, no, I suppose there is not," said Justine. "We are in the country after all."

"So I am not a host in myself," said Dudley.

"It is known to be better for the country to be like itself," said Sarah, who found this to be the case, as it was the reason of her acquaintanceship with the Gavestons.

Thomas looked up with a faintly troubled face.

"This is a very charming person, who has been a great deal with me," continued Matty, as if these interpositions did not signify. "Her parents have lately died and left her at a loose end; and if I can help her to gather up the threads of her life, I feel it is for me to do it. It may be a thing I am equal to, in spite of my—what shall I call them?—disadvantages."

"I always tell you that your disadvantages do not count, Aunt Matty," said Justine.

"I feel that they do, dear. They must to me, you see. But I try not to let them affect other people, and I am glad of any assurance that they do not."

"Do you mean Maria Sloane?" said Blanche. "I remember her when we had just grown up and she was a child. She grew up very pretty, and we saw her sometimes when we stayed with you and Father."

"She grew up very pretty; she has remained very pretty; and she will always be pretty to me, though she is so to everyone as yet, and I think will be so until she is something more."

"It is odd to see Aunt Matty giving her wholehearted

admiration to anyone," said Justine to Mark. "It shows that we have not a complete picture of her."

"It also suggests that she has one of us."

"It is pleasant to see it in a way."

"We may feel it to be salutary."

"She has only seen one or two of my many sides," said Dudley.

"Miss Sloane has not married, has she?" said Blanche.

"No, she is still my lovely Maria Sloane. I don't think I could think of her as anything else. A rose by any other name would smell as sweet, but it seems that marriage might be a sort of desecration of Maria, a sort of plucking of the rose." Matty ended on an easy note and did not look into anyone's face.

Sarah regarded her with several expressions, and Blanche with an easy and almost acquiescent one.

"Mrs. Middleton has been plucked," murmured Aubrey. "Mr. Middleton has plucked her."

Thomas gave a kindly smile which seemed to try to reach the point of amusement.

"Is she well provided for, Aunt Matty?" said Justine in a clear tone.

Sarah nodded towards Justine at the pertinence of the question.

"I think so, dear; I have not heard anything else. Money seems somehow not to touch her. She seems to live apart from it like a flower, having all she needs and wanting nothing more."

"Flowers are plucked," said Aubrey.

"They look better when they are not, dear."

"Money must touch her if she has all she needs," said Clement. "There must be continual contact."

"Well, I suppose she has some, dear, but I think it is not much, and that she does not want any more. When you see her you will know what I mean."

"We have all met people of that kind, and very charming they are," said Justine.

"No, not anyone quite like this. I shall be able to show you something outside your experience."

"Come, Aunt Matty, think of Uncle Dudley."

"I could not say it of myself," said her uncle.

"Yes, I see that you follow me, dear. But there is no one else who is quite as my Maria. Still you will meet her soon, and I shall be glad to do for you something you have not had done. I take a great deal from you, and I must not only take."

"Is she so different from other people?" said Blanche, with simple question. "I do not remember her very well, but I don't quite know what you mean."

"No, dear? Well, we shall see, when you meet, if you do know. We can't all recognise everything."

"Would it be better if Mother and Aunt Matty did not address each other in terms of affection?" said Mark. "Is it supposed to excuse everything else? It seems that something is."

"Well, perhaps in a way it does," said Justine, with a sigh. "Affection should be able to stand a little buffeting, or there would be nothing in it."

"There might be more if it did not occasion such a thing," said Clement.

"Oh, come, Clement, people can't pick their way with their intimates as if they were strangers."

"It is only with the latter that they attempt it."

"Father and Uncle behave like friends," said Aubrey, "Mother and Aunt Matty like sisters, Clement and I like brothers. I am not sure how Mark and Clement behave. I think like strangers."

"No, I can't quite subscribe to it," said Justine. "It is putting too much stress on little, chance, wordy encounters. Our mild disagreement now does not alter our feeling for each other."

"It may rather indicate it," said Clement.

"We should find the differences interesting and stimulating."

"They often seem to be stimulating," said Mark. "But I doubt if people take much interest in them. They always seem to want to exterminate them."

"I suppose I spend my life on the surface," said Dudley. "But it does seem to avoid a good deal."

"Now that is not true, Uncle," said Justine. "You and Father get away together and give each other of the best and deepest in you. Well we know it and so do you. Oh, we know what goes on when you are shut in the library together. So don't make any mistake about it, because we do not."

Edgar's eyes rested on his daughter as if uncertain of their own expression.

"Do you live on the surface, Aunt Matty?" said Aubrey.

"No, dear. I? No, I am a person who lives rather in the deeps, I am afraid. Though I don't know why I should say 'afraid,' except that the deeps are rather formidable places sometimes. But I have a surface self to show to my niece and nephews, so that I need not take them down too far with me. I have a deal to tell them of the time when I was as young as they, and things were different and yet the same, in that strange way things have. Yes, there are stories waiting for you of Aunt Matty in her heyday, when the world was young, or seemed to keep itself young for her, as things did somehow adapt themselves to her in those days. Now there is quite a lot for Aunt Matty to talk about herself. But you asked her, didn't you?" Matty looked about in a bright, conscious way and tapped her knee.

"It was a lot, child, as you say," said Oliver.

"Aubrey knew not what he did," said Clement.

"He knew what he meant to do," said Mark. "Happily Aunt Matty did not."

"We both used to be such rebels, your aunt and I," said Blanche, looking round on her children. "We didn't find the world large enough or the time long enough for all our pranks and experiments. I must tell you all about it some time. Hearing about it brings it all back to me."

"Being together makes Mother and Aunt Matty more alike," said Mark.

"Suppose Mother should become a second Aunt Matty!" said Aubrey.

"Or Aunt Matty become a second little Mother," said Justine. "Let us look on the bright side—on that side of things. Grandpa, what did you think of the two of them in those days?"

"I, my dear? Well, they were young then, as you are now. There was nothing to think of it and I thought nothing."

"We were such a complement to each other," continued Blanche. "People used to say that what the one did not think of, the other did, and *vice versa*. I remember what Miss Griffin thought of us when she came. She said she had never met such a pair."

"Miss Griffin!" said Justine. "I meant to ask her to come in to-night and forgot. Never mind, the matter can be mended. I will send a message."

"Is it worth while, dear? It is getting late and she will not be ready. There is not much left for her to come for. We will ask her to dinner one night and give her proper notice."

"We will do that indeed, Mother, but there is still the evening. And she is just sitting at home alone, isn't she, Aunt Matty?"

"Why, yes, dear, she is," said Matty with a laugh. "When two out of three people are out, there must be one left. But I think she enjoys an evening to herself."

"I see it myself as a change for the better," said Oliver.

"Now I rather doubt that," said Justine. "It is so easy, when people are unselfish and adaptable, to assume that they are enjoying things which really offer very little. Now what is there, after all, in sitting alone in that little room?"

"Cosiness, dear, perhaps," said Matty, with a change in her eyes. "I have asked that same question and have had an answer."

"The size of the room is well enough for one person," said Oliver. "That is indeed its scope."

"Mother dear, I have your permission to send for her?" said Justine, as if the words of others could only be passed over.

"Well, dear, if you have your aunt's. But I don't know whom we are to send. The servants are busy."

"There is no problem there; I will go myself. I have eaten enough and I will be back before the rest of you have finished."

"One of the boys could go," said Edgar.

"No, Father, I will leave them to satisfy their manly appetites. No one else will understand the exigencies of Miss Griffin's toilet, and be able by a touch and a word to put things right, as I shall."

"Certainly no one else will undertake that," said Mark.

"Should I come to help with the toilet?" said Aubrey.

"One of you should walk with your sister," said Edgar, without a smile.

Aubrey rose with a flush, stood aside for Justine to pass and followed her out of the room.

"Oh, my baby boy has gone," said Blanche, not referring to the actual exit.

"He has developed very much, dear," said Matty. "We shall have him like his brothers after all."

"Why should he not be like them?"

"Well, he will be. We see that now."

"He has always seemed to me as promising as either of them. A little less forward for his age, but that is often a good sign."

"It must be difficult to judge of children," said Mark, "when their progress must count against them."

"I can't think of a childhood with less of the success that spells failure," said Clement.

"Slow and steady wins the race," said Oliver, without actually following.

"He is not particularly slow. He is only different from other people, as all individual people are," said Blanche. "No one with anything in him is just like everyone else."

"That cannot be said of anyone here, can it?" said her sister. "We are an individual company."

"Yes, but no one quite so much so as Aubrey. He is without exception the most individual person I have ever met."

"Without exception, dear?" said Matty, bending her head and looking up from under it. "Have you forgotten the two young rebels we were talking about just now?"

"No, but even you and I did not quite come up to him in originality. He is something in himself which none of the rest has been."

"I think that is true," said Mark.

"Now what do you mean by that? If you mean anything disparaging, it is very petty and absurd. I wish Justine were here to take my part. I can only repeat that there is something in Aubrey which is to me peculiarly satisfying. Edgar, why do you not support me?"

"You do not seem—you hardly seem to need my help."

"But what do you think yourself of the boy? I know you always speak the truth."

Edgar, who had lately hoped that his son might after all attain the average, broke this record.

"I see there is much—that there may be much in what you say."

"Aubrey is the one with a touch of me in him," said Dudley. "I wish Justine were here too."

"Hark! Hush! Listen," said Matty. "Do not make so much noise. Is it Maria's voice in the hall? Blanche, do ask your boys to stop talking. Yes, it is my Maria; Justine must have brought her. She must have arrived this evening. It is a full moment for me, and I am glad for you all to share it." Matty broke off and sat with a listening expression and set lips.

"What a pity for her to come like this," said Blanche, "with dinner nearly over! I hope she has had something to eat, but Miss Griffin will have seen to that."

"Yes, Miss Griffin will have cared for her, but I am here to give her welcome. And I cannot get my chair away from the table; I cannot manage it; I am dependent upon others; I must sit and wait for help. Yes, it is her voice. Sometimes patience is very hard. Thank you, Dudley; thank you, Edgar; I knew I should not wait long. No one else, Jellamy; too many cooks spoil the broth. I am on my feet now, and I can arrange my lace and touch my hair and make myself look my best, vain person that I am; make myself look like myself, I should rather say, for that is all my aim."

"What relation is this friend to you all?" said Sarah, leaning towards Blanche.

"No relation, only an old friend. She lived near to our old home and my sister saw a good deal of her."

Sarah gave a grateful nod and leaned back, ready for the scene.

Justine spoke in the doorway.

"Now, I am simply the herald. I claim no other part. I found Miss Sloane already in the lodge and Miss Griffin at a loss how to manage the situation. So I took it into my own hands. And I feel a thought triumphant. I induced Miss Sloane, tired as she was, travel-stained and unwilling as she was, harassed and moithered by crossing letters and inconsistent trains, to come and join us to-night. Now do you not call that a success? Because it was a hardly earned one. And now you can all share the results."

A tall, dark woman of fifty entered the room, came towards Matty with a swift but quiet step, exchanged a natural embrace and looked round for her hosts. Blanche came forward in the character; Matty introduced the pair with an air of possession in each; Miss Griffin watched with the open and almost avid interest of one starved of interest and accordingly unversed in its occasions, and Justine took her stand at her side with an air of easy friendship.

"I do not need an introduction," said Blanche. "I remember you so well, Miss Sloane. I am afraid that my daughter has asked rather much of you, but we do appreciate your giving it to us."

"Miss Sloane has made a gallant capitulation, Mother, and does not want credit for it any more than any other generous giver."

"It is more than we had a right to expect," said Edgar.

"It is certainly that, Father. So we will take it in a spirit of simple gratitude."

"Well, stolen waters are sweet."

"Bravo, Father!" said Justine, smiling at Miss Griffin. "He comes up to scratch when there is a demand on him."

"I have less right to expect what I am having," said the guest, in a voice which did not hurry or stumble, shaking hands with several people without hastening or scamping the observance. "I am a travel-worn person to appear as a stranger."

"It is only a family gathering, Miss Sloane," said Justine. "We honestly welcome a little outside leavening."

"We are glad indeed to see you, my dear," said Oliver, who had got himself out of his chair. "You are a good person to set eyes on. I do not know a better."

"For heaven's sake sit down, Miss Sloane," said Justine, when they reached the drawing-room. "I shall feel so guilty if you continue to stand."

"Now I am dependent upon help to get into a place by my guest," said Matty, in a clear tone. "I cannot join in a scramble."

"Poor, dear Aunt Matty, the help is indeed forthcoming. And, boys, you must see that Miss Griffin has no chair. Thank you, Uncle; I knew you would not countenance that."

Maria Sloane was a person who seemed to have no faults within her own sphere. She had a tall, light figure, large, grey eyes, features which were good and delicate in their own way rather than of any recognised type, and an air of finished and rather formal ease, which was too natural ever to falter. Matty had said that money seemed not to touch her, and that when they saw her they would understand; and Edgar and Dudley and Mark saw her and understood. Justine and Sarah thought that her clothes were of the kind of simplicity which costs more than elaboration, but she herself knew that when these two qualities are on the same level, simplicity costs much less. Blanche simply admired her and Miss Griffin welcomed her coming with fervid relief. She had lost a lover by death in her youth, and since then had lived in her loss, or gradually in the memory of it. Her parents had lately died, and she had left the home of her youth with the indifferent ease which had come to mark her. She believed that nothing could touch her deeply again, and losing her parents at the natural age had not done so. Her brothers and sisters were married and away, and she now took her share of the money and went forth by herself, seeing that it would suffice for her needs, rather surprised at herself for regretting that they must be modified, and welcoming a shelter in the Seatons' house while she adapted herself to the change. She had rather felt of herself what Matty said of her, that she lived apart from money like a flower, but she had lately realised that not even the extreme example of human adornment was arrayed as one of these.

"Confess now, Miss Sloane," said Justine. "You would rather be in this simple family party than alone in that little house. Now isn't it the lesser of two evils? I think that nothing is so hopeless as arriving after a long journey and finding the house empty and a cheerless grate, and everything conspiring to mental and moral discomfort."

"Has Justine had that experience?" said Mark. "If so, we are much to blame."

"That could hardly have been the case, dear," said Matty, "with Miss Griffin and Emma in the house."

"I meant metaphorically empty and cheerless. We all know what that means."

"We are even more to blame," said Mark.

"Make up the fire, Aubrey dear," said Blanche, following the train of thought.

"It is metaphorically full," said her son from a chair.

There was laughter, which Aubrey met by kicking his feet and surveying their movement.

"Get up and make up the fire," said Clement, who found these signs distasteful.

His brother appeared not to hear.

"Get up and make up the fire."

"Now that is not the way to ask him, Clement," said Justine. "You will only make him obstinate. Aubrey darling, get up and make up the fire."

"Yes, do it, darling," said Blanche.

"Now I have been called 'darling' twice, I will. Why should I be obliging to people who do not call me 'darling' or 'little boy' or some other name of endearment?"

There was further laughter, and Aubrey bent over the fire with his face hidden. This seemed a safe attitude, but Clement observed the flush on his neck.

"Don't go back to the best chair in the room."

Aubrey strolled back to the chair; Clement intercepted him and put a leg across his path; Justine came forward with a swift rustling and a movement of her arms as of separating two combatants.

"Come, come, this will not do: I have nothing to say for either of you. Both go back to your seats."

"Will one of you help me to move the chair for your mother?" said Edgar, who did not need any aid.

93

"Yes, sir," said Aubrey, with almost military precision.

"Now I think that Aubrey came out of that the better, Clement," said Justine.

"The other fellow doesn't seem to be out of it yet," said Oliver, glancing at his second grandson. "I am at a loss to see why he put himself into it."

"Miss Sloane, what must you think of our family?"

"I have belonged to a family myself."

"And do you not now belong to one?"

"Well, we are all scattered."

"I do not dare to think of the time when we shall be apart. It seems the whole of life to be here together."

Thomas lifted his eyes at this view of a situation which he had just seen illustrated.

"Do you belong to a family, Miss Griffin?" said Dudley.

"I did, of course, but we have been scattered for a long time."

"I have lived in the same house all my life, and so has my brother," said Edgar.

"I have lived in two houses," said Blanche.

"I am just in my second," said Matty, "and very strange I am finding it, or should be if it were not for this dear family at my gates. The family at whose gates I am, I should say."

"Why should you say it, Aunt Matty?" said Justine. "What difference does it make?"

"I too have just entered my second," said Oliver, "though it hardly seemed worth while for me to do so. I had better have laid myself down on the way."

"And you, Miss Sloane?" said Edgar.

"I am on my way to my second, which must be a very tiny one. It will be the first I have had to myself."

"And you have not had your road made easier," said Oliver. "You have been dragged out of it in the dead of night, when you thought that one of your days was done. The way you suffer it speaks well for you."

"I have an idea that a good many things do that for Miss Sloane," said Justine. "But you make me feel rather a culprit, Grandpa."

"You have done a sorry thing, child, and I propose to undo it. Good-night, Blanche, my dear, and good-bye I hope until to-morrow. If it is to be for ever, I am the more glad to have been with you again."

"Father is tired," said Blanche, who would never admit that Oliver at eighty-seven might be near the end of his days.

"I am tired too," said Matty, "but after such a happy evening with such a satisfying end. I thank you all so much, and I am sure you thank me."

"We do indeed," said Justine. "You are tired too, Miss Griffin, and I am afraid after a very brief taste of happiness. But we will make up for it another time."

"Oh, I am not tired," said Miss Griffin, standing up and looking at Matty.

"Be careful, both of you, on this slippery floor," said Blanche. "I always think that Jellamy puts too much polish on it. Do not hurry."

"We shall neither of us be able to do that again," said Oliver.

Blanche followed her father and sister with her eyes on their steps, and perhaps gave too little attention to her own, for she slipped herself and had to be saved. Justine moved impulsively to Maria.

"Miss Sloane, I do hope that you are going to spend some time with them? It comes to me somehow that you are just what they need. Can you give me a word of assurance?"

"I hope they will let me stay for a while. It is what I need anyhow, a home and old friends at this time of my life."

"And there are new friends here for you. I do trust that you realise that."

"I have been made to feel it. And they do not seem

to me quite new, as they are relations of such old ones."

"Dear Aunt Matty, she does attach people to her in her own way."

"We have enjoyed it so much, Mrs. Gaveston. We shall have a great deal to think and talk of," said Sarah, able to express her own view of the occasion.

"We need not thank you," said Thomas, uttering the words with a sincere note and acting upon them.

"You did not mind the inclusion of Aubrey?" said Justine. "It is so difficult to keep one member of the family apart, and we know Mr. Middleton is used to boys."

"Can that give him only one view of them?" said Mark.

"Oh, come, he would not have given his best years to them if they had not meant something to him. I daresay he often finds his thoughts harking back to the old days."

"His best years!" said Sarah, laughing at youth's view of a man in his prime.

"Mr. Middleton, what do you think of the little boy?" said Justine in a lowered tone. "Don't look at him; he is enough in the general eye; but would you in the light of your long experience put him above or below the level?"

Thomas was hampered in his answer by being forbidden to look at the subject of it, a thing he had hardly done.

"He seems to strike his own note in his talk," he said in a serious tone, trying to recall what he had heard.

"Yes, that is what I think," said Justine, as if the words had considerable import, "I am privately quite with you. But quiet; keep it in the dark; tell it not in Gath. Little pitchers have long ears. You see I feel quite maternally towards my youngest brother."

Thomas was able to give a smile of agreement, and he added one of understanding.

"Do you think that we are alike as a family, Miss

Sloane?" said Blanche, willing for comment upon her children.

"Really, Mother, poor Miss Sloane! We have surely had enough from her to-night."

Maria regarded the faces round her, causing Aubrey to drop his eyes with a smile as of some private reminiscence.

"I think I see a likeness between your brother-in-law and your youngest son."

"A triumph, Miss Sloane!" said Justine. "That is a great test, and you are through it at a step. Now you can turn to the rest of us with confidence."

"But perhaps with other feelings," said Mark. "Miss Sloane will think that we have one resemblance, an undue interest in ourselves."

"In each other, let us say. She will not mind that."

"I think there are several other family likenesses," said Maria.

"And they are obvious, Miss Sloane. Quite unworthy of a discerning eye. You have had the one great success and you will rest on that. Well, I think that there is nothing more fascinating than pouncing on the affinities in a family and tracing them to their source. I do not pity anyone for being asked to do it, because I like so much to do it myself."

"Must it be a safe method of judging?" said Clement.

"Now, young man, I have noticed that this is not one of your successful days. I can only assure Miss Sloane that you have another side."

It now emerged that Matty and her father had reached the carriage, and the party moved on with the surge of a crowd released. Justine withheld her brothers from the hall with an air of serious admonishment, and assisted Edgar and Blanche and Dudley to speed the guests.

"Goodbye, Miss Griffin," she called at the last moment. "That is right, Uncle; hand Miss Griffin into the carriage. Good night all."

The family reassembled in the drawing room.

"Now there is an addition to our circle," said Justine.

"Indeed, yes, she is a charming woman," said Blanche. "I had not remembered how charming. It is so nice to see anyone gain with the years, as she has."

"I believe I have been silent and unlike myself," said Dudley. "Perhaps Justine will explain to her about me, as she has about Clement."

"Indeed I will, Uncle, and with all my heart."

"I find that I want her good opinion. I do not agree that we should not mind what other people think of us. Consider what would happen if we did not."

"Miss Sloane behaved with a quiet heroism," said Mark.

"Under a consistent persecution," said his brother.

"Oh, things were not as bad as that," said Justine. "She did not mind being asked to look at the family. Why should she?"

"She could hardly give her reasons."

"And she was not actually asked to look at Aubrey," said Mark. "If her eyes were drawn to him by some morbid attraction, it was not our fault."

"Don't be so silly," said his mother at once.

"I really wonder that she was not struck by the likeness between you and Uncle, Father," said Justine.

"We may perhaps accept an indifference to any further likeness," said Edgar with a smile.

"We have to make conversation with our guests," said his wife.

"I am glad that my look of Uncle flitted across my face," said Aubrey.

"Little boy," said Justine, pointing to the clock, "what about Mr. Penrose to-morrow? He does not want to be confronted by a sleepy-head."

"Good night, darling," said Blanche, kissing her son without looking at him and addressing her husband. "I do hope Matty enjoyed the evening. I could see that my father did. I am sure that everything was done for her. And Miss Sloane's arrival was quite a little personal triumph."

"I could see it was," said Mark, "but I did not quite know why. It seemed that it had happened rather unfortunately."

"Yes, dear Grandpa was quite content," said Justine. "He does like to be a man among men. We cannot expect him not to get older."

"We can and do," said Mark, "but it is foolish of us."

"I was sincerely glad of Aunt Matty's little success. It was something for her, herself, apart from what she was taking from us, something for her to give of her own. It seemed to be just what she wanted."

"I think Miss Griffin will enjoy having Miss Sloane," said Blanche, guarding her tone from too much expression.

"And I am glad of that from my soul," said Justine, stretching her arms. "I would rather have Miss Griffin's pleasure than my own any day. And now I am going to bed. I have enjoyed every minute of the evening, but there is nothing more exhausting than a thorough-going family function."

"You need not work so hard at it," said Clement.

"Clement has a right to speak," said Mark. "He has followed his line."

"Yes, anyhow I have done my best. I could spare myself a good deal if I had some support."

"Yes, that is true, Clement dear," said Blanche. "You ought to come out of yourself a little and try to support the talk."

"Is it worthy of any effort?"

"If it is worthy of Justine's, it is worthy of yours. That goes without saying."

"Then why not let it do so?"

"I had not realised that we were indebted to Clement for any regard of us," said Edgar.

"I believe I had without knowing it," said Dudley. "I believe I felt some influence at work, which checked my spirits and rendered me less than myself."

"Really, Clement, you should not do it," said Blanche, turning to her son with a scolding note as she learned his course.

Clement walked towards the door.

"We will follow—perhaps we will follow our custom of parting for the night," said his father.

"Good night, Mother," said Clement, slouching to Blanche as if he hardly knew what he did.

"Good night, dear," said the latter, caressing his shoulder to atone for her rebuke. "You will remember what I say."

"Father is sometimes nothing short of magnificent," said Justine. "The least said and the most done. I envy his touch with the boys. Good night, Father, and thanks from your admiring daughter."

Edgar stooped and held himself still, while Justine threw her arms about his neck and kissed him on both cheeks, a proceeding which always seemed to him to take some time.

"I was so proud of them all," said Blanche, when her children had gone. "I do see that Matty has much less than I have. I ought to remember it."

"You ought not," said Dudley. "You ought to assume that she has quite as much. I am always annoyed when people think that I have less than Edgar, because he has a wife and family and an income and a place, and I have not. I like them to see that all that makes no difference."

"Neither does it to you, because you share it all."

"That is not the same. I like it to be thought that there is no need for me to share it, that that is just something extra. I hope Miss Sloane thinks so."

"Has Miss Sloane as much as Blanche?" said Edgar, smiling.

"Yes, she has," said his wife, with sudden emphasis. "She is such a finished, satisfying person that anything

she lacks is more than balanced by what she has and
what she gives. I am not at all a woman to feel that everyone must have the same. I am prepared to yield her the
place in some things, as she must yield it to me in others.
And I think she will be such a good example for Justine."
Blanche put her needle into her work without alluding
to her intention of going to bed, and observing Dudley
retrieving her glasses and putting them into their case,
seemed about to speak of it, but let the image fade. "I
mean in superficial ways. It is the last thing we should
wish, that the dear girl's fundamental lines should be
changed. We are to have breakfast half an hour later:
did I remember to tell Jellamy? I must go and see if
Aubrey is asleep. Good night, Edgar; good night, Dudley.
I hope my father has got to bed. He seemed to be feeling
his age to-night. If you are going to talk, don't sit up too
long. And if you smoke in the library, mind the sparks."

"We must be a little later than Blanche means," said
Dudley, as he brought the cigars to his brother and sat
down out of reach of them himself. "I want to talk about
how Matty behaved. Better than usual, but so badly. And
about how Miss Sloane behaved. Beautifully. I do admire
behaviour; I love it more than anything. Blanche has
the behaviour of a person who has no evil in her; and
that is the rarest kind, and I have a different admiration
for it."

"I fear we cannot say much for Clement on the point."

"We will not say anything. The less said about it, the
better, and it is silly to say that and then talk about it."

"Do you think he is developing on the right lines?"

"People don't alter at his age as much as older people
think."

"How old is he?" said Clement's father, wishing to
know at this stage.

"Twenty-six the month before last. The change now
must be slow. Perhaps the lad ought to be a grief to me,
but I don't suffer a great deal; I hardly even think of him

as the lad. To tell you the truth, I feel so young myself
that I hardly feel I am any older than he is; but you will
not tell anyone that. And now I have made one confession, the ice is broken and I should be able to make
another. But do not look at me or I could not make it.
You are looking at me, and for the first time in my life
I cannot meet your eyes. Why don't you tell me to sit
down quietly on that little stool and tell you everything?"

"Well, do that."

"You know my old godfather?"

"The one who is ninety-six?"

"Yes, that one; I have no other. At least, of course
people have two godfathers, but the other is dead. And
now this one is dead too. I hope he was not feeling his
age, but I expect he felt as young as Clement. You know
he had no children?"

"Yes, I had heard it, or I think I had. Has he left you
any money?"

"Edgar, is it possible that your thoughts have run on
sordid lines?"

"I had not thought of it until this moment."

"I am glad of that. I should not like to feel that I had
lost my brother. It would be quite different from losing
a godfather."

"It would in the matter of money," said Edgar, with
his short laugh. "Is it surprising that a childless man
should leave money to his godson?"

"Yes, very. People have not any money. And they
always have a family. It is very rare to have the first and
not the second. I can't think of another case, only of the
opposite one. We see that Matty has relations."

"I did not know that he had much money."

"I see you will feel the shock as well. I am not alone
in my distress."

"Why is it distress? Why not the opposite feeling?"

"Edgar, you must know that money is the cause of all
evil. It is the root of it."

"How did he get so much?"

"He speculated and made it. I knew he speculated, but I thought that people always lost every farthing. And it is wrong to speculate, and he has left the fruits of his sin to me."

"The sins of the father are visited upon the children. And in default of them there is a godson."

"Unto the third and fourth generation. But I expect they have generally lost it all by then."

"Can you bring yourself to tell me how much it is?"

"No. You have only just brought yourself to ask."

"Is it very much?"

"Yes."

"How can I help you?"

"I must leave it to you. You have never failed me yet."

"Shall we wait and look at *The Times*?"

"No, that would imply a lack of confidence. There have never been secrets between us."

"Is it as much as a thousand a year?"

"Yes."

"As much as fifteen hundred?"

"Yes."

"As much as three thousand?"

"No. How easy it is after all! It is about two. I am glad you have not failed me. Now our danger point is past, and we know that we can never fail each other."

"Those letters you have had in these last days? That one you went away to answer?"

"I see there has been no secret between us."

"It will make a great deal of difference, Dudley."

"Yes, it will. I am not going to pretend that I don't think much of it. I think too much, as is natural. And I am not going to refer to it as a nice little fortune. I think it is a large one, though I am rather ashamed of thinking it. I don't know why people do such aggravating things. It must be because money brings out the worst in them. I shall never even say that I am a comparatively poor man. I have actually begun to push the thought from me."

The door opened and Blanche appeared with a lamp, pale and different in the half light, her loose, grey hair and straight garments giving her the look of a woman from another age.

"What are you talking about all this time? I had no idea that you had not come up. I went to get something from Edgar's room and thought he must be asleep. I can never get to sleep myself while I know that other people are about. I am so afraid of fire. You know that."

"Indeed I did not, Blanche," said Dudley. "At least, I thought that you slept in spite of your fear, like everyone else."

"I thought the same, assumed it," said Edgar.

"I cannot sleep when I feel that people are doing their best to set the house in a blaze every moment. How could I?"

"I don't see how you could. I did not know that Edgar did that when he sat up. It seems sly somehow, when he never does it in the day. And it does show that he ought to be in bed. But I do my best with quite different things. You can sleep in peace when you know that I am about."

"You will accept our excuse when you hear it, Blanche. Dudley has been left a fortune—a sum of money by his godfather."

"He hasn't," said Blanche in a petulant tone. "Not large enough to make all that talk and keep you up half the night. I know he was quite a poor man; I did not know why anyone had him for a godfather. Now come upstairs, both of you, and put out the lamps and push back the coals, as Dudley implies that he does it, and let us hear about it in the morning."

The brothers occupied themselves with these measures.

"How much is it?" said Blanche, shading her lamp with her hand and speaking as if she might as well hear while she waited.

"It is a large sum, my dear, really very large. You must be prepared."

"How much is it? It is very nice if it is large. I saw his death in the papers, and meant to speak about it and forgot. He was over a hundred, wasn't he?"

"He was ninety-six," said Dudley, "but that is old enough to make it excusable to forget his death."

"How much is it? Why do you not tell me? Is there some mystery?"

"No, there is not; I wish there were; I hate having to manage without one. Edgar, you are failing me at last."

"It is two thousand a year," said Edgar, "or probably about that sum."

"Two thousand pounds a year?"

"Yes, yes. About that, about two thousand pounds."

"Two thousand pounds a year or two thousand pounds?"

"Two thousand pounds a year."

"Why, how very nice!" said Blanche, turning to lead the way from the room, with her hand still over her lamp. "When did you hear? Dear Dudley, I do congratulate you. It is just what you deserve. I never was so glad about anything. And you were wise not to talk about it before Matty. It sometimes upsets her to hear that people have much more than she has. We might be the same in her place. Well, no wonder you stayed up to talk about that. We must talk it all over in the morning; I shall quite look forward to it. Well, I shall sleep very soundly after hearing this."

Blanche, meaning what she said and about to act upon it, went upstairs, guarding her lamp, and the brothers followed, pausing to whisper outside their doors.

"We have seen things out of their true proportion," said Dudley. "How is it that our outlook is so material? I was prepared to toss on my bed, and really we ought to sleep particularly well. I thought when I saw Miss Sloane, that she and I lived apart from tangible things. And really we have only been kept apart from them. Well, you can't separate yourself from me on this occasion. All that I have is yours."

A flash from Blanche's door sent Edgar into his room and Dudley on tiptoe to her side.

"Blanche, I am only waiting for the morrow, to come and pour it all into your lap. And I am sure the house is not in a blaze."

"Good night, dear Dudley," said Blanche, smiling and closing her door.

IV

"WELL, has your uncle told you his news?" said Blanche at breakfast, as she moved her hands uncertainly amongst the cups. "I heard it last night and I found it quite a tonic. I was feeling so very tired and it quite pulled me up. I slept so well and I still feel quite stimulated. I have been looking forward to talking about it."

"What is it?" said Mark. "Is Uncle going to be married?"

"No, of course he is not. What a thing to ask! There are other kinds of news."

"Well, I must say, Mother, it occurred to me," said Justine. "What interpretation do you want put upon your words? That would be quite a natural one. I was already feeling a mingled sense of excitement and coming blank. And people were springing to my mind as likely candidates. As you have created the void, you owe it to us to fill it."

"Perhaps your uncle would like to tell you himself."

"No, I should not; I do not talk about my own affairs. I have come down early on purpose to hear you do it."

"Or perhaps they would like to guess?"

"Really, Mother, we are not so young. And there is
nothing to put us on the track. If Uncle has neither become engaged nor been left a fortune, we clearly cannot
guess."

"I think you can," said Edgar. "Indeed you have almost done so."

"Have I? Oh, dear Uncle," said Justine, springing up
and hurrying round the table to Dudley. "Dear, dear
Uncle, who have given all your mind and your life to
other people, to think that you have something for yourself at last! I would rather it were you than anyone else
in the world. Far, far rather than that it were me."

"I would rather it were me too."

" I know you wouldn't. You would rather it were anyone and everyone. But it isn't this time. You are the hero of
this occasion. And utterly rejoiced we all are that it is so."

Blanche glanced from her daughter to Dudley with
eyes of modest but irrepressible pride.

"We should like to know just at what we are to rejoice," said Clement.

"I should not; I am quite indifferent. I just like to know
that a piece of luck has crossed Uncle's path; and what it
is and how much it is can stand over while I savour the
main truth. It is what I have always waited for."

"I suppose we all wait in case we shall be left a fortune," said Dudley. "But I never heard of anyone's waiting for other people to be left one. Because why should
they be? They have no claim. And we should spend part
of ours on them, and what can they want more?"

"Yes, that is what you want it for," said Justine, sighing. "To spend it on other people. And we shall all share
in it evenly and equally. It was idle to hope that you
would have anything for yourself. It hardly becomes us
to ask how much it is. Oh, what am I saying? What a
pass your dealings with us have brought us to! Somebody say something quickly to cover my confusion."

"Perhaps someone who does not assume that it is his as

much as Uncle's, may put the question," said Clement. "Our interest in Uncle may lead us to that."

"Well, who will do it?" said Mark.

"I cannot," said Justine, leaning back. "Leave me out of it."

"You were hardly anticipating that fate."

"They all feel sensitive about it," said Blanche, smiling at Dudley. "This is something outside their experience."

"But why should they feel like that? I do, of course, because I have something which I have done nothing to earn, and which makes me one of those people who have too much, when some people have not enough to live on; and anyone would be sensitive about that. I expect that is partly why rich people say they are poor. But only partly: they really think they are poor. I begin to understand it and to think I am poor myself, really to see that I am. So no one need feel sensitive for my sake. There is no reason."

"I need not say how I feel for my own," said Justine. "Oh yes, Father, you may look as if your only daughter could do and say no wrong. I crossed the bound that time."

"I don't see how we are to hear the main thing," said Clement.

"Can we ask who has left the money?" said Mark.

"My godfather," said his uncle.

"The man who was nearly a hundred?"

"Well, he was ninety-six."

"Well, we need feel no sorrow; that is one thing," said Justine, as if further complication of feeling would be too much.

"Is it a million pounds?" said Aubrey.

"Now, little boy, you are not as young as that."

Aubrey fell into silence as he found what he did by words.

"What proportion of a million is it?" said Clement.

"A terribly small one," said Dudley. "About a twen-

tieth, I should think. It is really very small. I have quite
got over my sensitiveness and am afraid that people will
think I am better off than I am. I see now how that happens. I am sorry I have so often said that people can
surely afford things, when they are so well off. I feel so
much remorse. I really don't like inheriting so little, except that now I suppose I should starve without it."

"Oh, we shall not find it so very little. Make no doubt
about that," said Justine, meeting the general laughter
with her own. "Well, why should we not speak the truth
after all?"

"You have seen no reason why you should not speak
it," said Clement. "I mean, as you see it. Don't sit grinning at me, Aubrey. It makes you look more vacant than
usual."

"It is an immense family event," said Mark. "I mean
a great event for Uncle. It seems that we cannot speak
without tripping, that all words mean the same thing."

"I hope you are not all forgetting your breakfast," said
Blanche.

"I am so ashamed of being excited and toying with my
food," said Dudley. "And all about my own little affairs!
I have explained how little they are. I am grateful to
Justine for taking the matter as concerning us all. It
makes me fell less egotistic, sitting here chasing morsels
round my plate."

"Would you like something fresh and hot, sir?" said
Jellamy, who had stood behind the table with prominent
eyes, and now spoke as if any luxury would be suitable
for Dudley in his new situation. "Shall I give the word
to Cook, ma'am?"

"No, you may go now. We have not really wanted you
all this time. We will ring if we want anything."

"No, ma'am; yes, ma'am," said Jellamy, going to the
door with a suggestion of coat-tails flying.

"Jellamy has had a good half-hour," said Mark, "and
will now have another."

"Well, we have all had that," said his sister.

"You have had the best," said Clement. "No one has been left anything but you and Uncle, and he had had his hour already."

"That is unworthy, Clement. And there is something I do not like in the tone of the speech. Father, are you not going to say a word on the great occasion? We know it is greater for you in that it concerns Uncle and not yourself. And we seem to want your note."

"Father said all that he felt last night," said Blanche, unsure of her husband under the demand.

"What did the godfather die of?" said Clement, with a retaliatory note, as if to add a touch of trouble and reproach.

"Of old age and in his sleep," said Dudley.

"He has shown us every consideration," said Mark, "except by living to be ninety-six."

"I have been kept out of my inheritance too long. I might have saved by now, and then I should not have had so little. But I must conquer any bitterness."

"There is little Mr. Penrose," said Justine. "Aubrey, you can put all this excitement out of your head."

"Perhaps I can have a fullsized tutor now."

"Now, now, none of that. This makes no difference to you, except that you rejoice with Uncle. Apart from that you can just forget it."

"He can indeed," said Blanche, looking up. "Are you paying attention, Aubrey?"

"Good morning, Mrs. Gaveston; good morning, Mr. Gaveston. May I offer you my congratulations upon the piece of news which has just come to my ears? Good morning, Mr. Dudley; I feel that I should have addressed you first on this occasion."

"So you meet an occasion when you do not find me second to my brother."

"Oh, I do not know that, Mr. Dudley," said Mr. Penrose, laughing. "I have never had any feeling of that kind. One naturally comes to the elder brother first. That has been all the distinction in my mind."

"So good news runs apace," said Edgar.

"How did you hear, Mr. Penrose?" said Justine.

"From your manservant at the door. I do not generally talk to the man, but to-day he addressed me and volunteered the information. And if I may say so, he was full of the most pleasant and spontaneous goodwill towards the family."

"I think we could not expect him to be silent upon such a piece of news."

"Indeed no, Miss Gaveston," said Mr. Penrose, laughing. "Not upon the accession of a quarter of a million to the family. It would indeed be much to expect."

"It is about a twentieth of a million," said Dudley.

"Well, well, Mr. Dudley, putting it in round numbers."

"But surely numbers are not as round as that. What is the good of numbers? I thought they were an exact science."

"Well, taking the bearing of the sum upon ordinary life, shall we say?"

"No, we will not say it. We will say a twentieth."

"Well, we may as well be numerically accurate," said Mr. Penrose, not pretending to appreciate any further difference. "Come, Aubrey, we must be setting out. I suppose, Mr. Gaveston—I suppose this modification of your affairs will not affect your plans for Aubrey's education?"

"No, no, not at all. As far as I can see, not at all."

"Oh, no, Mr. Penrose, not in the least," said Justine. "There is no difference in Aubrey's prospects."

"Thank you, Miss Gaveston, thank you. You do not mind my asking? It is best to be clear on such a matter."

"Poor little Mr. Penrose, he went quite pale," said Justine. "It would be sad if our rise in fortune should spell disadvantage for him."

"Let us talk of something else," said Dudley. "We have had enough of me and my affairs. Of course I don't mean that. I am so worried about the confusion in people's minds. Mr. Penrose has thoroughly upset me. You don't think he has any influence on Aubrey?"

"None," said Mark.

"Oh, I am sure he has," said Blanche, who had half heard.

"Well, that would be rather much to expect," said Justine, "that a tutor should be accepted as an influence by a pupil. But dear Uncle! I don't think I have seen you so much engaged with your own experience in all my life."

"There, wealth has already ruined me. And I have not got wealth. I must be in the stage where I only have its disadvantages. I have heard of that. Do you think that people will think more of me or less?"

"More of you," said Clement.

"Yes, well, I think we can hardly expect them not to do that in a way," said Blanche.

"So they have not thought as much of me as they could?"

"I am sure they have in one sense, in any sense that matters."

"Little Mother, you are coming out very nicely on this occasion," said Justine. "We could not have a better lead. And the occasion is something of a test."

Blanche gave her daughter a rather absent smile, put her needle into her work and rose and went to the window.

"Father and Matty, Edgar! I thought I caught a glimpse of them. Coming up the drive! Both of them and on foot! It must have taken them half an hour. What can it be?"

"I will go out and help them to come in," said Justine.

"What can Justine do?" said Clement. "Carry them in, in her strong young arms?"

"It would be a useful piece of work," said Mark. "They can hardly be fit to take another step."

"Oh, I am not at all ashamed of being strong!" called his sister. "I have no wish to be the other thing. It would seem to me a very odd ambition. I like to be a good specimen physically, as well as in every other way."

"I think we might all like that," said Edgar, smiling and at once changing his tone. "If arms are needed we all have them."

"I will go," said Dudley. "I must keep my simple ways. I must not let myself become different. That sounds as if I have admired myself, and in a way I have."

"Now, Grandpa dear, come in," said Justine, keeping her eyes on Oliver as if to see that he followed her direction. "We will have you established in a minute. Don't have any misgiving."

"Thank you, my dear, you take it all off me; I have none."

"Well, dear ones all," said Matty, pausing in the door as if she could go no further, "so here is a great occasion. I am come to share it with you, to rejoice in your joy. I could not remain in my little house and feel that so much had come—so much more had come to you in your big one, without coming to add my sympathy to all you have. For your happiness is mine. It shall be. And I shall have plenty if I can find it like that. And it is a lesson I have learnt, one that has come my way. And it isn't a hard lesson, to rejoice in the good of those so dear."

"My dear, nothing has come to us. It is to Dudley," said Blanche, emerging from her sister's embrace.

"Yes, and there is a difference, isn't there?" said Matty in an arch manner. "And we are all to see it? Well, we can't, and that is flat, as the boys would say. And that is a great compliment to him and to you."

"When do we say it?" said Mark.

"You can take that view too readily, Aunt Matty. Of course there is a difference," said Justine.

"But Justine ought to sympathise with Aunt Matty in the idea," said Aubrey.

"Of course, yes, of course," said Matty, looking at Dudley. "And you will let them say so? Well, I will not, I promise you. I will guard your reputation, I who know you almost as a brother. My sister's brother must be partly mine, as Blanche and I have always shared our good things. Now let me get to a chair and have my share of the news."

"How did you hear?" said Clement.

"Well, well, little birds flit about the chairs of people who are tied to them. And it would be rather a sad thing if they did not, as they would be the last to hear so much, when it seems that they ought to be the first. So the news came, I won't say how."

"I will do so," said her father. "It came through a tradesman's lad, who comes to our house after yours, or who comes to it on the way to yours and to-day chose to come again on his way back."

"So Jellamy was the bird," said Mark.

"Well, anyhow we heard," said his aunt. "But I should have liked to hear it from one of you, coming running down to tell me."

"We should have been down in a few minutes," said Justine.

"Would you, dear? But the minutes passed and nobody came. And so we came up to hear for ourselves."

"A bold step for anyone tied to a chair," muttered Clement.

"And came on foot!" said Blanche. "Whatever made you do that?"

"Well, dear, what were we to do?" said her sister, laughing and glancing at Edgar.

"You could have waited a little while."

"Well, it is true that the occupation palled," said Oliver.

"I expect Miss Griffin was very interested," said Justine.

"Well, now, let us settle down to hear the story," said Matty, in a tone of leaving a just annoyance, smoothing her dress in preparation for listening. "The full news of this happy quarter of a million. Let us hear it all from the first."

"My dear, it is not as much as that. It is not a quarter as much; it is about a fifth as much," said Blanche. "It is barely a fifth. It is about a twentieth of a million."

"Is it, dear? I am afraid they do not convey much to me, these differences between these very large sums. They have no bearing upon life as I know it."

"But it is just as well to be accurate."

"Well, you have been so, dear. So now tell me all about it. The exact sum makes no difference."

"Of course it does. The one is precisely four times the other."

"Well, but we don't have to think of proportions, after people have everything that they can have," said Matty, giving a glance round the room as if this appeared to her to be already the case.

"But you can't have everything you can have, from a moderate fortune belonging to somebody else."

"Oh well, dear, moderate. Your life has altered you more than I thought. Altered your attitude: of course you yourself are always my old Blanche. But a quarter of a million or some other proportion of one! We were not brought up to differentiate between such things. And belonging to somebody else! Dudley and I know better."

"It is not a quarter of a million or some proportion of one. I said it was barely a twentieth," said Blanche, her voice unsteady.

"You might say that fifty pounds is a proportion of one," said Mark.

"I had better go and lie down," said Dudley. "I may feel better when I get my head on the pillow."

"I don't care which it is," said Justine. "A simple life for me."

"Yes, and for me too, dear," said her aunt. "I always feel that in my heart."

"And keep it in your heart then," said her father.

"Well, let me hear all about it," said Matty, tapping her knee. "I have asked more times than I can count."

"Calculation does not seem to be Aunt Matty's point," said Mark.

"I want to hear the beginning, the middle and the end. Not the exact sum; I won't press that; but the romance of it from the first. That would be a small thing to deny your invalid, who is dependent on you for the interest of her life."

"Oh, how is Miss Sloane this morning?" said Justine, reminded of her aunt's other interests.

"That is another question, dear. Thank you, she is well and rested. And now for my own answer."

"My godfather died and left no heir. That is the romance," said Dudley.

"Left no heir!" said Matty, with a roguish look. "He has left an heir indeed, and very much we all rejoice with him. There is the romance in truth."

"That very old fellow," said Oliver, "who lived not far from us?"

"Yes, dear Grandpa, he was ninety-six," said Justine, smoothing Oliver's sleeve in tender recognition of an age that was approaching this.

"He must have seen a lot," said Oliver, making his own comparison.

"I remember him," said Matty. "Edgar and Dudley were staying at his house when Edgar and Blanche first met. I don't know why you object to the word romance. It all seems to me to fit together in quite a romantic way. So now tell me all about it. When you heard, what you heard, how you heard. How you felt and what you said. You must know all the things that I want to be told."

"They must by now," said Oliver. "I agree."

"We heard at breakfast this morning. Mother and Father had heard from Uncle last night," said Justine, in a running tone with a faint sigh in it. "It is only an hour or two ago. And what did we feel? I declare it already eludes me."

"That is really not fair on Aunt Matty," said Mark.

"Then I heard nearly as soon as you," said Matty, turning her eyes from her niece and nephew. "But my feelings do not play such tricks on me; no, they were too strong and eager for you for that. But I want to know how Dudley felt when the truth broke upon him. That is the main issue of the story."

"We heard last night, Edgar and I," said Blanche. "Edgar and Dudley sat up late, and when I came down to scold them, I was met by this piece of news. I told them it was quite a tonic. I slept so well after hearing it."

Matty looked at her sister and simply turned to other people.

"But what did you feel, Dudley? That is the main point."

"Uncle, gratify Aunt Matty's curiosity," said Justine. "She has every right to feel it."

"Well, dear, more than a right, I think, and curiosity is an odd word. It is natural and sympathetic to feel an interest in an important change for a friend. It would not even be quite affectionate not to feel it."

"No, no, Aunt Matty, you are all on the safe side. So now, Uncle."

"I heard a few days ago and kept the matter in my heart."

"Ah, that shows how deep it went."

"Oh no, does it? If I had known that, I would have brought it out. I thought it showed that I did not attach enough importance to it, even to mention it. I meant it to be showing that."

"Ah, we know what that kind of indifference means. Keeping the matter in your heart, indeed! And at last it got too big even for your big heart"—Matty gave Dudley a smile—"and you revealed it to your second self, to

117

Edgar. And didn't you have the tiniest feeling of interest? Not the least spark of excitement?"

"I had all the natural feelings. Shock, delight, excitement; compunction at having so much; worry lest I should be thought to have more than I had, though I did not know then how much reason there would be. Pleasure in what I could do for people; fear lest they should take it all for granted, or think I was conferring favours, and it does seem unlikely that they should avoid both. And then I told it all to Edgar, and the matter assumed its just proportions—you will remember that the sum is a twentieth of a million—and I went to bed feeling that my little affairs had a small place in the general scheme, and that it would all be the same a hundred years hence; which is not true, but it was right for me to feel it. And now I ought to say that that is the longest speech I have ever made, but I never know how people can be sure of that."

"There, Aunt Matty, there is a proper effort," said Justine.

Matty's swift frown crossed her face.

"You don't any of you seem to feel quite what I should have expected."

"Well, no, child, I am rather of your mind," said Oliver.

"We have not inherited anything," said Blanche. "It is Dudley who has had the good fortune."

"A good fortune in two senses. And what do the two young men feel, whose prospects are now so different?"

"They are nothing of the kind," said Blanche, with both her voice and her needle rising into the air. "This had nothing to do with them, and they are not giving a thought to it, except to rejoice in their uncle's happiness."

"I am not as bad as that," said Dudley. "Happiness depends on deeper things. Love in a cottage is the most important kind of love; no other kind is talked about so much. I can only hope to be allowed to share what I have with other people, and of course I shall feel that the generosity is theirs."

"I am sure you will," said Matty. "And now what about the unchanged positions of the two young men? Was I right or wrong in saying what I did?"

"You were wrong in saying it," said her father. "It was not a thing to say."

"Well, was I wrong—incorrect in thinking it?"

"Your sister says that you were, her brother-in-law that you were not. You must decide."

"Well, I decide that it was a true and natural thing to think, and therefore to say. And most heartily do I rejoice with them in the truth of it."

"Clement and I have all we need," said Mark. "We should have no right or reason to ask for more."

"And the people who do not ask for things, are the people who have them, I have heard. You would not ask, I am sure. Yes, I must not be denied my little bit of excitement for you. It is the one kind I have left, to let my spirits soar for other people, and I must be allowed to make the most of it. It is the best kind."

"I suppose it is, Aunt Matty. Anyhow it is nice of you to feel it," said Justine, "but there doesn't really seem to be much need. I am with the boys there. We have our home and our happiness and each other, and the simple tastes and pleasures which are the most satisfying. We do not ask or need anything more. I am quite sorry for Uncle that it is so, because he would like nothing better than to pour out his all upon us. But our simple lot suffices us, and there it is."

"They are all so self-reliant," said Blanche, with mingled apology and pride. "They have been brought up to be independent of things outside themselves."

Matty gave her glance about the room, this time with an open smile.

"Yes, I see what you are thinking," said her niece at once. "We have been brought up in a beautiful and dignified home; that is the truth. I should be the last person to deny it. But it has become our background, and that means that we are independent of it in a way. Not that we do not love it; I do from the bottom of my heart. And that brings it to my mind that I should be glad for something to be done for the dear old house, to prevent its falling into decay. I have long wished that its faithful service could be repaid. It would be a relief to Father, who sees it as a life trust and not as his own in any personal sense, so that he would not really be taking anything for himself. And Mark feels about it in the same way. Yes, I think I may say that we should all be grateful for succour for the fine old walls which have sheltered us and our forebears."

"Well, there is one bright spot in the darkness," said Matty to Dudley, changing her tone as she spoke. "I cannot but support my niece, though I must admit that my gratitude would have a personal quality."

"But the house has sheltered me and my forebears too," said Dudley. "Perhaps it does not count."

"Well, well, it may count a little. And anyhow it will cost a little. That must be your comfort."

"What do you say, Father?" said Justine.

"I must say what you do, my dear; I cannot but say it. It is a thing that your uncle and I could do together."

"Ah, that strikes the right note. That clinches the matter. You and Uncle can do it together. It stands that it will be done."

"Better and better," said Matty to Dudley with a smile.

"We can scarcely say that Father and Mark—that as a family we take nothing," said Clement. "The house hardly belongs to Father the less, that it will go to his descendants."

"No, I do not feel that I can say it," said Mark.

"No, you will not shirk your part as a benefited and grateful person," said Matty, in a tone of approval and sympathy.

"That is hardly straight, Aunt Matty," said Justine. "I wish you would not let these touches of unfairness creep into your talk. It gives to all our response that little undercurrent of defensiveness. We are not ungrateful because we want something beautiful preserved, which will be of advantage to future generations as well as ourselves, and because we realise that that is the case. You have admitted to the same feeling."

"I have it indeed, dear, but then I feel definitely grateful. It is a great thing in my life, this lovely background that I see behind you all, and feel behind myself at stated intervals. I should feel unthankful indeed if I did not appreciate it. And I ask your uncle to accept my gratitude for any service that he does to it."

"The east walls are crying for attention," said Edgar, as if his thought broke out in spite of himself. "I have hardly dared to look at them, but they must be sinking. I can almost feel it; I know it must be the case. You and I might go round, Dudley, and sketch out a plan for the work. This—I find this one of the days of my life."

Blanche looked up at her husband as if uncertain what she should feel.

"There, Uncle!" said Justine. "I congratulate you. That is what you want. You have what you would ask."

"Better still," said Matty to Dudley. "There is progress. I don't think you need fear."

"Justine dear, will you fetch my silks from my room?"

"No, Mother, I can't be sent out of the room like that, even if I have been a little frank and definite and may be so again. You must know me by now, and if you want me you must take me as I am."

"And as we cannot do without her, she has us in a tight place," said Matty, retrieving her position.

"It is half-past eleven," said Blanche, relinquishing her work as if her thoughts had not returned to it. "Matty dear, would you like anything? Or would Father? It is surprising how the time goes."

"Well, I really don't think it is to-day," said Justine. "I should not have been surprised to find ourselves at the last stroke."

"Well, dear, some coffee for me, and for Father a glass of wine and a sandwich," said Matty, somehow implying that in the risen fortunes of the house such requirements would hardly count. "I hope you are going to join us."

"Yes, we will all have something; I think our nerves need it," said Justine.

"Are you feeling guilty?" said Matty, in a low, mischievous tone to Dudley.

"Will Miss Seaton and Mr. Seaton be staying to luncheon, ma'am?" said Jellamy.

"Yes. You will be staying, won't you, Matty? Father won't find it too much? He can have his rest."

"We will quarter ourselves upon you," said Oliver. "You will put up with what comes to you to-day. I take it that you wouldn't alter it."

"Yes, they will both be here for luncheon, Jellamy."

"And Miss Sloane and Miss Griffin, Jellamy," said Justine, throwing a glance from her chair.

"My dear, have you heard that?"

"No, Mother, I have just decided it. I think we need the effect of their presence."

"But are they free, dear child?"

"Well, we can soon find out. If they are not, they cannot come, of course. But I fail to see what engagements they can have in a place where neither knows anyone."

"But Miss Sloane may not care to come. What does Aunt Matty say? Miss Sloane is her guest."

"Well, for that reason I should like to have her with me. It is a kind thought of Justine's. I was wondering if I could leave her alone, and how to send a message. But Miss Griffin finds it a change to be without us." Matty's tone quickened and her eyes changed. "And I find a certain relief in being only with my relations. So I will say what I mean in my family circle and feel it is said."

"You will be better apart, if I may still depend on my eyes and ears," said her father. "I do not know what Maria makes of it all. I do not ask. She could not give a true answer and a false one would be no help. You forget the size of the house, though you talk of it."

"Well, I am not used to it yet."

"You would do well to become so."

"Let me have my own way, Aunt Matty," said Justine, sitting on the arm of her aunt's chair. "Don't deny it to me because we have got a little across. Give it to me all the more for that."

"Well, well, take it, dear. You know how I like you to have it."

"You have your own way a good deal, Justine," said Blanche,

"Oh, well, Mother, a mature woman, the only sister amongst three brothers, Father's only daughter! What can you expect?"

Edgar looked up as if to see how his own name had become involved.

"Everyone must rejoice with me to-day," said Dudley. "That always seems to me an absurd demand, but I am going to make it."

"And if there is anyone for selfless rejoicing for other people, Miss Griffin is that person, if I know her," said his niece. "And I shouldn't be surprised if Miss Sloane has a touch of the same quality."

"Suppose we keep people apart, dear," said Matty in a light tone.

"Oh, Aunt Matty, Miss Sloane has not a touch of that feeling. She would not mind being coupled with Miss Griffin. Even being with her once told me that. I should think it is not in her."

"But keep her apart, nevertheless dear," said Blanche, in a low voice that was at once reproving and confidential. "She has nothing to do with anyone else."

"I am not sure that she would say that," said Justine

audibly. "She has the connection with Miss Griffin of a long friendship. I should say that she would be the first to recognise it."

"Well, well, dear, are you going to run down and ask them?"

"No, no, not I this time," said Justine, shaking her head. "I am not always going to present myself as the bearer of such messages. It would mean that we thought too much of them altogether."

"Clement and I will go," said Mark. "That will give a trivial air to the errand. And we can imply that we think little of it."

"That should be easy," said his brother. "We have only to be natural."

"Ah, that is not always so easy as you seem to think," said Justine.

"Perhaps you find it too much so."

"Well, run along, dears," said Blanche, in a neutral manner. "You can wait and bring them back."

"If they consent to come, Mother," said Justine, with a note of reproof.

"Well, you thought they had no other engagements, dear. Let the boys go now. It will be a breath of fresh air for them after their exciting morning. We can't have nothing but excitement."

"Do you know where to look?" said Matty to Dudley, in a mischievous aside.

"Mother talks as if we were guilty of some excess," said Clement to his brother as they left the house. "Our excitement has been for Uncle. Nothing has come to most of us."

"A good deal has come to Father, and in a certain sense to me."

"A good deal to you both. A house handed on intact is different indeed from one gaping at every seam, and sucking up an income to keep it over our heads. You are full of a great and solemn joy."

"And my happiness is not yours?"

"Any satisfaction of mine must come out of my own life, not out of other people's. But I ought to have some of my own. Father's money will be set free and Uncle has no one to spend on but us."

"What are your personal hopes?"

"Much as yours, except that they are on a smaller scale and yours are already fulfilled. I don't want a place or could not have one. But I do want a little house of my own in Cambridge. I hate the college and I am obliged to live in the town. And a little income to add to what I earn. Then I should not need to spend my spare time at home. I cannot suffer much more of Aubrey and Justine."

"And I can?"

"Your prospects are safe. You have no right to speak."

"I shall have nothing until Father dies, but the life which you must escape."

"Your future is bound up in the place. Mine has nothing to do with it. The house is a halting place for me."

"And for Justine and Aubrey what is it?"

"Aubrey is a child and Justine is a woman. There is no comparison."

"Aubrey will not always be a child and Justine not always a young and dependent woman. I can imagine her in her own house as well as you."

"Mine is the need of the moment."

"So is mine. I could do with many things. But I don't know if we can make the suggestions to Uncle."

"They may occur to him."

"Images will have to come crowding on his mind."

"I don't see why they should not. He must have seen our straitened life."

"He must have lived it," said Mark.

"You can make a joke of other people's needs, when your own are satisfied. He can hardly go on for ever, spending all he has on the house. All sorts of demands must arise. We have been held very tight and insensibly the bonds will be loosened."

"When Father dies, you will have your share of what there is. Both he and Uncle must leave what they have to us."

"And how long will that be to wait?"

"Clement, what manner of man are you?"

"The same as you, though you pretend not to know it. You can go in here and offer this invitation. Explain that we observe a piece of good fortune for one of us as a general festival."

"I am in command of such a situation. You are right to imply that you are not."

"There is Miss Griffin at the window. She is there whenever we come."

"She sees the shadows of coming events. Such a gift would develop in her life."

In due course the four emerged from the lodge and set off towards the house. Mark was ready to discuss the event; Clement was inclined to glance at Maria to judge of her view of it, and to try to talk of other things; Maria was lively and interested and Miss Griffin was alternately reflective and disposed to put sudden questions.

"Here is a fairy-tale piece of news!" said Maria, as she met the family. "I shall always be glad to have heard it at first hand. We must thank you for our experience as well as congratulate you on yours."

"Thank you, Miss Sloane. That is a pleasant congratulation indeed," said Justine, turning to her brothers to continue. "What a contrast to poor Aunt Matty's! What a difference our little inner differences make!"

"A quarter of a million pounds!" said Miss Griffin, standing in the middle of the floor. "I have never heard anything like it."

"Neither have I," said Dudley. "It is about a twentieth of a million."

"A twentieth of a million!" said Miss Griffin, in exactly the same tone.

"About fifty thousand pounds."

"Fifty thousand pounds!" said Miss Griffin, with the fuller feeling of complete grasp.

"We ought not to keep talking about the amount," said Blanche. "We value the thought and the remembrance."

"But if we leave it out," said Dudley, "people will think it is so much more than it is."

"I think it is better than that," said Maria. "It will not eliminate planning and contrivance from your life, and it will keep you in the world you know."

"Sound wisdom," said Justine. "How it falls from unexpected lips!"

"I feel very comforted," said Dudley. "People may realise my true position after all."

"It was deep sagacity, Miss Sloane," said Justine. "I daresay you hardly realise how deep. Words of wisdom seem to fall from your lips like raindrops off a flower."

"Justine dear, was that a little frank?" said Blanche, lowering her voice.

"Well, Mother, pretty speeches always are," said Justine, not doing this with hers. "But I don't think that a genuine impulse towards a compliment is such a bad thing. It might really come to us oftener. And Miss Sloane is not in the least embarrassed. It is not a feeling possible to her. I had discerned that, or I had not taken the risk."

"The impulse has come to Justine again," said Mark to his brother.

"And embarrassment is a feeling possible to the rest of us."

"Well, I have not been saying words of wisdom, perhaps," said Matty, in a tone that drew general attention. "But I have done my best to show my joy in others' good fortune. Though 'others' is hardly the word for people with whom I feel myself identified. Contrivance had not struck me as one of the likely results, but if they like to enjoy the poverty of the rich, we will not say them nay. It is only the poverty of the poor which we should not welcome for them. We have that enough in our thoughts." Matty's voice died away on a sigh which was somehow a thrust.

"I shall have to give to the poor," said Dudley. "It is a thing I have never done. It shows how nearly I have been one of them. I have only just escaped being always in Matty's mind."

"A dangerous place to be," said Mark.

"I suppose I shall subscribe to hospitals. That is how people seem to give to the poor. I suppose the poor are always sick. They would be, if you think. I once went round the cottages with Edgar, and I was too sensitive to go a second time. Yes, I was too sensitive even to set my eyes on the things which other people actually suffered, and I maintain that that was very sensitive. Now I shall improve things out of recognition, and then I can go again and not recognise anything, and feel no guilt about my inheritance."

"No one can help being left money," said Miss Griffin.

"That is not on any point," said Matty lightly.

"I don't know, Aunt Matty; I don't think I agree with you," said Justine. "But I have disagreed with you enough; I will not say it."

"Well, it may be as well not to let it become a habit, dear."

"Justine dear, come and sit by me," said Blanche.

"Oh, you mean to be repressive, Mother. But I feel quite irrepressible this morning. Uncle's good fortune sets my heart singing even more than yours or Father's would. Because he has been the one rather to miss things himself and to see them pass to other people, and to see it in all goodwill. And that is so rare that it merits a rare compensation. And that the compensation should come, is the rarest thing of all. 'My heart is like a singing bird, whose nest is in a water'd shoot.' "

"Are we all going to stay in the whole morning?" said Blanche. "Justine, it is not like you to be without energy."

"Surely an unjust implication," said Mark.

"Well, we can hardly bring Miss Sloane and Miss Griffin up here, Mother, and then escort them out again at once."

"They might like to join us in a walk round the park. I sleep so much better if I get some exercise, and I expect we shall sit and talk after luncheon."

"An indulgence which can be expiated in advance by half an hour in a drizzle," said Clement.

"Well, what do you feel, Miss Sloane?" said Justine.

"I should like to go with your mother."

"And you, Miss Griffin?"

Miss Griffin opened her mouth and glanced at the fire and at Matty.

"Miss Griffin prefers the hearth. And I don't wonder, considering the short intervals which she probably spends at it. So you set off with Miss Sloane, Mother, and the rest of us will remain in contented sloth. I believe that is how you see the matter."

Blanche began to roll up her silks without making much progress. Justine took them from her, wound them rapidly round her hand, thrust them into the basket and propelled her mother to the door with a hand on her waist. Maria followed without assistance, and Blanche shook herself free without any change of expression and also proceeded alone. Matty at once addressed the group as if to forestall any other speaker.

"Now I must tell you of something which happened to me when I was young, something which this occasion in your lives brings back to me. I too might have been left a fortune. When we are young, things are active or would be if we let them, or so it was in my youth. Well, a man was in love with me or said he was; and I could see it for myself, so I cannot leave it out; and I refused him—well, we won't dwell on that; and when we got that behind, he wanted to leave me all he had. And I would not let him, and we came to words, as you would say, and the end of it was that we did not meet again. And a few days afterwards he was thrown from his horse and killed. And the money went to his family, and I was glad that it should be so, as I had given him nothing and I could not take and not give. But what do you say to that, as a narrow escape from a fortune? I came almost as near to it as your uncle."

"Was that a large fortune too?" said Miss Griffin.

"It was large enough to call one. That is all that matters for the story."

"You ran very near the wind, Aunt Matty," said Justine. "And you came out well."

"I shall be obliged to take and not give, if no one will accept anything from me," said Dudley. "Because I am going to take. Indeed I have taken."

"You have not been given the choice," said Miss Griffin.

"Well, well, we all have that," said Matty. "But there is not always reason for using it. There is no obligation to seek out connections when there is no immediate family. This friend of mine had brothers."

"I wish you would not put such thoughts into words," said Dudley.

"I can't help wishing that he had not had them, Aunt Matty," said Justine. "You might have had a happier life or an easier one."

"An easier later chapter, dear, but I do not regret it. We cannot do more than live up to the best that is in us. I feel I did that, and I must find it enough." Matty's tone had a note of truth which no one credited.

"I find it so too," said Dudley. "My best is to accept two thousand a year. It is enough, but I do wish that people would not think it is more."

"Two thousand a year!" said Miss Griffin.

"Well, it is between a good many," said Matty. "It is so good when a family is one with itself. And you are all going to find it so."

"To accept needs the truest generosity," said Dudley. "And I am not sure that they have it. I know that people always underrate their families, but I suspect that they only have the other kind."

"It is that kind which is the first requirement," said Clement.

"Clement, that remark might be misunderstood," said Justine.

"Or understood," said Mark.

"I don't think I should find any difficulty in accepting something I needed, from someone I loved. But I am such a fortunate person; I always have all I need."

"There, what did I say?" said Dudley. "An utter lack of true generosity."

"I will go further," said his niece. "I will accept an insurance of the future of my little Aubrey. Accept it in my name and in that of Father and Mother. I think I am justified in going so far."

"It is all very well to laugh, Clement," said Dudley, "but how will you look when it appears that your brothers have true generosity, and you have none?"

"I can do as they do and without having it. It seems to me to be the opposite thing that is needed."

"Clement, be careful!" said Justine, in an almost stricken tone.

"People are always ashamed of their best qualities and describe them in the wrong way," said Dudley. "Clement will accept an allowance from me and let me forget that my generosity is less than his."

"Then he is a dear, sensible boy," said Matty.

"Sensible certainly," said her nephew.

"Well, Clement, I don't know what to say," said Justine.

"You can say what you will say to Mark and Aubrey."

"Well, I suppose that is fair in a way, but it does seem that there is a difference. But I will say nothing. The matter is taken out of my hands."

"It was never in them."

"Now don't take that line with your sister. That does not make matters better."

"I have no wish to improve them. I find them well enough."

"I am afraid you do, Clement."

"Now that is not sensible, dear, and perhaps not even quite kind," said Matty.

"It seems fair that all three brothers should have something, if two have," said Miss Griffin.

"Well, it is really a matter for the family."

"Aunt Matty, don't snub Miss Griffin in public like that," said Justine. "That is certainly not quite kind."

"My dear, you may have a way of coming between people, but between Miss Griffin and me there is our own relation."

"I am afraid there is, Aunt Matty."

There was a long silence.

"Dear, dear, money, money, money!" said Justine, leaning back and locking her hands above her head. "Directly it comes in, away fly dignity, decency, everything."

"Everything but true generosity," said Mark.

"Dignity and decency depend up to a point on money," said Clement.

"Indeed that is true," said Dudley. "You have only to go round the cottages. It seems absurd to say that money is sordid, when you see the things that really are."

"And that come from the lack of it."

"Why should it be sordid any more than any other useful thing?" said Matty.

"They say that it is a curse," said Dudley, "but I do

not find it so. I like being a person to confer benefits. There, that is the worst."

"Dear Uncle!" said Justine. "Enjoy your money and your generosity and all of it. You have never had a chance before."

"So you don't think that the things I gave were more valuable than money. I knew that people never really did."

"To talk about money's having no value is a contradiction in terms," said Clement.

"Now I think that is honest, dear," said Matty.

"Aunt Matty, you are going rather far in your implications," said Justine.

"You do not go in for such things, dear, I know."

Justine put back her head in mirth, the action so familiar in her aunt somehow throwing up her unlikeness to her.

"That may be fair, but we won't start another skirmish. And I don't take it at all as an insult, however it was meant. I am one for the direct and open line. Now here are the other elders, come in the nick of time to prevent our discussion from becoming acrimonious."

"They are running it fine," said Clement.

"Well, have you made up your minds how to spend your uncle's money?" said Oliver.

"Yes, we have," said Clement, pausing a moment to get the plan of his speech. "The house is to be put in repair for Father and Mark; there is to be an allowance for me; and something is to be done for Aubrey's future."

"Oh!" said Blanche. "Oh, it is too quick. I did not think it would all be arranged at once like that."

"Would it be better for being delayed?"

"I don't know what to say. It does not seem right somehow. I really feel almost ashamed."

"To tell you the truth, Mother, so do I," said Justine. "But I could not help it. I plead guilty to the suggestion about Aubrey's future, but otherwise I can hold myself apart."

"As a benefited person, I feel that my tongue is tied," said Edgar. "The mention of me was adroit."

"It was simply true," said Clement.

"Dudley, I don't know what to say," said Blanche. "What can you think of them all?"

"I feel that we are drawn closer. They will not spoil things for me by letting me feel alone. I don't think Clement and I have ever been so close before. And I expect them to share my joy, and people ought not to share a feeling without sharing the cause of it. I should not think it is possible. And I should be ashamed of feeling joy over a thing like money, if no one felt it with me."

"There is something in that, I suppose," said Justine.

"Well, it is nearly time for luncheon," said her mother. "I suppose I must not say any more. We have had such a nice walk. I feel all the better for it and Miss Sloane has quite a colour. It was so kind of her to come with me. Father, did you get your sleep?"

"I slept like a child, my dear, as is well for a person approaching his second childhood."

"That is not the speech of someone doing that, Grandpa," said Mark.

"Father, what a way to talk! Well, I must go and take off my things. Perhaps Miss Sloane would like to come with me. And then we should open these windows. You have all been in here all the morning."

"With all our selfish hopes and desires," said Clement. "But I wonder that Justine has not been like a breath of fresh air in herself."

"I expect she has," said Blanche, patting her daughter's cheek.

"I have certainly been a breath of something, Mother, but I believe it has been felt to be more like a draught. But it may have been fresh and wholesome."

"We did not talk about the good fortune all the time,"

said Matty. "We had our glimpse of other things. I gave them an early experience of my own, which amused them with its likeness to this one. Its likeness and its difference, shall we say? Well, what do you think of your aunt's varied history? I see you are not to be allowed to dwell on it. Your mother is directing our attention to more material things."

"The luncheon will not improve by waiting, dear, and I like it to be nice for you all. Let the boys help you out of your chair."

"Thank you, dears, Miss Griffin will do it. I am more used to her," said Matty, forgetting that she had objected to Miss Griffin's presence. "But she seems to be having a little nap. Wake up, Miss Griffin; even our pleasure days have their little duties, you know." Matty's tone of rallying reproof changed as she found herself alone with her companion. "You appear to have fallen into a trance. You can't come out just for enjoyment when you come with me. There is some thought of your being of a little use. You are not quite in the position of Miss Sloane."

"I did not know that you wanted any help."

"Of course I want the help you always give me. I cannot be deprived of the few little things I have, just because other people suddenly have so much. You need not lose yourself in their experience. It will affect no one but themselves. It will anyhow make no difference to you."

"You so often get out of your chair by yourself. I can hardly know when you want help."

"Well, understand that I always want it, when you are standing by doing nothing. It would not be suitable for me to manage alone, when it is easier for me with help, and you are there to give it. I wonder you do not see it. But then I suppose you see nothing."

"Just fancy all that money!" said Miss Griffin, who was used to meeting attacks as if she were unconscious of them. "I can hardly grasp it."

"You won't have to. That is the last thing you will have to do. So that is what you have been doing instead of keeping your eyes open for my convenience. I see that a break from routine does not suit you. I must remember it."

When a break comes very seldom, it does sometimes upset people," said Miss Griffin, in a lower tone.

"Oh, you are going to be like that! That is to be the result of a little change and pleasure. I must see that you do not have it. I see that it does not work. I must take counsel with myself and arrange for your life to be nothing but duty, as that is what seems to suit you." Matty, as she spoke, was accepting Miss Griffin's ministrations as if they were rendered by a machine, and indeed the latter could only perform them in this spirit. "Well, are we going in to luncheon, or am I going in alone? Perhaps you had better go straight home and be by yourself. That would probably make the best of you."

Miss Griffin followed Matty without reply, and seemed consciously to change her expression to one of anticipation.

"Come in, Miss Griffin," said Justine, as if Miss Griffin needed this encouragement and her aunt did not, an attitude more supported by fact than she knew. "Come in and sit by me. And Aunt Matty, take the seat by Father. And Miss Sloane on his other side, if she will."

"The seats are all arranged, dear," said Blanche.

"Yes, Mother, but a word of help is not amiss. They were all standing about like lost souls. A large family party is the most baffling thing."

"I will sit on the other side of Miss Sloane," said Dudley, "and go over everything from the beginning. She can hardly check me; she does not know me well enough."

"Do not abuse her indulgence, Uncle. Well, Mr. Penrose, what sort of a morning?"

"Well, to be frank, Miss Gaveston, not up to our standard. I am not disposed to make any complaint, as I think

the family news is responsible. It is natural and perhaps
not wholly undesirable that it should be so. And I hope
we shall atone for it to-morrow."

"Now, little boy, what sort of hearing is this? And
when Uncle has been thinking of you and your future!
What kind of return is this to make?"

"He did not know about that, dear," said Blanche.
"He has been excited about his uncle, as you all have.
And any difference for him will not be for a long time.
We must allow him his share of the pleasure, so I think
he might have a holiday this afternoon. We must not ex-
pect him to settle down so much sooner than anyone else.
You have all been shaken out of yourselves, and no
wonder. What do you say, Edgar?"

"What you do, my dear. It is—it seems to me the
thing to be said."

"And you, Mr. Penrose?" said Justine. "We should not
dream of upsetting the routine without your sanction."

"Well, I should be disposed to be indulgent upon the
occasion, Miss Gaveston."

"There, little boy, there is your holiday assured."

"Half holiday," said Aubrey.

"I am afraid it is nearer a whole one than it should
be."

"They will be able to go for a long walk," said Blanche,
"instead of having to be back by four."

"Well, really, Mother, I think Mr. Penrose might
have his share of the celebration. I should guess that he
is inclined to shake the dust of this house off his feet.
He has his own private life as much as we have."

"Well, Mr. Penrose will do as he likes, dear. Aubrey
can play by himself."

"It is very considerate, Mrs. Gaveston."

"Am I big enough to play alone?" said Aubrey.

"No, you are not," said his sister. "You are incapable
of managing your time. I will see that we both spend a
pleasant and profitable afternoon."

"You have all stopped talking about my inheritance," said Dudley. "Does it mean that you think enough has been said about it? Miss Sloane does not seem to think so. But she may not know how much has been said."

"I have thought of nothing else since I heard of it, Uncle."

"Neither have I," said Aubrey. "I have a witness."

"Neither have I," said Dudley.

"I should like to hear what your uncle is going to do for himself," said Blanche.

"I doubt if we shall have that satisfaction, Mother," said Justine, "great as it would be. Uncle is a man of few and simple desires. Unless he has a house of his own, which heaven forbid as long as we are all in this one, it is hard to see how he is to spend so much on himself. He has his interests and occupations and his brother. More he does not ask of life."

"He has all of us as well," said Mark. "That cannot be left out of account. Anyhow it has not been."

"Our desires have a way of getting bigger with our incomes," said Matty. "Just as they have to get smaller with them. I have had the latter experience, and rejoice the more that all of you are to have the first."

"Miss Sloane shows a great patience with our family drama," said Mark. "I am too enthralled by it myself to wonder."

"I have come on your family at a dramatic moment. Patience is the last thing that is needed."

"That is what I should have thought," said Dudley. "I am wounded by Mark's speech."

"Wait a moment, Miss Sloane, I am going to ask it," said Justine. "It is not a crime, if it is a little unconventional. Which do you consider the better to look at, my father or my uncle? Do not hesitate to say; they will not mind."

"I am afraid I do hesitate," said Maria, laughing. "And I had not thought of making a comparison."

"Oh, come, Miss Sloane, that is not quite ingenuous.
People always think of it; it seems inevitable. They can't
see the one by the other, without summing up their
respective characteristics and ranging them on different
sides."

"Dear Justine, Miss Sloane had not thought of it,"
said Blanche. "She has told us."

"Well, she will think of it now, Mother, as I ask her to.
I am sure she has never denied anyone without more
reason."

"I have never met two people whom I should see less
in terms of each other."

"Ah, now that is subtle, Miss Sloane. And I believe
you are right. Now I come to consider, neither have I.
It is simply superficial to talk as if one were a feeble copy
of the other."

"It is worse than that," said Dudley. "It is too bad."

"They should give more attention to the comparison,"
said Edgar, smiling at the guest. "My daughter seems
only to have grasped the essence of it at this moment."

"Oh, now, Father, you would like me to be perfect,
wouldn't you? Well, I am not, so you can make the best
of it."

"Father may claim to have done so," said Clement.

"I think we are better when we are greedy than when
we are clever," said Mark. "The one quality is natural to
us; the other is not."

"And your uncle can satisfy the one, but he can do
nothing for the other," said Edgar, with another smile.

"They might all do so much, Miss Sloane, if they
would only apply themselves," said Blanche, pursuing
the line of her children's ability.

"I suppose—have the arrangements you spoke of taken
any form?" said Edgar.

"Not definitely, Father," said Justine, "but they are
taking their course. Uncle has opened his purse in the
way that I knew he would, as I indeed foretold, though

my doing so raised an outcry. Clement is to have an allowance; Aubrey's future is secure; the house benefits in whatever way you have arranged; and what your private and personal benefits are to be, we do not know. They are between you and him and will be left so."

Blanche took something from a dish which Jellamy handed, as if it were no good to interpose.

"And what is my Justine to have from the open purse?"

"Oh, trust you to ask that, Father. My position is safe with you. Well, I am having peace of mind about Aubrey. It is what I asked and what was at once granted to me. I could think of no other need."

"Who was to depend on Father to that extent?" said Clement to his brother.

"Perhaps Justine did. If so, we see that she was right."

"Justine holds herself apart from my easy generosity," said Dudley, "so that to her I am what I have always been, simply her uncle."

"But you shall be more than that!" said his niece. "I will not stand aside a moment longer. You shall be generous to me. I will take a yearly subscription to my pet charity, to my old men and women in the village. Yes, I think I can ask that, without feeling that I am piling up a life already loaded. And you need not tell me that it is forthcoming, because I know it is. Actually for myself I ask nothing, holding myself already too rich."

"And I have only felt that about myself for a few days. How much better you are than I am! And I already think I am poor."

"You will soon be right," said Mark.

"You know I meant that a twentieth of a million was poor."

"One thing I say!" said Justine, suddenly raising her hand. "One stipulation I make. Uncle shall feel free to break off these undertakings at anytime, to stand as fully apart from them as if they had never been made. And this at any hint of demand from his own life. In one moment, at one fell swoop—at one swoop,what is his own is in his hands, to be deflected to his own purposes. It is on this understanding and this alone, that I subscribe to the engagements, and rejoice for other people and accept for myself."

"Well, that goes without saying, dear," said Blanche.

"Oh, no, it does not, Mother. And therefore it shall not on this occasion. I am not quite without knowledge of life, though you probably believe me to be. I know how to safeguard the future or how it should be safeguarded. And as no one else made a move, I did it myself; and I am glad to have done it and glad to have it behind."

"It is well to have it said once," said Edgar. "We will all remember it has been said."

"Thank you, Father. If I could not depend on you, where should I stand?"

"It is wise to say it for another reason. Your uncle can only use the income from his money. The capital is held in trust and cannot be touched."

"I can only will it," said Dudley. "So other people will have the use of it in the end. I am not in at all a selfish position. My godfather must have been afraid that I should rush to ruin. He did not mind if other people did. I do appreciate his special feeling for me. Indeed I approve of all his feeling."

"It may be a wise condition," said Maria. "You would be checked in any headlong course. I daresay you will live to be glad of it."

"I have done that already," said Dudley, lowering his voice. "We began to consider the repairs to the house, and I was checked almost at once. To do them all would take all my income and leave me as I was before, and I could not bear to be that. I think that fifty-three years must have made me tired of it."

"One thing I ask!" said Aubrey, raising his hand in

imitation of his sister. "And that is that Mother shall
have a new dress to celebrate the event."

"Yes, well, I think I can accept that," said Blanche, "as
it is for that reason." She turned to her son with more
feeling than she had yet shown. "My little boy does not
like his mother to be shabby."

"And so can I," said Justine, "and with all my heart.
And rejoice in other people's pleasure in it, which will be
greater than my own."

"Justine's advantages will not cost any less, that she
gets no personal benefit from them," said Clement to
Mark.

"And so can I," said Matty, smiling at Dudley. "And
so I will, to show that I rejoice as heartily as anyone in
your access to the world's good things. We will all have
one good thing for ourselves, to show our wholehearted
approval of them."

"Now that is nice of you, Aunt Matty, and nicely put,"
said Justine.

"They are all too kind," muttered Clement.

"I am so pleased with you all," said Dudley. "No one
wants me to feel any misery because I have more than he
has. I wish I had never said that anyone had more than
was right for any one person. I see now what a revealing
thing it is to say."

"It will not be true of you, Uncle," said Mark.

"I will have a new suit," said Aubrey.

"Now, now, little boy, no making a mock of what is
serious in itself. There *is* a certain generosity in accepting, as Uncle recognises."

"He has plenty of practice," said Clement.

"Miss Griffin will have a dress too," said Dudley. "She
does not grudge me my inheritance any more than anyone else."

"Inded I do not. Indeed I will, if it is to prove that,"
said Miss Griffin, flushed and conscious and cordial.

Matty gave her a friendly smile.

"Will Miss Sloane be allowed to escape?" said Mark.

"Shall we have Grandpa decked out for the occasion?" said Clement.

"Miss Sloane, it may be asking too much of you," said Justine. "But if it is not, you will give my uncle the privilege? It will be accepted as such."

"I think I will ask to have my congratulations accepted without any proof of them."

"And being denied does not form a large part of your experience? You will not be in this case. We should not dare to attempt it."

"We must not ask Maria to become one of us quite so soon," said Matty.

"I have seldom felt so much one of a family."

"Never at a loss for a graceful response!" said Justine, turning aside and sighing. "I wonder what it feels like."

"Miss Sloane turned her whole mind on my affairs," said Dudley. "I have never seen anyone do that for anyone else before."

"No, Uncle, you have rather been the one to do it for people yourself. But I daresay it has brought its own reward."

"It has," said Mark.

"Did you hear my mean little speech?" said Dudley to Maria. "I believe I think that I ought to be taken more seriously because I have money. Well, I suppose it had to make me deteriorate in some way."

"You are going to leave us, Blanche, my dear?" said Oliver. "You and the other women. I should like to have my smoke and talk while I have the strength for them."

"Grandpa is a privileged person, you observe, Miss Sloane," said Justine. "Things are permitted in him which would not be in other people."

"You know it is only for a short time, child, and show me that you do."

Aubrey rose with a glance at Clement and passed out of the door as if unconscious what he did. He disliked remaining with the men and facing his brothers' banter more than he disliked the status of a child. He sometimes wondered how he would fill any rôle but this.

"Now, Mr. Penrose, off with you; out of our house," said Justine. "You do not want to be with us a moment longer, and we do not want you, will not attempt to detain you. So off to keep your holiday in your own way."

"I am more than glad of the cause of it, Miss Gaveston."

"So am I," said Dudley.

The five men settled at the table, Edgar and Dudley to talk to Oliver, and Mark and Clement by themselves. It was at this stage that the latter would have turned their attention to their brother. Dudley presently pointed to Oliver, who had fallen asleep.

"Here is my chance to say something else. Would it be right to give some money to Matty? Would she dislike me more for keeping it or giving it? Both are such disagreeable things, and I must do one of them. No one can carry off either."

"We need not make a suggestion," said Clement. "We have shown the course we prefer."

"You have tried to make me happy. But your aunt may not really desire my happiness. She may wish me to pay for it."

"Well, you are proposing to do so."

"I mean pay with discomfort."

"She would rather you paid for it with money."

"Such simplicity is seldom the whole truth," said Edgar, without hesitation. "Your aunt has come on evil days, or days which she sees as such, and your uncle on good ones; and if she is struck by the difference it may not mean so much."

"It would make the difference less, if I gave her a little of the money and went without it myself. Or is it true that people want more, the more they have? Of course, she is not my real relation and others have a nearer claim. I am beginning to get the outlook of the rich. Do you hear me talk in their way? You would know how terrible it would be, if she wanted more, the more she had, if you had just inherited money."

"It would have to be a moderate, settled sum. It would be a pleasure to Blanche, Dudley. May I suggest—I will suggest an allowance of about two hundred a year."

"Thank you; that is real help. It is not too much or too little. I think that is the way rich people talk. Fancy saying that two hundred a year is not too little, when you have two thousand a year yourself!"

"That is no longer true," said Mark.

"Yes, you won't have so much more left than you can do with," said Oliver, raising his head. "We shall all be busy relieving you of it. I find I am doing my part, and I do it willingly. Why shouldn't I have my last days made easy? They are my very last. And my daughter has had enough ill fortune to render it worth while to make it less. Thank you, my boy, you are a pleasant person to take it from, and I pay you a compliment."

"Of course the generosity is yours. We have decided that."

"No, it is yours, which pleases me better and serves its purpose. Such a quality in me would serve none."

"What are the other allowances?" said Edgar. "I am still in the dark. It does not do to be shy about these things, if we can take them."

"What dreadful speeches reticent people make!" said Dudley. "I suppose it is want of practice."

"The lads are only like the rest of us," said Oliver.

"We do not know," said Clement, something in his tone showing that he was in suspense.

"I thought three hundred a year for Clement, and two hundred for Mark, as he has an interest in the house. And a hundred for Justine, as she will not spend it on herself and I am mean to a woman and good works. And Aubrey's future to be provided for as it develops. And any bitterness to be at once considered and the cause rectified. Causes of bitterness are always so just. And the rest to be for myself, to dole out as I please and earn gratitude and be able to call the tune. How despicable it sounds, and how I do like it!"

"So do we. Do not worry about our part," said Oliver, rising to his feet. "I will tell my daughter and spare you the scene. And having got what I can get, I will take my leave. Do not come after me. I can walk to the next room, where the women will busy themselves."

"I believe it was too little," said Dudley. "Unless I have reached the stage of expecting extravagant thanks for the least thing. I hope that is what it is. Of course it is a mean sum. Two hundred a year is a tenth of two thousand, and it must be mean to offer anyone a tenth of what you have. It sounds as if I were keeping nine times as much for myself. I hope Matty will not hear before she goes. People don't resent having nothing nearly as much as too little. I have only just found that out. I am getting the knowledge of the rich as well as their ways. And of course anyone would resent being given a tenth."

"I do not," said Mark. "I have the opposite feeling."

"I am overpowered," said Clement.

"I must not forget to thank you for your true generosity. Mine is the other kind and we begin to see what that is. Justine is to have a twentieth and she will appreciate it, which is true generosity indeed. I find myself actually looking forward to it, I am deteriorating so fast. There is her voice. The very sound of it ought to be a reproach."

"Well, so the occasion is at an end," said the voice. "Or the moment has come when it would cease to be a success. We really are seeing something of each other. It is such a good thing when those things don't fail to materialise. There is always the touch of risk. It is a tribute to us all that the risk has not even hinted itself in this case. Miss Griffin and I have had a talk to ourselves. We settled down as two women and made the most of each other."

"So we take our leave after hours so full of happiness," said Matty. "It is a pleasant weariness that follows a long rejoicing for others. I only wish I could call it by some other name, that there was some different word for cramped limbs and aching head. But the happiness outweighs it, and that is all I ask."

"Here is the carriage, dear," said her sister. "You won't have to take the walk a second time."

"Well, I could not do that, dear. We cannot go beyond our strength. Up to it willingly but not beyond. I shall be so glad when you have a second carriage, and it should not be long now. It is a thing I have wanted for you. We get into the way of planning things for other people when we must not imagine them for ourselves. And it is a good and satisfying substitute. We can be grateful for it. The cushion into the carriage, Miss Griffin. It won't walk in by itself."

"Jellamy will take it," said Justine, putting her arm in Miss Griffin's. "It will be safely in its place."

Edgar took the cushion and went to the carriage, and Miss Griffin stood within Justine's arm as if she would linger in its safety.

"Come, Uncle," said Justine, "tear yourself away from Miss Sloane. She gives no sign of relief in her escape from us, and most heartily do we thank her. But the moment has come for her release."

"Matty cannot know of my meanness," said Dudley, looking after the carriage. "She could not show her view of it as openly as that."

"Does Mother know of all your other meanness?" said Mark.

"Oh, I don't like to think of it," said Blanche, when she had heard the truth. "I cannot bear to feel that you have all taken so much. I ought to blush for my family."

"I don't think you need, Mother," said Justine. "I

147

should be more ashamed if I could not take Uncle's bounty openly and generously, as it is offered. It would show a smaller spirit. It is not for us to hold ourselves above the position of grateful people. We have to be able to accept. Anything else shows an unwillingness to grant someone else the superior place."

"Uncle must feel well established in that," said Mark.

"I have done what I can to help him. I have been able to take more pocket money," said Aubrey, kicking a rug with his eyes upon it.

"Aubrey looks down to get the advantage of the ostrich," said Clement.

"Which is very real," said his brother, instantly raising his eyes.

"Oh, is that what you and Uncle have been talking about?" said Blanche. "I don't know what to think of you all. I feel that I did not know my children. I am glad I am taking nothing for myself."

"Well, it is all for you in a way, Mother," said Justine. "You can't dissociate yourself from the benefits of your family."

"Poor Mother, that is rather hard," said Mark.

"No, that is why I feel it as I do," said Blanche to her daughter in a tone of simple rejoinder. "And Grandpa and Aunt Matty too! Well, I cannot do anything. Here is the carriage coming back. The coachman is bringing a letter."

"For Uncle from Aunt Matty," said Justine, handing it to Dudley. "We should not read the envelopes of letters, but this is an exceptional occasion."

"We can be sure that it will not repeat itself," said Mark.

"It would be very bad for us all," said Blanche.

"I will read it aloud," said Dudley, "and have the general protection. Suppose I have patronised Matty, or presumed on my connection, or thought that money meant something to her. I have taken a foolish risk."

"Read away, Uncle," said his niece. "We are all ranged on your side. But I shouldn't be surprised if Aunt Matty comes out well on this occasion."

"Is it an extreme test?" said Clement.

" 'MY DEAR DUDLEY,

'I cannot wait to give you my thanks and my father's for your thinking of us as part of my sister's family. We feel that we are related to you, and we can take from you what we would take from a son and a brother. And we thank you as much for being that to us, as for the help that sends us forward lighter of heart. And we rejoice with you in your joy.

'Your affectionate and grateful
'MATILDA SEATON.'

"I did not know that I was as near to them as that, and I have not given in that measure. I have kept nine times as much for myself. That in a son and a brother does seem dreadful. Riches are a test of character and I am exposed. And Matty still thinks that I have joy in having money, instead of pleasure in giving and other decent feelings. She may know me better than I know myself. People do have a terrible knowledge of sons and brothers."

"Mrs. Middleton is in the carriage," said Aubrey.

"My dears!" said Sarah, emerging on to the gravel with hands upraised. "What you must think of us! Your coachman picked us up as we were coming to hear your news. And I waited while your read your letter: I did not want to interrupt." Sarah spoke the truth; she had wished to hear to the end. "A quarter of a million of money! What a thing for you to face!"

"And to put to other purposes," said Thomas, appearing in his turn and using a tone of kindliness and pleasure.

"It is so good of you to be interested," said Blanche.

"It has been a great event for us all. We are still quite excited about it."

Sarah met Blanche's eyes.

"Poor Mrs. Middleton!" said Justine. "Do satisfy her curiosity."

"Yes, I want to hear, dear," said Sarah, almost with pathos. "I want to know how it came about, before we talk of it."

"My godfather's lawyers wrote to say that my godfather had died and left me all he had," said Dudley. "He died a few days ago as a very old man. I am so glad that you would like to hear; I was afraid that people might be getting tired of the subject."

"He had no children, Mrs. Middleton," said Justine, in a benevolent tone. "Indeed he seems to have had no relations."

"Then it was natural that he should leave his money to your uncle?" said Sarah, her face lighting at this clearance of her path.

"Quite," said Dudley. "I have every right to it. But I did not know that he had any. I heard a few days ago and told my brother last night, and to-day we all discussed it at breakfast."

"You did not tell them all at once?"

"No, I waited to get confirmation. It was not needed, but I felt that I wanted to have it."

Sarah bowed her head in full understanding.

"And my father and sister came in to learn all about it," said Blanche, "and have just gone. I found the news such a tonic yesterday. I thought I was too tired to sleep, and I had the best night I have had for months."

"That is right, both of you. Tell Mrs. Middleton succinctly all she wants to know," said Justine.

"We are indeed glad to know that," said Thomas, putting a sincere note into his tone.

"How had they heard?" said Sarah, her eyes just crossing Justine's face. "They came quite early, didn't they?"

"They came soon after breakfast," said Justine with indulgent fluency. "They had heard from one of the tradesmen, who had heard from Jellamy. We had discussed it at breakfast in the latter's hearing." She gave a little laugh. "And already it seems quite familiar knowledge. How did you hear?"

"My dear, it is all about everywhere," said Sarah, now able to follow a lead into the drawing room. "And what a sum! A quarter of a million!"

"A twentieth of a million," said Dudley. "No more to do with a million than with any other amount. I do not know why people mention a million. Everything is a fraction of one."

"And this is really a twentieth?" said Sarah, pausing with a world of knowledge in her tone. "Well, I don't know whether to congratulate you or the rest of them. I expect they have already made their wishes known."

Her voice asked for further enlightenment, and Mark sat down by her side and gave her as much as he chose.

"A little house in Cambridge for Clement," she said, as she rose at the moment of her satisfaction. "And this house to be put in order for your father. Ah, that will be a joy to you all. This beautiful inheritance! And Aubrey to have what he needs as time goes on. And your dear sister to be helped in her useful work. Well, I will leave you to rejoice with each other. It is pretty to see you doing it together."

"Let us send you in the carriage," said Blanche, who had resumed her work.

"No, we will walk and perhaps drop in on your sister. My husband will like a chat with your father. The men like to talk together."

"The women may not object to it on this occasion," said Thomas, with a smile. "I may say how very pleased I am."

"Now do you feel fully primed, Mrs. Middleton, with

all that you want to discuss?" said Justine, as she went to the door with the guests.

"Yes, dear, I know it all, I think," said Sarah, resting her eyes once more on Justine's face. "I don't like things to pass me by, without my hearing about them. We are meant to be interested in what the Almighty ordains."

"Mrs. Middleton gives as much attention to the Almighty's doings as He is supposed to give to hers," said Mark.

"I am glad the Almighty has given half a million to Uncle," said Aubrey.

"Half a million!" said Dudley. "Now I am really upset."

"What did you think of Mrs. Middleton's account of her curiosity, Justine?" said Clement.

"Poor Mrs. Middleton! We can't call it anything else."

"She can and did," said Mark.

Sarah went on to the lodge, desiring to know the Seatons' share in the fortune and hoping that it was enough and not too much. The matter was not mentioned and her compunction at overhearing the letter vanished. She saw that she could not have managed without doing so.

V

"UNCLE is walking with Miss Sloane on the terrace," said Aubrey to his sister.

"Well, that is a normal thing to do, little boy. I notice that Uncle is often with Miss Sloane of late. It may be that it gives Aunt Matty a chance to talk to Father."

"He has been helping her up the steps. She goes up them by herself when she is alone."

"Well, when you are older you will learn that men

often do things for women which they can do for themselves. Uncle is a finished and gallant person, and there
has been a late development in him along that line. He
seems to be more aware of himself since he had this
money. I hope it does not mean that we took him too
much for granted in the old days. But the dear old days!
I can't help regretting them in a way, the days when he
gave us more of himself, somehow, though he had less of
other things to give. I could find it in me to wish them
back. I don't take as much pleasure in my new scope as
I did in the old Uncle Dudley, who seems to have taken
some course away from us of late. Well, I have taken
what I can get, and I am content and grateful. And I
hardly know how to put what I mean into words."

Blanche looked up at her daughter as if struck by
something in her speech, and rose and went to the
window with her work dropping from her hand.

"Mother, what is it? Come back to the fire. Your
cough will get worse."

Blanche began automatically to cough, holding her
hand to her chest and looking at her daughter over it.

"It is true," she said. "They are walking arm-in-arm.
It is true."

"What is true? What do you mean?" said Justine,
coming to her side. "What is it? What are we to think?"

"We are spying upon them," said Aubrey, his tone
seeming too light for the others' mood.

"Yes, we are," said his sister, drawing back. "No, we
are not. I see how it is. Uncle is choosing this method of
making known to us the truth. We are to see it and grasp
it. Well, we do. We will let it stand revealed. So that is
what it has meant, this strange insight I have had into
something that was upon us, something new. Well, we
accept it in its bearing upon Uncle and ourselves."

"Dear Dudley!" said Blanche, picking up her work.

"Dear Uncle indeed, Mother! And the more he does
and has for himself, the dearer. And now go back to the

fire. You have grown quite pale. It cannot but be a shock. Aubrey will stay and take care of you, and I will go and do as Uncle wishes and carry the news. For we must take it that that is what his unspoken message meant."

"We must beware how we walk arm-in-arm," said Aubrey.

Blanche extended a hand to her son with a smile which was absent, amused and admonitory, and remained silent until her other sons entered, preceded by their sister.

"Standing at the landing window with their eyes glued to the scene! Standing as if rooted to the spot! Uncle chose his method well. It has gone straight home."

"My Justine's voice is her own again," said Blanche, looking at her sons as if in question of their feeling.

"Well, Mother, I am not going to be knocked down by this. It is a thing to stand up straight under, indeed. I found the boys in a condition of daze. I was obliged to be a little bracing, though I admit that it affected me in that way at first. This is a change for Uncle, not for ourselves. It is his life that is taking a new turn, though ours will take its subordinate turn, of course, and we must remember to see it as subordinate. But dear Uncle! That he should have come to this at his age! It takes away my breath and makes my heart ache at the same time."

"Are we sure of it?" said Mark.

"Let us build no further without a foundation," said his brother.

"Look," said Justine, leading the way to the window. "Look. Oh, look indeed! Here is something else before our eyes. What led me to the window at this moment? It is inspiring, uplifting. I wish we had seen it from the first. We should not have taken our eyes away."

Edgar was standing on the path, his hands on the shoulders of Maria and his brother, his eyes looking into their faces, his smile seeming to reflect theirs.

"Is it not a speaking scene? Dear Father! Giving up his place in his brother's life with generosity and courage.

We see the simplicity and completeness of the sacrifice, the full and utter renunciation. It seems that we ought not to look, that the scene should be sacred from human eyes."

"So Justine stands on tiptoe for a last glance," said Aubrey, blinking.

"Yes, let us move away," said his sister, putting his words to her own purpose. "Let us turn our eyes on something fitter for our sight." She accordingly turned hers on her mother, and saw that Blanche was weeping easily and weakly, as if she had no power to stem her tears.

"Why, little Mother, it is not like you to be borne away like this. Where is that stoic strain which has put you at our head, and kept you there in spite of all indication to the contrary? Where should it be now but at Father's service? Where is your place but at his side? Come, let me lead you to the post that will be yours."

Blanche went on weeping almost contentedly, rather as if her resistance had been withdrawn than as if she had any cause for tears. Aubrey looked on with an uneasy expression and Clement kept his eyes aside.

"I am quite with Mother," said Mark. "It is all I can do not to follow her example."

"Has the carriage been sent for Aunt Matty?" said Aubrey.

"Ought it to be?" said Blanche, sitting up and using an easier tone than seemed credible. "We must ask Miss Sloane to stay to luncheon, and I suppose your aunt must come too. It is she who first brought her to the house. We little knew what would come of it. But not Miss Griffin, Justine dear. We had better be just a family gathering. That is what we shall be, of course, now that Miss Sloane is to be one of us."

"We will have it as you say, little Mother. I will send the message. And I commend your taste. It is well to be simply as we are. And in these days there is no risk of the promiscuousness and scantiness which did at intervals mark our board." Justine broke off as she recalled that her uncle's open hand might be withdrawn.

"Are we to take it as certain that Miss Sloane and Uncle are engaged?" said Mark. "The evidence is powerful, but is it conclusive?"

"Conclusive," said Justine, with a hint of a sigh. "Would a woman of Miss Sloane's age and type be seen on the arm of a man to whom she stood in any other relation? Uncle is not her father or her brother, you know."

"Unfortunately not," said Clement. "That should be a certain preventive."

"Come, Clement, it is in Uncle's life that we shall be living in these next days. He has had enough of living in ours."

"It is odd that we are surprised by it," said Mark.

"I suppose we are," said Justine, with another sigh. "But we have had an example of how to meet it. Father has given it to us. Don't remind me of that scene, or I shall be overset like Mother."

"You were unwise to call it up, but I admit the proof."

"Wait one minute," said Justine, going to the door. "I will be back with confirmation or the opposite. I shall not keep you long."

"I must go and make myself fit to be seen," said Blanche in her ordinary tone. "I have been behaving quite unlike myself. I suppose it was thinking of your uncle, and his having lived so much for all of us, and now at last being about to live for himself."

"It is enough to overcome anyone," said Clement, when his mother had gone. "It puts the matter in a nutshell."

"You mean that Uncle may want his own money?" said Mark.

"It seems that he must. Nearly all the balance after the allowances are paid has gone on the house. It seemed to need all but rebuilding. Houses were not meant to last so long. Can things be broken off at this stage?"

"They can at the end of it. I suppose they will have to

be. Uncle had very little money of his own. There is so little in the family apart from the place. He was a poor man until he had this money. And he can only use the income; the capital is tied up until his death. And he will want to give his wife the things that go with his means. And she will expect to have them, and why should she not?"

"Because it prevents Uncle from giving them to us," said Aubrey.

"We do not grudge Uncle what is his own."

"We only grudge Miss Sloane what has been ours."

"How about your extra pocket money?" said Clement.

"I grudge it to her. And I thought she liked Father better than Uncle. She always looks at him more."

"I did not think about which she liked better," said Mark. "I thought of her as Aunt Matty's friend."

"Perhaps she did not find Aunt Matty enough for her," said Aubrey. "I can almost understand it. Well, we shall have her for an aunt and she will be obliged to kiss Clement."

"Well, I bring confirmation," said Justine, entering the room in a slightly sobered manner. "Full and free support of what we had gathered for ourselves from the full and frank signs of it. It was not grudged or withheld for a moment. I was met by a simple and open admission such as I respected."

"And did they respect your asking for it?" said Clement.

"I think they did. They saw it as natural and necessary. We could not accept what we could not put upon a definite basis. They could not and did not look for that."

"So you did not have much of a scene?"

"No—well, it was entirely to my taste. It was brief and to the point. There was a natural simplicity and depth about it. I felt that I was confronted by deep experience, by the future in the making. I stood silent before it."

"That was well."

"Are we all ready for Aunt Matty?" said Aubrey.

"Yes, we are not making any change," said Justine. "That would imply some thought of ourselves. We are meeting to-day in simple feeling for Uncle."

"Just wearing our hearts on our sleeves."

"Now, little boy, why are you not at your books?"

"Penrose is not well. He sent a message. And directly his back was turned I betrayed his trust."

"Well, well, it is not an ordinary day. And I suppose that is the carriage. Are we never to have an experience again without Aunt Matty? Now what a mean and illogical speech! When we may owe to her Uncle's happiness! I will be the first down to welcome her as an atonement."

"So you are not too absorbed in the new excitement to remember the old aunt. That is so sweet of all of you. And I do indeed bring you my congratulations. I feel I am rather at the bottom of this. So, Blanche, I have given you something at last. I am not to feel that I do nothing but receive. That is not always to be my lot. I am the giver this time, and I can feel it is a rare and precious gift. And I do not grudge it, even if it may mean yielding up a part of it myself. No, Dudley, it is yours and it is fully given. You and I are both people who can give. That is often true of people who accept. And you find yourself in the second position this time."

"There have to be people there or giving would be no good."

"We are all there together," said Blanche, who looked excited and confused. "Edgar's sister will be a sister to me, as his brother has been my brother."

"We have always valued the relation," said Matty, taking Blanche's hand. "And now we are to be three instead of two, we shall have even more to value. I must feel that I also am accepting. I shall try to feel it and not dwell upon what I relinquish."

"I do not feel that I am losing anything. I know Dudley too well."

"Well, if I feel I am giving up a little, I yield it gladly, feeling that others' gain is more than my loss, or more important. For I have been a dependent person who has had to make demands; and now there has come a demand on me, I am glad to meet it fully. I have had my share of weakness and welcome a position where I have some of the strength."

"I need not talk about what I am accepting," said Maria, "in this house where it is known. I am giving all I have in return."

"Simple and telling, Miss Sloane, as we should have expected," said Justine. "But we did not need you to say it, and hope that it was not at any cost. And we will all give you on our side what is right and meet. And rest assured, Aunt Matty, that we are not unmindful of your sacrifice. If we seem to be a little distant to-day, it is because the march of affairs is carrying us with it. Let us make our little sally and return in course."

"Edgar, we must have a word from you," said Matty. "It may seem hard when you are giving up the most, but you are a person from whom we expect much."

"Surely not in that line," said Clement.

"Well, Aunt Matty, I think it *is* hard," said Justine. "And you have given the reason. Well, just a word, and then we must make a move. We must eat even on the day of Uncle's engagement. Uncle's engagement! Who could know what the words mean to us?"

"I think that will do for my speech," said Edgar.

"Then that is enough," said Justine, taking his arm and setting out for the dining room.

"Dudley must sit by Miss Sloane," said Blanche, "and then that is the whole duty of them both."

"Shall I say my little original word?" said Aubrey.

"Now, little boy, silence is the best kind of word from you."

"I should like to see Clement come out of himself."

"You go back into yourself and stay there."

"Does Miss Sloane know how bad notice is for Clement?"

"You must forgive him, Miss Sloane; he is excited," said Justine, giving an excuse which both satisfied the truth and silenced her brother.

"Blanche, your cough is worse," said Matty. "I believe you ought to be in bed."

"I could not be, dear, on a day like this. What would happen to them all? I am indispensable."

"You are indeed, my dear. That is what I mean."

"Mother was condemned to remaining in one room," said Justine, "but I had not the heart to carry out the sentence. Our little leader shut up alone, with the rest of us observing this celebration! My feelings baulked at it."

"It is a mistake to be all heart and no head," said Clement.

"I am quite well," said his mother. "I am only a little worked up. I cannot sit calmly through a day like this. I was never a phlegmatic person. I feel so keenly what affects other people. I get taken right out of myself. I almost feel that I could rise up and float above you all. I don't know when I have felt so light all through myself. I don't believe that even your uncle feels as much lifted above his level."

"I see that people really do rejoice in others' joy," said Dudley.

"You have done your share of it, Uncle," said Justine. "And it is well that something else has come in time. A spell of natural selfishness will do you good. Give yourself up to it. We have schooled ourselves for the experience. It will be a salutary one. And a proportion of your thoughts will return to us, supported by someone else's."

"So for the time I have no uncle," said Aubrey.

"You will have a second aunt, dear," said Matty. "Come and sit by your first one. Aunts can be a compensation, and you shall find that they can."

"Perhaps I shall be Miss Sloane's especial nephew."

"You do not deserve it, but I have an idea that you may be," said Justine. "Naughty little boy, to have a way of being people's favourite and knowing it! Confess now, Miss Sloane, that you already look upon him with a partial eye."

Maria smiled at Aubrey but was not in time to check a glance at his brothers.

"Ah, now, you may not be so much the chosen person this time. You can take it to heart and retire into the background," said Justine, as Aubrey did both these things.

"Mother, you don't seem to know what you are doing," said Mark. "You keep on beginning to eat and forgetting and beginning again. You have not accomplished a mouthful in the last ten minutes."

"I am a little wrought up, dear. I can't treat this as an ordinary day. Your uncle has never been engaged before."

"Never and may not be again," said Clement. "He will not spoil Mother's appetite many times."

Blanche began to laugh, pursuing something with her fork and continuing her mirth as she had continued her tears, as if she had not the strength to overcome it.

"Mother, you are over excited," said Justine. "You are on the point of becoming hysterical. Not that that is any great matter. It is pleasant for Uncle in a way to see how you feel yourself involved in his life. It is not your own interest that looms large to you, is it?"

Blanche looked up as if she did not follow the words.

"You are faint from want of food, Blanche," said Edgar. "You ate nothing at breakfast. You must make an effort."

"I can't make an effort," said his wife, in another tone. "I don't feel well enough. And I do not like being told what I am to do. I am used to doing what I choose. I am able to judge for myself." She thrust her plate against her glass, and sat watching the result in a sort of childish relief in having wreaked her feeling.

"Mother is not herself," said Justine, rising to deal with

the damage, and speaking for her mother's ears, though not directly to her. "She is at once more and less than herself, shall we say?"

Blanche watched the process of clearing up with vague interest.

"That is one of the best table napkins," she said, reaching towards it. "That wine does not stain, does it? I only put them out last week." Her voice died away and she sat looking before her as if she were alone.

"We must take—it would be well to take her temperature," said Edgar.

"That was in my mind, Father. I was waiting for the end of luncheon."

"Send Jellamy away," said Blanche suddenly. "He keeps on watching me."

"Jellamy can fetch a thermometer," said Mark, giving an explanatory smile to the man. "That will kill two birds with one stone."

Jellamy vanished in complete good-will towards his mistress, and Blanche gave a laugh which passed to a fit of coughing, and sat still and shaken, with her eyes moving about in a motionless head.

"Mother's breathing is very quick and hard," said Clement.

"She must have been feverish all day," said Mark.

"We all see that now," said Justine sharply. "It is no good to wish that someone had seen it before. That will not help. We can only deal with things as they are."

"I thought perhaps no one would notice, if I did not speak," said Blanche, as if to herself. "Sometimes people don't see anything."

Edgar had come to his wife's side. Dudley and Maria had risen and were talking apart. Matty sat with her eyes on her sister, her expression wavering between uneasiness and irritation at the general concern for someone else. Aubrey looked about for reassurance. There was the sudden stir and threat of acknowledged anxiety.

The thermometer told its tale. Blanche lost her patience twice and delayed its action. Matty and Dudley talked to amuse her while she waited. She was interrupted by her cough, and they all realised its nature and its frequency. Her sister's face became anxious and nothing else.

"I heard Mother coughing in the night like that," said Aubrey.

"Then why did you not say so?" said Clement.

"That is no good, Clement," said Justine. "We all wish we had taken earlier alarm. It was not for Aubrey to give us the lead."

Blanche was found to be in high fever, and seemed to take pleasure and even pride in the discovery.

"I never make a fuss about nothing," she said, as she sat by the fire while her room was warmed. "I have always been the last to complain about myself. When I was a child they had to watch me to see if I was ill. I never confessed to it, whatever I felt."

"That was naughty, dearest," said Matty. "And you are not a child now."

"An ignorant and arrogant boast, Mother," said Mark.

"Poor Uncle!" said Justine, in a low tone, touching Dudley's sleeve. "On your engagement day! We are not forgetting it. You know that."

"I am oblivious of it. I am lost in the general feeling."

"I often kept about when people less ill than I was were in bed," continued Blanche, her eyes following this divergence of interest from herself. "I remember I once waited on my sister when my temperature was found to be higher than hers. I daresay Miss Sloane remembers hearing of that."

"Don't tell such dreadful stories, dear," said Matty.

"But I often think that not giving in is the best way to get well," said Blanche, putting back her hand to a shawl that was round her shoulders, and glancing back at it as a shiver went through her. "Staying in bed lowers people's resistance and gives the illness a stronger hold. Not that

I am really ill this time, though a bad chill is something near to it. I shall not give in for long. I am a person who likes to do everything for herself."

"It is not always the way to do anything for other people, dear."

"You will do it once too often, Mother," said Clement, glad that his words were broken by the opening door.

The room was said to be ready. The doctor was heard to arrive. It seemed incredible that an hour before the household had been taking its usual course, even more incredible that the course had been broken as it had.

Blanche sat still, with her eyes narrower than usual and her hands and face less than their normal size, stooping forward to avoid the full breath which brought the cough.

"I think people know what suits themselves. I have never done myself any harm by keeping about. I shall not stay in bed a moment longer than I must. The very thought of it makes me feel worse. I am worse now just from thinking about it. People's minds do influence their bodies." Her tone showed that she was accounting for her feelings to herself.

The doctor gave his word at a glance. Blanche was wrapped up and taken to her room. Her sons returned with the chair which had carried her, and glanced at each other as they set it down.

"What a very light chair!" said Clement, giving it a push.

"People who are light are often stronger than heavier ones," said his brother.

Aubrey began to cry.

"Come, come, all of you," said Justine. "Mother can't have got any lighter in the last days. She can never have weighed much. I always feel a clodhopper beside her."

"When is the nurse coming?" said Mark.

"As soon as she can," said Matty, who had returned from seeing the doctor. "That is good news, isn't it? And

I have some better news for you. We are sending for Miss Griffin. Your uncle and Maria have gone to fetch her, and she is the best nurse I have ever known. That is why I am yielding her up to you. So Aunt Matty provides the necessary person a second time."

Miss Griffin arrived with her feelings in her face, concern for Blanche and pleasure in the need of herself, and settled at once into the sickroom as her natural place. She had more feeling for helpless people than for whole ones, and it was Matty's lameness rather than the length of their union, which made the bond she could not break. She began to talk to Blanche of Dudley's engagement, feeling it an interest which could not fail, and making the most of the implication that Blanche was bound up with ordinary life.

But Blanche had taken the news more easily than Miss Griffin, and had a lighter hold on the threads of life, though she seemed to have so many more of them. Her lightness of grasp went with her through the next days, working for her in holding her incurious about her state, against her in allowing her less urge to fight for life. With petulance and heroism, childishness and courage she lived her desperate hours, and emerged into peace and weakness with remembrance rather than realisation of what was behind.

Her family was new to such suspense and lived it with a sense of shock and disbelief. After the first relief they accepted her safety and resented that it had been threatened.

When Matty and Maria came to share the rejoicing, they found it took the form of reaction and silence. The first evening after the stress might almost have been one at the height of it.

Justine extended a hand to her uncle as though she had hardly strength to turn her eyes in the same direction.

"We must seem selfish and egotistic, Uncle, in that we do not remember your personal happiness."

"Just now we are sharing yours," said Maria.

"And I am afraid we cannot be showing it," said Dudley.

"We can all share each other's," said Matty. "I can give my own illustration. My joy for my sister to-night only gives more foundation to my joy for my friends. Yes, that other happiness which I feel here is very near to my heart."

"You are fancying it," said Dudley. "Maria and I have laid it aside."

"You have pushed it deeper down. Into a fitter place."

"I am appalled by the threat and danger of life," said Mark.

"It may be good for us to realise that in the midst of life we are in death," said his sister.

"What benefit do we derive from it?" said Clement.

"Oh, don't let us talk like that on this day of all days. It is not suitable or seemly. Our nerves may be on edge, but we must not hold that an excuse for crossing every bound."

"We may have no other excuse," said Edgar, "but our guests will accept that one. We have been tried to the end of our strength and I fear beyond."

"We are not guests, dear Edgar," said Matty. "As a family we have been in darkness, and as a family we emerge into the light. And perhaps it is a tiny bit ungrateful not to see the difference."

"We do not find the light dazzling," said Clement.

"No, so I see, dear. Now I do find it so, but to me the darkness has been so very dark." Matty was easily tried by depression in others, being used to support and cheer herself. "You see, my sister and I are so very near. From our earliest memories our lives have been bound in one. And not even the mother's tie goes back so far."

"Really, Aunt Matty, that is too much," said Justine. "Or I should say it was, if it were not for the occasion."

"It is that which makes it so," said Mark.

"So the occasion does mean something, dears?"

"Aunt Matty, if you do not beware, you will have us turning from you with something like shrinking and contempt," said Justine, allowing her movement to illustrate these feelings.

"Something very like," said Clement.

Edgar looked up as if weariness held him silent.

"Well, well, dear, perhaps I betrayed something of such feelings myself. We are all wrought up and beyond our usual barriers. We must forgive each other."

"I do not see why," said Clement.

"And I am indulging in personal joy all through this," said Dudley. "And Matty said that she shared it. So I suppose this is what joy for others is like. No wonder people rather avoid feeling it."

"Miss Sloane, come to our rescue," said Justine. "We need some sweetness and sanity to save us from ourselves."

"It is the anxiety that is to blame. A happy ending does not alter what has gone before."

"That is what I say," said Clement. "Why should we hold a celebration because Mother's life has been threatened and just saved?"

"Poor little Mother! Are we in danger of losing her experience in our own?"

"Surely not, dear," said Matty. "No, I do not think that you and your brothers would find yourselves coming to that."

Justine gave a laugh which was openly harsh in its acceptance of her aunt's meaning.

Matty raised her brows in perplexed enquiry.

"Come, come," said Edgar.

"No, I shall not come, Father. I shall not rise to that bait any more. I shall not rise to those heights. I will not be forbearing and tolerant through any strain. It is not a fair obligation on anyone. I shall be hard and snappish and full of mean and wounding insinuation like anyone else. Oh, you will find a great difference. You will find that I mean what I say. I feel the strain of temper and malice which is in the family, coming out in me. I am a true daughter of the Seatons, after all."

"Well, you are your mother's daughter, dear," said Matty. "And we will ask nothing better, if you can be that."

"But I cannot. I am not even now saying what I mean. I am not Mother's daughter as much as your niece. That is what I should have said; that is what I did say in my heart. I have nothing of Mother in me. That strain of heroism and disregard of self is wanting in me, as it is in you, as it is in all of us."

Edgar made a sound of appeal to Maria, and she rose and came to his daughter and allowed her to throw her arms round her neck and weep.

"I hope I am not the cause of this," said Matty.

"What is your ground for hope?" said Clement.

Edgar threw his son a look of warning.

"I am not surprised to hear that heroism is not one of my qualities," said Mark, trying to be light. "I have always suspected it."

"Heroism and disregard of self," said Matty, giving a little laugh. "Has my poor little sister had to show such things?"

"Oh, what will you all think of me?" wept Justine. "What of my poor little boy who is looking at me with such baffled eyes? What is he to do if I fail him?"

"We think you have had more strain than other people, and been of more use," said Maria.

"Indeed, indeed," said Edgar. "The chief demand has fallen on Justine and Miss Griffin. My wife is not happy with strangers, and the actual nursing is a small part of what has been done."

"Father has surpassed himself," said Justine, sitting up and using a voice which became her own as she spoke. "There, I am myself again. I have had my outburst and feel the better for it. And I don't suppose anyone else is much the worse." She wiped her eyes and left Maria and returned to her place.

"I am very shaken," said Aubrey, speaking the truth.

"You have all been very good," said Miss Griffin, who had witnessed the attack on Matty with consternation, pity and exultation struggling through her fatigue, and now lifted eyes that seemed to strive to see.

"You are very tired, Miss Griffin. You had better go home and rest," said Matty, somehow betraying a desire to deprive the family of Miss Griffin's service.

Miss Griffin looked up to speak, assuming that words would come to her and finding her mistake.

"It cannot be good for you or for anyone else, for you to go on in that state."

"It is the best thing for Mother," said Justine. "She will be happier if she knows that Miss Griffin is sleeping in the next room. We shall see to-night that it is real sleep."

"Well, that is a good way of feeling indispensable. Too sound a way to be given up. We shall all be useful like that to-night. I shall be able to sleep for the first time, and I shall be glad to feel that I am doing some good by doing it."

"Well, I think you will be, Aunt Matty," said Justine, who was right in her claim that she was again herself. "Doing what we can for ourselves does make the best of us for other people. And not sleeping is the last thing to achieve either."

"We are certainly more useful—have more chance of being of use when we are not tired out," said Edgar, "though it is only Miss Griffin who seems to be indispensable at the moment of sleep."

"Then she is continually useful," said Matty, glancing at Miss Griffin and using a tone at once light and desperate.

Miss Griffin rose with a feeling that movement would be easier and less perilous than sitting still.

"I will go and take Mrs. Gaveston's temperature. That was the doctor's bell. I will bring it down so that she need not be disturbed again to-night."

"You see us all human again, Dr. Marlowe," said Justine.

"He would hardly have a moment ago," said Clement.

"We could not be more human than we have been in the last week," said Dudley. "We have sounded the deeps of human experience. I am very proud of all we have been through."

"Father, you were going to say some formal words of gratitude to Dr. Marlowe," said Justine. "But there is no need. He is no doubt as skilled in reading people's minds as their bodies."

"Then it is well that he was not here just now," said Aubrey.

"So, little boy, you have found your tongue again," said Justine, stooping and putting her cheek against his.

"Weren't you glad to hear my authentic note?" said Aubrey, glancing at the doctor.

"I meant to sound mine too," said Dudley.

"We heard it, Uncle, and happy we were to do so. But you have had your own support in the last days."

"My feelings have been too deep for words like anyone else's."

"I think we hear our Justine's voice again," said Matty, with an effort to regain a normal footing.

Justine crossed the room and sat down on the arm of her aunt's chair.

"What a thing affection is, as exemplified between Aunt Matty and Justine!" said Mark.

"A thing indeed but not affection," said Clement.

"I think this thermometer must be wrong," said Miss Griffin, in the measured tones of one forcing herself to be coherent in exhaustion. "I used it myself and it has gone up like this. I don't know what can be wrong with it. It has not had a fall."

The doctor took it, read it, shook it, read it again and was suddenly at the door, seeming to be another man.

"Come with me, anyone who should. There may be no time to be lost. The temperature has rushed up suddenly. I hoped the danger was past."

The family followed, at first instinctively, then in grasp of the truth, then with the feelings of the last days rushing back with all their force. The late hour of reaction might have been an imaginary scene, might have been read or written.

They reached the bedroom and Edgar took his daughter's arm. Justine pushed Aubrey back into the passage and then walked forward with her father. Her brothers stood with them, and Dudley a step behind. Maria drew back and waited with Aubrey on the landing.

"You feel hot, Blanche, my dear?" said Edgar.

"Yes—yes, I do feel hot," said his wife, looking at him as if she barely saw him and hardly wished to do more. "What have you all come for?"

"To say good night to you, Mother dear," said Justine.

"Yes, I am better," said Blanche, as if this accounted for their presence. "I shall soon feel better. Of course it must be slow."

"Yes, you will be better, Mother dear."

"But I don't want Miss Griffin to go," said Blanche, with a sharpness which was her own, though her voice could hardly be heard. "I don't want to have to get well all at once. I am not going to try."

"Of course you are not," said her husband. "You must just lie still and think of nothing."

"I don't often think of nothing. I have a busy brain."

Edgar took her hand and she drew it away with a petulance which was again her own.

"Is Aubrey in bed?"

"He will be soon. He wanted to come and see you, but we thought you were too tired."

"Yes, I am very tired. Not so much tired as sleepy."

"Shut your eyes, Mother, and try to sleep," said Mark.
Blanche simply obeyed but opened her eyes again.

"I want Miss Griffin to be where I can see her. You
make her go away."

Miss Griffin drew near and Blanche gave her a smile.

"We are happy together, aren't we? My sister does not
know."

"I am very happy with you."

"My bed is right up in the air. Are you all up there
too?"

"We are with you, dear," said Edgar. "We are all
here."

"It is too many, isn't it?" said Blanche, in a tone of
agreement. "Has Matty been here to-day?"

"She is downstairs, waiting to hear how you are."

"She cannot come up here," said his wife, with a note
of security.

"No, she will wait downstairs."

"Her brain is not really so much better than mine."

"No, we know it is not."

"Father does not know that I am really a nicer person.
But it does not matter, a thing like that."

"We all know it, Mother," said Mark.

"But you must be kind to Aunt Matty," said Blanche,
as if speaking to a child.

"Yes, we will be, Mother."

"She wants too much kindness," said Blanche, in a
dreamy tone.

"Shut your eyes, dear, and try to sleep," said Edgar.

"Are you that tall man who asked me to marry him?"
said Blanche, in a very rapid tone, fixing her eyes on his
face.

"Yes, I am. And you married me. And we have been
very happy."

"I did not mind leaving Father and Matty. But I don't
think that Father will die."

"No, not for a long time."

172

"Dr. Marlowe is watching me. A doctor has to do that. But I don't like it when Jellamy does it."

"He shall never do it again," said Edgar, stumbling over the words.

The doctor moved out of her sight, and Dudley felt his brother's hand and came to the bed.

"They are not really so alike, when you get to know them," said Blanche to Miss Griffin.

"Mother, try to rest," said Mark.

"Try to rest," echoed his mother, looking before her.

"Perhaps you are a little near to the bed," said the doctor.

"They moved away.

"Where have you all gone?" said Blanche at once.

"We are here, dear," said Edgar. "You are not alone."

"Alone? That would be an odd thing, when I have a husband and four children."

"We are all here, Blanche, all with you."

"Matty does not mind not having any children. Some women do not mind."

Justine came closer and her mother saw her face.

"Are you my beautiful daughter?" she said, again in the rapid tone. "The one I knew I should have? Or the other one?"

"I am your Justine, Mother."

"Justine!" said Blanche, and threw up her arms. "Why should we want her different?"

"I am here, dear," said Edgar, bending over her, and saw that his wife was not there.

For another minute they were as silent as she.

Then Miss Griffin spoke.

"I got to love her so much. She was so good. She never made a murmur and it must be dreadful not to be able to breathe. We could hardly wish her to linger like that."

The speech, with its difference of thought, of word, of class, seemed to shock them back into life. Edgar turned from the bed as if forcing himself to return to the daily world. Clement moved towards the door. Dudley turned to speak to the doctor. Mark tried to lead his sister away. Aubrey met them in the passage and stood with the expression of a man before he broke into a child's tears. Maria went down to tell Matty the truth. The day which had been at an end was ending again. Another end had come.

"We must go down and say good night to Aunt Matty," said Justine, as if feeling that normal speech and action were best. "And then Miss Griffin must go to bed. Uncle, you have Father in your charge. Dr. Marlowe will understand us. We cannot say much to-night."

Matty was sitting in her chair, waiting for them to come. She held out her arms to them, one by one, going through an observance which she had had in her mind, and which seemed to suggest that she offered herself in their mother's place.

"My poor children, your mother's sister is with you. That is the light in my darkness, that I am here to watch over you. It must have been put into my thoughts to come to your gates, that you might not be alone when your sorrow came."

They stood about her, heedless of what she said, and her voice went on on the same note, with another note underneath.

"There is one little comfort I can give you, one poor, sad, little comfort. You have not suffered quite the worst. You have not sat still and felt that you could not go to her side. You were able to obey your hearts."

They did not answer, and as Matty's face fell from its purpose a look of realisation came. Her world would be different without her sister; her place in it would be different. She rose to go and found that she must wait while Dudley and Maria took their leave.

"Come, dear, I must get home to my father. I have more to go through to-night. And if I do not face it now, my strength may fail. I feel I have not too much." She broke off as she remembered that Blanche would not hear and suffer from her words. They would fall on other ears and she must have a care how they fell.

"Well, I must leave you to take care of yourselves, of yourselves and Miss Griffin and each other. I must believe that you will do it. And I will go home and take some thought for myself, as there is no one else to do that."

"There is not, Aunt Matty," said Justine, in a clear, slow, almost ruthless voice. "We cannot tell you that there is. We have all lost her who watched over us. We are all desolate. We cannot tell you that that place will be filled."

VI

"WELL, my son," said Oliver, as he entered Edgar's house on the day after his daughter's funeral. "I hope I may always call you that. It is what she has left to me. It is the wrong thing that she is taken and I am left. No one feels it more than I do."

Edgar was silent before the difference made by death. His father-in-law had never used the words before.

"No, Grandpa, you must not feel that," said Justine, walking with her arms about him. "We do not take one person in terms of another. She never did and we do not."

"It is kind of you, my dear, but I cumber the ground in her house."

"If Grandpa had had the choice of sacrificing himself for Mother," said Mark to Clement, "I should have taken it ill if he had not done so."

"I wonder if he would have. There are only records of the opposite feeling."

"Mrs. Middleton, this is kind," said Justine, "and I ought to have greeted you. But I instinctively waited for someone else to do it."

"My dear, if kindness could do anything!"

Thomas stood aside, as if he would suppress a possibly unwelcome presence.

"Well, dear ones," said Matty, looking at her nephews as though uncertain of her new position with them. "Now is anyone good and brave enough to say that he has had a good night?"

"Brave in what sense?" said Clement.

"I am not going to admit that I have no heart and no feeling," said Mark. "I think that is the sense."

"So you slept well, dear?" said Matty.

"They are still in a daze," said Sarah with compassion.

"I wish I could have taken refuge for longer in that first numbness. But it has passed and left me without defence. I have nothing left to me but courage, and I am sure my boys and girl have that. Is it enough for them to tell me that they are better and brighter this morning?"

"We seem to have told her," said Mark.

"Because I have not been able to summon mine as yet," said Matty, lowering herself into a chair with a weakness at once assumed and real. "No, I cannot give a very good account of myself. I am not much of an example."

"We none of us are," said Justine. "It is rather soon to expect it."

"Yes, it is, dear, but I catch a return of spirit in those words, a note of hope and resolve for the future. I fear that I have not got so far. I feel to-day as if I may never do so. There is a confession to make. That is not much of an aunt to boast of."

"We should be out of sympathy with any other feeling."

"That is kind, dear. And I must try to sympathise with your hope and looking forward."

"We must be allowed to live in the moment, Aunt Matty."

"But I must be in sympathy with your moment. I must not feel that it is like my eternity."

Justine gave her aunt a glance and turned away, and Matty sank lower in her chair, in apprehension and remembrance.

"Can't you occupy yourself, little boy?" said Justine.

Aubrey began to cry. Matty looked up and held out her arms, and he faltered towards her and stood within them. Justine did not speak; she would take no more on herself. Sarah sent her eyes from face to face and then put up her hand to steady them.

"What will Father do without either Mother or Uncle?" said Clement to Mark. "I can't imagine his life."

"I shall have to spend more time with him."

"And that will fill the double blank?"

"It will be doing what I can. More than you will do by living your time for yourself."

"If I had it carried on for me, as you have yours, I could be more free with it."

"Boys, boys!" said Justine, with a hand on their arms. "It is a dreadful day, a day which puts more on us than fits our strength, but we shall gain nothing by being conquered by it."

"Will you come into the library?" said Edgar to his father-in-law. "We can do no better than keep to our old ways."

"I will do what you tell me. I have not come here, seeing any good in myself. I must take what is done for me. And who but you will do anything?"

"Whatever is done, is really done by Mother, Grandpa," said Justine, accompanying him to the door.

"I am in no doubt about the bond between us, child."

"Are we to hear your uncle's voice to-day?" said Matty. "Is he to give us anything of himself?"

"He is in the garden with Miss Sloane," said Aubrey. "Perhaps he has given all of it."

"Little boy, I like to see you try to do that with yourself," said Justine in her brother's ear. "We know who would have liked it."

"We do not grudge them to each other," said Matty. "I do not, who gave them. But it seems that they might spare a little of what they have to-day. I might feel now that I went almost too far in giving. I must rise above the feeling, but to-day it seems far to rise."

"They may hesitate to intrude their happiness on our sorrow," said Justine.

"They might give us a little of the one, dear, and share a little of the other. Your uncle lived with your mother for thirty years. It might be that he missed her. If he knew how I envy him those years!"

"Oh, Aunt Matty!" said Justine, shaking her head and turning away, and then turning impulsively back again. "Poor Aunt Matty, you are old and helpless and alone, and we give ourselves to our own sorrow and forget your greater need. For your need is greater, though your sorrow is less."

"Yes, that is how you would see me, dear. That is how I should seem to you all, now that my sister is gone. I must thank you for trying to feel kindly towards what you see."

Clement gave a faint laugh, and Matty looked at him as if in surprise at such a sound.

"They keep on passing the library window and looking in," said Mark.

"Oh, I know," said Justine. "They are waiting for Grandpa to go, so that Uncle may go in to Father. Their minds are full of us, after all. Miss Sloane is waiting to yield up Uncle to his brother. They say that sorrow makes us sensitive to kindness, but I am touched by that."

Matty sat with her lips compressed and her hands on her chair, as if trying to face the effort of rising. Sarah watched her but did not offer her aid, knowing that it would not be welcome.

"Well, we will go, dear, if they are waiting for that, if that is what we can do to help you. We came to try to give our help."

"Dear Aunt Matty, I believe it would be doing what you can. Grandpa has had his word with Father, and can go, strengthened by it. And Father can have the support of Uncle's companionship. He is hardly in a state to give virtue out himself to-day."

Matty turned and went to the door, hardly looking at her niece.

"Where is Miss Griffin?" she said, in a tone of asking for something that went as a matter of course.

"I don't know. She may not be up yet. We leave her to sleep late. She may not know that you are here."

"Well, no, dear, not if she is not awake. If she were, she would know that I should not have stayed away."

"I will go and see if she can come down."

"She can come down, dear."

"Well, I will go and see."

"Send her down, and then your grandfather can come with me. Until she comes he had better stay with your father."

"She may not be ready, Aunt Matty. Would not Miss Sloane go home with you?"

"We are talking about Miss Griffin, dear," said Matty, with a smile and a sigh.

"We may have to keep you waiting."

Matty turned and went back to her place, loosening her cloak and drawing off her gloves in preparation for this period.

She sat down with her nephews, and began to distract their thoughts with lively accounts of their mother's youth, which neither saddened them nor required them to suppress their feelings, seeming to forget her own trouble in her effort to help them in theirs. When Justine returned she hardly looked up, and maintained her talk as if fully occupied with it.

"Miss Griffin will be ready quite soon. She has only to put her things together."

Matty gave two bright nods in her niece's direction, as if in reference to something that went without saying, and continued to talk.

Miss Griffin came down, a little abashed, a little out of heart, a little the better for her time under another roof. Matty just threw her a glance and gave herself to ending a tale. Then she looked round in faint question, as if expecting something to be taking place.

"Are you ready for Grandpa, Aunt Matty?"

"Yes, dear, I have been ready since we talked about it, since you said that things would be the better for our going. But I don't think my nephews were quite so inclined for me to leave them."

"Shall I fetch him for you?"

"Yes, dear," said Matty, in a tone of full encouragement. "But I see that Aubrey is going for you. He is better and brighter in the last half-hour."

"Mrs. Middleton, I feel that we are dismissing you," said Justine. "And it has been so kind of you to come."

"We have had our glimpse of you, dear," said Sarah, in an unconsciously satisfied tone, having had a full sight of the situation.

Thomas departed with a bare handshake, as though he would impose the least demand. He uttered no word as a word would have required an ear.

"Well, it becomes easier for me to leave you all," said Oliver. "I have those who belong to me on both sides. It gets to make less difference to me on which side I am."

His grandsons looked at him with incredulous eyes, startled by the faith of a man who was in other respects a normal being. They had no grasp of the mental background of Oliver's youth.

"I suppose Grandpa is saved," murmured Aubrey.

"People always are," said Clement. "That is the plan. It is specified that sins may be of any dye and make no difference."

"There are arrangements for those who are not," said Mark, "permanent ones. They seem indeed to err on the side of permanency."

"I suppose Aunt Matty is saved," said Aubrey. "Sins being as scarlet——"

"Boys dear," said Justine, "isn't this rather cheap jesting upon subjects which are serious to many people? Do you know, at this moment I could find it in me to envy Grandpa his faith?"

"I see that he has the best of it," said Mark.

"We should like to have some comfort," said Aubrey, his grin extending into the grimace of weeping, as he found himself speaking the truth.

Justine stroked his hair and continued to do so while she addressed her aunt.

"Aunt Matty, as you are taking Miss Griffin and you also have Grandpa, will you leave us Miss Sloane? I feel we need someone to break down the barriers of family grief. And I begin to find it much, this being the only woman in the family."

"Yes, dear, take anything from me; take anything that is mine," said Matty, proceeding on her way. "I am willing to be generous."

Justine ran after her and flung her arms round her neck.

"Dear Aunt Matty, you are generous indeed. And we do value the gift."

Her aunt walked on, perhaps not wishing to go further in this line.

Justine sighed as she looked after her.

"I believe I have put something definitely between Aunt Matty and me. That is what I have done in the first days without Mother. Well, we can't expect to do so well without her."

"Is Miss Sloane remaining with us in simple obedience?" said Mark.

"I should like to stay with you all."

"I will give her to you for a time," said Dudley. "I
must learn to talk like a husband."

"And Aunt Matty has given her," said Aubrey.

"Father, she is yours, if you will have it so," said
Justine. "No one counts with us as you do."

"Justine has also given Miss Sloane," said Aubrey.

"Then I will talk to your father," said Maria. "And
you can have your uncle."

Justine waited for the door to close.

"Uncle, I don't think it is too soon to broach a subject
which Mother would wish to be dealt with. This does
not seem the wrong day to carry out what may have been
her last wish. You know what I would say?"

"Can't you try to say it? Because I cannot. And if your
mother would have wished it, you must."

"It goes without saying," said Justine, with a casual
gesture. "It is yours, that which you gave us in your
generosity when it was yours to give. Now it belongs to
another, and we are glad that there is the nearer claim.
The lack of it was the shadow over your good fortune.
Mother felt it for you and just had time to know that it
was lifted. You must have known her feelings."

"What about your old men and women in the village?"

"I shall give them what I gave them before, the work
of my heart and head. They like it better, or rather I like
it as well for them, as it does not touch their independence. Do not fear, Uncle. There is no sacrifice in rendering to you the things that are yours."

"It seems that there must be sacrifice in rendering
things. What does Mark feel about the house?"

"Am I so much worse than Justine?"

"I should think you must be rather worse. Anyone
would be. And it is on the weaker person that the greater
sacrifice falls."

"Sacrifice? Faugh!" said Justine. "What Father can bear, Mark can, and with as good a grace, I hope, as someone who is less affected and matters less."

"I did not know all that about Mark. And I am still ill at ease. To give a thing and take a thing is so bad that I cannot do it. It must be done for me. And I am glad that a beginning is made."

"We can go on," said Clement, quickly. "Everything is in your hands. Have you anything to tell us of your future home?"

"Do you remember," said Justine, "how I almost foresaw the need of some readjustment like this, and made a stipulation to meet it? Everything was to be as it had been. That is how it is."

"Mark has not told me that he will like to see the house decay. I wish he would."

"I can tell you how glad I am to have parts of it saved, and the parts in most danger, and how glad to feel that you will have a home of your own."

"Here is a little man who is as ready as anyone to make what you will call his sacrifice," said Justine. "He is too shy to say so, but he feels it none the less."

"I am ready indeed," said Aubrey at once, showing his sister's rightness and her error.

"And it is not really a sacrifice," said Dudley. "He will tell me that it is not."

"There is no need to do that, Uncle."

"Haven't you enjoyed the money I gave you? It is dreadful to want you to enjoy it and then to give it back. But am I the only person in the world who really likes money?"

"We have savoured it to the full," said Justine, "but not as much as we shall savour the sense that you are using it for yourself."

"I do not like the sound of that. I want to eat my cake and have it. I had better let Aubrey keep his pocket money. Then I shall feel that I am letting my brother's family have all I can. That is all I can let them have. Five shillings a week."

"Well, the little boy will appreciate it, Uncle. And he will feel that he has shown himself willing to fall into line."

"Aubrey will eat his cake and have it," said Clement.

"So he will," said Dudley. "And I shall keep my cake and give away the smallest morsel of it. I think that is what people do with cakes. I shall have to be like people; I cannot avoid it."

"You cannot," said Justine. "You are caught in the meshes of your own life. It has come at last, though it has been so long delayed."

"You don't think I am old, do you?"

"No, not at all. You are in time to give your full prime to her who has won it. Accepted it, you would like me to say. And I think it may be the truer word."

"And some people always have a touch of youth about them."

"Yes, and you are indeed one of them."

"Thank you, I think that is all. And yet I feel there is something else. Oh, Clement has not told me that he is pleased to give up his allowance."

"It goes without saying, Uncle."

"I see it will have to. And I am taking everything and giving nothing. That is terribly like people. I have so often heard it said of them."

"The tables are turned on you at last," said Justine. "Brace up your courage and meet the truth."

"Of course people never can really part with money. You seem to be the only ones who are different from them. I am getting to know myself better. I knew people before."

"You will have a larger charity."

"Is it larger? It is certainly not the same. Perhaps it is what people have when they give their sympathy and nothing else? I am more and more as they are. I shall have to face it."

"Well, I don't think it does us any harm to look at that straight. I have always regarded it squarely myself."

"But you have never given a thing and taken a thing. You may not really be like people. You can cling to that in your heart."

"I wonder if I do," said Justine, in a musing tone.

"I am going," said her uncle. "I may be told that I am like people and you are not. Saying a thing of yourself does not mean that you like to hear other people say it. And they do say it differently."

"Well, we have come to it quickly," said Clement. "I wonder that Uncle liked to bring another change to our life at once."

"It was Justine who chose the time," said Mark.

"I liked the way he did it," said Justine, still musingly. "It was the way I should have chosen to see him carry it through. My heart ached for him as he tried to keep his own note throughout. And he succeeded as well as anyone can, who attempts the impossible. And I think that I spared both him and us by grasping the rope in both hands."

"You could not have helped him more," said Mark.

"Miss Sloane and I are to share his money," said Aubrey. "It should knit us closer."

"I am glad you are not to make a sacrifice, little boy. You are young to take that sort of part in life."

"I regret that I have to make one," said Clement.

"I would rather that Uncle had the money than I. I am only so glad that he wants it."

"I can't understand his wanting it all at once like this. Our little allowances can't make so much difference."

"He has spent too much on the house," said Mark. "It has taken much more than we foresaw. He has overdrawn his income and the capital he cannot touch. He must actually be in debt. If he did not have this money, he would have nothing for the time. If he had not inherited it, he could not have thought of marrying."

"He would have had to see Miss Sloane quite differently," said Aubrey. "We see the power of wealth."

"He could easily borrow money," said Clement.

"You talk as if you did not know him," said Mark. "He would not do that; he would hardly dare. You must allow for the effect of his life upon him and for his own character. And it may be less easy to borrow when your securities are in trust."

"The income would soon accumulate. He is not going to be married to-morrow."

"Let us face the truth," said Justine suddenly. "Uncle has lost himself heart and soul in Miss Sloane. Nothing counts beside her and his desire to lavish all he has upon her. His old feelings and affections are for the time in abeyance. We must face it, accept it, welcome it. Anything else would be playing a sorry part."

"And he has to take a house and do the part of an engaged man," said Mark. "He will have expenses."

"We shall have to see that we have none," said Clement.

"And quite time too," said Justine, "if it makes us feel like this. It is a good thing that the change has come before we are quite ruined."

"You are all ruined but me," said Aubrey.

"Make an end to your selfish complacence," said Clement to his sister. "You are giving up nothing."

"Justine has spent what she had on other people," said Mark. "Her old men and women are the sufferers."

"Oh, I have spent on them very wisely, very circumspectly. I have seen to it that they should take no risk. They will feel no sudden change. I have had a care for them."

"Is Aunt Matty to give up her money?" said Clement.

"No. Uncle indicated to me in an aside that there would be no question of that. It is to remain as it is."

"He should have had an aside about Clement," said Aubrey.

"Mother has left her money to Father, hasn't she?" said Clement.

"Yes, most of it. A small legacy to Aunt Matty. She had very little."

"Will Aunt Matty be ruined, Justine?" said Aubrey. "What will she be like then?"

"Poor Aunt Matty!"

"Rich Aunt Matty!"

"Oh, come, she is an invalid woman, living in a small way. It is not for us, in this house and in comparative luxury, to grudge her any extra that she has. And it will make a difference to Grandpa's last years."

"Grandpa is not an old man in the village. Only in the lodge."

"And you are a naughty little boy. We must have Mr. Penrose back. We must make an end of this doing nothing because of our sorrow. We have lost our leader, but we are in no doubt about her lead. We shall get into the way of hiding a good deal of laziness under our grief. I am in her place and I must represent her."

"Your own place entitles you to direct Aubrey," said Mark.

"We must take up our burdens and go forward."

"People say that kind of thing so cheerfully."

"I am at a standstill," said Clement.

"Things go deep with people of Clement's saturnine exterior," said Aubrey, glancing at his brother with a wariness which was not needed, as the latter's demeanour showed that he had not noticed his words and would notice no other words from him.

"I do see his point," said Justine. "But it will not hurt him to show a little grit in his youth."

"Things like that ought to be guaranteed or not given," said Clement. "People can't have credit for giving things just while they do not want them."

"Uncle asked no credit."

"No, but he had it, and we shall have none for giving

them up when we are becoming dependent on them. People's outlook alters a great deal in a few months."

"Really, Clement, I don't see that you deserve any praise for your kind of relinquishment. We have not had enough giving up in our lives. We see it as a thing which has to be learnt. I am not quite so pleased with my part in it as I perhaps implied; but in a way I welcome it and look forward to getting my teeth into it and going forward without a sign. We may look back on this early lesson and be grateful."

Aubrey looked at his sister in surprise at the place she gave the lesson in her life.

"What will Father do now?" he said. "There will be no one to be with him."

"Ah," said Justine, shaking her head, "is that ever out of my mind? Does anything matter beside our real problem? We can snap our fingers at any other."

"Yes, we see you can," said Clement.

"We must all do our best," said Mark.

"Mark has confidence in himself as a substitute for Mother and Uncle," said Clement, irritated by this attitude towards problems.

"Now I don't think what he said suggested that, Clement."

"We can't help fate," said Mark.

"We can't help it," said his sister, sighing, "in any sense."

"I suppose all problems solve themselves."

"Why do you think that?" said Clement. "Yours does. My problem and Father's have no solution. We shall have to cut the knots, and the result will be the usual mess and waste."

"Come," said Justine, beckoning with a slow hand and moving to the window. "Come. Perhaps the answer to our question is here."

Maria and the brothers were walking together below.

"Is that our solution? May it be."

"May it," said Clement. "It has served so far for several seconds."

"Come," said his sister, beckoning again. "Is it unfolding itself before our eyes?"

Dudley had left his place in the middle and taken Maria's other arm, leaving the one he relinquished, for his brother."

"There may be the lifting and laying of our fear, the final token of the future."

"You build rather much on it," said Mark.

"I feel it is symbolic, emblematic, whatever you call it. I cannot feel that the future will be left to itself, with Uncle's eyes upon it, with Uncle's hand to steer its way. And by the future I mean Father's future, of course."

"No one else has one," said Clement. "But it is natural that Father should not escape Uncle's thoughts at this time. He has just lost his wife, and his brother is leaving him after fifty years. It is not an average situation."

"Well, I feel that we have had a sign. But you are determined to be contrary until your own little share in the change becomes familiar."

"Why is it little? Because yours is? There is no other reason."

"Look at that and keep it in your heart," said Justine, pulling the curtain further. "Of what do you consider that a sign? What kind of an omen?"

Dudley had gone, and Edgar and Maria were walking together.

"Is not Uncle sharing everything even as Father has shared it?"

"Uncle has his own ways of sharing. He may withdraw it at his pleasure."

"Even their married lives are at the disposal of each other. It is a sobering and cheering thing."

"Boys," said Aubrey, blinking and pointing to the window, "what of the lesson of another pair of brothers?"

"And they are walking in step," pursued Justine, bending over the sill, "Uncle's brother and future wife. Is not that prophetic? I choose to see it so."

Clement came to her side and stood looking down with her.

"May you be able to abide by your choice."

"Away now," said Justine, resuming her ordinary voice. "Away to your daily employment. We must not go on dreamily, self-indulgently, deaf to the normal demands of life. Father has set us the example. He is up and about and turning his eyes on the future. At who knows what cost to himself? We must not be behind him, who has so much more to face. He hears the call of life and obeys it."

Edgar looked up as if feeling eyes upon him.

"They are watching us, those four who are my charge and whom I know so little. My brother has taken too much of my life, and you will not find that hard to understand. I must use the time I shall have to myself, to get to know my children. It may be too late to do anything except for myself."

Maria did not realise the unusual freedom of his words.

"You may find that you know them better than you think. It may be difficult to live with people and not know them, anyhow young people. I think we seem to know them when anything brings them out. Have you often been surprised by these?"

"I think perhaps I have not. I think they are themselves under any test. And if I have not served them much, I have made little demand. I have not much debt to pay. It might speak better for me if I had. I have not set myself apart from the normal relations of life, and I should have done better in them."

"Justine will solve many problems for you and will make none."

"Perhaps that in itself may be a problem."

"You do not often find people good all through as she is."

"You like my Justine?" said Edgar, with what he felt should be his feeling.

"I like good people," said Maria, with the simplicity which in her had its own quality, something which might have been humour if she could have been suspected of it. "I never think people realise how well they compare with the others."

"You have thought about people?"

"I have been a great deal alone and perhaps thought more than I knew. I should have learned more by meeting them."

"You must help me, if Dudley will let you. And I see that he will."

"I will if I can. I have been afraid of coming between you."

"You can hold us together from there. Dudley has put you between us. I do not know what I should do if he had not. It helps me to face the future, to face my double loss. I feel there is something—someone in the place."

Justine turned from the window as her uncle entered.

"Uncle!" she said, extending her hand towards the scene below.

"Perfect. To think that I am the possessor of all that!"

"It is all yours. Your full meed was delayed to come at last. When I look at those two tall figures, walking in step as if they would walk so all their lives, I see you between them, still walking somehow self-effacingly, there to do your part by both. I take it as an augury."

"Perhaps I am marrying for the sake of others. I could not think of myself at such a time. If I could, I might feel that I was doing so, or other people might. I don't suppose we ever feel that we are thinking of ourselves."

"Do you think we do not know you, Uncle?"

"I have been afraid you were getting to know me."

"Go your way, Uncle. Set your heart at rest. Forget yourself and go forward. If there is any little thing on which you do not like to turn your eyes, turn them from it and pass on. Take your life in your own hands. It is yours."

"You are certainly getting to know me."

"I declare this is the first time that I have felt cheerful since Mother left us. But the sight of Father with you and Maria—yes, I will say the name—has helped me to it. I feel I can emulate you and go forward."

"I can't be so very bad, if you are going to be the same."

Justine walked out of the room as if carrying out her words, and passed her brothers on the landing.

"Yes, it is a fascinating spectacle. I don't blame you for standing with your eyes riveted to it. But do not let it be a snare to lure you from righteousness. Life will be rushing by and leaving us in a backwater. Father has embarked upon the stream. We must not be behind him."

"Is that what has happened to Father?" said Clement to his brother. "Or has the stream sucked him in unawares? It has taken him already some distance. I wonder if he knows."

"Knows what?"

"Is it like Father to wander about alone with a strange woman?"

"It is like very few of us, but that is not what he is doing."

There was a pause.

"When is Uncle going to be married?"

"I don't know. I suppose not too soon after Mother's death."

Clement remained at the window after his brother had left him. He was to stand there several times in the next two months. At the end of them he came to the room where his sister was alone.

"Are not Father and Uncle going away in a few days?"

"Yes. Uncle has to see his godfather's lawyer, who manages his money. It may be about settlements or something. I have not asked. It is between him and Miss Sloane."

"Then they are going near Grandpa's old home. It was when he and Father were visiting the godfather that Father and Mother met."

"Yes, so it was. Yes, they must be going there. It will do Father good to get away alone with Uncle."

"But surely this will not be the suitable change for him. Are we simply passing over Mother's death and expecting him to do the same?"

"Oh, I had not thought. Of course he must not go there. I had forgotten the place. I will speak to Uncle. Poor Father, no wonder he was not very eager over the plan."

"Grandpa and Aunt Matty are more and more anxious to sell their house and the furniture they left in it," said Clement, strolling to the window and twisting the blind cord round his hand, while his eyes went down to what was beneath. "The agent who is supposed to be doing it seems to need some pressure and supervision. Could not Uncle try to put it through and come home a little later? It would put an end to Aunt Matty's talk."

"Does she talk so much about it? She must talk to you and not to me. It suggests that I am in disgrace. I daresay Uncle could do it. It is a good idea. We will ask him."

"And I believe that Miss Sloane wants something done in her old home."

"Well, he will certainly be glad to do that. She can ask him herself; I will remind her. And I will also remind Aunt Matty. It will make a good approach and help to bridge the rift. What a thoughtful boy you grow!"

Clement still twisted the cord.

"You seem tied to the window in every sense. What is there to be seen from it? If we light upon any uplifting scenes, we are only concerned with them as onlookers. For us there remains the common task."

' I AM just the person who should not be going away,"
' said Dudley.

"Courage, Uncle," said his niece. "Absence makes the
heart grow fond. And we will all keep an eye on her for
you."

"Do you want to give me any instructions as the person
in charge?" said Matty.

"I have not had my own yet. I am waiting to be told
to take care of myself and to come back as soon as I can.
I must take the will for the deed, though that always
seems to be giving people too much credit."

"Come away from the hall," said Justine. "Leave the
engaged pair to enact their little scene in privacy and
peace. They do not want eyes upon them at every
moment. Someone give an arm to Aunt Matty."

"I think I may stay here, dear. I am not so able-
bodied as to keep running away on any pretext. And I
am to take Maria home as soon as your uncle has
gone."

"I think it would be better to forget your office for once.
Too duenna-like a course is less kind than it sounds."

"It did not sound kind, dear. And the words are not in
place. There is nothing duenna-like about me. I have no
practice in such things. I have been a person rather to
need them from other people."

"Yes, I daresay, Aunt Matty. I did not mean the word
to be a barbed one. Well, come along, Father. Leave
Aunt Matty to carry out her duty in her own way. It
would not be my way, but I must not impose my will
on hers."

"You can only do your best," said Mark. "And that
you have done."

"Come, let the engaged couple have anyhow only one
pair of eyes upon them."

"They are still accustomed to being apart," said Edgar, as he moved from his place. "Their life together is not to begin yet."

"No, but common sense will hardly play much part in their feelings at this time. Whatever they feel, logic will not have much to do with it."

"If they don't want people's eyes they may not want their tongues."

"Father, protect me against this unchivalrous brother."

Edgar edged by his daughter and walked down the hall. She misinterpreted his abruptness and followed and put her hand through his arm. He shook it off and went on, giving one backward glance.

"Father's look at Uncle goes to my heart," she said, as she joined her brothers.

Clement looked at her and did not speak. He also had followed his father's eyes.

"Some things are too sacred for our sight," said Aubrey. "They can only bear Aunt Matty's."

"Yes, that is the inconsistence I can't quite get over," said Justine. "It does not seem fair, but we are not allowed to prevent it."

"They have all their lives to be alone with each other," said Mark.

"Oh, why can't people see that the whole of their lives has no bearing on this moment?" said his sister, beating her hands against her sides. "All those moments added together will not make this one. It is one of the high water marks of life, the first parting after an acknowledged engagement. Why must we be so uncomprehending about it all?"

"We need not grasp more than is there," said Edgar, who had returned and now spoke with a smile. "The parting is to be a short one. Your uncle is hardly making so much of it."

"A fortnight or more. You don't know how long a fortnight can be in certain circumstances, Father."

Edgar again turned away, and Justine was after him in a moment, putting her hand in his.

"Oh, Father, what a crass and senseless speech! Why do I talk about people's want of comprehension? Why do I never take a lesson myself? Well, I have had one this time. I hope I shall never again take a fall like that. I hope there is one self left behind."

"It is hard on the people who assist Justine's rise on her dead selves to higher things," said Clement.

Edgar stood with his hand in his daughter's, silent in service to his duty.

"Come, Father, and just wave a farewell," she said, as if she thought heroism the best course. "And then we will go and look at the work that was done before the men left. There is one piece of security for the future."

Edgar went with her, without taking the first step, and Mark spoke to his brother.

"Father does not miss Mother more than he will miss Uncle."

"He will miss someone else as much as either."

"Has he fallen in love with Miss Sloane?" said Aubrey.

"Get away," said Clement. "Why do you think we want you here?"

"I don't think so, but why should that make any difference?"

"You should not be always listening to grown-up talk."

"I wasn't. Only you two boys were talking."

"That is too childish even for you."

"Well, I am Justine's little boy. And she likes me to be with other boys as I do not go to school."

"Go and hang on to her apron strings. No one else in the house wants you."

Aubrey recoiled, glanced about the room and burst into sudden tears.

"What is the matter?" said Mark.

Neither of his brothers gave the answer they both knew.

"Boys, boys!" said Justine, appearing with a promptness which struck her brothers as natural, but which was caused by her father's wish to be alone. "What is all this? Can I not leave you for a moment without coming back to find disturbance and tears?"

"You have not contrived to this time," said Mark.

"I shall have to learn to be in several places at once."

Aubrey gave a laugh to indicate that his emotion was of an easy nature.

"Tell me what it is."

"It seems to be nothing," said Mark.

"Nothing," Aubrey supported him with a sob.

"Well, I refuse to be left in the dark."

"It appears that you will be," said Clement.

"Clement, what is it?" said Justine, her voice deep with suspicion.

"Nothing at all. We told Aubrey to go out of the room, and he refused and some words resulted."

"You did not touch him?"

Clement raised his shoulders in contempt of her thought, and Aubrey supported him by a derisive laugh at it.

"Am I to conclude that it is absolutely nothing?"

"It is my own conclusion," said Mark.

Justine cast a glance at Clement and another at Aubrey, as though to trace some connection between them.

"Well, little boy, when are you going to show your face?"

Aubrey did not reply that this would be when he found the courage.

"Are you going to cry all day?"

Aubrey saw the awkwardness of the prospect but no means of averting it.

"Tell me what it is, Clement. I can see that you know."

"I told him to hold on to your apron strings and produced this result."

"Poor little boy, he has no others to hold on to. Oh, that is what it is." Justine held out her arms to her brother as his renewed crying gave her the clue. "You must be more careful. And what a silly thing to say! A child is always in the charge of women. You were yourself not so long ago."

"I told him that we were all boys together," said Aubrey, with tears and mirth. "That is what he did not like. He tries to think he is a man."

"Is anyone hurt?" asked Edgar at the door.

"No, Father, only someone's feelings. And they are already soothed," said Justine, encircling Aubrey's head in a manner which for once he welcomed, as it hid his face. "So we need not worry you with it."

Edgar looked at his eldest and youngest children, as they went together from the room.

"There is a good deal on your sister. I hope you will be a help to her. I will ask you both to do your best. A house like this goes ill without an older woman. It will run for a time of itself as it has been set on its lines. But if any part goes off, the whole must follow. We must support that one of us who may be destined to strive and fail."

"I hope that Uncle will live near to us," said Mark.

"I hope so; I think he will do his best. But a separate household will not keep this one to its course. I trust the lines may run together; I trust they may."

Edgar left the house and walked on the path where he was used to walking with his brother. He held his head upright and his hands behind his back, as if seeking a position to replace the old one. His face was still and set, as though he would not yield to any feelings that would cause a change. He looked at his watch, surprised by its slowness, and at once replaced it and walked on.

Justine, watching from a window, left her place and hastened to her room. Coming downstairs in outdoor clothes, she passed her brothers with a sign.

"Do not ask me where I am going. Do not see me. Do not remember I have gone. Go on with what you are doing and leave me to do the same."

"Where is she going?" said Mark. "What is the mystery?"

"I suppose to see Aunt Matty. She may be about to make some scene. It is a good thing to be out of it."

"Is Aunt Matty very lonely without Mother?"

"She must miss the concern which it had taken sixty years to work up. I should think it could not have been done in less. It is no good for anyone else to begin it."

"It is a pity that Grandpa is too old for a companion to Father."

"You are less sure of yourself in that character?"

"That aspect of me does not seem to strike him," said Mark, with his easy acceptance of the truth. "And I hesitate to bring it to his notice."

"We shall be a wretched household if Uncle—when Uncle goes. And I shall be obliged to spend more time in it."

"You take your usual simple attitude."

"What would happen to me if I did not?"

"You might devote yourself to doing a mother's part by Aubrey."

"You might have more success in that part yourself than as a wife for Father."

"Successful!" called Justine's voice, as her rapid feet bore her through the hall. "Successful and you need not ask in what way. That is in my own heart and I do not need to reveal it. I am content with my own sense of satisfaction."

Clement paced up and down, silent and as if pre-occupied. When Maria came up the drive he glanced through the window, and continued pacing as if unaware of what he had seen.

Three weeks later Aubrey came to the others.

"I saw Father and Miss Sloane saying goodbye."

"Did you?" said his sister. "Well, that was not much of an event. They must meet and part every day."

"Do people—do men kiss the women their brothers are going to marry?"

"Oh, that is what you saw? So that is what it has come to. Well, I am glad it has. They can carry that off, being the people they are. I don't know whether it is conventional between brothers and sisters-in-law, but that does not matter with these two. No doubt they felt that. They must know themselves as they are."

"Father will miss Miss Sloane when Uncle marries," said Clement.

"And shall we not all miss several people? A great part of our life will be a blank. This is something to be a help to him until the break comes. It is sad that we should think in that way of the consummation of Uncle's life, but we can hardly help it. I question indeed whether I have been wise in throwing Father and Maria so much together. I meant it for the best; God knows I did; but it will be something else to be relinquished. And I have been so glad to see him brighter and hear the old spring in his step. Well, we will not anticipate trouble. It will be on us soon enough."

"He must be better for being helped through the first stage. When that is over, he will have himself in hand and can look to his future. He must be used to his loss, before he is master of his own life."

"And people get used to anything," said Mark. "Even if he never gets over it, he must get used to it."

"He will get over it," said Justine. "To be honest, we know he will. His feeling for Mother was sound and true, but it was not that, not the kind to live by itself when its object was gone. You do not misunderstand me?"

They did not, and she stroked Aubrey's hand to help him over this initiation into the life of truth.

"We are all leaving our loss behind," said Clement.

"And it is the better for us and for other people, the sooner it is done."

"I hope it does not mean that our little mother is drifting away," said Justine, frowning as she tried to think of another meaning. "But what dear, good boys you are in these days! You will not leave your sister alone at the helm. It is only Father whose future troubles me. He does seem to be separated by a wide gulf. Mark and I hoped that we could bridge it, but we found our mistake. That is why I am glad if Maria can get even a little way towards the self which is hidden. Somehow he seems to want to keep it so. Somehow I feel that there is a higher barrier between us than there was. There is something which I can't put into words about it."

"Does Father like Miss Sloane better than Mother?" said Aubrey.

"Now, little boy, you know better than to ask such questions. It is not worth while to answer them. But Father's life is not my affair, if he does not wish it to be. It was presumptuous to feel that I could in any way take Mother's place. I am content that Maria should do so to any extent that she can. The trouble is that it cannot be for long."

"Then Father likes Miss Sloane better than you, Justine."

"Oh, come, I am Father's only daughter, since Mother died the only woman in his family. You will know better when you are older, what that means. He may not want to mix up other relations with it. He has a right to have it by itself, simple and intact, if he wishes."

"Uncle is coming back to-morrow," said Clement.

"And Father's life will be full for the time. And we will not look further."

"Uncle has written to Miss Sloane every day," said Aubrey. "I saw the pile of letters on Aunt Matty's desk."

"Really, little boy, I don't know what to say to that.

I hope they remained in a pile; I am sure they did; but even then I don't know what has become of my training."

"I don't think she writes to him as often," said Mark. "I took their letters to the post one day, and there was not one from her to him."

"My dear boys, what has come to you? I suppose you must have your little curiosities, but this goes too far. People must have their private lives and you must leave them. In some ways convention is a good thing. Mark, you are too old not to be quite certain about it."

"It is a wonder that the young are not worse than they are, when everything is condoned in them," said Clement. "We do all we can to prevent their improvement."

"Do you think Clement is softened lately, Justine?" said Aubrey.

"He has been more at home," said Mark. "I hoped, Justine, that our combined influence might do something for him. And I am not wholly disappointed."

"Don't talk nonsense. It will only end in a quarrel. And one thing I want to say. When Uncle comes back and meets Miss Sloane, don't all stand round in a circle, gaping at them. Let them have their moment."

"I do not remember grouping ourselves in that manner or with that self-indulgence. It was not a conscious effect."

"Well, you know what I mean. Anyhow you all seem to know a good deal. Talk about the curiosity of women! I seem to have much the least. Keep away and allow them their first hour. I expect even Father will do that. And it will be more to him, a foretaste of the time when he will be deserted. For that is what I fear he will feel in spite of his children. Dear, dear, I hardly dare to look at the future."

Edgar did not do as his daughter foretold. He met his brother, standing at Maria's side, and shook hands with his eyes on his face, as if he felt it was his duty to meet his eyes. Dudley took a step towards them, but stopped short, warned by some instinct that things were not as they had been. He drew back and waited for them to speak, feeling with his natural swiftness that this imposed on them the most demand and gave him the fullest chance. Maria's letters came to him, and he saw in a flash that this was not how she wrote. He waited to hear that she wanted release and had enlisted his brother's support. What he heard was always to return to his mind, each word sharp and heavy with all its meaning.

"Dudley, I must say what I must. Everything comes from me. You must hear it from my lips. Maria wishes to be released from you and has consented to marry me. We would not continue in a lie to you for a day. I cannot ask you to wish us happiness, but I can hardly believe, with my knowledge of you, that you will not wish it. And I can say that I wished it to you, when it seemed that things were to be with me as they are with you."

Dudley looked at his brother with motionless eyes, and in an instant recovered himself and met the moment, seeming to himself to act a part over unrealised feeling.

"So I am to be a hero. Well, it will suit me better than it would most people, much better than you, Edgar. I see how unheroic you are. And I return to my life of living for others. I don't think that they have really liked my doing anything else. And I see that it is nicer for them. And I shall keep you both instead of giving up one for the other. I expect that is what you have been saying. It sounds an improvement, but I shall not let you think it is. I must have some revenge for being put in this position. I shall look so foolish, standing aside in simple renunciation."

"You will indeed keep us both," said Edgar, in so low a voice that he seemed to feel it unfitting that he should speak.

"I ought to have thought of this myself. It would have come better from me. It does not come at all well from you, Edgar. I wish I could have the credit of suggesting it. I suppose I can't have it? We can't pretend that it did come from me?"

"It did in a way, Dudley. You gave us so full a share of each other."

Dudley recoiled but in a moment went on.

"And you have both taken a larger share than I meant. That is the worst of kindness; people take advantage of it. You really have done so. It will give me a great hold on you both."

His words, and his voice more than his words, laid a spell on his hearers and kept them still. Maria did not speak. She had nothing to say, nothing to add to what Edgar had said. Dudley looked at her, aloof and silent, and over his tumult of feeling continued to speak. He felt that he must get through the minutes, get them behind, that he must meet his brother's children and break the truth, before he went away alone to face the years. He could not face them with anything more upon him.

"I will go and tell Justine and the boys that I am to remain in their home. I suppose you do not wish me to leave it? You don't feel as guilty before me as that. They will betray their pleasure at the news, and I suppose that will be balm to my sore heart. I may be fortunate that I have never needed any balm before. They would rather have me than you, Edgar. I suppose I have really been the only father they have known. It is a good thing that you have not to face this ordeal. You would be quite unequal to it. You have been very awkward in this last scene. I see what people mean when they say that I am the better of the two."

"So do I, Dudley."

Dudley left them with a light step and they still stood apart. But as he paused to get his grasp on himself, he saw them move to each other and lift their eyes. Their ordeal was over: his had begun.

He paused at the door of the upper room and listened to the sound of voices. Justine and Aubrey and Mark were playing a game. Clement was standing on the hearth, as he had stood while the scene went on below. Dudley had not thought to dread this moment as much as he dreaded it. It had seemed that his main feeling must drown any other, and a thought just came that he could not be suffering to the last. He stood just inside the door and said the words which he felt would be his.

"I bring you a piece of good news. You are not going to lose me. I am to remain the light of your home. You thought that my gain was to be your loss, but I am not going to have the gain. It seemed impossible that I should be going to marry, and it is impossible."

"What do you mean, Uncle?" said Justine. "Have you changed your mind?"

"No, I am better than that. I have been rejected in favour of my brother and I have risen above it. I am the same person, better and finer. The last little bit of self has gone. It was rather a large piece at our last interview, but that does not matter, now it has gone."

"Tell us what you mean," said Mark.

"I don't think I can be expected to say plainly that Maria has given me up and is going to marry your father. Surely you can save me from the actual words. I shall soon have said them. Surely you have taken the hint."

"It is really true, Uncle?"

"Yes, you have taken it," said Dudley, sinking into a chair as if in relief.

"We are to accept this as definite and acknowledged? It affects us as well as you."

"It does, doesn't it? I had not thought of that. I am glad that you are to share the embarrassment. A burden is halved if it is shared, though it almost seems that it would be doubled. And you must be very uncomfortable. It is very soon for your father to want to marry."

"But Father can't marry Miss Sloane," said Aubrey. "He is married to Mother."

"No, dear," said Justine, in a low tone. "Mother is dead."

"But she would not like him to have another wife."

"We do not know, dear. Hush. Mother might understand."

"So that is what it has meant," said Mark, "their being so much together."

"Is that what it was," said Aubrey, "when I saw them——"

Justine put her hand on his to enforce his silence.

"Yes," said Dudley, "all of it was that. It is bad enough to bring out the best in me, and it has had to be the very best. And your position is not so good. Your father is losing no time in filling your mother's place. I must make one mean speech; I can't be the only person to suffer discomfiture. But of course you see no reason why I should suffer it, and of course I see that your mother would have wished this to happen, and that your father is simply fulfilling her wish."

"We cannot but rejoice that we are to keep you, Uncle," said Mark.

"Yes, we must feel that for ourselves," said Justine.

Clement and Aubrey did not speak.

"I don't wonder that you are ill at ease. And I must embarrass you further and tell you that you will have your money back again. I want you to feel some awkwardness which is not caused by my being rejected. No doubt you see that I do. But you will have the money after you have proved that you could give it up. It is just the position one would choose. And I have simply proved that I could take it back. My situation would not be chosen in any way. What do you think people will think of me? Will they despise me for being rejected? I do not say jilted. A vulgar word could not pass my lips."

"They will think what they always have of you, Uncle," said Justine.

"That I am second to my brother? Well, they must

think that. Do you think a vulgar word could pass their lips?"

"I am sure it could not in connection with you."

"That is a good thing. Perhaps I am a person who can carry off anything. I must be, because that is what I am doing. You will have to support me and not show it. I should not like it to be thought that I needed help from others. And as I am still well off, people won't entirely despise me."

"You are many other things, Uncle."

"They are not the kind of things that people would see. People are so dreadful. I am not like them, after all."

"When will Father marry Miss Sloane?" said Aubrey.

"We do not know, dear. No one knows," said his sister. "Some time will have to pass."

"That seems so unreasonable," said Dudley. "Why should people wait to carry out their wishes? Of course they should not have them. I see that; I like to see it. I am not a man without natural feelings. I could not rise above them if I were without them. And that seems the chief thing that I do."

"Will you be taking up the repairs to the house again?" said Justine, in a practical tone, as if to liberate her uncle from the thrall of speech.

"Your father will think of that. It will be to his advantage. Oh, I must not let myself grow bitter. People are ennobled by suffering and that was not the speech of an ennobled man. And I thought of my advantage when my turn came. That came as a shock to people; I like to remember that it did. I was not a person who could be trusted to think of himself; they actually hardly expected it. If I had not become engaged, my true self would never have emerged. And now I shall never be thought the same of again. But I suppose nobody would be, whose true self had emerged."

"Is Father's self made manifest now?" said Aubrey.

"Yes, it is, and we see that it is even worse than mine."

Justine rose and shook out her skirt with a movement of discarding the traces of some pursuit.

"People's weaker side is not necessarily their truer self," she said, in a tone which ended the talk and enabled her uncle to leave the room.

A silence followed his going.

"Are men allowed to marry someone else as soon as they like after their wives are dead?" said Aubrey.

"How many weeks is it?" said Mark.

"I do not know. We will not say," said his sister. "It can do no good."

"It may have been the emotion of that time which prepared the way for the other."

"It may have been. It may not. We do not know."

"Is it often like that?" said Aubrey.

Justine sat down and drew him to her lap, and as he edged away to save her his weight, suddenly raised her hands to her head and burst into a flood of tears. Her brothers looked on in silence. Aubrey put his knee on the edge of her chair and stared before him.

"Well, that is over," she said, lifting her face. "I had to let myself go at first. If I had not, it would only have been bottled up and broken out at some inopportune time. Witness my passages with Aunt Matty. Well, I have betrayed my feelings once and am in no danger of doing it a second time. I can feel that Uncle will be able to face his life, and that I shall be able to face seeing him do it."

"Shall we all be able to, or must we all cry?" said Aubrey, who was himself taking the latter course.

"Well, women look into the depths more than men. But you need not fear that I shall reveal myself again."

"Shall we all follow Justine's example?" said Aubrey, glancing at his brothers to see if they had done so.

"Uncle did a difficult thing well," said Mark.

"I wondered when he was going to stop doing it," said Clement.

"Clement! Ah well, it is your feeling that makes you say it," said Justine.

"Justine helped him to stop," said Mark. "I wonder what would have happened if she had not."

"He would have managed for himself. I had no real fear. I only wanted to spare him all I could."

"It seems that we have been blind," said Clement.

"Have we?" said his sister. "Did we see anything? Dir we foresee it? Shall we ever know?"

"Of course we shall," said Mark. "We know now that we have had a shock."

"It seems that there must have been signs, even that there were. Well, then, so it was."

"I wonder what the scene was like between Uncle and Father," said Clement.

"We need not wonder. We know that it was an exhibition of dignity and openness on the one side and generosity and courage on the other."

"Miss Sloane was there," said Aubrey. "I saw them all go into the library together."

"And what quality did she contribute?" said Mark. "But there was surely no need of any more."

"I wonder which of them one's heart aches for the most," said Justine.

"For Uncle. Mine only aches for him."

"I don't know. If I know Father, he has his share of the suffering."

"I think it is clear that we did not entirely know him. And Uncle is reaping the reward."

"Yes, yes, that in a way," said Justine, putting her hands round her knee and looking before her. "That, indeed. And yet there is something so stimulating in the thought of Uncle's course. It is such a tonic sadness. One wonders if such things are ever not worth while."

"Not for Uncle, I am afraid. The benefit is for other people."

"Do you know, I don't know?" said Justine, beginning

again to gaze before her but checking herself. "Well, I must go and pursue the trivial round. Even such things as these bring duties in their wake. Miss Sloane will be staying to dinner, and I suppose Aunt Matty must come to preside at this further involvement of her fortunes with ours."

"Is that the best thing?" said Mark.

"Yes, my dear," said Justine, simply. "It saves Uncle the most. He gets it all over in one fell swoop and has his path clear. Let him go to bed to-night feeling that his hard time is behind, that he has finished with heroism and has only to look forward in his old way to the happiness of others."

"Finished with heroism!"

"Well, begun it then, begun the real part. Begun to serve his sentence, even if it is for life. That is not so foreign to Uncle. We are not on his level. We can trust him to go further than we could."

"And fare worse, it seems."

"And fare as he may," said Justine with a sigh. "Now we have to take our thoughts from him and think of Father."

"A less elevating subject."

"No, no, Mark. We will not cross our proper bounds. Though Father is changing his life and ours, we are none the less his children."

"Will Aunt Matty be any relation of Father's now?" said Aubrey. "It was because of Mother that he was her brother."

"Oh, what a muddle and mix-up it all is! Well, we must leave the future. We have no right to mould or mar it. Aunt Matty is Mother's sister and has a right in our home. And she is also Miss Sloane's friend. It is strange that I do not feel inclined to say Maria now. But I dare-say that is littleness and perhaps, if I knew, self-righteousness. She has brought this happiness into Father's life, and we must not forget it, though we have counted the

cost. Let me see bright faces now. It is due to Father and
to her, yes, and to Uncle too, that we should show a
pleasant front to those who are managing their lives in
their own way."

"Certainly not ours," said Mark.

"The whole point is the feeling between Father and
Miss Sloane," said Clement. "It is best for things to
happen according to the truth underneath."

"We can't help resenting the truth; that is the trouble,"
said his sister. "We shall have to hide our feelings, and
we shall not be the only people doing that. It is surprising how little we are in control of our minds. I found myself wishing that Mother were here, to help us out of the
muddle which has come through her death."

"Well, she is not, and Father has to make his life without her. And he would be a more tragic figure alone than
Uncle, if only for the reason that he would be lonely
and Uncle will not."

"Not on the surface. We shall all see to that. But there
is such a thing as being alone in a crowd. And perhaps
we had some feeling that Father ought to be lonely at
this time. Well, if we had, we had; I don't know what it
says for us. Now will you walk across to Aunt Matty, and
break the news cheerfully, gently—oh, how you please,
and come back and tell me if she is coming to-night? To
see her friend taking her sister's place may be a thing
she can face, and it may not. Only she can know. Dear,
dear, I don't see how things are to straighten out."

"I believe that you are a contributing cause of all this,"
said Mark to Clement as they set off. "It was your idea
that Uncle should stay away to serve Aunt Matty. That
is how things had the chance to turn themselves over.
They could hardly have done it otherwise."

"It was a good thing they had it, with all this working
underneath. It would not have done for the future to go
on without any root in the truth."

"Have you had any base thoughts in your mind?"

"What do you mean?"

"Have you begun to think of having your money?"

"Oh, that. Uncle said something about it."

"He said the one significant thing."

"I suppose I shall come to it: I see you have done so."

"I was wondering if my mind were baser than anyone else's. I see it is baser than yours."

"Oh, all our minds are alike," said Clement. "Everyone is base in a way."

Dudley came across the grass behind them, raising his voice.

"Are you going to see your aunt? Then I will come with you and get the last piece of my ordeal over. I have shown you how a person should bear himself under a reverse, and now I will give the same lesson to Matty. We do seem to feel that she needs lessons, though I begin to see that her failings are not so bad as such things go."

Matty's voice came to their ears, raised and almost strident.

"Of course I should not be treated like this. You seem to be devoid of any knowledge of civilised life. Here have I been sitting alone all day, imagining everything, anxious about everyone, yearning for some word or sign! And here I am left as if I were nothing and nobody, and had nothing to do with the people who are the nearest in my life. I have lost my sister, but her children are my charge, and the woman who is to take her place is my friend. I am deeply involved in all of it and it is torment to be kept apart."

"I only said that they must have had a shock, and may not have thought of sending anyone down."

"Then don't say it; don't dare to say it. Sending anyone down! As if I were some pensioner to be cast a scrap, instead of what I am, the woman who stands to my sister's children in the place of a mother! You have never felt or had any affection, or you could not say such things."

Miss Griffin looked at the window, opening her eyes to prevent any other change in them, and Matty broke off, touched her hair, laid her hands on her flushed cheeks and leaned towards the door.

"Come in, whoever you are, and find a poor, wrought-up woman, tired of knowing nothing, tired of being alone. You have come to put an end to that. I am not quite forgotten. And do I see three dear faces? I am not forgotten indeed. But I have been feeling quite a neglected, sad person, and I am not going to sympathise with anyone. I have used up that feeling on myself. I know how the day was to go; I had my place behind the scenes; and I am just going to congratulate two of you on keeping your uncle. I know that I am striking the right note there."

The three men greeted the women, Mark guessing nothing of the scene, Clement part of it, Dudley the whole.

"Well, so I am to hear what has happened, all of it from the beginning. You tell me, Dudley. You are too interested in the whole panorama of life to be biased by your own little share. You know that I use the word, little, in its relation to your mind, not to mine. So tell me about it, and when it is all to take place, and what you will do with your wealth, now that it has come back into your hands. You won't think there is anything I do not want to hear. I include all human experience in my range. You and I are at one there."

"I think you have got me over my first moment better than anyone," said Dudley, reminded of Blanche by her sister and catching the deeper strain in Matty's nature. "I can really pretend that I feel no embarrassment. We ought not to feel any when we have done nothing wrong, but there are so many wrong things people do without feeling it, and so few they can have done to them. And being rejected in favour of a brother is not one of those. People will say that I am behaving well, but that I shall keep the most for myself by doing so, and how wise I am. They said it thirty-one years ago, and I remember it as if it were yesterday, and now it is happening again to-day. And you just said that my wealth had come back into my hands. And that is one of those words which we carry with us. I have never heard anyone say one of those before."

Matty flashed her eyes over his face and touched the chair at her side.

"Now you and I have to suffer the same sort of thing. I feel that my sister's place will be filled, and that I have not quite the same reason for being here as I had, and not quite the same claim on her family. And people will say the things of me, as you say they will of you."

"Do you really think they will? I like someone else to have things said, but I expect we can depend on people."

"Miss Griffin, suppose you run away and find something to do," said Matty, in such a light and expressionless tone that she might almost not have spoken.

Miss Griffin, whose eyes had been fastened on the scene, withdrew them and went to the door, with her face fallen and a step slow enough to cover her obedience to a command. Matty turned to her nephews.

"Well, you thought that you were to have a new aunt, and you are to have a new—what can we say? Well, we can't say it, can we? You and I can't. So we will just say that you are only to have one aunt after all. We do not want to cloud other people's happiness, and we will not; we shall be able to steer our way; we will keep to the strait and narrow path. But now we have made our resolve, we will get what we can out of it for ourselves. Let us have our gossip. That is much less than other people are getting, and if we do not grudge them their big share, they must not grudge us our little one. So when did you see the first hint of change, the cloud no bigger than a man's hand?"

"We saw no cloud until it broke," said Mark.

"Let me get my word in at once," said Dudley, "or I shall feel more awkward. It is best to take the bull by the horns. That is a good figure: it shows that we are talking of a terrible thing. Well, the cloud fell on me, sudden and complete, and I lifted my head and went forward. I told people myself; I went through my strange task, shirking nothing, and adding my own note with what was surely the most heroic touch of all. I am sure you would not dare to pity me. If you would, I must just face the hardest part."

"Well, you know, I do not feel that about pity. I often feel that I deserve it and do not get my share. People so soon forget to give it."

"That is another kind thing to say. But is pity really better than forgetfulness? Then I have still to suffer the worst indeed."

"Justine wants to know if you will join us at dinner, Aunt Matty," said Mark. "We can send the carriage when you like."

"Mark thinks I am talking too much about myself. Forgetfulness is already coming, and I see how bad it is. And coming so soon too! It is the only thing that could do that."

"What time, Aunt Matty? Justine was firm on the point. She wants an exact answer."

"Dear Justine! A time is always exact, I should have thought. Well, a quarter to seven, if that is not too early, if she can do with me so soon. She is still the regent in the house."

"I suppose Mark wanted to save me from myself. He is afraid that I may run on and not dare to stop, for fear of the silence that may follow. He has noticed that is my tendency. So will someone speak at once?"

"Well, perhaps half past six," said Matty, with immediate and smiling response. "Half past six and brave, bright faces. We have all made up our minds. So goodbye for the moment and good luck to our resolve. And tell Justine exactly half past six."

"You go on and take the message," said Dudley to his nephews. "And I will have a word with Miss Griffin. I find her regard for me very congenial. This trouble has come from someone's being without it."

Miss Griffin was lingering in the hall with almost open purpose.

"Well, you and I have more than ever in common, Miss Griffin. People think too little of both of us. I have been rated below my brother, and I am wondering if it will add to me to accept the view. Everyone feels that that ought to be done for me just now, and keeps trying to do it. And we ought to do what we can for ourselves."

"We don't all think you are below him."

"Most people do, and I expect I shall accept the judgement of the many, though it is known to be a silly thing to do. I am glad you are not so foolish."

"I am not indeed; I mean, I don't accept it."

"Of course I may be inferior to him. It is true that when I inherited money, I thought it put me on a pedestal. And when I gave it away, I thought it was wonderful. To give away money that cost me nothing to gain. But between ourselves I am still inclined to think it was. And I am not sure that he would have done it."

"Anyhow it was unusual."

"So now I am going to give it back, because if you can part with money, you can do something that very few people can do."

"I suppose people could do it if they liked," said Miss Griffin, in sincere thought.

"No, they could not. They are the slaves of money, not its masters."

"It seems funny, doesn't it?"

"I used not to understand it. But when I had money myself, I understood. I had to act quickly in case I became a slave. I nearly became one."

"But you did not quite."

"No, but soon afterwards I did. I feel I must speak so that you can only just hear. I asked for the money back again."

Miss Griffin smiled as if at a child.

"Did you not know that?"

"No."

"Isn't it extraordinary that such news does not spread? I should like so much to hear that about anyone. I did not know that people were so unimportant. And they are not: everyone is important."

"Of course everyone is."

"Do you feel that you are?"

"Everyone ought to be."

"I am afraid I am thought important because of what I can do. And it may be the same with you."

"I cannot do much for anyone."

"I thought you did everything for Miss Seaton."

Miss Griffin looked aside.

"It is extraordinary how people put things to themselves. I daresay my nephews will take back their money with a sense of doing something to improve my position. And Miss Seaton probably thinks that you lead the same life as she does. And my brother may say to himself that he is saving me from a loveless marriage, when everyone knows that it is wise to found a marriage on other feelings. And Miss Sloane must have those for me now, when everyone makes such a point of it. And I will tell you something that I have told to no one else. I think it is ordinary of her to prefer my brother to me. It already makes me like her less. Our marriage might not have been loveless, but I think our new relation may be. It seems so obvious to choose the eligible brother."

"Is he more eligible? A widower with a family? Everyone would not say so."

"Perhaps he is not. Perhaps she really does prefer him to me. Then that makes me like her less still. I am glad if she is making a bad match. I wonder if people will recognise it. People have such average minds. It is something that I can speak of her in this detached way. I wish she knew that I could. Do you like her?"

"I did very much, until——"

"Until you heard that she had rejected me. So she has lost some of your affection and mine in the last hours. There is no gain without loss. And I shall make the loss as great as I can. That sounds unworthy, but it is natural. We really only want one word for natural and unworthy."

"There is Miss Seaton!" said Miss Griffin.

Matty came towards them with her slow step, her deep eyes fixed on their faces. Dudley caught a footfall on the stairs and looked up to address her father.

"We have been waiting for you to come down, sir. Miss Griffin said it would be soon. Are you going to join us to-night and be a witness of my courage?"

"Your virtues are your own, my boy, and will be no good to me. So I do not look for a chance to enter my daughter's house, and see her husband cheating himself that he can forget two-thirds of his days. Perhaps you will remain a moment and let me hear a human voice. And then you can take my poor Matty to do what she must in the home that was her sister's."

"Isn't it nice that we are all in trouble together?"

"It is better than being in it alone. It is the truth that we find it so. We will remember it of each other."

"We are sure to do that," said Dudley. "I shall not deny myself anything at such a time."

Miss Griffin and Matty had gone to the latter's room in silence. During Matty's toilet they hardly spoke, Miss Griffin fearing to be called to account and Matty uncertain whether to probe the truth. Matty maintained an utter coldness, and feeling for the first time an answering coldness in Miss Griffin, resented it as only someone could who had wreaked her own moods through her life. She left her attendant without a word, appearing unconscious of her presence. As she reached the hall and heard her step moving lightly above, she paused and raised her voice.

"Miss Griffin, will you bring my shawl from the bed. You did not give it to me. I am waiting for it."

Miss Griffin appeared at once on the landing.

"What did you say, Miss Seaton?"

"My shawl from the bed! It was under your eyes. You can run down with it in a minute."

Dudley took less than this to run up for it, and more to receive it from Miss Griffin, and Matty turned and walked to the carriage in silence.

"Oh, my shawl; thank you," she said, taking it as if she hardly saw it.

Dudley took his seat beside her, indifferent to her mood, and she felt a familiar impulse.

"Well, how are things to be to-night? Is it to be an evening of rejoicing or of tactful ignoring of the truth? In a word, are we to consider Edgar's point of view or yours?"

Dudley read her mind and felt too spent to deal with it.

"Well, are we not to have an answer to an innocent question?"

"It was a guilty question and you will have no answer."

"Well, we will try to do better. Let us take some neutral ground. Justine remains safe and solid. How does she feel about yielding up her place? Dear, dear, these are days of relinquishment for so many of us."

"Justine thinks very little about herself."

"Then I know whom she is like," said Matty, laying her hand on Dudley's.

Dudley withdrew his hand, got out of the carriage and assisted Matty to do the same, and, leaving Jellamy to hold the door, went upstairs to his room. Matty passed into the drawing room, unsure of her own feelings.

Maria was sitting alone by the fire. The others had gone to dress, and it was not worth while for her to go home to do the same. And it seemed to her that any such effort for herself would be out of place.

"Well, Matty, you see the guilty woman."

"I see a poor, tired woman, who could not help her feelings any more than anyone else. I began by liking Edgar the better of the brothers, and Blanche liked him better too; so if you do the same, both she and I ought to understand. And I feel she does understand, somehow and somewhere, my dear, generous Blanche."

Maria looked up at Matty, sensing something of her mood.

"I am not troubled by its being a second marriage. That has its own different chance. Nor about having made a mistake and mended it. But I wonder how things will go, with me at the head, and Edgar's children living under a different hand. It does not seem enough to resolve to do my best."

Matty regarded her friend in silence. So she did not disguise her own conception of the change. Her simplicity came to her aid. She saw and accepted her place.

"Perhaps Justine will take most of it off you. She may remain in effect the head of the house. And things will not go far awry while she is there."

Maria met the open move with an open smile. She knew Matty better since she had lived in her house.

"She will not do that. Her father would not wish it, and she is the last person to feel against him. And I must set her free to enjoy her youth."

"My poor sister! How ready people are to enjoy things without her! But you will not have much freedom for yourself."

"I shall give up my freedom. I have had enough and I have made no use of it."

"It is dead, dear, the old memory?" said Matty, leaning forward and using a very gentle tone.

"It is not dead. But the cause of it is. I ought to have realised that before."

"You knew it at the right moment. Dear, dear, what a choice you had! Your understanding of yourself came in the nick of time."

"That can no longer be said. We must forget that I had a choice, as both of them will forget it."

"Stay there, stay there," said Justine, entering and motioning to Maria to keep her seat. "That is the chair which will be yours. Remain in it and get used to your place. Father will sit opposite, as he always has. There has to be the change and we will take it at a stride. It is best for everyone."

"Yes, you do welcome it, dear," said Matty.

"Now, Aunt Matty!" said Justine, sinking into a chair and letting her hands fall at her sides.

"Now what, dear?"

"Already!" said Justine, raising the hands and dropping them.

"Already what? Already I face the change in the house? But that is what you said yourself. You called out your recommendation from the door."

There was silence.

"Well, it is the replacement of one dear one by another," said Matty.

There was silence.

"It is good that they are both so very dear."

There was still silence. Maria lifted a fan to her face, screening it from the fire and from her friend. A current seemed to pass between her and Justine, and in almost unconscious conspiracy they held to their silence. Matty looked at the fire, adjusted her shawl with a stiff, weak movement, saw that it stirred a memory in her niece, and repeated it and sat in a stooping posture, which she believed to be her sister's in her last hours downstairs.

"No, no, Aunt Matty," said Justine, shaking her head and using a tone which did not only address her aunt. "That is no good. Conscious acting will do nothing."

Matty altered her position, and instantly resumed it, a

flush spreading over her face. Justine held her eyes aside as if she would not watch her.

As Edgar's sons entered, Maria rose and went to a bookcase and Justine took her seat.

"What a long day this has seemed!" said Mark, speaking to avoid silence.

"Yes, I expect it has, dear," said his aunt with sympathy. "It has taken you from one chapter of your life into another. We cannot expect that to happen in a moment. It generally takes many days. This has been a long one to me too. I seem to have lived through so much in the hours I have sat alone. And it has not been all my own experience. I have gone with you through every step of your way."

"Yes, we have taken some steps," said Justine, "and in a sense it has been an enlarging experience. I don't think Miss Sloane minds our talking about it. She knows what is in our minds, and that we must get it out before we leave it behind."

"And she knows she is fortunate that it can be left," said Matty.

"It will fall behind of itself," said Maria.

"The first touch of authority!" said Justine. "We bow to it."

"It was not meant to be that. I am here as the guest of you all."

"It was just a little foretaste of the future," said Matty. "And quite a pleasant foretaste, quite a pretty little touch of the sceptre. I think we must hurry things a little; I must be taking counsel with myself. We must not leave that capacity for power lying idle. Now this is the sight I like to see."

Edgar and Dudley entered, at first sight identical figures in their evening clothes, and stood on the hearth with their apparent sameness resolving itself into their difference.

"This is what I used to envy my sister in her daily life,

the sight of those two moving about her home, as if they would move together through the crises of their lives. I used to feel it was her high water mark."

"And they have just gone through a crisis and gone through it together," murmured Justine. "Yes, I believe together. Miss Sloane, it must be trying for you to hear this family talk, with my mother always in the background as if she still existed, as of course she must and does exist in all our minds. But if it is not to your mind, put a stop to it. Exert your authority. We have seen that you can do so."

"I should not want to do so, if I had it. I know that I have not been here for the last thirty years. I shall begin my life with you when I begin it. That is to be the future. We all have our past."

"And we will share with you what we can of ours."

"I hope you will. I should like it."

"Is Justine glad that Father is going to marry Miss Sloane?" said Aubrey to Mark.

"She is glad for Father not to be alone. It is wise to make the best of it. We can do nothing for people who are dead."

"It is a good thing that Mother does not know, for all that," said Aubrey, with an odd appeal in his tone.

"Yes, we are glad to be sure of it."

Aubrey turned away with a lighter face.

"Edgar," said Matty in a distinct tone, "I have been thinking that I must be making my plans. Come a little nearer; I cannot shout across that space; and I cannot get up and come to you, can I? The wedding will be my business, as Maria's home is with me. And I think I can make the cottage serve our needs. You will like a simple wedding, with things as they are? And it cannot be for some months?"

"I shall know about such things when I am told."

"I thought we ought to save you that, Aunt Matty," said Justine, sitting on her aunt's chair and speaking into her ear. "It does not seem that it ought to devolve on Mother's sister."

"Why, you are not sparing yourself, dear, and you are her daughter. And that is as close a tie, except that its roots are of later growth. I shall be doing what I have done before for your father. It is fortunate that I am so near. And I think we need not be troubled for your mother. If we feel like that, this should not be happening. And she will go forward with us in our hearts."

"No," said Edgar, suddenly. "She will not go forward. We shall and she will not."

"Her wishes and her influence will go on."

"They may, but she will not do so. She has had her share, what it has been."

"I can see her in all her children," said Maria. "I shall get to know her better as I get to know them."

"And yet Edgar can say that she does not go on."

"She does not, herself. It will make no difference to her."

"We cannot serve the past," said Mark, "only fancy that we do so."

"Only remember it," said Justine, looking before her.

Maria and Edgar exchanged a smile, telling each other that these days had to be lived. Matty saw it and was silent.

"I shall be best man," said Dudley. "I think that people will look at me more than at Edgar. I shall be a man with a story, and he will be one who is marrying a second time, and the first is much the better thing."

"You need not worry about any of it," said Matty, with apparent reassurance. "People's memories are short. They too will feel that they cannot help what is gone, and they will not waste their interest. You will soon be a man without a story again."

"Do you resent a tendency to look forward?" said Clement.

"No, dear, but it seems to me that people might look

back sometimes. Not for the sake of what they can do for the past, of course; just for the sake of loyalty and constancy and other old-fashioned things. My life is as real to me in the past as it is in the present, my sister as much alive as she was in her youth. But all these things are a matter of the individual."

"Aunt Matty," said Justine, in a low tone, bringing her face near to her aunt's, "this house is moving towards the future. It is perhaps not a place for so much talk of the past."

"They are a matter of age, I think," said Mark. "The young are said to live in the future, the middle-aged in the present, and the old in the past. I think it may be roughly true."

"And I am so old, dear? Your old and lonely aunt? Well, I feel the second but hardly the first as yet. But I shall go downhill quickly now. You won't have to give me so much in the present. I shall be more and more dependent upon the past, and that is dependent upon myself, as things are to be."

"People are known to be proud of odd things," said Dudley, "but I think that going downhill is the oddest of all."

"Yes, you forget about that, don't you?" said Matty, in a sympathetic tone. "About that and the past and everything. It is the easiest way."

"Miss Sloane, what has your life been up till now?" said Justine, in a tone of resolutely changing the subject. "We may as well know that piece of the past. You know our corresponding part of it."

"The man whom I was going to marry died," said Maria, turning to her and speaking in her usual manner. "And I did live in the past. It may not have been the best thing, but it seemed to me the only one."

"Then long live the future!" said Justine, slipping off her aunt's chair and raising her hand. "Long live the future and the present. Let the dead past bury its dead.

Yes, I will say it and not flinch. It is better and braver in that way. Mother would feel it so. Aunt Matty, join with us in a toast to the future."

"Aunt Matty raises her hand with a brave, uncertain smile," said Aubrey, as he himself did this.

VIII

"NOW all to the fore," said Justine, "and in a natural way, as if you were thinking of Father and not of yourselves. It is his occasion, not ours, you know. People do not return from a honeymoon every day."

"It is not the first time for Father," said Mark. "And Maria planned it for herself before."

"I wonder if Father will think of last time," said Aubrey.

"Now I should not wonder that sort of thing," said his sister. "Just take it all simply and do what comes your way. The occasion is not without its demand. I do not find myself looking forward with too much confidence."

"Boys, can you look your father straight in the eyes?" said Aubrey.

"Will he want just that?" said Mark ."Will he be able to do it with Uncle?"

"Oh, why should he not?" said Clement. "He need not hang his head for behaving like a natural man."

"That is a thing I never thought to see him do."

"I can still only think of Uncle as he was at the wedding," said Justine. "Easy, self-controlled, courteous! It was a lesson how to do the difficult thing. We have only to think of that example, if we find ourselves at a loss."

"Is Father in love with Maria?" said Aubrey in a casual tone.

"Yes, we must say that he is. The signs are unmistakable. We could not be in doubt."

Aubrey did not ask if the same signs had been seen between his father and mother: he found he could not.

"Come, Mr. Penrose," said Justine, as the latter edged through the group. "If you want to slip away before the arrival, we will not say you nay. We know that it is our occasion and not yours."

Mr. Penrose responded to this reminder by hastening his steps.

"Were you wondering about me?" said Dudley, approaching from the stairs. "The scene would lose its point if I were not here. I shall not try to acquit myself as well as I did at the wedding. There are not enough people here to make it worth while. I hope the memory of me then will remain with them."

"It remains with us, Uncle."

"Justine spoke quietly and simply," said Aubrey.

"That is not what I meant. Does it remain with Mr. Penrose?"

"Yes, indeed, Mr. Dudley. Mrs. Penrose and I found it a most enjoyable occasion. We have several times spoken of it."

"Oh, away with you, Mr. Penrose," said Justine, with a laugh. "Your heart is not in the occasion as ours is. And indeed why should it be?"

Mr. Penrose did not admit that he saw no reason.

"I am most interested, Miss Gaveston."

"Of course you are, most interested; and what a feeling compared with ours! Away with you to the sphere which claims your feeling."

Mr. Penrose obeyed, but with some feeling over for the sphere he left.

"Oughtn't Aunt Matty to be here?" said Mark.

"No," said his sister. "No. I decided against it. You do not suppose that I have not given the matter a thought? We must break the rule that she is to be here on every occasion. We must not hand on such rules to Maria, ready made. Things cannot be quite the same for Aunt Matty here in future. Maria has a debt to her and doubtless will repay it, but the manner and method thereof must be her own. It may not be her choice to be confronted by her husband's sister-in-law on her first homecoming. Aunt Matty will be with us at dinner, and that is as much as I felt I could take on myself."

"You and I are wasted on this occasion, Justine," said Dudley. "It must be enough for us if we have our own approval. My trouble is that I only care for other people's."

"Uncle, you know you have enough of that."

"Is Maria very old to be a bride?" said Aubrey.

"Not as old as Father to be a bridegroom," said Mark.

"Well, men marry later than women," said Justine.

"Welcome to the bride and bridegroom," said Aubrey, raising his hand.

"Welcome to your father and his wife," said his sister, gravely.

"Welcome to my brother and the woman who preferred him to me," said Dudley. "I am equal to it."

"I should not be, Uncle," said Justine, in a gentle aside. "I should put it out of my mind, once and for all. That is the way to gain your own good opinion and mine. Oh, here are the travellers! I feel we ought to raise a cheer."

Aubrey gave her a glance.

"I should suppress the impulse," said Clement.

"Oh, you know what I mean."

"Well, so would everyone else."

The scene was over in a minute. Maria was simple and ready, kind and natural; Edgar was stilted and sincere; and both were themselves. Dudley shook hands with both as if after an ordinary absence. His natural spareness and the flush of the occasion covered his being worn and pale. Maria kissed her stepchildren as if she had thought of nothing else, and took the head of the tea table without demur. She made some reference to Blanche in the course of supplying her family, and joined in the talk of her which followed. They felt that the situation was safe, and had a sense of permanence and peace. They had begun to talk when a trap drove up to the door.

"Aunt Matty!" said Aubrey.

"That high trap!" said Justine.

"Is she not expected?" said Edgar.

"Not until dinner, Father. I thought it was all arranged. And that fidgety horse! Will she ever get down?"

Dudley and Mark and Jellamy were perceived to be approaching the scene, and Matty was set upon the ground.

"Perhaps she has come to welcome me," said Maria.

"She has come for no other reason," said Clement.

"She comes!" said Aubrey.

Matty came in and went straight up to Maria, her eyes seeking no one else.

"My dear, I was so sorry not to be here to welcome you. The trap I had ordered did not come in time, and Miss Griffin had to go for it. I would not have had you arrive without a familiar face from the old world. You have so many from the new one."

"I have had a very good welcome."

"Yes, they are good children and mean to continue to be so. They are my own nephews and niece. But I feel that I am the bridge between the old life and the new, and I could not let you cross the gulf without it. The gulf is so much the widest for you."

"I am safely on the other side, with the help of them all."

"So you are, dear, and I will sit down and see it. I will have a chair, if I may. Thank you, Dudley; thank you, Mark; thank you, my little nephew. You are all ready and willing; you only want a little reminder. I will sit near to Maria, as it is she who is glad of my presence. Do not let me displace you, Edgar; that is not what I meant. We will sit on either side of her and share her between us. We are used to that sort of relation. I want to feel that this second time that I give you your life companion, is as much of a success between us as the first." Matty gave Edgar a swift, bright look and settled her dress."

There was a pause.

"We did not know you were coming," said Justine, "or we would have sent for you."

"You asked me to come, dear. I should have done so, of course, but you did remember the formality. But it was for dinner that you said. I did not know that they were expected so early. I only found it out by accident."

"We did not mean to give a wrong impression."

"No, dear? But you said for dinner, I think."

"I did not know you expected—that you would want to be here for their arrival. We thought they would have a rest, and that you would see them later."

"Have a rest, dear?" said Matty, with a glance round and a twitch of her lips.

"Well, stay with us for a little while, and then go upstairs by themselves and meet everyone at dinner."

"Maria never rests in the day, even after a journey," said Matty, in the casual tone of reference to someone completely known to her."

"I am finding all this a rest," said Maria.

Matty looked round again, with her mouth conscientiously controlled, but with a gleam in her eyes.

"Well, can it be true?" said Clement.

"I am finding it a great strain," murmured Aubrey.

"Hush, don't whisper among yourselves," said their sister.

"I think I will have some tea," Justine dear," said Matty. "Or am I to remember that I was only asked to dinner?"

"Really, Aunt Matty, I shall not reply to that."

"I am afraid I am pouring out the tea," said Maria, laughing and taking up the pot.

"Are you, dear? I thought you were having a rest, and

that Justine would still be directing things. I have had no directions except from her."

"You could not have them from me until I returned."

"You did not write to me, I thought you would want to arrange your first day yourself."

"I did not think of it. I was content just to come home."

"No, no, Aunt Matty. You will not make bad blood between Maria and me," said Justine, shaking her head.

"Bad blood, dear?" said her aunt, in a low, almost troubled tone. "I did not think there was any question of that. I had put the thought away. I am sure there is none any longer. I am sure that all the little pinpricks and jealousies have faded away."

"Justine does not know what such things are," said Edgar.

"Well, I said they had faded away, and that amounts to the same thing."

"It is on the way to the opposite thing."

"Dear Father, he has come back to his only daughter," said Justine.

"Incontrovertibly," said Aubrey, looking down.

"Well, am I to have any tea?" said Matty.

"When you stop holding everyone rooted to the spot," said Clement. "As long as they are petrified, they cannot give you any."

"Well, I must lift my spell. I did not know it was so potent. Some people have more power than others and must be careful how they wield it. Thank you, Dudley, and a penny for your thoughts."

"I was thinking that I had never made a speech which carried a sting."

"I was wondering when we were going to hear your voice. I have never known you so silent."

"I recognise the sting. I almost think that the gift of speech is too dangerous to use."

"What should we do without your talent in that line?"

"I believe that is a speech without a sting."

"Oh, Aunt Matty, if you would only do it oftener!" said Justine, sighing. "You don't know how far you could go."

"Don't I, dear? I sometimes think I should be left in a backwater. I admit that I sometimes feel driven to apply the goad."

"Aunt Matty, how wrong you are! If only you would realise it!"

"It must be a trying obligation," said Maria.

"If you can manage without it in your ready-made family, you are fortunate."

"I see that I am."

"And we all see that we are," said Mark.

"I am sure—I hope we have many happy days before us," said Edgar.

"Rest assured, Father, that we are not poaching on your preserves," said Justine. "Maria is yours, root, barrel and stock. We claim only our reasonable part in her."

Aubrey looked at his sister.

"You don't understand my wholehearted acceptance of our new life, do you, little boy? When you get older you will realise that there is no disloyalty involved."

"It is a rich gift that I have brought you," said Matty, smiling at Edgar. "So do you think I may have it in my own hands for a time, while you and Dudley go and make up your arrears, and the young ones play at whatever is their play of the moment."

The word was obeyed before it was considered. Edgar withdrew with his brother and his children found themselves in the hall.

"If I were Maria," said Clement, "I would not let Aunt Matty order the house."

"She will not do so for long; do not fear," said his sister. "There are signs that she is equal to her charge. I am quite serene. And I was glad to see Father and Uncle go off in their old way. Uncle still has his brother. I don't think anything has touched that."

Edgar and Dudley were sitting in their usual chairs, their usual table between them, the usual box of Dudley's cigars at Edgar's hand.

"The young people have given no trouble?"

"None."

"You have not lavished too much on them?"

"Nothing. They keep to what they have."

"Is there anything to tell about the house?"

"The work goes on. Mark and I have had our eye on it."

"Dudley," said Edgar, keeping his voice to the same level but unable to control its tones, "I have always taken all you had. Always from the beginning. You did not seem to want it. Now, if I have taken something you did want——"

"Oh, I am a great giver. And giving only counts if you want what you give. They say that we should never give away anything that we do not value."

"It is the rarest thing to be."

"Well, I don't wonder at that. It seems to be one of those things which may end anywhere. We see that it has with us. But I had to follow my nature. It may have been my second nature in this case. It would be best to hide a first nature quickly, and I was very quick. I hope people admire me. To be admired is one of the needs of my nature; my first nature that would be. But I should only expect them to admire the second. It would not often be possible to admire first natures. I used to think that you and I only had second ones, but now we have both revealed our first, and it gives us even more in common."

Edgar looked at his brother, uncertain whether to be cheered or troubled by the tangle of his words.

"You find you are able—you can be with Maria and me?"

"Yes. There is not so much of my first nature left as you fear. And I daresay it is best that I should not marry.

If a man has to forsake his father and mother, he ought to forsake his brother, and I find I could not do that. I suppose you have forsaken me in your mind? You should have."

Edgar looked up with a smile, missing what lay behind the words, and the cry from his brother's heart went unanswered.

When Elgar's children came down to dinner they found their aunt alone.

"Well, here is the first evening of our new life," said Justine. "I feel easy and not uncheerful."

"Yes, I think so do I, dear," said Matty. "I think I can see my Maria over you all, as I could not see anyone else."

"I already see her taking her place at the table in my mind's eye," said Justine, leaning back and closing her other eyes to give full scope to this one. "Easily and simply, as if she had always had it."

"Well, perhaps not quite like that, dear. That might not be the best way. I think she can do better."

"That would be well enough," said Mark.

"I daresay she will take her place like anyone else," said Clement.

"I think the boys admire their young stepmother, Justine," said Aubrey.

"Well, we are at a difficult point," said Matty. "We are the victims of a conflict of loyalties. We must be patient with each other." She smiled at them with compressed lips, seeming to exercise this feeling.

Maria took her seat at the table as if she were taking it naturally for the first time.

"The place is taken," murmured Aubrey.

"And as I said it would be," said Clement.

"Well, I want a little help in taking my place," said Matty. "I am not able to take it quite like that. Thank you, Edgar."

"I shall so enjoy shelving the household cares to-morrow," said Justine. "No housewife ever parted with her keys with less of a pang."

"You will give what help you can?" said Edgar.

"No, I shall not, Father. I know it sounds perverse, but a house cannot do with more than one head. Nothing can serve two masters. I go free without a qualm."

"I only serve one master," said Aubrey. "Penrose."

"Do you feel you would like a change?" said Maria.

"No, no, don't pander to him, Maria; he will only take advantage. I mean, of course, that that is what I have found. You will form your own conclusions."

"Perhaps I shall find that I have learnt more from Penrose than many another lad at a great public school."

"I don't know what ground you have for the view," said Mark.

"It was just one of my little speeches. What would the house be without them?"

"It would be better with Uncle and no one to copy him," said Clement.

"Now, Clement, come, there is a real likeness," said Justine.

"Clement is jealous of my genuine touch of Uncle."

"Does Dudley see the likeness?" said Matty, with a faint note of sighing patience with the well worn topic.

"I should think it is the last thing anyone would see, a likeness to himself," said her niece.

"Should you, dear? The opposite of what I say. We are not all like your uncle."

"I make no pretence of lightness and charm. I am a blunt and downright person. People have to take me as I am."

"Yes, we do, dear," said Matty, seeming to use the note of patience in two senses.

"Clement thinks that I try to cultivate them," said Aubrey, "and it makes him jealous."

"You may be wise to save us from taking you as we take Justine," said Clement.

Aubrey gave a swift glance round the table, and sat with an almost startled face.

"Maria, what do you think of our family?" said Justine. "It is full experience for you on your first night."

"It is better not to have it delayed. And I must think of myself as one of you."

"This is the very worst. I can tell you that."

"I have often been prouder of my sister's children," said Matty.

Edgar and Dudley turned towards her.

"I believe the two brothers are so absorbed in being together that no one else exists for them."

There was a pause and Matty was driven further.

"Well, it is a strange chapter that I have lived since I have been here. A strange, swift chapter. Or a succession of strange, swift chapters. If I had known what was to be, might I have been able to face it? And if not, how would it all be with us? How we can think of the might-have-beens!"

"There are no such things," said Edgar.

"We cannot foretell the future," said Mark. "It might make us mould our actions differently."

"And then how would it all be with us?" repeated Matty, in a light, running tone. "Maria not here; Justine not deposed; nothing between your father and uncle; everything so that my sister could come back at any time and find her home as she left it."

"Is it so useful to have things ready for her return?"

"It is hardly a dependable contingency," said Clement.

"No, no," said Justine, with a movement of distaste, "I am not going to join."

"So my little flight of imagination has fallen flat."

"What fate did it deserve?" said Edgar, in a tone which fell with its intended weight.

"Did you expect it to carry us with it?" said Mark.

Matty shrank into herself, drawing her shawl about

her and looking at her niece almost with appeal. The latter shook her head.

"No, no, Aunt Matty, you asked for it. I am not going to interfere."

"What do you say to the reception of a few innocent words, Dudley?"

"I have never heard baser ones."

Matty looked at Maria, and meeting no response, drew the shawl together again and bent forward with a shiver.

"Have you a chill, Matty?" said Dudley.

"I felt a chill then. There seemed to be one in the air. I am not sure whether it was physical or mental. The one may lead to the other. I think that perhaps chills do encircle you and me in these days."

"That is not true of Uncle," said Justine. "He is safely ensconced in the warmth of the feeling about him."

"And I am not? I am a lonely old woman living in the past? I was coming to feel I was that. Perhaps I ought not to have come to-day, sunk as I was in the sadness of this return." Matty ended on a hardly audible note.

"It was certainly not wise to come with no other feeling about it," said Mark.

"No, it was not, because that was how I felt. So perhaps it is not wise to stay. I will make haste to go, and lift the damper of my presence. I feel that I have been a blight, that your first evening would have been better without me. I meant to come and join you in looking forward, and I have stood by myself and looked back. I am glad it has been by myself, that I have not drawn any of you with me." Matty kept her eyes on Mark's, to protect herself from other eyes. "But I have been wrong in not hiding my heart. My father sets me an example in avoiding the effort destined to fail. I thought I could follow your uncle: I meant to take a leaf out of his book. But I can't quite do it to-day. To-day I must go away by myself and be alone with my memories. And I shall not find it being alone. And that is a long speech to end up with, isn't it?"

"Yes, it is rather long."

"Very well, then, go if you must," said Justine.

"What does my hostess say?"

"Oh, of course, I should not have spoken for her," said Justine, with a little laugh.

"Justine has said the only thing that can be said. But the carriage cannot be here at once."

"Well, I will go and sit in the hall. Then I shall have left the feast. There will no longer be the death's head at it. I shall be easier when I am not that. That is the last thing I like to be, a cloud over happy people. We must not underrate happiness because it is not for ourselves. It ought to make us see how good it is, and it does show it indeed."

"Who is going to see Aunt Matty out?" murmured Aubrey.

"Perhaps Dudley will," said Matty, smiling at the latter. "Then he and I can sit for a minute, and perhaps give each other a little strength for the different effort asked of us."

Dudley seemed not to hear and Maria signed to her husband.

"Aunt Matty would have been burned as a witch at one time," said Clement.

"Does Clement's voice betray a yearning for the good old days?" said Aubrey.

"Witches seem always to have been innocent people," said Mark.

"That will do. Let us leave Aunt Matty alone," said Justine. "She may merit no more, but so much is her due."

"What does Maria say?" said Dudley, in an ordinary tone.

"We are all moving forward. And if Matty does not come with us, she will be left behind."

"She may pull herself up and follow," said Justine.

"She will probably lead," said Clement.

"She will not do that," said his father, returning to the room.

"Has Aunt Matty gone already, Father?" said Justine.

"No. She asked me to leave her, and I did as she asked."

After dinner it was the brothers' custom to go to the library. Blanche had had her own way of leaving the room, pausing and talking and retracing her steps, and any custom of waiting for her had died away. Dudley put his arm through Edgar's, as he had done through his life. Edgar threw it off with a movement the more significant that it was hardly conscious, and waited for his wife, giving a smile to his brother. Dudley stood still, felt his niece's hand on his arm, shook it off as Edgar had done his own, and followed the pair to the library. He sat down between them, crossing his knees to show a natural feeling. Edgar looked at him uncertainly. He had meant to be alone with his wife and had assumed that his brother understood him. This withdrawal of Dudley's support troubled him and shook his balance. Something was coming from his brother to himself that he did not know.

"Does Maria mind smoke?" said Dudley, knowing that she did not mind, knowing little of what he said.

"No, not at all. I am used to it."

"I do not smoke; I never have; I get the cigars for Edgar."

"I could not afford them for myself," said Edgar.

"I must give you some as a present," said his wife, feeling at once that the words would have been better unsaid.

Dudley looked at her and met her eyes, and in a moment they seemed to be ranged on opposite sides, contending for Edgar. Edgar sat in a distress he could not name, moving his strong, helpless hands as if seeking some hold.

"They come from some foreign place," said Maria,

taking up the box. "We shall have to depend on Dudley for them."

Dudley lifted eyes which looked as if he were springing from his place, but held himself still. The silence held, grew, swelled to some great, nameless thing, which seemed to fill the space between them and press on their hearing and their sight. Edgar rose and showed by his rapid utterance as well as by his words how he was shaken out of himself.

"What is this, Dudley? We cannot go on like this. We should not be able to breathe. What is it between us? It is not fair to give me everything, and then turn on me as an enemy."

"Not fair to give you everything?" said Dudley, rising to bring his eyes to the level of his brother's. "Do you think it is fair? Does it sound fair as you say it? For one person to do that to another? For the other person to take it? Or do you take it all, as you always have, you who know how to do nothing else? And turn on you as an enemy? What have you been to me but that? If you have never thought, think now."

"So it has come to this, Dudley. It has all been this. This has been before us, and so between us, all our lives. You have given me nothing. You wanted to have me in your hands in return. No one can give really, not even you; not even you, Dudley. I shall not think that any more of you. You are not different. Why did you let me think you were? I would not have minded; I could have taken you as you were; I did not want anything from you. And now I have lost my brother, whom I need not have lost if I had known."

Edgar turned his face aside, and the simple movement, which Dudley knew was not acting, pierced him beyond his bearing and flung him forward. His pain and his brother's, the reproach which he suffered in innocence and sacrifice, flooded his mind and blurred its thought.

"You have lost your brother! Then know that you have

lost him. Know that you speak the truth. You may be glad to be left with your wife, and I shall be glad to leave you. I shall be glad, Edgar. I have always been alone in your house, always in my heart. You had nothing to give. You have nothing. There is nothing in your nature. You did not care for Blanche. You do not care for your children. You have not cared for me. You have not even cared for yourself, and that has blinded us. May Maria deal with you as you are, and not as I have done."

Maria stood apart, feeling she had nothing to do with the scene, that she must grope for its cause in a depth where different beings moved and breathed in a different air. The present seemed a surface scene, acted over a seething life, which had been calmed but never dead. She saw herself treading with care lest the surface break and release the hidden flood, felt that she learned at that moment how to do it, and would ever afterwards know. She did not turn to her husband, did not move or touch him. The tumult in his soul must die, the life behind him sink back into the depths, before they could meet on the level they were to know. She felt no sorrow that she had not shared that life, only pity that his experience had not found cover as hers had found.

Dudley went alone from his brother's house, taking nothing with him but his purse and covering from the winter cold. He went, consciously empty of hand and of heart, almost triumphant in owning so little in the house that had been his home. As he passed Matty's house, forming in his mind some plan for the night, he heard a sound of crying behind the hedge, which seemed to chime with his mood. He followed the sound, thinking to find some unfortunate who would make some appeal, and willing for the sense of being met as a succourer, and came upon Miss Griffin bent over the bushes in hopeless weeping. She raised her head and came forward at once, spreading her hands in abandonment to the open truth.

"Miss Seaton has turned me out. I have been out here for some time. I haven't anywhere to go, and I can't stay here in the dark and cold. And I can't go back." She looked round with eyes of fear, and something showed that it was Matty in relenting mood, with an offer of shelter, that she feared.

Dudley put his arm about her and walked on, leading her with him. She went without a word, taking her only course and trusting to his aid. Her short, quick, unequal steps, the steps of someone used to being on her feet, but not to walking out of doors, made no attempt to keep time or pace, and he saw with a pang how she might try the nerves of anyone in daily contact. The pang seemed to drive him forward as if in defiance of its warning.

"You and I are both alone. People have not done well by us, and we have done too well by them. We should know how to treat each other. We will keep together and forget them. We had better be married, and then we need never part. We have both been cast out by those who should have served us better. We will see what we can do for ourselves."

"Oh, no, no," said Miss Griffin, in an almost ordinary tone, as if she hardly gave Dudley's words their meaning. "Of course not. What a thing it would be! We could not alter it when it was done, and of course you would want to." Her voice was sympathetic, as if her words hardly concerned herself. "And what would people think? You can help me without that." The words stumbled for the first time. "If you want to help me, that is, of course."

"I was trying to serve myself," said Dudley, too lost in his own emotions to feel rebuff or relief. "I must serve you in some better way. You can think of one yourself. And now we must hurry on and get you under a roof."

He walked to Sarah Middleton's house, seeing his companion's thinly covered feet and uncovered head, and the scanty shawl snatched from somewhere when she was driven into the cold. On the steps of the house she looked up to explain the truth, that he might know it and express it for her.

"She came back from the house very early and very upset. I could hardly speak to her. Nothing I said was right. And she did not like it if I did not speak. It was no good to try to do anything. Nothing could have made any difference. Mr. Seaton had gone to bed and we were alone. At last she flew into a rage and turned me out of doors. She said it drove her mad to see my face." Miss Griffin's voice did not falter. She had felt to her limit and could not go beyond.

Dudley asked to see Sarah and told her the truth. She heard him in silence, with expressions of shock, eagerness, consternation, delight and pity succeeding each other on her face. When at last she raised her hands, he knew that his task was done. He saw her hasten into the hall and bring the hands down on Miss Griffin's shoulders. Her husband rose and put a chair for the guest, keeping his face to the exact expression for the action.

"You will be safe, my dear; we will see that you are safe," said Sarah, showing that Miss Griffin was not the only person in her mind.

Miss Griffin parted from Dudley with eager thanks, and he saw her go in to food and fire with greater eagerness.

He left the house, feeling soothed and saner, and found himself imagining Sarah's experience, if she had known his own solution for her guest. He went to the inn to get a bed for the night, indifferent to surprise or question, finding a sort of comfort in the familiar welcome. He slept as he had not slept since his brother's engagement, the sense of suspense and waiting leaving him at last. He found that his mind and emotions were cleared, and that his feeling for Edgar had taken its own place. He had been lost in the tumult of his own life, and the hour passed in another's had done its work. Edgar stood in his heart above any other. The knowledge brought the relief of simplified emotion, but fed his anger with his brother, and confirmed his resolution to remain out of his life.

He went to Miss Griffin in the morning in almost convalescent calm, prepared to live his life without hope or eagerness. She came into the hall to meet him, wishing to see him without Sarah, as her sympathy with curiosity did not lessen the trial of response.

"Oh, it was everything to be warm and safe. I shall never forget that waiting in the cold. I don't know what would have happened if you had not come."

"What would you like to do now? And in the future?"

"I should like to get away from Miss Seaton," said Miss Griffin, meeting his eyes in simple acceptance of his knowledge. "It seems a dreadful thing to say after all these years, but every year seems to make things worse. I should like to have some peace and some ordinary life like other people, before I get old." Her voice broke and her eyes filled, both actions so simple that she did not heed or disguise them. "I don't feel I want to have had nothing: it doesn't seem right that anyone should go through life like that. You only get your life once. Of course, if people were fond of you, that would be enough; but Miss Seaton seems to hate me now, and I don't know what to do to make it different. I only want to be peaceful somewhere, and not always driven and afraid, and to be able to do something for someone else sometimes." Her eyes went round the hall as if its narrow comfort satisfied her soul.

"You would like a cottage of your own, and a little income to manage it on, and perhaps a friend to live with you, who needed a home."

"Oh, I know two or three people," said Miss Griffin, in gladness greater than her surprise. "I could have them in turn to make a change for me and for them. Oh I should like it. But I don't know why you should do as much for me as that." Her voice fell more than her face. She depended on Dudley's powers, and would have liked

so much to do this for someone, that she hardly conceived of his not feeling the same.

"I shall like to do it, and I can do it easily. I shall be
the fortunate person. We will arrange for the money to
come to you for your life. I shall not be living here, but
that will make no difference."

Miss Griffin hardly heard the last words. She stood with
a face of simple joy. She believed that Dudley would not
miss the money, would have been surprised by the idea
of his doing so, and saw her life open out before her,
enclosed, firelit, full of gossip and peace.

"What will Miss Seaton say?" she said, in a tone which
was nervous, guilty, triumphant and compassionate.
"Well, she will soon get used to it and settle with someone else." A spasm crossed her face but did not stay. She
had been tried to the end of her endurance, and knew
that she could not continue to endure. "Perhaps you
could come and tell Mrs. Middleton. Then I need not
talk about it, and other people will hear."

Sarah was startled, incredulous, rejoiced, desirous that
Miss Griffin should have enough for her ease, anxious
that she should remain a much poorer person than herself, relieved when it was apparent that she would; and
betrayed her feelings partially to Dudley and completely
to Miss Griffin, without surprising or estranging either.
Miss Griffin's thought followed hers. She did not want
a whit more than she needed, felt that the money would
have more significance if every coin had its use, looked
for the pleasures of contrivance, and allowed for a touch
of laxness in herself, which Matty had combated with
bitterness, with an open self-knowledge which to Sarah
was sensible, and to Dudley comic and touching. She did
not stress her gratitude, almost betrayed a faint sense of
envy of anyone who could give so much without sacrifice. If she had not forgotten the offer of marriage, she
behaved as if she had, and he saw that in effect they
would both forget it, that she saw it simply as an impul-

sive offer of rescue. If she divined that it had some root in his own life, she saw the life as too far removed from her own to be approached.

Dudley left her with the natural sense of elation, and as it fell away, walked on with the single intention of going further from his brother, thinking and caring for nothing beyond.

IX

EDGAR and his wife were left looking at each other. Maria was the first to speak.

"We must go on as if nothing had happened. We could not help it. I do not think we could. We might have seen it had to come. But I thought it would not come, with Dudley. Did you think that?"

"I thought it," said Edgar, hardly parting his lips. He was summoning up his brother's experience, grasping at its meaning as his brother had lived it. He had taken from him the thing he had asked, taken and held it for himself, and let him move aside to walk alone, but near him that he might give his support. The demand was exposed, and he felt that he could not believe in the sight. Maria saw that it was useless to be with him, that each was alone.

By common consent they remained apart that night. When they met in the morning they felt it was a new meeting, that it came after a sudden separation and brought them to a new future. It almost made a fresh bond between them, giving them a common knowledge out of all they knew.

"Well, this is a sobering morning," said a voice, which seemed to be neither Aubrey's nor Justine's, but was really the former used in imitation of the latter. "But we shall be stimulated by it. We must live in Father's life and not allow ourselves to cross the bound. I will take it all at one fell swoop and lead the way into the room."

"You both look tired after your long day," said Mark.

His father felt that his words should cover that part of the day he did not know.

"Maria is tired," he said.

"She will soon be rested in her own home," said Justine. "I already enjoy a personal sense of relief. I am a mere unimportant child of the house again."

"Will you wait breakfast for Mr. Dudley, ma'am?" said Jellamy.

"No. He is not coming back so early."

"Where has he gone?" said Clement.

"Away for a time, I am afraid," said Edgar. "He felt he wanted a change. I fear that he found the sight of the two of us together too much."

"Well, I think it is a thoroughly good idea," said Justine at once. "Uncle has been attempting altogether too much of late. He can't go on being superhuman. Even he is subject to the rules of mortal life. I wanted to suggest his having a break, and would have done so if I had dared."

"He has done his duty in giving you a welcome, and feels he is free," said Mark, realising the false impression he gave.

"He has taken no luggage, ma'am," said Jellamy.

"And does that prevent your bringing in the breakfast?" said Edgar.

"He will be sending for what he wants, I expect," said Maria. "He had to get away at once. Yes, bring in the breakfast."

"I thought it might imply that he would be back this morning, ma'am."

"You heard that he was not coming back," said Edgar.

"Bring in the breakfast, Jellamy, and make no more ado," said Justine. "You will forgive me, Maria; the words slipped out. I can't keep my tongue from leaping out at that man sometimes."

"I feel with Jellamy," said Mark to Clement, as they followed the others to the table. "He wants to know why Uncle has suddenly gone, and so do I. And the luggage is a point. Either he is coming back at once or he has left in storm and stress."

"Don't whisper, boys," said Justine, turning and lowering her own voice. "Things are difficult and we must do our part. Pull yourselves together and remember that we are mere pawns in the game of skill and chance which is being played."

"Are we as essential to the game as that? I feel a mere spectator. And it is really a simpler game."

"Well, don't look as if we were making some mystery."

"We could hardly contrive to do so. It is clear on what lines the break came, if break there has been."

"Shall I remove Mr. Dudley's place, ma'am?"

"No," said Edgar, as he saw the traces of his brother about to be obliterated. "Leave it as it is. It is likely—it is possible that he may come back."

"We will all take our own places," said Justine. "Then Uncle can return and find his place ready for him, and the others occupied round him, as will be right and meet."

"Not a gap in the circle," said Aubrey, flushing as he realised his words.

"No one can be expected to show himself in Uncle's place," said Mark.

"Yes, to take it would be even less easy—would be almost as difficult," said Justine—"oh, what a time this is for innocent and inapposite speeches!"

"No one tries to take anyone's place," said Maria. "Empty places remain and new people make their own."

"Of course. Why cannot I put things as you do?"

"If you knew the reason," said Clement, "I am sure you would deal with the matter."

"Well, that comes well from you. We don't see much sign in you of a gift for words."

"Should we have said that silence was golden, if we had only known Clement?" said Aubrey.

Maria laughed, and Edgar looked up and smiled more at the sound than at his son's words.

"Yes, cheer up, Father," said Justine. "You have not lost everything with Uncle. And he will come back and everything will be as it has always been—everything will be straight and well."

"Silence is golden," murmured Aubrey.

"Oh, I don't know. I believe I would give all the silence in the world for a little healthy, natural speech."

"Well, you have always done so," said Clement.

"And I do not regret my choice."

"Clement raises his brows," said Aubrey.

"Aubrey is readier with his words than you will ever be, Clement."

Aubrey looked at the window.

"Can you see through the curtain?" said his brother. "If you can, it is still dusk outside."

"I can see the wide, wintry expanse with my mind's eye."

Edgar looked up, with his mind following his son's, and meeting the picture of his brother with no refuge before him or behind. He turned to his wife and knew that she saw the same.

"Did Uncle say anything?" said Justine. "Did he—oh, I will take the bull by the horns, as he does. Has he any plans? Did he leave any address?"

"He had none to leave. He went suddenly," said her father. "He may—it will be possible for him to send one later."

"We know all," murmured Mark to Clement.

"You know all we can tell you," said Edgar.

"A flush mantles Mark's cheek," said Aubrey.

Maria was again amused, and her stepson showed his

249

nonchalance by rising and walking to the window and pulling the curtain aside.

"Aunt Matty! Coming across the snow!"

"Across the snow? Aunt Matty?" said Justine.

"She must be coming across the snow if she is coming," said Mark.

"Did you know she was coming, little boy? Why did you go to the window?"

Aubrey did not give his reason.

"Boys, get your coats and go to meet her. Perhaps she has some news of Uncle."

Edgar rose.

"I hardly think so," said Maria. "She would not be coming herself."

Matty was approaching with her halting step, holding a wrap across her breast, holding something to her head in the wind, pressing forward with a sort of dogged resignation to her slow advance. She gave a faint smile to her nephews as she suffered them to lead her in.

"You have come alone, Aunt Matty?"

"Yes, I have come alone, my dears. I had to do that. I shall be alone now. My dear father has left me, and left me, as you say, alone." Matty sank into a chair and covered her face. "I must be content alone. I must learn another hard lesson after so many."

She kept her hand to her brow and sat without moving, as the family gathered about her.

"Yes, I have had a life of deep and strange experiences. It seems that I ought to be used to them, that I ought to have that sad protection."

There was silence.

"Losing her father when she is over sixty herself is not a startling one," said Clement.

"Is Grandpa dead?" said Aubrey.

"That is a better way of putting it," said Mark.

"Well, his life was over," said Justine. "It was not hard to see that."

Matty was continuing to Edgar and his wife.

"He had gone to bed early as he was very tired. And I sent up something, hoping that he would eat before he slept. And it was found that he was already sleeping, and that he would not wake again."

"We cannot improve on that," said Mark.

"Yes, it was a good way to go," said Matty, misinterpreting his words. "He was full of years. His harvest was gathered; his sheaves were bound. For him we need not weep. But I must grieve for myself, and you will grieve for me a little."

"Dear Aunt Matty, we do indeed," said Justine. "And Mother would have suffered equally with you."

"Yes, dear. That is my saddest thought, that I have no one to do that. But I will be glad that yours is the lighter part. I had thought that my sister and I would sorrow together in this natural loss. But so much was not to be for me."

Maria took the seat by Matty, and Matty gave her her hand, putting the other over her eyes, but in a moment laid both hands on her friend's and looked about with a smile.

"Well, I must not fail in resolution. I must be myself. I must be what I always was to my father. I must not be lonely when I am not. I will not be."

"Look round and see the reason," said her niece.

"Yes, I see all my reasons," said Matty, looking about as if to discover the truth. "All the dear reasons I have for clinging to life, the dear faces which I have seen growing into themselves, the dear ones whose link I am now with one side of their past. Well, it should forge the link strongly. We shall go forward closely bound."

"How was dear Grandpa found? Did Miss Griffin go in to him?"

"No, dear, the maid went in and found him as I say. As she thought at first, sleeping; really in his last sleep."

"Poor Emma, it must have been a shock for her. Was she very much upset?"

"Well, dear, I was the more upset, of course. She was troubled in her measure. And I was sorry for her, and glad that she only had her natural share of the shock. Your grandfather had been always good to her. But she is not a young woman. There was nothing unsuitable in her being the one to find him. One of us had to do so, and I am not in the habit of going up and down stairs, as you know."

"And now Miss Griffin is managing everything?"

"No, dear; Dr. Marlowe is seeing that everything is done for me. He is a good friend, as you have found. There would not have been much for Miss Griffin to do."

"She will feel it very deeply. I daresay she is too upset to be of much use. It is a long relation to break."

"Yes, well, now I must tell you," said Matty, sitting up and using an open tone. "You will think that I have had a stranger life than you thought, that I seem to be marked out for untoward experience. Well, I was sitting in my little room alone, waiting for the shadows to close in upon me. It seems now that I must have had some presentiment; I had been so wrought up all day; you must have had your glimpse of it. And it was found that Miss Griffin had left me, that my old friend with whom I had shared my life for thirty years had vanished and left me alone in my grief. Well, what do you think of that for an accumulation of trouble, for what the Greeks would have called a woe on woe? I seem to be a person born for trial by flame. I hope I may emerge unscathed."

There was silence.

"When did Miss Griffin go?" said Justine. "Did anyone know when she went? Did she suddenly disappear?"

"Well, I must try to answer all those questions at once. But I only know what I have told you. I was sitting alone in the parlour, as you call it, finding the time rather drag as it moved on towards my trouble. I see that the boys are smiling, and I should not have wished to hasten it, if I had known. And I seemed to need the sound of a human voice, and I opened the door of the house—Miss Griffin had run into the garden on some pretext that I had sent her out, or something. You know I left you rather out of sorts; things here had upset me—and I found—— Well, you find my tale amusing? I am making a mountain out of a molehill? It is a trifle that I am exaggerating because I am personally involved? Well, we have all done that. You will not find it hard to understand."

"Then Miss Griffin did not leave you after Grandpa died? She had gone before? Yes, I know you implied that she had. But you said that you were alone in your grief. I did not quite follow."

"I meant my grief for your mother, dear. I happened to be remembering. But it was not the time for you to do so, as I had found. Well, I will get on with my story. So I found that was how it was, that my old friend had left me—well, we won't say alone in my grief—alone in a dark hour. And what do you say to that for a sudden revelation? I won't say that I have nourished a viper in my bosom; I won't say that of Miss Griffin, who has been with me through so many vicissitudes, and whom I have spared to you in yours. I will just say—well, I will say nothing; that is best."

"I don't think we can say anything either. We must find out where she has gone unless she returns very soon. But in the meantime tell us how you are yourself, and if you are staying here for the time."

"Well, it is to Maria that I must answer that question," said Matty, turning to her friend. "Answer it as a matter of form, because I must remain with you. I cannot go back to that house alone. So the formal question is answered, and I can settle down in as much content as I can, in as much as will prevent my being a damper on other people."

"Would you like anything fetched from your house?" said Maria.

"No, dear, no; Justine can lend me things of her mother's. I need not trouble you for anything."

"I hope you will trouble anyone for anything you need."

"Yes, dear, I know it would not be a trouble," said Matty, with a faint note of correcting the term. "But I am a person of few wants, or have learned to be. Now shall we leave me as a subject and go on to all of you? Or would you like to hear more of the old friend, or old aunt, or old responsibility, or whatever you call me to yourselves?"

"We should like to know all we can. Have you given any thought to the future? You clearly have not had time. But will you settle down in your house or will you be too much alone? Did you mean to stay there after your father died?"

"One moment, Maria. One thing, Aunt Matty," said Justine, leaning forward with a hand on Maria's arm. "Is Emma alone in that house? Let us get that point behind."

"No, dear, she has a sister with her. You have not reached the stage of arranging such things for other people as a matter of course. And that being so, it was a natural anxiety. Well, what was Maria saying? Yes, I was to stay here after my father died. He meant me to, and so did my sister. And I shall follow what I can of their wish. It will seem to bind me to them closer, to carry out our common plan. So I shall be too much alone: I must answer 'yes' to that question. But I shall not be too proud to accept any alleviation of my solitude." Matty smiled at the faces about her. "I have no false notions about what exalts people. I have my own ideas of what constitutes quality."

"We will do all we can for the sake of the past, for your sake," said Edgar. "Maria will do it with us, as she will do everything."

"Thank you. So we shall all have helped each other. We have done our best with Blanche's place in filling it and finding that we cannot fill it." Matty turned the smile on Maria. "And now we must do what we can with another, and I know you will do your part. We are used to striving together to meet a common loss."

"I read Aunt Matty like a book," murmured Aubrey. "I wonder if it is suitable for Justine's little boy."

"And we hope that Miss Griffin will come back and be with you, Aunt Matty," said Justine. "I cannot imagine the two of you apart."

"It is a relief not to have to think of them together," said Aubrey, turning to meet his brothers' eyes. "Yes, I am sure that is what Uncle would have said. You can see that I am trying to prevent your missing him."

"Cannot you, dear?" said Matty to her niece. "I have had to go a little further. You see I am having the experience. But shall we leave my prospects to the future, as we cannot in the present say much for them? I am holding you up in your breakfast. I will sit down and try to go on with it with you. I must make as little difference as I can."

"Here is a place all ready for you."

"Is there? How does that come to be? Had any news reached you? No, you were unprepared. Did you expect me to stay last night and order a place for the morning? Well, I must be glad that I went home to my father. Something seems to guide us in such things."

"The something took a clumsy way of doing its work," said Mark.

"So it was to be my place?" said Matty, seeming pleased by the thought. "Perhaps you hoped that the truant guest would return and expiate her sins?"

"It is Dudley's place," said Maria, knowing that the truth must emerge. "We thought that you would not be here. But he has followed Miss Griffin's example and left us for the time."

"Has he? Dudley? Has he run away and left you? Do we all manage to make ourselves impossible to those near and dear to us?" said Matty, her voice rising with her words. "Is it a family trait? Well, we can all assure each other that our bark has quite wrongly been taken for a bite."

"Barking may be enough in itself," said Mark. "It may not encourage people to wait for the next stage."

"Our Dudley? Has he found things too much? Well, I can feel with him; I find things so sometimes. But running away is not the best way out of them. They will not get the better of him, not of Dudley. I should have been glad to get a sight of him, and borrow a little of his spirit. It seems that people who show the most have the most to spare. Theirs must be the largest stock. Well, I must have recourse to my own, and I have not yet found it fail. It is not your time to need it, but you may look back and remember your aunt and feel that you took something from her."

"Why had Aunt Matty not enough spirit to give some to Miss Griffin?" said Aubrey.

"She gave her a good deal, or she got it from somewhere," said Mark.

"Yes, it is Miss Griffin, is it?" said Matty, with a different voice and smile. "Miss Griffin who takes the thought and takes the interest? That is how it would be. The person who has suffered less makes less demand. And we who suffer more must learn it. Well, we must not make a boast of spirit and then not show it."

There was silence.

"I think we ought to find out where Miss Griffin has gone," said Justine. "I do really think so, Aunt Matty."

"Yes, dear, I said she would be in your minds. And I think as you do. I shall be so glad to know where she is, when you can tell me."

"I suppose we have no clue at all?"

"That I do not know, dear; I have none."

"You have no idea where she may have gone?"

"None as she has not come here. I had a hope that she might have. I am so used to finding the house a refuge myself"—Matty gave her niece another smile—"that I did not think of her being perhaps struck by it differently. Especially as she has spent her time in it in another way."

"We are all very grateful to her. I am very hurt that she has not come here."

"Yes, dear? She has hurt us all."

"Has she any home?" said Mark.

"Her home has been with me. I know of no other."

"She has no relations she could go to?"

"She has relations, no doubt. But, you see, to them she would be, as you say, a relation. It is to you that she is the person outside the family."

"She has no friends in the neighbourhood?"

"She has those to whom you may have introduced her. She can have no others."

"Aunt Matty, I know that you think we might have introduced you to more people," said Justine. "But the truth is that when the house was running at full pressure, with all of us at home and you and Grandpa coming in, Mother could manage no more. It worked out that your coming here to meet our friends meant that you could not meet them. It implied nothing more and I am sure you know it, and Maria may manage better; but as concerns the past that is the truth. It seemed to be a rankling spot, and so I have let in a little fresh air upon it."

"No, dear, that is not the line on which my thoughts were running," said Matty, lifting her eyes and resting them in gentle appraisement on her niece. "They were on the death of my father, as they hardly could not be. And friends and houses and Miss Griffin all came second to it. Indeed only Miss Griffin came in at all."

"We have no clue either to my brother's whereabouts," said Edgar, taking the chance of opening his mind. "It is a strange fashion, this silent disappearance. We must try to get on the tracks of them both. Was Miss Griffin prepared for going? It is very cold."

"As far as I know, she went out of the garden without hat or coat or anything. The action was sudden and unpremeditated and she will probably be back at any time. She may be back now, in which case my father's death will have been a great shock to her."

"Did she wander in the garden without hat or coat in this weather?" said Clement.

"Take care; Aunt Matty must have driven her out," said Mark. "And she did not wait to be called back, but went on her own way. And if she freezes or starves or dies of exposure, and it seems that she must do all those things, she will be better off than she has been."

"Had she money, Aunt Matty?" said Justine.

"I do not know—yes, dear, more than I have at the moment."

"And had she it with her?"

"I can only know that when you find out and tell me. That thought has been in my own mind from the first."

"She cannot have gone far," said Maria, who had listened in silence. "We could send someone to drive about the country and look for her. We had better do it at once."

"May I interpose, ma'am?" said Jellamy.

"Yes, if you have anything to tell us."

"Mr. Dudley and Miss Griffin were perceived to be walking together last night, ma'am."

"Oh, they were together. That is a good thing. How did you hear?"

"The information came through, ma'am."

"You are quite sure?"

"The authority is reliable, ma'am."

"Well, that is the worst off our minds about both," said Justine. "We need not worry about anyone who is in Uncle's charge, or about anyone in Miss Griffin's. Each is safe with the other. They both have someone to think of before themselves, and that will suit both of them."

"It is a mercy that their paths crossed," said Mark. "What would have happened to Miss Griffin if they had not?"

"She would have gone home, dear," said Matty, with a change in her eyes.

"Well, they did cross, so we need not think about it," said Justine.

"We can hardly help doing that," said Maria. "It was the purest chance that your uncle passed at the time."

"There are inns and other shelters," said Edgar, glancing at the window.

"For people who have money with them. She seems to have gone out quite unprepared."

"I told you that the action was unpremeditated," said Matty. "But they would have trusted her as she is known to live with me."

"People might not trust a person who was leaving the house where she was employed."

"Maria, it is a great feat of courage," whispered Justine, "and I honour you for it. But is it wise? And is it not an occasion when indulgence must be extended?"

"Your aunt had not lost her father when she turned Miss Griffin out of doors."

"Oh, you have your own touch of severity," said Justine, taking a step backwards and using a voice that could be heard. "We shall have to beware. It may be a salutary threat hanging over us."

"Well, what of Dudley?" said Matty. "Are we to hear any more about him, now that Miss Griffin is disposed of? Have you any room for him in your minds? Do you take as much interest in his comings and goings? Did he go out prepared for the weather? Had he any money? Did you have notice of his going? Tell me it all, as I have told you. We must not deal differently with each other."

"We will tell you, Aunt Matty. We admit that he went

suddenly," said Justine. "And that we do not know the manner or the wherefore of his going."

"Mr. Dudley was sufficiently equipped for the weather, ma'am," said Jellamy. "Miss Griffin was perceived to be wearing his coat when they were observed together."

"Was she? Then he was no longer in that happy state," said Matty, going into laughter rather as if at Jellamy and his interruption than at Dudley's plight. "We can keep our anxiety to him. Miss Griffin no longer requires it. What about scattering some coats and hats about the road, for people to pick up who have fared forth without them? It is really a funny story. Somebody from the large house and somebody from the small, running away into the weather without a word or a look behind! Well, people must strike their own little attitudes; I suppose we none of us are above it; but I cannot imagine myself choosing to posture quite like that. And if I had had to pick out two people to scamper off into the snow with one coat and hat between them, I should not have pitched on Dudley and Miss Griffin." Matty bent her head and seemed to try to control her mirth. "It was a good thing that the coat belonged to Dudley, if they were to wear it in turn. He could not have got into hers."

No one joined in the laughter, and Matty wiped her eyes and continued it alone, and then stopped short and adjusted her skirt as if suddenly struck by something amiss.

"I have heard better jokes," said Mark. "The weather is icy cold and one coat is not enough for two."

"I wonder who was wearing the hat," said his aunt in a high voice which seemed to herald further laughter.

"Miss Griffin was perceived to be wearing a shawl about her head, ma'am."

"Oh, what a picture! It sounds like a gipsy tableau. I wonder if they intended it like that. I wonder if they had a caravan hidden away somewhere. I know that Miss Griffin has plenty of hats in her cupboard. Some of them

I have given her myself. What can be the reason of this sudden masquerade?"

"Perhaps she had none in the garden," said Clement.

"We know they have not a caravan," said Mark. "And it is hard to see how they are to manage without one."

"There is the inn," said his father, in a sharp tone.

"Of course there is, Edgar," said Matty in a different manner. "They all seem to think that the scene is staged on a desert island. But the scene itself! I can't help thinking of it. I shall have many a little private laugh over it."

"But no more public ones, I hope," muttered Mark.

Maria rose from the table, and Justine, as if perceiving her purpose, instantly did the same. Matty followed them slowly, using her lameness as a pretext for lingering in Edgar's presence. She came to the drawing room fire in a preoccupied manner, as if the cares of her own life had returned.

"Well, you are well in advance of me. I came in a poor third."

"We know you like to follow at your own pace," said Justine.

"I do not know that I like it, dear. My pace is a thing which I have not been able to help for many years."

"Well, we know you prefer people not to wait for you. Though Father and the boys have waited. I suppose they saw that as unavoidable."

"Yes, I expect they did, dear. I don't think we can alter that custom."

"No, naturally we cannot and we have not done so. But poor Aunt Matty, of course you are not yourself."

"No, dear, of course I am not," said Matty, with full corroboration. "And it has been silly of me to be surprised at seeing all of you so much yourselves. This morning is so different from other mornings to me, that it has been strange to find it so much the same to other people. You have not had days of this kind yet. Or you have put them behind you. Sorrow is not for the young, and so you have set it out of sight. And you have filled your empty place so wisely and well, that I am happy and easy in having helped you to do it. Any little shock and doubt and misgiving has melted away. But my father's place will be always empty for me, and so I must remain a little out of sympathy—no, I will not say that—a little aloof from the happiness about me. But I am glad to see it all the same. I must not expect to find people of my own kind everywhere. They may not be so common."

"I should think they are not," said Clement.

"You mean you hope not, naughty boy?" said Matty, shaking her finger at him in acceptance of his point of view .

"You do not want to think they are."

"I only found myself noticing that they were not."

"We might—perhaps we might see ourselves in other people more than we do," said Edgar.

"We all have our depths and corners," said Justine.

"And we all think that no one else has them," said Mark.

"Dear, dear, what a band of philosophers!" said Matty. "I did not know I had quite this kind of audience."

"Do you see yourself in us more than you thought?" said Clement.

"No, dear, but I see a good many of you at once. I did not know you were quite such a number on a line. I had thought of you all as more separate somehow."

"And now you only see yourself in that way?"

"Well, dear, we agreed that I was a little apart."

"I don't think we did," said Mark. "You implied it, but I don't remember that you had so much support."

"I am going to end the talk," said Maria, rising. "Your aunt is more tired than she knows and must go and rest. And when I come down your father and I will go to the library, and you can have a time without us."

"How tactless we have been!" said Justine. "We might have thought that they would like an hour by themselves. But what were we to do while Aunt Matty was here?"

"What we did," said Mark. "No one could have thought that the scene was to our taste."

"I do admire Maria when she gives a little spurt of authority."

"She did not like to think of Miss Griffin wandering by herself in the snow," said Aubrey, bringing this picture into the light to free his own mind.

"Little tender-heart!" said Justine, simply evincing comprehension.

"Without a coat or hat, and I suppose without gloves or tippet or shawl," said her brother, completing the picture with ruthlessness rather than with any other quality.

"It is odd that we feel so little about Grandpa's death."

"Aunt Matty's life puts it into the shade," said Mark.

"Well, he was old and tired and past his interests, and we really knew him very little. It would be idle to pretend to any real grief. It is only Aunt Matty who can feel it."

"And it does not seem to drown her other feelings."

"Perhaps that is how sorrow sometimes improves people," said Aubrey.

"No, no, little boy. No touch of Uncle at this moment. It is too much."

"We might all be better if our feelings were destroyed," continued Aubrey, showing that his sister had administered no check.

"Poor Aunt Matty! One can feel so sorry for her when she is not here."

"You do betray other feelings when she is," said Mark.

"I suppose I do. We might have remembered her trouble. Even Father and Maria seemed to forget it."

"Well, so did she herself."

"She will be very much alone in future. I don't see how we are to prevent it."

"Will grief be her only companion?" said Aubrey.

"Well, she has driven away her official one," said Mark.

"She will be confined to rage and bitterness and malice," said Clement.

"So she will be alone amongst many," said Aubrey.

"No, no, I don't think malice," said Justine. "I don't think it has ever been that. I wonder what Miss Griffin and Uncle are doing. But their being together disposes of any real problem. I think Uncle may safely be left to arrange the future for them both."

"Uncle has been left to do too much for people's futures," said Mark. "And not so safely. We can only imagine what happened last night."

"You are fortunate," said Clement. "I cannot."

"Or unfortunate," said Aubrey, who could.

"I have been keeping my thoughts away from it," said Justine.

"They have had enough to occupy them," said Mark. "But they will return. Grandpa's death, Miss Griffin's flight, even Aunt Matty's visit will all be as nothing. We may as well imagine the scene."

"No, my mind baulks at it."

"Mine does worse. It constructs it."

"Maria was there," said Aubrey.

"Yes, poor Maria!" said Justine. "What a home-coming! It never rains but it pours."

"I think it nearly always rains. We only notice it when it pours."

"Yes, it is Uncle. Clear, natural and incontrovertible," said Justine, with a sigh, as if this fact altered no other. "Well, you may be clever boys, but you have a depressed sister to-day."

"How would it all have been if Maria had kept to Uncle?" said Aubrey.

"That is not Uncle," said Clement.

"Little boy, what a way of putting it!"

"Miss Griffin would still have run away; Grandpa would still have died; Aunt Matty would still have paid her visits," said Mark. "Only it might have been Father

264

instead of Uncle who met Miss Griffin. And that might not have worked so well. He would have been more awkward in offering her his coat. So perhaps it is all for the best. That is always said when things are particularly bad, so there could hardly be a better occasion for saying it."

"Look," said Justine, going to the door and holding it ajar. "Look at those two figures passing through the hall, as two others used to pass. What an arresting and almost solemn sight! Do we let our hearts rejoice or be wrung by it?"

"We will take the first course if we have the choice."

"Which is better, the sight of two beautiful men or of a beautiful man and a beautiful woman? I do not know; I will not try to say."

"I am letting my heart be wrung," said Aubrey, grinning and speaking the truth.

"Will they ever be three again? Ought we to wish it? Or ought we just to hesitate to rush in where angels fear to tread?"

"We might be imagining them four," said Aubrey, in a light tone.

"How I remember Mother's slender figure moving in and out between the two taller ones! That is a different line of thought, but the picture somehow came. And it brings its own train. Mother would have wished things to come right between them. And it may be that they will do so, and the three tall figures move together through life. But I fear it cannot be yet. Uncle was heading for trouble, and at the crucial moment it came. He could not go on too long, keyed up to that pitch. The strain of the last months can only be imagined. None of us can know what it was."

"Is Justine transfigured?" said Aubrey.

"Well, I am affected by the spectacle of intense human drama. I do not deny it."

"It were idle to do so," said Clement.

"It would have been better to go away at once," said Mark, "and not attempt the impossible."

"I don't know," said his sister, gazing before her. "It was a great failure. Surely one of those that are greater than success."

"I never quite know what those are. I suppose you mean other kinds of success. The same kind involves the same effort and has a better end."

"And a much more convenient one," said Clement.

"Yes, yes, more convenient," said Justine. "But what we have seen was surely something more than that."

"Something quite different indeed," said Mark.

"Surely it was worth it."

"From our point of view, as spectators?"

"Well, in the sense that all human effort must achieve something essential, even if not apparent."

"Well, now the human drama goes on in the snow," said Aubrey.

"Oh, surely they have got under shelter by now," said Justine, laughing as she ended. "Oh, what intolerable bathos! You horrid little boy, pulling me down from my heights!"

"You could not have gone on too long any more than Uncle."

"I don't know. I felt I was somehow in my element."

"That may have been what Uncle thought. I believe it was," said Mark.

"A greater than Uncle is here," said Aubrey.

"And they are different heights," said Clement.

"I think Clement is making an effort to conquer his taciturnity, Justine."

"Oh, don't let us joke about it. Do let us turn serious eyes on a serious human situation."

"Miss Griffin and Uncle walking through the snow, with Miss Griffin wearing Uncle's coat and hat!" murmured Aubrey.

"She was not wearing his hat. She—she"—said Justine,

going into further laughter—"had a shawl round her head. Oh, why are we laughing? Why cannot we take a serious view of what is serious and even tragic in itself? Miss Griffin's long relation with Aunt Matty broken! Because I suppose it is the break. And her life at sixes and sevens, because that must be the truth. And we cannot see it without being diverted by silly, little, surface things which in themselves have their tragic side, just because they touch our superficial sense of humour." Justine's voice quavered away as this again happened to her. "I suppose we are half hysterical; that is what it is."

"That is the usual explanation of unseemly mirth," said Mark.

"Well, happiness is a good thing," said Edgar, smiling in the door, his voice as he said Matty's frequent words illustrating the difference between them. "Maria and I are going to walk outside—that is, we are going for a walk before Mark and I begin to work. Your aunt is resting upstairs."

"Oh, Father, it seems that we ought not to be in spirits on the day of Grandpa's death and Aunt Matty's desolation, and all of it," said Justine, taking hold of his coat. "But we are in a simple, silly mood. We have agreed that we must be hysterical."

"Your grandfather's death can only seem to you the natural thing it is. He has not been much in your life and he has had his own." Edgar's voice was calm and almost empty, as if his feelings on one thing left him none for any other.

"But Aunt Matty's loneliness and all that has happened," said Justine, standing with her face close to the coat and bringing the lapels together. "You do feel that you have an anchor in your children?"

Edgar turned and walked away.

"Oh, I suppose I have said the wrong thing as usual. I might have known it was hopeless to attempt to do anything for him. In my heart I did know."

"It is good to follow the dictates of the heart," said Clement.

"Yes, you can be supercilious. But what did you attempt after all? I did try to show Father that he had something to depend on in his home."

"And he showed you that he could not take your view."

"I suppose Maria has taken my place with him. Well, it would be small to mind it. I have never done much to earn the place. And it is better than her taking another. She does not feel she has taken that. We can think of that little place as open and empty, free for Mother's little shadow."

Aubrey turned and slouched out of the room, kicking up his feet. He came upon Maria, who had been to fetch a cloak and was following her husband.

"Are you going upstairs?" she said. "What is the matter? Come back in a minute and tell me."

Aubrey threw back his head, thrust his hands into his pockets and turned and sauntered back.

"Odd days these."

"Yes, they are strange and disturbed. But they will pass."

"Days have a way of doing that. It is the one thing to be said for them."

"Too much happened yesterday indeed."

"Indeed."

"Your grandfather had had his full share of everything. And there is no greater good fortune than sudden death."

"No," said Aubrey, his face changing in a manner which told Maria her mistake.

"And he knows nothing now," she said, "not even that he is dead. And that can be said of all dead people."

There was a pause.

"You have had your share of things," said Aubrey, with terse and equal understanding.

"We have all had that and found it enough."

"Too much for me. Quickly up and quickly down at my age. But if I am thought callous one minute, I am thought sensitive the next."

"We need not mind being thought callous sometimes," said Maria, seeing the aspect preferred.

"No. The heart knoweth," said her stepson, turning away.

X

"SHALL I say what I can see?" said Mark. "Or does it go without saying?"

"Let us not go to meet her," said Clement. "Let us begin differently and hope so to go on."

"Your aunt is already in the hall or we should meet her," said Edgar with a vision of his brother going swiftly to such a scene.

Matty came forward without exhibition of her lameness or of anything about herself.

"Now I am afraid you must see me as the bearer of ill tidings. And I may deserve to have to bring them. I have made myself the harbinger of sadness and now I am not to come without it. But you will make my hard task easy. You will know that the tidings are sad for me as well as for you."

"What is it?" said Edgar at once. "Is it my brother?"

"Yes, you have helped me. And now I can help myself and tell you that it is not the worst, that all is not lost. There is still hope. He is lying ill at a farmhouse twenty miles away. He walked for days when he left this house, and got wet and got weary, and ate and slept where he could; and came at last to this farm one night, hardly able to say who he was or whence he came." Matty dramatised what she had to tell, but spoke without actual thought of herself. "And the next day they fetched Miss Griffin to nurse him, and a message came from her to me this morning, to say that there is trouble on the lungs and that she does not dare to hide the truth. She has a doctor and a nurse, and the woman at the farm is good. So all we have to do is to go to him at once. All that you have to do. What I have to do is to stay here and keep the house until your return. And if it seems to me the harder part, I will still do it to the best that is in me. I will do what serves you most and what saves you anything."

Edgar had already gone, followed by his wife. Matty suggested some things which might be of use, and before they were ready he had set off on horseback by himself.

"Someone should go with Father," said Justine. "But it is too late."

"Is Uncle a strong man?" said Mark.

"He has seemed to be in his own way. But the troubles must have lowered his resistance, and the wet and cold have done the rest."

"He saved Miss Griffin," said Aubrey; "himself he could not save."

"My dear, think what you are saying. What makes you talk like that?"

"Excess of feeling and a wish to disguise it," said Aubrey, but not aloud.

"Where has Miss Griffin been?" said Mark.

"At the Middletons' house, where your uncle took her on the day when your grandfather died," said Matty, stating the fact without expression. "I know no more."

"We must go. Goodbye, Aunt Matty," said Justine. "Maria is in the hall. Keep Aubrey with Mr. Penrose, and the house to its course. We can't say yet just what we may require of you."

"Command me dear, to any service," said Matty, with a hint of dryness in her tone.

"You can send me word," said Aubrey, "and I will command my aunt."

Edgar was in advance of his family and was the first to enter his brother's room. Miss Griffin met him at the door, and the way she spoke of Dudley, as if he could not hear, warned him of his state.

"He is very ill. He must have been ill for days. He will have me with him; he will not be left to the nurse." She stood, stooping forward, with her eyes bright and fixed from want of sleep. "He is like Mrs. Gaveston in that. The doctor says that his heart is holding out and that he may get well."

Dudley was raised a little in his bed, the limpness of his body showing his lack of strength to support himself, his breathing audible to Edgar at the door. His eyes were still and seemed not to see, but as his brother came they saw.

"What is the time?" he said in a faint, rapid voice between his breaths. "They do not tell it to me right."

"It is about twelve o'clock."

"No, it is the afternoon," said Dudley, with a cry in his tone. "I have been asleep for hours."

"Yes, you have had a sleep," said Miss Griffin, in a cheerful, ordinary voice, which she changed and lowered as she turned to Edgar. "It was only for a few minutes. He never sleeps for more."

"It will soon be night," said Dudley.

"Not just yet, but it is getting nearer."

Dudley lay silent, his expression showing his hopeless facing of the hours of the day.

"Does the time seem very long to him?" said Edgar.

"Yes, it is so with very sick people. It is as if he were living in a dream. A minute may seem like hours."

Dudley fell into a fit of coughing and lay helplessly shaken, and under cover of the sound Miss Griffin's voice became quicker and more confidential.

"Oh, I am glad I could come to him; I am glad that he sent for me. It was a good thing that I was not with Miss Seaton. She might not have let me come. She said she would never let me nurse anyone but her again. But I don't expect she would have kept to that."

"I am sure she would not," said Edgar. "Is there anything my brother would like?"

"If only it would stop!" said Dudley, looking at Edgar as he heard the word of himself.

Edgar turned to him with so much pain in his face, that he saw it and in the desperation of his suffering tried to push it further.

"If only it would stop for a second! So that I could get a moment's sleep. Just a moment."

"He is not like himself," said Edgar. "It seems—it reminds me of when my wife was ill."

There were the sounds of the carriage below and Miss Griffin spoke with appeal.

"Is anyone coming who can help? I have been with him all day and all night. He cannot bear to be with strangers, and he should not be nursed by anyone who is too tired."

"My wife and daughter are here," said Edgar, the word of his second wife bringing the thought that he could not replace his brother. "And any help can come from the house at once. In the meantime my sons and I have hands and ordinary sense, and can be put to any service."

Maria came into the room and Dudley saw her.

"It is the afternoon," he said, as if she would allow it to be so.

"Not yet," she said, coming up to the bed. "You did not send for us, Dudley. That was wrong."

"I sent for Miss Griffin."

"Yes, but you should have sent for Edgar and me."

"I only want to have someone here. I don't think you are different from other people," said Dudley, in a rapid, empty tone, which did not seem to refer to what she said, looking at her with eyes which recognised her and did no more. "It doesn't matter if we are not married. I like Edgar best."

"Of course you do. I knew it all the time. And he feels the same for you."

"If I could get to sleep, the day would soon be gone. And this is the longest day."

Maria turned to speak to her husband and Dudley's eyes followed her, and the moment of attention steadied him and he fell asleep.

Justine entered and kept her eyes from the bed, as if she would fulfil her duty before she followed her will.

"I have come to take Miss Griffin to rest, and then to wait upon anyone. The boys have gone on some messages. Father, the doctor is here and can see you."

Dudley was awake and lay coughing and looking about as if afraid.

"Is it another day? Shall I get well?"

"Of course you will," said the nurse. "It is the same day. You only slept for a little while. But to sleep at all is a good sign."

"People are here, are they? Not only you?"

"Justine and I are here," said Maria.

"Why are you both here?"

"We both like to be with you."

"Is it the afternoon?"

"It will be soon. Would you like me to read to you?"

"Will you put in any feeling?"

"No, none at all."

"Who is that person who puts in feeling? Matty would, wouldn't she? And Justine?" Dudley gave a smile.

"What book will you have?"

"Not any book. Something about——"

"About what?" said Maria, bending over him.

"You know, you know!" said Dudley in a frightened voice, throwing up his arms.

The movement brought a fit of coughing, and as it abated he lay trembling, with a sound of crying in the cough. Edgar and the doctor entered and seeing them broke his mood, though he did not seem to know them.

"Well, I haven't much to live for," he said to himself. "I am really almost alone. It isn't much to leave behind."

He tried to raise himself and spoke almost with a scream. "If I die, Miss Griffin must have some money! You will give her some? You won't keep it all?"

"Yes, yes, of course we will. She shall have enough," said Edgar. "But you will not die."

Something in the voice came through to Dudley, and he lay looking at his brother with a sort of appraisement.

"You don't like me to be ill," he said, in a shrewd, almost knowing tone. "Then you should not make me ill. It is your fault."

"He does not know what he is saying," said the nurse.

"I do," said Dudley, nodding his head. "Oh, I know."

"How long will it go on?" said Edgar to the doctor.

"It cannot be quick. He is as ill as he can be, and any change must be slow. And the crisis has yet to come."

The crisis came, and Dudley sank to the point of death, and just did not pass it. Then as he lived through the endless days, each one doubled by the night, he seemed to return to this first stage, and this time drained and shattered by the contest waged within him. Blanche's frailer body, which had broken easily, seemed to have stood her in better stead. But the days which passed and showed no change, did deeper work, and the sudden advance towards health had had its foundation surely laid. The morning came when he looked at his brother with his own eyes.

"You have had a long time with me."

"We have, Dudley, and more than that."

"Do they know that I shall get better?"

"Yes, you are quite out of danger."

"Did you think I should get well?"

"We were not always sure."

Dudley saw what was behind the words, but was too weak to pursue it.

"Shall I be the same as before?"

"Yes. There will be no ill results."

Dudley turned away his head in weakness and self-pity.

"You can go away if you like. There is nothing you can do. Where is Miss Griffin?"

Miss Griffin was there, as she always was at this time. The lighter nursing of this stage was within her powers. Dudley reached out his hands and smiled into her eyes, and Edgar watched and went away.

These moments came more often and at last marked another stage. Then the change was swift, and further stages lay behind. Dudley was to be taken to his brother's house to lie in his own bed, but before the day came even this stage had passed. The change was more rapid in his mind than in his body. In himself he seemed to be suddenly a whole man. The threat of death, with its lesson of what he had to lose, had shown him that life as he had lived it was enough. He asked no more than he had, chose to have only this. His own personality, free of the strain and effort of the last months, was as full and natural as it had been in his youth.

His return to the house as an essential member of it was too much a matter of course to be discussed. It was observed with celebration, Dudley both expecting and enjoying it. Maria went home in advance to get order in the house, and Edgar and Miss Griffin were to manage the move and follow.

Matty had been an efficient steward, but the servants did not bend to her simply autocratic rule, and Jellamy was open in his welcome. She seemed to be oppressed by her time of solitude, and kept to the background more than was her habit, seeming to acknowledge herself as bound less closely to the house. She knew that Maria realised her effect on its life, and was trying to establish a different intercourse, welcoming her as a family connection and her own friend, but keeping the relation to this ground.

The family waited in the door for the carriage to appear.

"Well, what a moment!" said Justine. "To think that

our normal life is to be restored! It seems almost too much. It shows us what rich people we are."

"That has hardly been true of us of late," said Mark.

"Yes, it is partly the force of contrast. The sharp edge of our appreciation will blunt. So we will make the most of it."

"I deprecate the method of enhancing our feeling."

"Our worst chapter is behind, our very worst. And I mean what I say; I use the words advisedly. You need not all look at me. You see, our grief for Mother was unsullied. This would have had its alloy."

"Relief from anxiety gives the impression of happiness," said Clement.

"Then let us have that impression," said his brother.

"Here they come! We must set our faces to disguise our emotion," said Aubrey, doing as he said.

"I don't want to disguise it," said his sister, wiping her eyes. "I do not care how much of it is seen by Uncle or anyone else. I should not like to go away and nearly die, and come back to unmoved faces."

"Neither should I," said Dudley's voice. "I could not bear it. I do not like people not to show their feelings. If they do not, they are no good to anyone but themselves, and they don't enjoy them nearly so much as the people who cause them. And it is better to have proof of everything, anyhow of feelings."

"Oh," said Justine, with a deep sigh, "the old touch!"

"I must pay great attention," said Aubrey. "I have been a long time without an example."

"Stay," said his sister, thrusting a hand behind her as she strode forward. "I am going to help Uncle out. I am going to use my feminine privilege in an unusual way."

"She looks equal to it," said Matty, smiling at Maria.

"Oh, someone else is to come out first," said Justine, turning and ruefully raising her brows. "Oh, it is Miss Griffin. Uncle does not forget to be himself. Well, it will give me great pleasure to help them both."

276

"How do you do, Miss Seaton?" said Miss Griffin, as she set foot upon the ground, embarking on her ordeal at once.

"How do you do, my dear?" said Matty, shaking hands with cordial affection. "We owe a great deal to you."

"What a good thing it is that I am spared!" said Dudley, descending on his niece's arm. "It is generally the valuable lives that are cut off, but I can feel that a real attempt was made on mine."

"You helped yourself a great deal," said Miss Griffin.

"And heaven helps those who do that. But I really don't remember any help but yours."

"Now up to your room. No more talking," said Justine, bringing her hands together. "Not another moment in this chilly hall. Maria, you do not mind my taking matters into my own hands. You see, Uncle has been bound up with the whole of my life."

"It is well that Maria feels as you say," said Clement.

Justine's words brought a sense of what was behind, and Edgar cleared a way through the hall. Dudley was assisted by his nephews to his room. He would have been able to walk with Edgar's help, but the brothers shrank from following their natural ways, as yet unsure of their footing. The uncertainty had come with Dudley's return to health.

"Well, what are we to do to celebrate the occasion?" said Matty, with something of her old tense touch.

"Go into the drawing room and sit quietly down," said Justine, in a rather loud tone, "and give ourselves to thankfulness."

"Yes, dear, that is what we feel inclined to do. So we are to indulge ourselves," said Matty, putting her niece's inclinations on their right level, and taking her seat by the fire in silence.

"Uncle will come and join us for an hour when he is rested."

"Well, I will wait for that, if Maria will let me."

"You will wait for it, of course, with all of us," said Maria.

Mark and Clement returned.

"Uncle is resting in his own room and Miss Griffin in another."

"Not in the same room?" said Aubrey.

"Now, little boy, no foolishness on this occasion."

"Those two great, clumsy lads carried Uncle up with hands as gentle as a woman's," said Aubrey, blinking his eyes.

"Poor Miss Griffin, I am shocked by her appearance," said Justine. "She looks more worn than Uncle."

"Yes, dear, I am troubled too," said Matty. "It seems sad that her connection with us should bring her to this. I have never seen her looking in this way before."

"You must have, Aunt Matty, at the times of your own illnesses."

Matty gave a smile and a sigh, as if it were no use to make statements doomed to rejection.

"This was arduous nursing," said Maria. "It could not be helped."

"Of course not, dear. If it could have been it would have. That is the thing that makes us sorry."

"The nursing has not been much for some time," said Edgar. "Miss Griffin is looking fairly well. She was upset by the motion of the carriage."

"And Father behaved with simple chivalry," said Aubrey. "Well, it would have been no good for Clement to be a witness."

"Oh, I believe she always is!" said Justine, sitting up straight.

Matty gave a laugh.

"That sort of thing does make people look ill for the moment," said Maria.

"And Miss Griffin is not used to driving," said Justine.

Matty put back her head in mirth.

"Did you know, Aunt Matty, that she was to have a

little house of her own?" said Justine, driven to the sudden announcement. "Uncle is to make it possible."

"No, dear," said Matty, with her eyes dilating. "I did not know. How could I when I was not told? When was that arranged?"

"When they met after—before Uncle was ill."

"Well, I am glad, dear; glad that our long relation is ending like this; glad that I brought her to a family who were to do this for her. It is good that our friendship should have this culmination."

"It was not the one which Aunt Matty planned when she turned her out of doors," said Mark to his brothers. "There was no question of any alternative roof."

"I am sure you are glad, Aunt Matty," said Justine.

"Are you, dear? So you accept something that I say."

"And I am sure it will be the beginning of a new relation with Miss Griffin."

Matty gave a little trill of laughter.

"Now, Aunt Matty, what exactly amuses you?"

"My relation with her, when you have all used her as a sick nurse and nothing else!" said Matty, bending her head and speaking in an impeded voice.

"Maria, would you advise me to move out of hearing of my aunt?"

Matty sat up and looked from her niece to her friend.

"If you think there would be anything gained," said Maria.

Justine rose and went to a distant seat, and her aunt looked after her with open mockery.

"So I am too dangerous a tinder for my niece's flint and steel. Or is it the other way round?"

"Either account will serve," said Clement.

"Well, well, then we must try not to come against each other. Perhaps we are too much alike."

"No, I don't think that is it, Aunt Matty," said Justine. "Oh, what is the good of my moving to a distance if I must communicate from it?"

279

"No good," said her brother.

"I should move back again, dear," said Matty, easily. "I don't think it does achieve anything."

Justine returned and sat down even nearer to her aunt, raising her shoulders.

Matty looked at her for a moment and turned to Maria.

"You have the whole of your family at home?" she said, stooping as if unconsciously to free her dress from contact with her niece.

"They are all at home as a usual thing. Clement is away for the term, but he gives us a good deal of time."

"He hasn't the house of his own yet?"

"I don't want it yet; I am putting it off," said Clement, in a quick, harsh tone. "I am thinking about it. I shall have it before long."

"I have rather an uncompromising nephew and niece."

"Well, we say what we mean, Aunt Matty," began Justine. "Oh, it is not worth while to waste a thought on us. Here is the person who matters! We might be twice as good or twice as bad and still be as nothing. And Father in attendance, after hovering about upstairs until he should wake! So that is why he crept away. I need not have wondered."

"Can we all quite agree that we are as nothing?" said Matty in a low, arch, rapid tone, looking up at Dudley as he passed. "I have never felt it of myself, or had it felt of me, if I can judge by the signs. So I must hold myself apart from that generalisation, though it is not a thing that matters on this occasion."

"This is the occasion in question," said Clement.

"I have not had any sleep," said Dudley. "I could not lose myself. I may be better down here amongst you all. If you see me dropping off, you could all steal quietly away. Perhaps your talk will lull me to sleep unawares."

Edgar followed his brother, looking as if he had no

connection with him and holding his face to prevent an encounter of their eyes. Dudley sat down by the fire and signed for a cushion. His niece was at his side in an instant, settling the cushion behind him and thrusting a rug down on either side of his knees.

"I think Justine is a little more than nothing," said Matty, with a smile.

"I am Uncle's willing slave. That is all I ask to be."

"Well, I would ask nothing better, if I were permitted such a character. But, as I have said, it has not been the one assigned to me."

"Well, you have been an invalid," said Justine, making a sally towards the rug where it was working up.

"Justine explains it," said Aubrey.

"Not always, dear. Not when I was your age, for instance."

"I don't think this talk will lull me to sleep," said Dudley.

"Well, I may not be a slave," said Matty, holding up a piece of needlework for his eyes, "but I have been willing in your service. A little bit of something made by a friend means more, I hope, than the same thing bought out of an ample purse."

"Is every stitch in it worked by loving hands?"

In an instant Justine had the work out of her aunt's hands and before Dudley's eyes.

"Gently, dear, the stitches will unravel," said Matty, leaning forward.

"Barely an inch or two. Nothing compared to the satisfaction of proving to Uncle that the work is all your own."

"He would have taken Aunt Matty's word," said Mark.

Matty retrieved the work and placing it on her knee, set herself to remedy the damage.

"Not much harm done, is there?" said her niece.

"A piece to be worked again, dear. It does not matter. I have all the time to do it, as no doubt you thought."

"Let me do it, just the piece that came undone. Then you will have worked the whole of it once."

"I only want loving thoughts stitched into it," said Dudley.

"You shall have them," said Matty, in a full tone. "Every thought shall be loving and every stitch mine, some of them doubly done."

"Oh, we forgot to ask, Aunt Matty, how you have been managing without Miss Griffin," said Justine, recalled by her aunt's industry to the fact that she was used to aid.

"Forgot to ask!" said Mark to Aubrey. "I would have died rather than do so."

"I think I shall die, now it is done. If I don't I don't know how to manage."

"Don't talk about dying in that light way," said Dudley. "You have no right. You have no idea of what it is to hover between life and death."

"No experience of the valley of the shadow," said Aubrey.

"None at all. I suppose there will be something in my face now that there is not in yours."

"Don't let us talk about that time," said Justine, with a shudder. "Let us only remember it enough to be thankful that it is past."

"And to feel the value of my presence in your home."

The words recalled the other way in which Dudley might have been lost to them. Justine moved to her uncle and stood stroking his hair, and her father's eyes followed her hand.

"Father might like to help Justine to smooth Uncle's hair," murmured Aubrey, "to help his only daughter."

"Well, Aunt Matty, what have you to tell us about yourself?" said Justine, putting more energy into her hand. "We have been too lost in our own troubles to give a thought to things outside."

"Your aunt has been in similar case," said Edgar.

"Now there is a nice, understanding word," said Matty. "And it is indeed a true one, even though in my case the things were not outside myself."

"Aunt Matty threw Father a grateful glance," said Aubrey.

"So I did, dear. I do not get too much understanding since Mother died, and Grandpa," said Matty, adapting her words to her nephew. "So much of it went with them. I do not mean that I expect more than I have. It would be idle indeed to do so. But I am the more grateful when it comes."

"Well, let us all emerge from that stage and take more interest in each other," said Justine. "You tell us of your plans and we will hear them."

"Well, dear, I have none as yet, as your father would know. Plans need thought and attention, and they have not been forthcoming."

"Try to do what you can about them at the moment," said Maria.

"Shall I, dear? I have been wondering when I should hear your voice. All these loquacious young relatives of mine seem to overwhelm you."

"I have never been a talkative person. Perhaps I have not much to say."

"Don't be afraid, Aunt Matty; Maria can hold her own," said Justine.

"Well, now, I have been asked for my plans. So I must make them and make them at once, so as not to keep people waiting. Well, as Miss Griffin is no longer to depend on me for a home, I must look for someone else who will find it a help to do so. For I cannot rely upon a maid-servant for the greater part of my companionship."

"Indeed no," said Justine, "though it would not be the greater part. You are wise to fill Miss Griffin's place, in so far as you can do so."

"Yes, dear, we all have to deal like that with places, or we all do. And, you know"—Matty gave her niece a

283

different smile—"I do not make a sorrow of a friend's good fortune."

"Ought the next person who is to depend on Aunt Matty for a home," said Aubrey, "to be told that it may be in the garden?"

"I have heard that snow is a warm covering," said Mark. "I don't know if Aunt Matty had."

"Uncle had not, or he need not have given Miss Griffin his coat."

"Depend does not seem a word to use of Miss Griffin," said Justine. "She earned her independence, if anyone did."

"It is clear what your aunt means," said Edgar.

"Father, I believe you are jealous of me for my proximity to Uncle," said Justine, hastening away from Dudley with no idea that her words had any real truth.

Edgar, who only knew it at the moment, put a chair for his daughter and smiled at her as she took it.

"Dear Father, with his one ewe lamb!"

"Suppose Father had more than one," said Aubrey.

"Well, Miss Griffin has certainly earned her independence in these last weeks," said Matty. "And she is to have it. That is so good to hear."

"Uncle had arranged to give it to her before he was ill," said Justine.

"Had he, dear? Well, that does not make it any less good. And if she had not earned it then, she has now. Or if she had earned it then, she has now earned it doubly. Let us put it like that. So she has a right to it. And I shall like so much to see her in her own home, as she has always seen me in mine."

"I really believe you will, Aunt Matty."

Matty appeared once more to strive with her laughter.

"Where is Miss Griffin?" she said, looking round as she overcame it. "Does she not want to be with you all? Or is she afraid of so many of us?"

"She is afraid of one of us," said Mark, "And so am I."

"Where has Clement gone?" said Edgar.

"I expect to his room," said Aubrey. "He is always slinking away by himself."

"Well, he has seen me," said Dudley, "and satisfied himself that I am on the mend."

"And to do him justice, Uncle, he did not go until he had done that," said Justine. "And he has his work. And we shall have someone else disappearing to-morrow. These holidays are at an end and they come too often. Maria and I are agreed."

"Aubrey could not work while he was gnawed by anxiety."

"Well, the relief will be a tonic now."

"I may wish to give myself to thankfulness for a time," said Aubrey.

"We all feel inclined for that, but the world has to go on."

"I suppose it would have gone on if I had died," said Dudley. "That is what we hear about the world. I think the world is worse than anything. Even Aubrey's lessons stopped."

"They are about to begin again," said Justine, with resolute descent to daily life. "There are many things in Clement which he might emulate."

"And Clement might take many lessons from his quiet little brother," said Aubrey, looking to see his stepmother smile and inconsistently looking away as she did so.

"I suppose you will all understand each other better now," said Dudley. "People do that after anxiety. I can feel that I have not been ill in vain."

"It seems that there ought to be more undertsanding," said Matty, with a faint sigh.

"Oh, people are not often as ill as I was."

"How does it feel to be so ill that you might die?" said Aubrey, with a desire to know.

"I can hardly say. Perhaps I was ready. I really don't understand about people who are not. When you are delirious and do not recognise people, it is hard to see how you can feel remorse for a lifetime and prepare yourself for eternity. I cannot help thinking that even people who die, are not as ill as I was. I think they are sometimes surprisingly well, even perhaps at their best."

"It is the few lucid moments at the last," said Justine.

"Well, I did not have those, of course. It is odd to think that we are all to have them. It does make me respect everyone. But long conversations and meetings after years of estrangement must be so difficult when you cannot recognise people. And it hardly seems worth while for a few moments, even though they are lucid. And I see that they must be. When people's lives are hanging by a thread, it seems enough to break the thread. And I think it must do so sometimes, if people die when they are equal to so much, more perhaps than they have ever been before."

Justine looked at Dudley uncertainly, and Matty with a smile.

"Have you been reading the books in the farmhouse, Uncle?" said Mark.

"Yes, I read them while I was getting well. And if I had known I was to be so ill, I would have read them at first."

"I love to hear him talk like his old self," said Matty, glancing at her niece.

"Don't you notice that a new note has crept in? Perhaps it marks me as a person who has looked at death. I think that Justine has noticed it."

"Yes, I have, Uncle," said his niece quietly. "It is the weakness of convalescence."

"Convalescence seems to be a little like the lucid moments at the last. I may not have got quite far enough away from them."

"You will soon forget it."

"I shall not. You will. I see you are doing so."

"I know what you mean," said Matty, keeping her eyes

on Dudley's face. "I too sometimes feel rather apart, as I live in my memories and find that other people have lost them. But I would not have them oppressed by what I can carry alone."

"I would; I had no idea that I should have to do that. I thought that people would always be as they were at my sickbed. They were so nice then; I thought a great change had come over them, and it had. They must have been expecting the lucid moments and getting themselves up to their level. And now they have returned to their old selves, as you were saying of me. But they have really done it."

"Are you joking, Uncle, or not?" said Justine.

"I am joking, but with something else underneath, something which may return to you later. If it does, remember that it is only convalescence. And now I will go and have another rest. Being here with you has not lulled me to sleep."

"Mark had better go up with you," said Maria. "You are not quite steady on your feet."

Dudley crossed the room, touching something as he passed and letting Mark take his arm at the door. His brother rose the next moment, adjusted something on the chimney-piece, went to the door and swung it in his hand and followed.

"Father cannot keep away from Uncle and I cannot either," said Justine. "I am going to follow at a respectful distance, more to feast my eyes on him than to be of any use. I am not going to grasp at the privilege of waiting on him. I bow to Father's claim."

"I will bring up the rear," said Aubrey, "and feast my eyes on Justine."

"And Maria and Aunt Matty can have the hour together for which I suspect Aunt Matty has been pining."

"I shall enjoy it, dear, but so I hope will Maria. It is a thing which depends on us both."

"Yes, have it your own way. Enjoy it together. Forget

us; agree that we are in the crude and callow stage; anything; I am quite beyond caring. Oh, I am so happy that I could clap my hands; I could leap into the air." Justine proved her powers. "I am in such a mood that it would be idle to attempt to contain myself."

Aubrey gave a grin towards his stepmother, and opening the door for his sister, followed her with his head erect.

"Quite a finished little man," said Matty. "You should not have much trouble with him. In what order do they come in your affections? They are already there, I can see."

"I hardly know the order. There will be one, of course. I think perhaps Mark comes first; then Justine; then Aubrey and then Clement. I hardly feel that I know Clement yet."

"I think I would put them in the same order," said Matty, who had lost her tenseness. "Except that perhaps I would put Mark after Justine. Yes, I think that my niece comes first, even though we try to quarrel with each other. We never succeed and that says a great deal."

"Why do you make the effort? It seems to be a rather constant one."

"Ah, you are catching the note of my nephews! You are to be a true Gaveston after all. You are not going to be left behind." Matty broke off as a noise came from the stairs.

Dudley had mounted the first flight, and coming to the second, had shaken off his nephew's hand and gone on alone. His limbs gave under him and he fell forward. Edgar sprang after him; Justine gave a cry; Mark turned back and raised his voice; Aubrey ran up the last stairs; Clement broke from his room and hurried to the scene. Dudley was helped to his nephew's bed, hardly the worse. Edgar stood by him, looking as if his defence had broken before this last onset. Clement made a movement to cover something on his desk, stumbled and made a clutch at the desk and sent a mass of gold coins in a stream to the floor.

Justine started and glanced at them; Aubrey paused for a longer moment and stared at his brother; Mark left the bed as he saw that no harm was done, and stood looking from the floor to the desk. Clement touched the coins with his foot, kicked a cloth towards them and thrust his hands into his pockets.

"How nice you all looked!" said Dudley, who had seen what they all saw. "Just as you did when I was ill."

"And we felt like it for a minute," said Justine, turning from her uncle as she spoke.

Edgar sat down and looked at his son, as if he ought to have some feeling over for him.

"Father looks paler than Uncle," said Mark.

"But anyone can see that I am the one who has been ill," said Dudley.

Maria appeared at the door with Jellamy behind, and Clement had the eyes of the household turned on the secret corner of his life.

"Is Dudley hurt?" said Maria. "Was it Dudley who fell?"

"Yes, it was me. It was a silly thing to do. You will get quite tired of all my disturbances and think less of them. It never does to wear out people's feelings."

"Is that money, Clement?" said Justine.

"If it is not, I will leave you to guess what it is."

"Have you been saving?"

"I have been putting by something to spend on my house. You know that I am going to have one, and that I do not spend what I have."

"Why do you keep it in that form?"

"It is like that at the moment. Or some of it is. I have to have some in hand for various things. And I don't care about having interest up to the last moment."

"Clement is a miser," said Aubrey, who accepted this account and did not know how the words struck other ears.

"Well, are you going to leave me?" said his brother, who was strolling up and down, enabled by the smallness of the space to turn round often and hide his face.

"Or are you going to settle in my room? Perhaps you forget that it is mine."

"You can allow Uncle time to recover," said Mark.

"He does not need to do so, as you know."

"And the rest of us to get our breath."

"I admit that I took that away from you," said Clement, with a laugh.

"Clement, that is no good," said Justine. "It is not a pretty thing that we have seen, and you will not make it better by showing us anything else that is ugly."

"I have no wish to show you anything. I don't know why you think so. It is your own idea to pry about in my room. I don't know what you keep in yours." Clement turned to Aubrey, who was touching things on the table. "Stop fingering what is not your own and get out of the room. Or I will throw you out."

"Don't do that," said Dudley. "If anyone else has a fall, I shall not be the centre of all eyes. And if you won't share things with Aubrey, why should I?"

"Is anyone of any use to Uncle? And ought not Maria to be in the drawing room, giving tea to Aunt Matty?"

" 'The king is in his counting house, counting out his money;
   The queen is in the parlour, eating bread and honey,' "

quoted Aubrey in the door.

Clement took one step to the door and kicked it to its latch, indifferent to what he kicked with it. It opened smoothly in a moment.

"Miss Seaton wished to be told if any harm was done, ma'am," said Jellamy.

"None is done in here," said Mark. "I don't know about outside."

"Master Aubrey has knocked his head, sir."

"Oh, I had better go," said Justine.

"We will come with you," said Maria. "Clement did not ask us in here."

Edgar followed his wife, and Dudley got off the bed and strolled to the desk.

"I am glad that you value your money, Clement. I like you to take care of what I gave you. And it shows how well you behaved when I asked for it back. I can't think of that moment without a sense of discomfort. We all have a little of the feeling at times. To know all is to forgive all, but we can't let people know all, of course. Does it give you a sense of satisfaction to have money in that form?"

"I don't know. Some of it happened to be like that."

"I wish you would tell me. Because, if it does, I will have some of mine in it."

"I suppose some people sent it in that form, and I put it all together. It will not remain so for long."

"Of course I am not asking for your confidence."

"I hope you have not killed Aubrey, Clement," said Mark.

"Justine would have come back and said so if I had. She would think it worthy of mention."

"I should not like Aubrey to die," said Dudley. "I only nearly died, and it would give him the immediate advantage."

"You must come to your room, Uncle," said Mark. "It was my duty to see you there."

"I am not going there," said Dudley on the landing. "I am going downstairs again. I have lost my desire for rest. I can't be shut away from family life; it offers too much. To think that I have lived it for so long without even suspecting its nature! I have been quite satisfied by it too; I have had no yearning after anything further. Matty is going and the gossip can have its way. It will be a beautiful family talk, mean and worried and full of sorrow and spite and excitement. I cannot be asked to miss it in my weak state. I should only fret."

"You won't find it too much?"

"I feel it will be exactly what I need somehow."

Matty waved her hand to Dudley and continued her way through the hall, as if taking no advantage of his return.

"Now I feel really at ease for the first time," he said as he entered the drawing room. "I do not mind having fled from my home in a jealous rage, now that Clement is a miser. It was a great help when Matty turned her old friend out into the snow, but not quite enough. Now I am really not any worse than other people. Not any more ridiculous; I don't mind if I am worse."

"You know you are better," said Justine, "and so do we. Now, little boy, sit down and keep quiet. You will be all right in an hour."

"You need not change the subject. I really am at ease. I don't need Aubrey to take the thoughts off me. I don't even like him to."

"Clement believed that I had attained his size before I had," said Aubrey, assuming that thoughts were as his uncle did not prefer them.

"Well, are we to talk about it or are we not?" said Justine.

"Of course we are," said Dudley. "You know I have already mentioned it. "I hope you do not think that it would have been fairer to Clement if I had not. If you do, I shall never forgive myself, or you either. But of course you would forgive me anything to-day; and what is the good of that, if there is nothing to forgive?"

"It is fairer to Clement to talk of it openly, reasonably and without exaggeration."

"Justine speaks with decision," said Aubrey.

"It may be better still just to forget it," said Maria. "We came upon it by accident and against his will. And it may not mean so much. We all do some odd things in private."

"Do we?" said Dudley. "I had no idea of it. I never do

any. As soon as I did an odd thing, I did it in public. I am so glad that life was not taken from me before I even guessed what it was."

"How much money was there in gold?" said Aubrey.

"Now, little boy, that is not at all to the point."

"If Clement is to have a house, it will take all he has," said Edgar.

"A less simple speech than it sounds," said Justine. "There is the solution, swift, simple and complete."

"Perhaps he will starve behind his doors," said Aubrey, "and put his gold into piles at night."

"Someone deserved to have his head broken," said Edgar.

"He may suffer from reaction and be driven into extravagance," said Dudley. "We shall all mind that much more. It must be difficult for young people to strike the mean."

"The golden mean," murmured Aubrey. "Clement may like to strike that."

"He will have a good many expenses," said Mark. "A housekeeper and other things."

"We already detect signs of extravagance," said Dudley.

His nephew strolled into the room.

"Well, am I to flatter myself that I am your subject? I am glad that you can take me in a light spirit. I was fearing that you could not."

"We were wondering if you could afford to run a house," said Maria.

Clement stopped and looked into her eyes.

"Well, I shall have to be careful. But I think I can manage with the sum I have saved. I am keeping part of it in money for the first expenses. They are always the trouble."

"Do you think of having the house at once?" said his father.

"Well, very soon now. I shall be going to Cambridge to see about it. I have enough put by for the initial outlay."

Clement went to the window and stood looking out, and then pushed it open and disappeared.

"Is it wise for a young man to spend all he has?" said Mark. "Let us now transfer our anxiety."

"So it is over," said Dudley. "Clement is a victim of the rashness of youth. I hope he will not waste his allowance."

"And all our thought and talk about it are over too," said Justine, rising. "We are not saying another word. Come, Aubrey; come, Mark. Come, Maria, if I may say it; we are really following your lead. We know you want us to leave Father and Uncle alone."

Edgar looked at the door as it closed, and spoke at once.

"The boy has hardly had a father."

"No, you have failed in one of the deepest relations of life. And you are faced by one of the results. Because there is more in this than we admit. I am not going to get so little out of it. I am sure people got more out of my running away from home."

"I hope he will go along now. This may be the result of too little to spare all his life. Your help may be a godsend in more than one sense."

"It seems to have been the cause of the trouble. You can't be a miser with no money."

"You can be with very little, when it is scarce."

"I rather liked Clement to be a miser; I felt flattered by it. It was taking what I gave him, so seriously."

"We may be making too much of the matter."

"Maria will not let us make enough. I will not give up the real, sinister fact. Why should I not cling to the truth?"

"Maria will be a help to us with all of them."

"To us! You knew the word that would go straight to my heart. But you ought to be a success as a brother, when as a father you are such a failure. What can you expect but that the tender shoots should warp and grow

294

astray? They had no hand to prune or guide them. I don't believe you even realised that Clement was a shoot. And he was so tender that he warped almost at once. I think you are very fortunate that he was the only one."

"How much has happened in the last fourteen months!"

"Yes. Matty came to live here. I inherited a fortune. I was engaged to Maria. Blanche fell ill and died. You became engaged in my place. You and Maria were married. Matty's father died. Matty drove her old friend out into the snow. I ran away from my home. I am not quite sure of the order of the last three, but they were all on the same night, and it was really hard on Matty that it happened to be snowing. On a mild night she would not have been blamed half so much. I rescued Miss Griffin and took her into my charge. It was hard on us that it happened to be snowing too. I decided to provide for her for her life. It seemed the only thing in view of the climate. At any time it might snow. I was sick almost to death, and was given back to you all. In more than one sense; I must not forget that. Oh and Clement was gradually becoming a miser all the time. You would have thought he had enough to distract him."

There was a pause.

"Dudley, I can ask you a question, as I know the answer. Maria does not mean to you what she did?"

"No, not even as much as you would like her to. I cannot see her with your eyes. I have returned to the stage of seeing her with my own. I nearly said that to me she would always be second to Blanche, but it would be no good to echo your own mind. And of course to both of us she is only just second to her. But I think that you married her too soon after Blanche died, and that you may never live it down. You can see that I am speaking the truth, that I feel it to be my duty. I know that Blanche had a good husband, but it would never be any-one's duty to say that."

"I was carried away. I had not been much with

women. And I think that emotion of one kind—I think it may predispose the mind to others."

"Why do some people say that we are not alike? We seem to be almost the same. But grief for a wife is a better emotion than excitement over money. Your second feelings had a nobler foundation and deserved success. But no wonder there are no secrets between us. I only have one secret left. But it shows me what it was for Clement, when his only secret was exposed."

"Are you going to tell me?"

"Yes, I am, because it is proof that I have lost my feeling for Maria. I have already proposed to someone else."

"What?" said Edgar, the fear in his tone bringing final content to his brother. "You have not had time. You were ill a few days after you left this house."

"Well, I proposed to her a few minutes after. You see that I lost my feeling for Maria very soon. And she refused me. Women do not seem to want me as the companion of their lives."

"Miss Griffin?" said Edgar, with incredulity and perception.

"How affection sharpens your wits! But you should have said: 'I want you, Dudley.'"

"I think—I see that the sun is coming out."

"So we can go out and walk as we have all our lives. The only difference will be that I must lean on your arm. I have had to say it for you. Saying it in your own way does not count. I said it in anyone's way. I am the better of the two."

"I think you might for twenty minutes, for a quarter of an hour."

The pair went out and walked on the path outside the house, and Justine, catching the sight from a window, rose with a cry and ran to fetch her brothers.

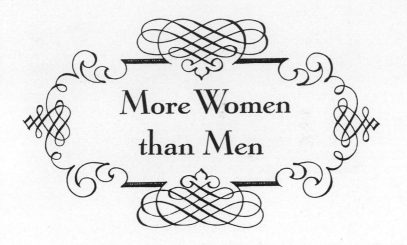

More Women
than Men

CHAPTER I

"IT is with an especial feeling that I welcome you back
to-day," said Josephine Napier, rising from her desk
and advancing across her study to greet the woman who
had entered it. "I do not forget that you are embarking
upon your eighth year on my staff. Believe me, I have not
been unmindful of my growing debt. May I say that I
think no one has lived a more useful seven years? You
will allow me to say just that to you?"

Josephine Napier, the head of a large girls' school in a
prosperous English town, was a tall, spare woman of fifty-
four, with greying auburn hair, full hazel eyes, an im-
pressive, high-featured, but simply modelled face, a conscious sincerity and simplicity of mien, rather surprisingly jewelled hands, and hair and dress arranged to set
off rather than disguise experience.

Miss Theodora Luke, a mistress in her school, was an
erect, pale woman of thirty-eight, with a simply straight-
forward and resolute face, smooth, coiled hair, grey eyes
with a glance of interest and appreciation, and an oddity
of dress displayed in the manner of the university woman
of Victorian days, as the outward sign of the unsuspected
inner truth.

"Indeed I will allow you to say it, Mrs. Napier," she
said in a quick, deep voice, with a quick, deep laugh. "It
definitely smoothes my path towards decrepitude."

"I think that maturity has very few disadvantages in-
herent in itself," said Josephine, speaking as if simply
from her own experience, and adding by way of putting
the full gulf of years between her companion and herself:
"Did you have a pleasant journey, my dear?"

"Yes, very pleasant, thank you. The train was rather
crowded. But I see no reason myself for objecting to the
presence of my fellow creatures." Miss Luke looked full
at Josephine as she set forth her individual view. "It is

299

extraordinary how seldom we meet unpleasant people, or see an unpleasant face. Have you ever met a repulsive person, Mrs. Napier? I think I have not."

"No, I think all faces I have met have had their human dignity and charm. But then I have spent my life amongst educated and intelligent people. I would not say that some faces might not show signs of—shall we say a different history? I hope"—Josephine bent towards her companion with a humorously guilty smile—"that you had none of those in your carriage?"

Miss Luke yielded for a moment to laughter.

"Well, what I always feel, Mrs. Napier, in meeting such people, is simply respect for their harder experience. I pay the rightful homage of the highly civilised—yes, that is what I choose to call myself—to those whose lives are spent at the base of the civilisation. Surely no other view should be admissible?"

"No, indeed it should not. I think you have given more thought to the matter than I have; to the equality of all kinds of usefulness. Possibly I have been too busy with the practical observance of it. Now, if I may claim your attention for a humdrum matter not within your province, I have to tell you that your room is changed." Josephine took up some slips of paper. "Yes, it is on the left side of the second corridor, with the south facing. You remember that the doctor said you were to have sun? I hope you will not mind making the adjustment?" She raised her eyes with her pencil on her lips, concerned simply with her programme.

"Mind? What a question, Mrs. Napier! I hope the change did not involve too much trouble. I am most grateful."

"Grateful?" said Josephine, in a faintly perplexed tone, still preoccupied. "And I have put Miss Rosetti next door. I like to feel that intimate friends are together. In a case of sudden sickness that may mean a good deal. It is good of you all to make my task of general so light."

"Ah, I hardly think it can be that," said Miss Luke.

"Well, so pleasant then. And that would be my choice. I have no desire for any lessening of my labour. I hope you are happy to come back to yours?"

"Well, yes, the ayes have it," said Miss Luke.

"I am glad that there is a pull on the other side," said Josephine, looking at her with searching kindness. "That means at once more for you, and for other people. And now you must want your tea, and anyhow I want it for you. Crowded railway carriages need an antidote. So go and do your duty to yourself and to me."

Josephine rose for a moment as her companion rose, and then sat down at her desk and took up her pen, but in a minute rose again to welcome the successor. This was a grey-haired, foreign-looking woman, taller and frailer and some years older than Miss Luke, with finely chiselled features, pale, dreamy eyes, with a cynical look that came as a surprise, and openly languid movements, whom Josephine greeted in a manner which showed her less assured of her own impression.

"Well, you have followed close upon Miss Luke. I remembered that your trains were near together. I hope you have escaped her experience of a crowded carriage?"

"No, I have not escaped it. I have been sitting upright in the middle of one row of people, and opposite another," said the newcomer, in a deep, dragging voice, a movement of her shoulders implying that the posture she mentioned was unnatural.

"Well, I suppose we have no reason for objecting to the presence of our fellow creatures," said Josephine, continuing in Miss Luke's line.

"I had reasons for objecting to the presence of these creatures. And I don't know why they were my fellows: I saw no basis of fellowship."

"I confess it does not always strike the eye," said Josephine, giving a full smile. "Though we should not dare to say so to Miss Luke. At least, I should not. Perhaps you, as one admitted to greater intimacy, would have more courage."

Maria Rosetti had been born of Italian parents and brought up in France, and was qualified by these means, and by others in herself which Josephine recognised, as an exponent of modern languages.

"Well, I trust your holiday has been pleasanter than your journey back to us?"

"I have not had a holiday; I have been in a holiday post. It is wise for me to earn what I can, while I can. I have been happy and well."

"Well, I hope you will have a pleasant term. We must see that your work is not too much. Or rather I must see to it; for I do not believe I can trust you." Josephine considered a time-table fastened to her desk. "Could we cut out your afternoon conversation classes? Yes, I think we might do that." She drew her pencil through them. "Then I shall feel that your afternoons are your own."

"My holiday work has nothing to do with my work in the term, Mrs. Napier."

"Has it not?" said Josephine, on a musical note. "But it has to do with my opinion of your fitness for it. I am glad you have told me: I quite see that that was a piece of luck."

"I am quite fit for my work, Mrs. Napier."

"You need not tell me that," said Josephine gravely. "It is easy, indeed, for you to be fit for work so well within your powers. I often wish I had duties for you more up to them. But failing that, I must feel that the daily round is not enough to be a burden."

"My work is hardly up to me," said Miss Rosetti, in a level voice. "I do not give it the whole of myself, as it does not claim it. I have been waiting to say that, if you ever have an opening for a partner, I should be grateful for it. I am in a position to meet the material demand; or why should I not say, pay for it?"

"Now, I hope I do not seem to you self-sufficient," said

Josephine after a pause, leaning over her desk with an open expression. "Believe me, I am only hard-working, and unused to having anyone to take the work off my hands. And at the moment I am grateful, for your giving me this mark of your confidence early enough for it to have its meaning. I will bear it in mind for the future; and bear it in mind for the present for my own encouragement. And we must see that the common task is not a tax upon capacities too rare for it. I think a little lightening of it will secure that."

"You are very kind, Mrs. Napier."

"No. Why am I kind?" said Josephine, seeming to speak in an aside from jotting something down. "You have always done all you can for me."

"I will certainly do it, Mrs. Napier," said Miss Rosetti, her eyes just resting on Josephine's empty page, as she left the room.

She was succeeded in course by a short, rather ponderous woman of faintly comical aspect, who advanced towards Josephine with an expression that suggested an appreciation of her own ambling gait. She had a fresh, round face, nondescript features, unmarked for her fifty years, drab-coloured hair arranged at the least expense of effort, and prominent, vague, bright eyes, that roved and suddenly withdrew as if their owner were informed.

"How do you do, Mrs. Napier? I have come back to-day because the term begins to-morrow."

Having uttered this greeting, Miss Emmeline Munday stood at ease and in silence.

"That is very considerate. I hoped we should see you to-day. Miss Luke and Miss Rosetti have arrived, and will be waiting in your common room. I hope you are one of those people who find holidays agreeable? Which do you find the more enjoyable, the holidays or the term?"

"The holidays," said Miss Munday, looking steadily at Josephine.

"I should rather ask, which gives you the more satisfaction?"

Josephine paused for the corresponding amendment.

"The holidays," said Miss Munday, her lip twitching.

"Well, that is healthy," said Josephine, not prone to be dissatisfied. "Have you any suggestion to make to me before you join your friends?"

"No," said Miss Munday, blinking her eyes.

"Nothing about your hours, your classes, your number of pupils; anything? You know you are my senior mistress; you have been with me longer than any member of my staff; and I have nothing to ask of you, but that you will consult yourself in any matter that arises. You know that that could be my only wish for you?"

"Yes," said Miss Munday, and upon her corroboration turned and left the room.

The fourth arrival was the only married member of Josephine's staff, a small, harried-looking woman of forty-five, with a small, brown, untidily-featured face, small, brown, flurried hands, unkempt, noticeable clothes, and the alert, enquiring, engaging aspect of some little woodland beast. Her husband had been blamed for leaving her without provision, but with some injustice, as she was qualified for teaching English literature, by being the widow of a man who wrote. The senior branch of this subject Miss Munday conducted, by virtue of a degree, thus indicating the place of her colleague's equipment in the scale. Mrs. Chattaway seldom referred to her wedded life, and her companions, in spite of their sincere deprecation of the married state, assigned her reticence to her sense of loss; whereas the truth was, as they might consistently have guessed, that the memory was uncongenial.

"Oh, I am sure I am later than all the others; I am so ashamed. But I have had a dreadful journey. My train was late, and while I was waiting for it, it went on without me. I did not notice it; it was my own fault. So I had to wait for the next."

"Well, I am glad that that one did not go on without you," said Josephine, smiling and retaining the speaker's hand. "It is not at all the duty of trains to us, to go on while we are waiting. We cannot be expected to do more than arrive and wait. I am afraid you must be very tired?"

"I am not so much tired as flustered and vexed with myself. And I feel so hopelessly untidy; I cannot guess how I must look." Mrs. Chattaway remedied this inability by glancing in the mirror, but seemed to take advantage of her distraught condition to pass over what she saw. "I am so very sorry to begin again by being late; I know you like us to be here for tea."

"Well, if I like that, it is for your own sake. And if you are going to arrive as troubled as this, I feel I am right. But you are mistaken in thinking that you are so late; the others have only just arrived. And if you were, fresh tea could be sent up to you. Though I admit that I do not care for you to run your meals too close, as nothing is more prejudicial to appetite. Now, may I depend on you to take the rest you need to-morrow, whether in working hours or out of them? You will serve me in that matter?" Josephine's manner was held in lighter check with this member of her house.

"You are too kind, Mrs. Napier. It is quite like coming home to come back to work here."

"Well, I should hope it is. You give me two-thirds of your life; and it would be a pretty thing if my house did not seem like home to you. There would be something very wrong with me if that could be so. If there is ever any little thing that would make it seem more home-like, you will tell me of it? May I trust you?"

"Indeed I will; indeed you may, Mrs. Napier. Not that there ever is anything; it is all thought of before we can imagine it. We do appreciate your kindness. I think you do a great work in making a self-supporting life so pleasant for the women who have to lead it."

"I am sorry you feel that about your life. May I congratulate you on hiding it so well? For it must need courage."

"Oh no, Mrs. Napier; indeed it does not. There is nothing to hide. I don't know what I meant by saying it. And of course I should not foster a feeling that might unfit me for my work."

"A feeling of that kind, even if not fostered, does unfit you for your work," said Josephine in a serious tone. "But may I pay you a compliment, and say that I do not think you can have it? I have watched you—No, no! No more and no less than it has been my duty to watch you —and I think that the feeling was a part of the disturbance of your life, when you first joined us—Believe me, I saw it with great sympathy—and that it has since vanished. Am I not right?"

"Yes, indeed you are, Mrs. Napier; I had not realised it myself. I am glad to be shown how happy I am in my life. I should be most ungrateful if I were anything else."

"You would be most unfortunate. Not to be contented in a life of useful work, that is within our power, is indeed to be unfortunate. I can imagine no lot more satisfying, and I am speaking from my own experience. I am not a person to speak lightly from a position that is not my own. And now I have preached at you long enough; I will not keep you from your tea another moment. And here is your new colleague, Miss Keats, arrived in time to share it with you! Run away, and if you will do me a kindness, ring for fresh tea for yourself and for her. Thank you very much."

Mrs. Chattaway literally ran away, and a tall, thin girl of twenty-three advanced towards Josephine, lifting her pale grey eyes from her small, pale, lively face, alert to turn to the ends of her own tongue whatever might be said.

"I am glad indeed to see you safely under this roof after your long journey. You have been in my thoughts more than once to-day. I hope you found it a good one?"

"I must shatter that hope," said Miss Helen Keats, in her soft, staccato voice, meeting Josephine's eyes with her expression unsteady. "I found it a bad one. A girl's school was returning; and as this school returns to-morrow, I knew that they were returning on the wrong day. I did not say to them: 'This is the mistresses' day.' I realised that the time for controlling myself with girls was at hand."

Josephine stood smiling into her face, looking as if she would bend her head, if the face were not on a level with her own.

"You must be tired, and ready for tea and rest."

"Yes, I find that girls in numbers have that effect. It augurs well for my appetite here, if not for my work."

"I hope the appetite will not wait until tomorrow for the numbers. The tea is ready now. And you will not see much of the numbers, my dear. Nothing except in school hours; and then your classes will be small. I do not make it difficult for people to use their gifts."

"It sounds as if I had brought with me a healthy aversion from the class of beings I am concerned with. I may see the better how to improve them."

"My dear, you have brought with you a brave spirit, or you could not have joined us at all. Believe me, I am not thinking little of it, your first plunge into professional life. My own memories are not so blunt. Will you remember that a woman older than your mother is waiting here for you, if you can put her to any of the uses that youth has for middle age? And now go and make some use of that appetite you were boasting of. If you remain so pale and slender, I shall think it was an empty boast. Your common room, the senior mistresses', is on the upper floor to the right. You are very young to belong to it, but people must be in their own place. No, I will not come up with you. The room is yours, not mine. You will hear the voices through the door."

Helen went upstairs and knocked at the door described.

"Is this where I am to be?" she said.

"Yes, it is, though I don't wonder that it strikes you as improbable," said Miss Luke, coming cordially forward. "So you are the glimpse of youth promised to our failing eyes; and we—there is nothing stranger than truth —are your future companions! Did Mrs. Napier warn you that you would find us all in the sere and yellow leaf?"

"Yes, I believe she did just warn me," said Helen.

Miss Luke showed amusement at finding her surmise correct, and recovered herself to introduce Miss Munday.

"I am the eldest, the senior mistress," said Miss Munday, lifting herself from the sofa to offer her hand, and sinking down again with her eyes on the floor.

"It is thoughtful of you to arrive after the rest of us, so that we are assembled to look at you," said Miss Rosetti, in the mellow tones of some of her moods, her eyes roving over Helen's form.

"You look so fresh and charming after your journey, that I can hardly believe it," said Mrs. Chattaway. "I dare not think how I must look beside you. I hardly liked to appear before Mrs. Napier, kind though she is. I think she was especially kind to-day."

"I noticed that her standard was high," said Helen.

"It is wonderful how she enters into the lives of all the people about her. If I had known it when I first came, I should have had a happier beginning."

"I suppose she forgot to tell you," said Helen. "She cannot remember with everybody."

Miss Rosetti laughed, and Miss Luke a little dubiously did the same.

"She may think that self-praise is no recommendation," said Mrs. Chattaway.

"I think she meant it for a recommendation," said Helen. "I don't see what other purpose it could serve."

"I think it often is a recommendation," said Miss Luke, standing rather squarely. "A little self-praise may augur a good deal of quality. We none of us like to praise our-selves as much as we deserve." She laughed.

"I think Mrs. Napier would like it. But I admit that she only hinted at the whole."

"Ah, she is a large person, our principal," said Miss Luke, looking round. "You should all support me when I say a thing like that. You make me feel I have been fulsome."

"I support you most warmly," said Mrs. Chattaway.

Miss Rosetti raised her eyebrows, and Mrs. Chattaway at once turned towards her.

"You are too clever and cynical, Miss Rosetti, to see the ordinary good qualities the rest of us see in people," she said, intending no disparagement of anyone involved.

"I see a great many qualities in Mrs. Napier, some of them good, and very few of them ordinary."

"We have a remarkable employer, head mistress," said Mrs. Chattaway.

"We have both," said Miss Luke, gently and frankly.

"It must be trying to be the head of a school," said Mrs. Chattaway.

"It is surely the least undesirable position in it," said Miss Rosetti.

"Let me get you all some more tea," said Mrs. Chatta-way. "It is too humble a duty for any of you."

"We must wait on our qualified women," said Miss Rosetti, coming to her aid.

"They say that more and more women are qualifying every year," said Mrs. Chattaway, her sequences of thought vague.

Miss Luke fell into open mirth.

"I did not mean that you were not unusual. I meant that more women were struggling to your level, who did not find it so easy."

"Oh, it was not done so easily," said Miss Luke.

"Even Mrs. Napier is not qualified, is she?" said Mrs. Chattaway.

"No," said Miss Luke, in a colourless tone.

"It is a privilege for me to have your friendship, your companionship."

"Oh, don't grudge us the status of friendship. Don't be so snubbing to mere spinsters," said Miss Luke.

"I don't think we must call Miss Keats a spinster yet; I mean, she has not reached the age of final decision."

"Are you sure that was what you meant?" said Miss Luke, with a roguish eye.

"Can anyone tell me where I am to lay my head?" said Helen.

"On the landing above, in number forty-three," said Miss Luke. "It seems that I have been probing into what is no concern of mine."

"That is very convenient for me. I will go and take advantage of it."

"Well, what is our verdict?" said Miss Luke.

"A most charming girl!" said Mrs. Chattaway. "It is extraordinary to think she has been to Oxford and taken such a high place. She gives no sign of it at all."

"The rest of you find the matter requires consideration?" said Miss Luke, glancing at Miss Rosetti.

"What do you think yourself, Miss Luke?" said Mrs. Chattaway.

"Well," said Miss Luke in a judicial tone, "perhaps a thought self-assured for a young girl and a new-comer, among the middle-aged and established. No, well, that is rather needless. Why should she not be assured? I am sure she has every reason. But definitely and consciously a significant young woman."

"But surely that is not to her disadvantage?" said Mrs. Chattaway.

"Certainly not; to her advantage," said Miss Luke.

"And not to the disadvantage of anyone else?" said Mrs. Chattaway.

"Certainly not," said Miss Luke. "What a line to take,

to be critical of the valuable gift of young confidence, to be blind to the claim of youth!"

Must we lay the burden of our middle age on the girl?" said Miss Rosetti. "As you said, she did not lay the burden of her youth on us. And I think she was right."

"She was undoubtedly right; and so are you; and I am wrong," said Miss Luke.

Mrs. Chattaway looked at Miss Luke with appreciation.

"I think I will follow her example and go and unpack," said Miss Rosetti.

"I will do the same," said Miss Luke.

Mrs. Chattaway sat with her eyes going after the pair.

"That is a wonderful case of devotion," she said to Miss Munday.

"Yes," said Miss Munday, looking at her empty teacup.

Mrs. Chattaway ran to replenish the cup, and came up to her companion.

"It must be a great thing in a life like this, such a friendship."

"Yes," said Miss Munday, stirring the cup and then raising her eyes. "It must."

"Are you interested in different human relationships?" said Mrs. Chattaway, on a more urgent note.

"Yes," said Miss Munday.

"You are more interested in abstract theories, I am sure," said Mrs. Chattaway, with compliment. "But some human relationships, that arise out of certain conditions, are worthy of attention."

"Yes," said Miss Munday.

"Both Miss Luke and Miss Rosetti have great gifts for intimacy."

"Yes, they have," said Miss Munday.

"You have watched them, have known them, ever since they have been here together?"

"Yes," said Miss Munday. "I was here before either of them."

311

"And they both have great powers of affection?" said Mrs. Chattaway, pausing for result at length to arise from her words.

"Yes, I have found them both very affectionate," said Miss Munday, going to the door.

"I think Miss Rosetti is the less constant," said Mrs. Chattaway, taking some running steps after her.

"I have found them both quite constant," said Miss Munday.

Miss Luke and Miss Rosetti mounted arm in arm to the second floor, and pausing outside their adjoining rooms, confronted each other.

"The new young woman is along the corridor, is she not?" said Miss Luke.

"I hope so, as that was the direction you gave her."

"Is not her room the next but one to mine, next door to yours?"

"I hope so again, as that is what you said," said Miss Rosetti, pushing the other against the wall, and looking into her face.

"Did you approach Mrs. Napier on the matter of the partnership?"

"With no avail."

"She can do without you?"

"That is what she was obliged to explain, at some cost to herself and to me."

"Yes, it must have been at cost to her," said Miss Luke in a low, quick tone.

Miss Rosetti was silent.

"I am at once glad and sorry," said Miss Luke. "Glad to keep you, and sorry not to see you rising above us."

"I am only sorry."

"Ah, you have come to the end of us. But Miss Keats is fresh ground for you to plough, until you can approach your ultimate goal. I believe you have an unconscious affection for our head."

Miss Rosetti turned from Miss Luke, and sauntering past her own door, knocked at the next.

"You are settling in?" she said. "Why not sit down and let me unpack for you?"

"I see no reason against it," said Helen. "At least none that need weigh with me, if it does not with you."

"This is your first post?"

"Yes; or perhaps I should be prepared to be unpacked for by my seniors. It is a custom here? A way of putting new-comers at their ease?"

"Well, I have done it before."

"If it is not invariably done, it does not put me at my ease."

"Is this the latest fashion, and this the one before?" said Miss Rosetti, handling some dresses with open interest.

"It does not put me at my ease to be told that my second gown is out of date. Have you never been taught about poverty not being a thing to be ashamed of?"

"I have always been ashamed of it. I would save anyone in my power from it. I have done so in the one case I could. I can alter the dress so that it bears no hint of it. I am a better dressmaker than I have had any reason to be. You need not be afraid of my old maid's history."

"But why should you trouble about other people's clothes? And I have not convinced myself that poverty is shameful."

"The clothes are not other people's. They are yours. And things like poverty and old age and death are shameful. We cannot help them; but that is the humiliation. To accept conditions that would not be your choice must be a disgrace."

Miss Rosetti went to the door, swinging the dress and whistling to herself.

CHAPTER II

"MY father has written to me for my birthday," said Felix Bacon, holding out a letter in his long, pale hand. "He congratulates me on completing my fortieth year. Last year he congratulated me on entering it. It seems inconsistent to congratulate for both, and a little tactless to congratulate for either. He says it is absurd to be doing nothing at that age. He said the same thing when I was twenty and thirty, and everyone knows that different things are absurd at different ages. Do I realise that he has paid for every meal that I have eaten? I had not actually realised it, meal by meal; he must be always thinking about food. That I have been a daily expense to him? Of course, it is a daily expense to pay for a person's meals; but he does not really consider them; it is a false implication. I don't know anyone who thinks less about his child's meals."

Felix crossed the room with a dancing step, and standing before a much older man, who sat by the hearth, waved the letter towards him.

"He says that forty is not too late to turn over a new leaf. Then why make this trouble about it, if it is not too late? I thought the lateness was the point. And he does not say a word about my looking so young for my age."

Felix surveyed in the mirror his small, light frame, his smooth, black hair, his narrow, green eyes, his pale, narrow face, his prominent, narrow features and his subtle, alert expression.

"My figure is remarkably supple and lithe," he said. "But when my father treats me as if I had the gift of perennial youth, I do not believe he is thinking about my figure."

"You have it indeed, my boy, and it is the rarest gift. You have to be old, to realise how rare."

Jonathan Swift rose from his seat, and, putting a hand

on Felix's arm, regarded the contrast they made in the glass, his own girth double that of his companion, and the latter's head barely at his shoulder. He was a tall, vigorous man of seventy, with rather formless features, with a likeness to those of his sister, Josephine Napier, the remains of bushy, auburn hair, emotional, roving, gold-brown eyes and an expression at once benevolent and unrestrained. His parents, realising that he bore the surname of a famous man, had given him also the Christian name, by way of doing all in their power towards equality; and possibly reflecting that for his father the precaution had been omitted, and equality had not been the result. They had further put him into the same profession of the Church; and he had himself continued in the line by turning his attention to letters, so that the difference in their practice of these was the only difference between his predecessor and himself. With regard to this difference he had observed that his writings were not in accord with the present taste, and could not be published with advantage during his life. He had helped himself through this period by taking pupils; and the last of these, Felix Bacon, had remained with him for twenty-two years, ever since he had arrived as a youth of eighteen in the escort of his father, a country squire, whose difference from Jonathan's family was illustrated by his ignoring the advantage of the name of Francis for his son.

"My father has not sent me my usual birthday cheque," said Felix, "because I must not get to depend upon it. He must know that habits get set at my age, when he has so often warned me about it. The best way of learning a thing is to teach it to another. He will not pay another tailor's bill this year. I should not want him to; it would look as if my personality depended on externals. But he is really rather womanly in the way he thinks of my food and clothes. Of course he knows that I am motherless."

Felix put the letter in his pocket, indicating by a gesture that it was near his heart.

"My boy, it is the wish of my life that I may cease to be a burden. It is hard on my friends that my work is not for their time."

"The judgement of posterity is known to be the only true one. So there seems no point in getting any other. I wonder so many people do it. You seem to be very wise."

"Ah, they get something besides judgement. But I may get some ordinary work, while I can do it, and do justice with it. God knows, I hope so; God knows, I do."

"He may do something about it, now he knows. I think it must be impressed on him. But perhaps he feels it hardly matters what I wear, as I carry off shabby clothes so well."

"Your father may take his view," said Jonathan, giving his gruff, deep laugh.

"Well, it is natural that they should think about me on the same line, when they bear the same relation to me; especially as the one claims to follow the other."

"I am not going to make a business of accepting what I need from one I love," said Jonathan. "I am simply grateful, as I ought to be."

"I would have a sale of my drawings, if they were good enough to be sold for anything but charity. It is a tribute to human nature that people will only pay for things they don't want, to help good works. What a mean criticism, that they ought to help them for nothing! If I were a woman, I should always serve at bazaars; I never know why men do not serve at them. I should have a regular employment. My father should have had a daughter."

"Does he wish he had had a daughter?"

"Yes. He says he would have found one a consolation. He says, too, that I might be a woman, for all the difference he can see. That seems to show that I have tried to be a comfort to him."

"Is he lonely?" said Jonathan.

"You know he is. Pray do not upset me."

"And I am not lonely owing to him."

"Entirely owing to him. He has the first claim. I could not bear to be the object of only one claim."

"We don't often get a chance of a talk like this. Young Fane seems always to be everywhere. I can't think when he does his work."

"I never think about people's work. Work is a thing I do not like to think about. It is odd that my father always connects me with it. He can hardly separate the two ideas."

"Does he suggest anything definite?"

"That I should save him the expense of an agent, and the discredit of having a son who will not live in his house. I don't mean that he actually suggests the whole of that."

"He does not sound addicted to work himself."

"Of course he is not addicted to work. Please do not speak unsuitably about my father."

"You may have inherited his liking for leisure?"

"Children must not be levelling in what they inherit. My father has a great dislike for what is levelling. I should be shocked if he worked. I must always work before him, as I recognise work to be degrading. I am not one of those modern people; I try always to seem a survival from the old world."

"It is generous of your father to continue your allowance."

"Yes, that often comes over me, and I resolve to amend my life. Could I teach drawing to the girls in your sister's school? The post is vacant, and I am the soul of delicacy."

"How would that appeal to your father?"

"Well, he says I might be a woman; and he wants me to work, though it is dreadfully unchivalrous of him; it would never do for him to teach in a girls' school. And women who work generally teach girls. Great women have done it, and I had better choose them for my model.

317

I can't help thinking that my drawing is better than theirs."

"Good afternoon," said a strident, self-confident voice, as there entered a spare, vigorous man of thirty-five, with definite movements, openly penetrating eyes, and strongly aquiline features set aslant. "And what are you wagging your tongues about so busily? I hope, as the children say, it was not about me, or I shall perforce interrupt your colloquy."

"I have no respect for people who cannot have their colloquies interrupted," said Felix. "We were not talking about you, but of course we might often do so. I should never suggest anything else to a person who thought he was being talked about. But we generally talk about my father."

"I hope you have arrived at some satisfactory conclusions concerning him," said the new-comer, spacing his words as if they called for note.

"Yes; I have said some generous things."

"Well, it is never too late to mend."

"It is quite early for me to mend. I really think I am one of those people who are as old as they look."

"Well, I don't know what my looks do for me," said Mr. Fane, facing Felix as though without intention. "I may appear a thought jaded at this time of the day. I have earned my cup of tea, whether or no anybody else has."

"Nobody else has. It is extraordinary how many people talk about earning meals. My father is really typical."

William Fane was a local lawyer, who had been introduced to Jonathan as a paying guest, by a former pupil, evincing his sentiments towards his own late educator. It was a need of his nature to feel self-esteem, and as he had no unusual quality but the power of sinking below his class, he esteemed himself for being a man and a potential husband; which human attributes were, to do him justice, less general than many he possessed.

"Well, I have the pleasant weariness that comes after a day of hard and not unremunerative effort. I am a tired but contented man."

"I am glad you do not regard work as an end in itself. But I could never be both tired and contented. I don't think I understand about pleasant weariness. But I am upset when I hear that doing nothing is the most ageing thing in the world. I get into the way of busying myself with little services to others." Felix poured out the tea and brought a cup to Fane.

"You ought to marry, and find scope for your gifts as a family man."

"Please do not look at me with a masculine expression. I may not have the power of making a woman happy."

"A woman asks very little beyond a home and a husband."

"She could not ask for a home from me. My father would have to offer her his; and I do not see how she could be happy with my father."

"I suppose your mother was happy with him."

"Why do you suppose that?" said Felix.

"Well, he has always been very kind and polite to me when we have met."

"He may have made differences between you and my mother."

"Well, I don't see why your mother should have died of a broken heart."

"She died when I was born. It was if she had lived, that I should have broken her heart, my father tells me. It was I, and not he, who had to cause her death."

"You seem quite obsessed by your father."

"So do you," said Felix. "I quite understand it."

"No, no, come, that is not possible."

"It seems to me inevitable, when you have met."

"I repeat that he was very kind and polite."

"Yes, you do repeat it."

"Well, come now, if you ask me, you and he would be

doing more for women if you gave a couple of them mates."

"I should not dream of not asking you. You seem to know everything about it; though you have rather soon forgotten my mother. But I have heard that women like men to work."

"Yes, that is a true word," said Jonathan. "Look at my sister, who is to be with me to-night. She likes people to work indeed, dear, good woman that she is! She has been the saving of my boy. She and I are the last of our family, the eldest and the youngest, the first and the last. Yes, that is the right description in another way."

"Oh, a dinner-party to-night, is there?" said Fane.

"No, just my family to see me, if you will bear with it. My sister and her husband, and my son."

"I wonder you do not have your son to live with you, now he is a grown man."

"Surely you do not, when my sister has brought him up from babyhood, and is more than a mother to him."

"Yes, she is more than that," said Felix.

"I think I will go and take a nap, as people are coming to dinner," said Fane. "I don't want to be a damper on the proceedings."

"It will be nice to see him at his best," said Felix. "I suppose he is generally a damper. I wish my father could really observe a person who did regular work."

"My boy, you have had a happy twenty years with me?"

"I have. And you remember my father asked you to make me happy. The one thing he has asked of you, you have done for him."

Felix danced towards Jonathan and took a seat on his knee, the older man moving his arm as if accustomed to the position.

"What would your father say, if he knew all our life together?"

"I don't think he uses words about everything."

"He deserves to be more respected than I am."

"Well, I think he gets what he deserves."

"Do people despise me?"

"Some people admire you for being a writer, but I think more people admire my father for being a squire."

"Well, I believe it is the rarer thing. But I would rather earn my admiration. But I am not of the men who have the facile trick of putting all of themselves on to paper."

"Is it really facile? I daresay they would say it was. We must go and dress. Your family is never late."

Felix ran upstairs and called to the man, who, with the aid of his wife, conducted Jonathan's household.

"I will wear my ordinary evening clothes, as they give an impression of greater ease than the new ones. I ought to be a person whose clothes never look new; it shows that no one really conforms to type. But one thing about me is that limpness gives the effect of grace."

CHAPTER III

JONATHAN followed Felix downstairs, clad in an old evening suit which he had worn nightly for years, and in which he appeared at once disreputable and dignified.

"Well, I am not dressed for the ladies," observed Fane. "For the lady, to be exact. I am assuming that Mrs. Napier will excuse it."

"That will put your mind at rest," said Felix.

"I am sure she will not mind my little omission."

"It is an advantage to have certainty."

"I make no claim to your elegant appearance. I am content with my own type."

"We most of us are," said Felix. "I am myself. It is the oddest thing in life."

"Now, what exactly do you mean by that?"

"Not at all what you thought I meant. How could you have thought I meant it?"

"I should know Josephine's bell in a thousand," said Jonathan.

"We don't have to distinguish it among so many," said Fane. "Our party is hardly so large."

"I am so looking forward to the evening," said Felix. "My attitude is as fresh and youthful as a boy's."

"Well, it does not do to get too blasé," said Fane, doing his best for his own expectant words.

Josephine led her family into the room, and greeted the men in a quiet manner that was not without a consciousness of her womanhood. Her embrace of her brother seemed to stress the comparative rareness of the salute between the sexes. Her husband followed at a seemingly greater than his actual distance, a tall, slight man of the same age, who gave the impression of being frail and old, with delicate, aquiline features, fluttering grey eyes, and a high, narrow head that filled and broadened at the brow. He shook hands in a gentle, interested manner, turning fully from one to another his courteous, physically feeble gaze.

A youth of twenty-three brought up the rear, Josephine's nephew and Jonathan's son, whom Josephine had adopted before the dawn of his memory, on her brother's return from a sojourn abroad, a widower with an infant boy. He was a tall, auburn-haired, rather handsome young man, with nervous movements that did not interfere with his impression of ease, and a manner rather elaborate and strained. He began to speak in quick, high, conscious, cultured tones.

"Well, we members of a family meet with all the politeness of strangers! We have never seen the weaker side of each other. I am convinced that my father has no weaker side. It seems to me unnatural for a son to live under his father's roof."

322

"So it does to me," said Felix.

"My dear Gabriel, my dear boy!" said Jonathan, standing with his hand on his son's shoulder, looking into his face. "I have been living all day in this moment; tomorrow I shall live in the memory of it. I don't think I live less with you, than other fathers with their sons."

"Don't let us talk of other fathers and their sons," said Felix.

"I should say that Gabriel is better off for parents than most people," said Josephine.

"It would come better from me than from you, Josephine," said Gabriel.

"The young man makes free with your Christian name, Mrs. Napier. You allow that?" said Fane.

"I am not asked if I will allow it," said Josephine, slightly raising her shoulders. "There came a moment when it just began, when I suppose it seemed to him that we were a man and woman together. I have no objection if it does not lead to unseemliness; and there has been no sign of that."

The ruling element in Josephine's life had come to be her feeling for Gabriel. She was a woman of emotions rather than affections, and her love for her husband, passionate for years, had failed before the demand of youth.

"He does not call you Simon, sir?" said Fane to Mr. Napier.

"No, he does not give his attention to his address of me," said the latter in his quiet, rather hopeless manner.

"He is making a long stay at home," said Fane.

"Yes, he has left Oxford. He is marking time. Well, time is at his disposal. He will see many things that we shall not."

"Well, we have seen many things that he has not," said Fane. "You have more than I."

"Yes, yes, there is more behind than in front; the past stretches further, the future less far," said Simon, speaking partly to himself. "The road before gets short."

323

"I admire you for saying that," said Felix.

"We should have admired you more," said Gabriel, "if your saying it three times had not shown how you admired it yourself."

"I admired it more each time," said Felix. "I could hardly believe it the third time."

Simon sank into gentle laughter.

Dinner was announced, and Josephine rose and moved across the room, with simple acquiescence in the convention of her leading the way. Simon followed at a gesture from Jonathan, and Fane stepped at this point into the line, with an air of easy acceptance of the rules of precedent. Jonathan came at the end, with his hands on the arms of Felix and his son.

"I am assuming that you are here as the son of the house, in going in before you," said Fane to Gabriel.

"I try to cultivate that position in as many houses as I can."

"I do not," said Felix.

"To-morrow we are swept away on the full tide of the term," said Josephine.

"I suppose the tide ebbs and flows, Mrs. Napier?" said Fane, surveying the effect of this masculine exactitude.

"No, that is just what this tide does not do," said Josephine, causing Simon to smile. "It flows without any ebb and carries us all away with it."

"The force of nature is nothing to that of my aunt, Fane," said Gabriel.

"You do your part by the tide by watching it," said Fane.

"He is watching it at the moment," said Josephine. "There is a great deal in it that is instructive for him. His own profession is to be education. He can do it for a little longer yet."

"It is hard to be reminded how short the time is, between the preparation for life and the living of it," said Gabriel.

"But better than being reminded how long it is," said Felix. "My father wrote this morning about mine, and its being over twenty years. In my birthday letter."

"Many happy returns of the day," said Josephine, turning to him with a smile.

"Thank you so much; I do hope I shall have them."

"It seems a natural hope," said Simon. "Yes, and it may be a sound one."

"Well, I have already had them," said Jonathan. "But I can do with more, if other people can do with me."

"Well, I come of a very long-lived stock," said Fane, looking round.

"I come of a rather short-lived family," said Josephine in a distinct, open tone. "Both my father and grandfather were fine men while they lasted; but they did not last. They both died in the sixties. It seems strange to me that my brother has already lived longer than either of them."

"You are doing a good work, Father, in getting the family out of this habit," said Gabriel. "I hope by the time I attain to three score years it will be definitely broken."

"Would any of us like to know how long we shall live?" said Jonathan.

"That is all very well for you, when you are already sure of so much life," said his son.

"Ah, that would make a difference between us," said Simon, shaking his head.

"No one would like a definite end put to himself," said Gabriel.

"Ah, we cannot guess at our appointed time," said Fane.

"Don't say it in that open manner," said Felix. "You should lower your voice when you speak of death."

"Well, I think one does, if one actually speaks of it," said Fane.

"I think that ignorance on such matters is best," said

Josephine. "It is natural; and whatever is natural is sound."

"Perhaps with the exception of death," said Gabriel.

"I should be sorry to know that I should live beyond the age of usefulness," said Josephine.

"That seems to me the most embarrassing age," said Felix. "I shall begin to be at ease when I am past it."

"Your duties begin to-morrow, my dear," said Jonathan to his sister. "They won't crowd too thickly on the first day of the term."

"Now that shows what you know about it. The first day is the foundation for the other days. And things do not stop in the holidays; there happens to be the post. You seem to be unaware of that, but I am kept aware of it."

"So am I," said Felix.

"Ladies are never averse from finding an outlet for their energies," said Fane. "They have a great amount of vitality."

Simon lifted his eyes to the speaker's face.

"Surely they vary in that way, and in other ways, as men do," said Josephine; "as all human beings must."

"Oh yes, I was not meaning that they were all on the dead level. I meant that their vitality was often out of scale with the rest of them. You must have noticed that, in dealing with women wholesale."

"No, I had not noticed it. What I have noticed, since you bring it to my mind, is that in highly developed people the mental force is often out of scale with the physical. I have found that with men as well as with women. I do not think"—Josephine lifted her eyes in reflection—"that it is a sex difference. And I must just say that I do not deal with women wholesale, but as individuals."

"Oh yes, of course," said Fane, his eyes rather wide open on her face.

"Which is it better to be, a man or a woman?" said Gabriel.

"Ah, that would lead us into thorny paths," said Simon.

"I do not at all mind saying I would rather be a man," said Felix.

Fane glanced at Josephine, as his own content became uneasiness.

"Well, a woman would not make a man, nor a man a woman," he said.

"Is that so?" said Simon, "I know it is said to be."

"So you are a feminist, are you, sir?" said Fane.

Simon smiled and made no reply.

"I cannot imagine any useful and self-respecting person of either sex wishing to belong to the other," said Josephine.

"Neither can I, a person of that kind," said Felix.

"I can't imagine him wishing anything at all," said Gabriel.

"I think you are probably useful in ways we do not know," said Josephine to Felix.

"It is to have it known, that I should be useful. But don't you get tired of usefulness even as recognised as yours?"

"Well, I would not say that it does not sometimes get to be much, as the ball rolls and gathers; but I have never yet found myself in a temper of rebellion. Though the question of recognition had not occurred to me."

"Suppose you did find yourself so? I can't help imagining it in that case."

"Well, I should just have to conceal it; that would be the only course open to me."

"Did you work the school up yourself, Mrs. Napier?" said Fane.

"From a dozen girls," said Josephine, turning fully to him and speaking in a clear tone. "I could not afford more than a moderate sum to buy the goodwill. A large sum it seemed to me then; a smaller one now, of course. It was all that I could muster at the crucial moment. And a very crucial moment it seemed, a great venture, a great risk. But all's well that ends well; and it has ended as I hoped, and not as I feared."

"You were a brave girl, Josephine," said Jonathan.

"I was not a girl. I was over thirty. It was not long before you returned from abroad, and made me a present of your son."

"Take care, Mrs. Napier," said Fane. "You are furnishing us with data, from which we may deduce your age."

"I need not give you the trouble of deducing it. I am nearly fifty-five."

"I was not going to deduce it," said Felix.

"Well, no one would guess it, Mrs. Napier," said Fane at the same moment.

"Well, there wasn't much fear about you, girl or not," said Jonathan.

"There was a good deal underneath. But if I did not show it, I dealt with it in the way it is best to look back on. I am glad it bothered no one but myself. And I soon had my husband's support." Josephine looked round the table and rose.

"You are not leaving us, Josephine?" said her brother. "Wait until we escort you into the drawing-room."

"No," said Josephine, standing to confront the group. "If a woman comes by herself to a party of men, she must abide by her position and fall in with the custom. I think there can be no two opinions. She is one by herself, and must not mind being by herself. I have no objection to my own company, and I see that, in a certain sense, some of you might have an objection to it; and so the matter ends."

She swept her skirts across the room, seeming to be conscious of this difference from her companions, inclined her head as the door was opened, and passed without looking behind her into the hall.

Felix returned to his seat, his face expressionless. Jonathan looked with proprietary affection after his sister.

Fane leaned back, as if freed from some conventional ban on ease. Simon gave a faint sigh.

"I don't believe in sex distinctions," said Felix.

"Ah, a wise woman knows we cannot manage without them," said Fane.

"I always manage without them."

"I saw you open the door for Mrs. Napier."

"But I did not see you. And you and she do believe in sex distinctions. You both keep explaining it. I was adapting myself to others. And I don't call that a sex distinction."

"Living in a stream of women as you do, you must be qualified to judge," said Fane to Simon.

"Living in the stream?" said Simon, looking up. "I should rather say that I watch it flowing, and every now and then get touched by the spray."

Fane regarded him in silence.

"You do no other work besides what you do in your school?"

"No, no other. And the school is my wife's."

"What a way to talk!" said Gabriel to Fane. "What work do you do, besides what you do in your office?"

"You are interested in your work?" said Fane, not taking his eyes from Simon.

"Yes, I am interested. I could wish that my pupils were sometimes more so," said Simon, between a smile and a genuine sigh.

"If I ever work, I shall try to have just that touch," said Felix. "I don't think my father talks more about work than other people."

"Let us talk about something else, for heaven's sake," said Jonathan.

"And for my sake," said Gabriel. "I am conscious of my present position."

"That is the worst of a temporary arrangement, said Felix. "One is never at ease. It is better to make it permanent."

"Could I let my aunt support me?"

"Yes, if you don't believe in sex distinctions. Men often support people. Nearly always, my father tells me."

"You have to be able to accept, my boy," said Jonathan, looking with affection at Gabriel. "It is one of the things we have to learn. Unwillingness implies a lack of generosity, a reluctance to grant anyone else the superior place."

"My father has never appreciated me," said Felix.

"I suppose that is why a gift is so often called a loan," said Gabriel.

"Ah, a good deal is done under the guise of borrowing," said Fane. "I have never borrowed; I can say that for myself."

"I have never borrowed. But I have accepted," said Jonathan.

"Two noble things instead of one," said Gabriel.

"Well, good things enough," said Jonathan. "Let us go into the other room. We are forgetting that your aunt is alone."

"We are, for the advantage we have taken of her absence," said Gabriel. "She left us to be men together, and we have decided vaguely against borrowing."

"Well, this is a subject it is safe to broach with you, Mrs. Napier," said Fane, entering the sitting-room. "You have never borrowed. I am sure of that."

"Yes, I have borrowed," said Josephine, laying down her book. "I borrowed a small sum from a friend in the early stages of my school, the very early stages." She paused with an almost grim smile. "I paid it back within three months."

"So you had to be thankful without any permanent benefit," said Gabriel.

"I was very thankful. And I began to earn as fast as ever I could."

"Do you know many people who earn?" said Felix.

"Yes, a great many. And a goodly proportion of them I have put in the way of earning myself."

"Could you put me in the way of it? I have heard that you want a drawing-master; and my drawing is very good; and my father says that I might be a woman."

"Now I think that is a foolish joke. I do not regard teaching of any kind as a matter for jesting. You will forgive my taking my own profession seriously?"

"Of course, when it is my profession."

"Now," said Josephine, leaning back and betraying in her voice a hope that it might be as she said: "am I to take you as being in earnest or not?"

"It shows what harm I have done to my reputation. I am like a man out of prison. If no one will employ me, how can I redeem my character?"

"You would not object to having a man teaching in your school, Mrs. Napier?" said Fane.

"No," said Josephine. "I do not see any reason for objecting to it. With certain things granted, of course."

"They are all granted with me," said Felix. "I do not even like to have such things talked about."

"Do you feel you have a gift for teaching?" said Josephine, looking straight into his face.

"I feel I have a gift for drawing. And that has always been a reason for teaching it."

"Yes, and there might be worse reasons," said Josephine, sitting back and speaking as if to herself.

"Thank you so much for engaging me. I will try to do my duty. And I will write to my father to-night."

Simon fell into rather doubtful mirth.

"The whole business is settled, then?" said Fane, looking about.

"Are you thinking about my stipend?" said Felix. "I am not at all ashamed of talking about it."

"You ought to be, if you talk about it like that," said Gabriel.

"Why should you be?" said Josephine. "The labourer is worthy of his hire."

"Yes, that is it, I know," said Felix. "But I have conquered myself."

"Now I hope," said Josephine, "that you have no feeling of its being beneath you to teach, or to teach girls?"

"I see now why workers have unions against employers."

"Well, shall we proceed to the practical side the next time we are alone?"

"The practical side! That is what I should have said. Are we ever alone?"

"Do you know what my last drawing mistress, teacher had?" said Josephine, in a voice that seemed to be lower, in spite of herself.

"It was a mistress," said Felix. "I have found out what she had."

"Then what about half as much again?" said Josephine, bringing her tones to an open level.

"You are not in favour of equal pay for equal work! Fancy being as experienced as that!"

"No," said Josephine, leaning back. "Men have more material responsibilities than women. I do not pretend to think that the same standards can apply."

"I am glad you do not take my father's view of me."

"Did your last teacher live in the school, Mrs. Napier?" said Fane.

"My drawing master or mistress is never resident."

Simon frowned slightly, his eyes down.

"Would not a woman serve your purpose as well?" said Fane.

"Yes," said Josephine. "Fully as well. But no woman of suitable attainments has presented herself."

"Pray do not conspire against my livelihood, Fane," said Felix.

"You are not allowed a say—do not have a say in the matter, sir?" said Fane to Simon.

"He is very kind in giving me his advice," said Josephine. "The school owes him a great deal."

"Well, you will have a companion in distress," Fane said to Felix, unable to adapt himself beyond a point.

"How many companions shall I have, Mrs. Napier?"

"I do not remember at the moment the exact number." Fane looked at Josephine.

"All ladies but the two gentlemen here?"

"No, not all."

"Oh, you have other men in your school?"

"Yes."

"And what do they teach?"

"Each his own subject," said Josephine, speaking the truth of her visiting masters.

"Oh, it would be regarded—it is a high class of school?" said Fane.

"I should soon give it up, if it did not merit some description of that kind. The keepers of schools cannot but be the makers of the future. I would not face the responsibility of not doing the work faithfully."

"Of course everyone goes to school," said Felix. "It does exalt my profession."

"Will you put your nephew into the school, Mrs. Napier?" said Fane, feeling that matters might go so far.

"No," said Josephine in a full, rounded tone. "He and I have lived so much on equal terms, that I feel he might not fancy me as a task-mistress. He looks to me for other things. And we must not put all our eggs into one basket. My school might fail like anyone else's."

"Then I should be out of work," said Felix.

"No," said Josephine quietly. "No one would be out of work. My testimonial would secure that. The school has its past. And now we have talked of school out of school long enough."

"Thank you all for taking an interest in my future," said Felix.

"It would be shocking to be a woman, and have less pay for the same work," said Gabriel. "For more work in many cases."

"Yes, on the whole, women are harder workers than men," said Josephine, her voice making no comment on this difference.

"There doesn't on the face of it seem any reason for it," said Jonathan.

"No," said his sister.

"You find that you get more out of your women than your men, Mrs. Napier?" said Fane.

"No, I do not find that," said Josephine, bending her head as if to suppress a smile. "But I have to inculcate more lessons on the sparing of themselves."

"They have fewer interests for their leisure," said Fane. "Public matters mean less to them."

"I think that if you were to hear my debating society, you would modify your opinion there."

"Perhaps the women you employ are hardly average women."

"Well, you would hardly apply the term 'average,' to a Cambridge wrangler, and two first classes at Oxford, women or not," said Josephine, looking at the window.

Simon slowly raised himself in his chair.

"I wonder they don't want to try their wings further afield," said Fane.

"Further afield?" queried Josephine.

"I mean in a more significant sphere."

"What sphere is more significant than education?"

Fane did not suggest one.

"Pray do not belittle my calling, Fane," said Felix.

"Does an element of self-sacrifice add to a life or take from it?" Simon asked himself in a low tone. "Some great men have seen no beauty in it. Well, so it is."

"There is very little self-sacrifice in the life of my mistresses," said his wife. "I see to that. And very ashamed I should be of myself if I did not."

334

"I am very fortunate," said Felix.

"Now, make no mistake," said Josephine. "I expect your best, your whole best, and nothing but your best. Then you shall find yourself as fortunate as I can make you."

"I need not suppress any charm that is natural to me, need I?"

"You need not indeed. I am the last person to want my pupils to be blind to charm, or to belittle it myself in my staff. I am fortunate in having got together a good deal of it."

"Do you think I shall have the most charm on your staff?"

"Well, I can hardly say," said Josephine in a serious voice. "There are some very charming women on it. I am sometimes struck by it, when I come on them unawares. I must be on my guard against taking a rare thing for granted."

"Yes, you must," said Felix.

"I will indeed," said Josephine. "And now it is time for me to get my cloak. Men of mine, be ready to escort me home."

"What purpose are you serving by this scheme?" said Gabriel to Felix.

"I want to see some life, and to wear out and not rust out, and to retaliate on my father."

"You won't see much life in a girls' school."

"That is where you are so superficial. I shall see an unusual sort of life."

"Yes, a school is a miniature world," said Jonathan, giving a yawn.

"That is just what it is not," said Felix; "or I should not take any interest in it. My father is a man of the world. It is little, unnatural corners of the world that appeal to me. I am very over-civilised."

"That is nothing to be proud of," said Fane.

"Oh, I don't agree with you," said Felix.

335

"No, it is hard to agree to that," said Simon, shaking his head.

"I will go and get a telephone call to my father," said Felix; "and tell him that his birthday letter has fulfilled its purpose, and led me to work; and that as he compares me to a woman, I thought it would be best to teach drawing in a girls' school."

"You will do nothing for our friendship by this," said Gabriel, following him into the hall.

"I don't want to do anything for it," said Felix, dancing towards the telephone. "It is not a thing I take any interest in. We are on the telephone at my father's expense. He does not approve of modern inventions, but he knows that I cannot be homesick when I can always hear his voice."

Josephine appeared on the stairs and bent smilingly from her height.

"You are going to telephone?" she said in a pleasant manner.

"Yes, to my father," said Felix.

"Will you please remember me to him," said Josephine in the same manner.

"My boy," said Jonathan to Gabriel, "the evening has meant much to me. You will spare me another? I make no claim; I have no claim. I depend on your generosity."

"I think you depend a little on my generosity, too," said Josephine, adjusting her wrap with her husband's aid.

"I know it; I am grateful. I have a great deal to be thankful for; I hope I am thankful. Good-bye, my dear sister. Good-bye, my son."

Jonathan embraced both his sister and his son, according to his custom, while Felix stood with his eyes averted, as if by chance, from the family scene, and Fane with his attention held by it.

"Well, I have a great deal in my life," said Jonathan. "They give me a generous affection that I have done little to deserve. Is that the telephone? Any message for me?"

"No, it is for me," said Felix. "A word from my father on the coming change in my life. I will be back in a few minutes."

"It must be quite that," said Fane at length. "Ah, we thought your time would be up, Bacon."

"I refused a second allowance of minutes. It was astonishing how much we said in the first. I began to realise how it would be, if we did not waste a moment of our lives."

"Well, what does your father say to your plan?"

"That it was what he would have expected. That is quite untrue. He would never have expected me to teach in a girls' school. That if I choose to behave in an undignified manner for a pittance, it is my own affair. That is the best definition of work I have heard. When do my so-called duties start? I said the day after to-morrow. Shall I wear petticoats to fulfil them in? I said I should wear my two everyday suits alternately, that I had no petticoats. As he pays the bills for all my clothes, he ought to know that."

"I admit it seems odd work for a gentleman," said Fane. "I don't make any secret of it."

"My father didn't think it was a secret either. To me any work seems odd for a gentleman; but I think that is rather a secret."

"There is plenty of work suitable for a man of any position. We have conquered the old prejudice against the learned professions."

"Teaching ought to be a learned profession. Have we conquered the prejudice?"

"Wouldn't it be better to teach boys, if you must teach?"

"My father said that, too. It is impossible to think of anything he did not say. And then they asked if I would have some more time! How clever it was to hit on the amount that just gets everything in!"

"Well, I will go to bed," said Fane. "I have a day's work before me."

"I wonder if I shall say that as often as other people."

"Ah, it is easy to begin to work. It is when the novelty wears off that the crux comes."

"I shall be glad when the novelty wears off."

"He is an inquisitive fellow," said Jonathan, as the door closed.

"Well, it is natural to be curious about my teaching drawing to girls. I am sorry to think my own affairs interesting, but I do think they are at the moment."

"Ah, Felix, your mind will be on Gabriel, and I shall be forgotten."

"I shall come home to you a tired bread-winner. I suppose I am a bread-winner, even if all the bread I win is for myself. Bread-winners' own bread hardly seems to count. But there has been so much talk about who pays for my meals."

"Felix, I ask you earnestly not to do for Gabriel what I have done for you."

"People are so open about wanting others to learn by their mistakes, instead of feeling that the less said about them the better. They almost seem to have made them for others to learn by. I have heard that there is self-indulgence in all sacrifice."

"Ah, I will conquer myself: I know I am thinking of myself: I do not think of the boy. I am a miserable old man, useless at the work I love, a burden on the friend I love, jealous of my own son. But I will be happy in what I have had, happy to give it up, now that the time has come. I am not one of those who have had nothing."

"I think I am going to be one of them," said Felix, taking his usual seat on Jonathan's knees. "I think I should have had something by now, if I were not."

CHAPTER IV

"WHY, Adela," said Josephine, shaking her latchkey at a maid who was waiting in her hall, "what is the good of my burdening myself with the insignia of a householder, if you are to stay up and make it useless? I undertake to be equal to the work of the morrow, late hours or not, but I have not the handicap of youth. A lady to see me, who insisted on waiting? Well, I have known people come at stranger times. Parent, pupil, former pupil, future parent? Which of them needs my help to the point of snatching my sleep?"

She entered the house, to be met by a clear, carrying voice, as a tall, dark woman broke out of a room to meet her, pushing back her veil to reveal the full, black eyes, the crinkling black hair, and the keenly cut nose and chin of a friend of her youth.

"Home, sweet home at last! Yes, it shall be sweet, though I have lost so much since I left it, and come back to it so old and poor and sad. I will have the spirit to make it so. You, who remember me of old, will not doubt the spirit. Both of you have had the early hopes fulfilled? I am too glad, for my heart to grow sick with my own still deferred. You will tell of the happiness to an ear so ready to listen."

"Elizabeth! Elizabeth Giffard!" said Josephine. "After all these years of silence! The voice struck my ears like an echo from the past."

"This meeting has been in my mind many times," said Simon, advancing with gentle eagerness. "The many imaginings have made it true."

"I had almost given up hope of it," said his wife. "And now it has come to pass, I think the heroine of the occasion should be sitting in this easy chair, and having a glass of this wine, and some of these sandwiches, that are not put here to be looked at. Now I think that is a great deal better."

"Such a lot of thought and kindness, that I am sure the old affection is underneath! It lies too deep in my own heart not to have its place in yours. So many storms have passed over it, and left it unscathed! Now, tell me of your life together, and the adopted son, and the success. Yes, I heard of the so brave ventures. I had no fear when I heard of them, when the little bird with the tidings flitted between you and me. Yes, little birds have known where they would find a welcome. I have not sent them back with only sad words to say. But now I will feel the happiness, though it is not mine. It shall be mine indeed."

"This is Gabriel Swift, our adopted son, my brother's boy," said Josephine. "I took him off Jonathan's hands, when he was a few months old, soon after I set up the school, and a short time before I married."

"Yes, yes, I know it all: I have not a short memory where my friends are concerned. And I heard you were to have a husband to help in the brave undertakings. My daughter was born at the time of your marriage, a few months after her father died, the father she never saw. So my child lost a father, and yours gained one. Well, that was how it was to be."

"It sounds a reproach to me," said Gabriel. "Is there anything I can do to atone?"

"Ah, I daresay there will be something. My girl will be glad to have a comrade. But at the moment my mind must be given to these old comrades of my own. I heard of the wedding when I could not write, when my baby was a few days old. I could only think of both of you. My heart was too full for anything else, too full of joy and sorrow. Both were there; yes, I will be just. And my heart found room for friends again; it was closed for such a little while. It was on your honeymoon that you heard that I had a daughter?"

"It was then that we heard of your husband's death," said Simon. "We heard the good and the sad tidings at the same time."

"I sent the other word to Josephine, when I was first alone; when I felt so weak, and remembered her as so strong. But it was not the moment for it; poor Josephine, it was not! I was so sorry afterwards to have sent such a sad, sad word. Yes, when I knew, I understood; I am not a person who misunderstands; I only feared I had done harm. But Josephine was herself, and went on her own brave way. And now I see her in the midst of all that came of it."

"We neither of us heard before our marriage," said Simon. "We had the letter that came on our honeymoon. I remember we sent the answer at once."

"Such a sweet answer! It gave me courage to go forward. I did not know how hard the world was to the widow and the fatherless. Well, I did not keep silence, to bring the sadness after all. So let me hear some of the dear, good news."

"I am sure we heard of your husband's death on our honeymoon," said Simon.

"I remember making it clear to you then, anyhow," said Josephine. "It would have been too much to be sure of accomplishing before. If Elizabeth meant to write a letter, or we meant to read one, when we were all immersed in the deeps of our experience, we shall none of us misunderstand."

"Well, a letter in the past is not to be compared with friendship in the present. I will take the one in exchange for the other with all my heart."

"Now, do you want this callow youth as witness of your reunion?" said Josephine. "I will spare you the constraint of his presence, and myself the discredit of missing our evening hour together, or any other lapse along that line. It is for my peace to keep in his good graces, but it makes less difference to yours. Don't think that I don't remember the old bond between you two. It is a pity for a tie of that kind to be broken. It seems to me such a sad thing, when the deep relations of life blot out the lighter memories that are the heritage from youth. So I will leave you to clasp your hands over the gulf of your experience. Don't think we want to be witnesses of that dramatic scene."

Elizabeth turned her smiling face from the closing door.

"So you heard that I was a widow, after you were married yourself, Simon?" she said, her voice making the sound of the name sweet.

"Yes, that is how I remember it," said Simon, his lips just framing the words.

"Well, and how did that come about? Well, it came about in one way or another. It was best for you to go to the chosen life, chosen, I am sure, so wisely for you, undistraught by anything that might lead you aside; or it was thought best. We are in the hands of—what shall we call it? Fate? Let us call it Fate. That is the best word, or shall we say the wisest?"

Simon did not speak.

"We must be good and wise. And it is never good and wise to think of what might have been, never good and wise to judge. I think that Josephine seems greater and wiser than ever now, Simon. Her face has gained with the years, if I may say a pretty thing to you about your wife. There is something there, that sits better on it than youth. But I did not realise that youth was so far behind: perhaps life is not always in such a hurry with its later gifts?"

"You have not let me hear from you for over twenty years," said Simon.

"Ah, you did not let me hear from you, when the months were as long as all the years afterwards."

"What are your plans for the future? I may ask that, even if I have no claim on the past."

"Ah, plans are for the more fortunate. They are not for lonely widows, lacking in the world's goods, not for the people who need them. I am lodging here, to live for

342

a while in my memories, and give my girl a glimpse of the scene of my youth. Through her childhood I have done whatever would keep her with me, always trying, trying to keep above it all. Trying with who knows how much success? I don't know what the verdict will be."

"Well, I do," said Josephine, returning to the room; "and one flattering enough even for you; and I remember how exacting you were in the matter of a compliment. Not that I think that any kind of work needs so much keeping above, you know. That is my own prosaic opinion. But what are you running away for? Can't you be comfortable here a little longer? I don't see anything in this room to frighten you."

"There is so much for me to see and appreciate and— no, I won't say envy—put from me as above my own claims, that I think I will run away, as you use that word. But I will run back again; a glimpse won't hurt me; it will only confirm that my friends still have the best. I have so prized our dear meeting after all these years. So now fare you well. Not that I need to say that to you. Does Simon have to leave the fire to speed poor me on my path?"

"Now, you stay where you are," said Josephine to her husband. "You and your chill have not yet parted company. Do you think I didn't notice your appetite at dinner, or your lack of it? I am used to doing the honours in this house. Such a great barrack of a place it seemed at first, for me to do the honours in!" She followed her guest to the door, continuing her speech. "Well, it is my lot, what I have undertaken. I meet it day by day, as it comes."

"Well, you have your husband to help you," said Elizabeth, walking in front. "He and I were great friends once, you know. You do know; you left us for a minute to remember it. We found the minute enough; we remembered many things; our old times together, his feelings when I was engaged, dear Simon, his surprise

343

when he heard too late of my husband's death. You thought it best he should have the surprise. Ah, poor, foolish girl that I was!"

"You were a woman when your husband died."

"Yes, poor, foolish woman that I was! It was more foolish in a woman. I should have known the risk; I had known you.' Elizabeth quickened her pace, almost as if she were fleeing from Josephine. "But yet I had not known you; perhaps I could not; perhaps the difference between us was too great. I have to blame my own innocence. Yes, it was strange in a woman of my age. You must find it strange. At the same age you had not that innocence."

"You know that Simon is always your friend," said Josephine, as the door of the hall brought them to a pause. "We did not suspect that you had this other feeling. Believe me, we did not; perhaps we had our own innocence. Your secret will be safe, even safe from Simon, and it is from him that you will want it to be safe."

"Yes, I think the secret is safe from Simon; that many things are safe from him."

"My dear, it was when you were the widow of another man, that you wrote to me, or thought you wrote. If Simon and I were blind to anything outside each other —perhaps we should admit we were for a time; well, we will both admit it—and a letter got passed over or put aside, it could have meant very little. It was when your future was dawning, that you wrote the letter to be answered, that could be answered by people in our state of mind. And we answered it at once; I remember reminding Simon, that it was his words rather than mine, that would bring you comfort. I was glad to hear you say that they brought it to you. He has to be kept to those little duties, as you who know him so well, must know; though that was a deep and pressing duty to both of us; you know that, too. But the things you have said, would give even me a wrong impression, if I let them.

But I will not let them; do not fear; do not let your hard experience warp your judgement. Tell me your troubles, and lean on me. I am so used to being leant on."

"My troubles," said Elizabeth, weeping into her hands, "are poverty and loneliness and anxiety for my child. I must earn my bread and hers, and I have nothing that people need. I have suffered to the last in eating bread they thought I did not earn, those people who seemed so much below me. It has been bitter bread; and no one in my life has helped me."

"Now can I help you?" said Josephine, in an open, considering tone, as if the foregoing talk had left little impression on her mind. "You would at least be with friends, if you took a place in my house. I have to replace my housekeeper, who is leaving me to be married. If her work would be easy for you, it is time you found things easy. And nobody would taunt you with eating bread you did not earn, even though it were a little more than bread. And in a school your daughter would find a place. I don't know how that sounds to you?"

"Such a blessing, such a breaking of light. I would accept it so gratefully, if I felt I was deserving. But I have said things out of the bitterness of my heart, when in yours there was kindness."

"Well, be thankful you said them to someone who knew you could not mean them. And tell me when you will come and bring your daughter, for both of us to care for together. I shall be grateful for your help as soon as you will give it, as I have put your predecessor's convenience before my own."

"Then I will come at once, to get used to my duties. Such sacred duties they will be to me, so faithfully discharged! So much I shall have to learn from you, and will learn so readily, or I should not be the woman I am. I think you remember my old self, though I have shown it through such a darkness. I am that old self still at bottom : I don't know if I look at all the same at the top?"

345

"You have altered much less than I have. People would hardly guess we were the same age. It is strange how differently the years deal with us, what divers things they give and take."

"So you have forgiven my yielding to bitterness at the contrast of our lots? It is seldom that I sink so low. But enough pressure forces us to anything, and I had had enough. My measure was full to overflowing, and it overflowed. I had drunk too deeply of the bitter cup; but it will be mingled with sweetness now." Elizabeth went with her light, quick steps towards the door. "Our old friendship is the basis of a new life together, with you at the top and me at the bottom, and such a lot of love in all the space between. The spirit that broke its bonds just now, has escaped. Your success shall be sweet to me. And so for such a short time, good-bye." She held out her hand, but Josephine drew her forward and kissed her on the cheek, and then, as if asking nothing in return, released her at once from her house and her embrace.

Simon hardly looked up as his wife returned.

"Well, still out of bed?" she said in a rather excited voice.

"You did not tell me, Josephine, when Elizabeth's husband died."

"Yes, I told you, and urged you to write her a letter, and had almost to sit over you while you did it, if my memory serves."

"That was on our honeymoon, when he had been dead for some months, if your memory serves there too. She said she wrote to you when he died."

"Well, now she says she did not write. And what an ugly, bitter, little voice! Poor Elizabeth! We need not load up on her every word she said, in a moment of emotion and what not. It is a good thing she chose to utter her retracting words to me. I could see her making her choice, and had mercy on her. You see, I knew her so well."

"Her voice did not sound as if she were uttering such words."

"Oh, we had the bout of emotion we were bound to have, as two weak women alone. You would not have expected her to have it with you. I had seen it gathering. Poor Elizabeth is often not mistress of herself."

"Did she retract her statement that she wrote to you at the time of her husband's death?"

"No," said Josephine, slightly drawing herself up. "I knew she was prepared to retract it, and so I did not require her to. I did not wish her to take more on herself than had to be: I saw she was not in a fit state. I don't want to push my advantage to the uttermost. I never have any use for that line."

"Are we to see her again soon? I hope we shall often meet."

"Well, I am glad to hear that," said his wife, with a faint note of triumph, "as she is settling here at once as housekeeper. We shall meet her every day, whether we want to or not. And we ought to want to; she is an old friend of us both." She ended with her voice dying away, and her eyes on the bookcase, and walking forward, took a book.

"Did you arrange that just now?"

"Well, it was obvious that we did not arrange it when she was in here," said Josephine, turning a page.

"Was it her wish?"

"My dear Simon, it was she who was worked up, because we did not see the desire in her mind, not I. Because I did not see it. She acquits you, I am sure; Elizabeth would always acquit a man. It is a woman whose instinct is supposed not to fail, as mine failed, I admit."

"She is coming here as housekeeper?"

"That is what she wanted. That is what I perceived her to want. That is what I ought to have perceived before. That is what I offered to her, when I perceived she wanted it. That is what she forgave me for not offering, when she accepted it. Well, is that all you want to know?"

"I am very glad," said Simon.

"So am I," said Josephine, in an open manner. "I am fond of Elizabeth, and shall enjoy having her working under me; working with me, for there is no question of top and bottom in my conception of work. She went about the business in a baffling spirit, but characteristic, poor, strung-up creature that she is!"

"I hope it will be a suitable post for her."

"Well, you are a nice kind of customer! Of course it is suitable, when she needs it, and has no other, and can have her daughter with her, when another might involve a parting."

"Her daughter will live here, will she?"

"My good Simon, how can we separate a mother and her child, when the mother is a widow, and the child of the dependent sex? You are not a fiend, and neither am I; so it is no good our pretending, convenient though it might be. And don't keep looking at me as if I were one. You have been adopting that expression for some time, and it is the reverse of becoming. You must see that what either of us wants, has no bearing on the matter."

"I do, indeed, see it, Josephine. I have been let into a sorry muddle."

"Well, don't keep harping on it. A muddle is not any better because it is sorry. The sorrier, the worse, in my humble imagination. I don't wonder that you became muddle-headed in meeting the romance of your youth. Don't think that I don't know about that. I heard enough of it at the time when her affections were in process of being transferred, and she was keeping you as a sort of second string to her bow, as far as I could gather. I even had a word of that time to-day, when she was referring, and frankly, too, to the changes that time had wrought in you and me. Ah, Elizabeth had her ways. A leopard does not change his spots, or change his feeling that spots are rather a credit. Well, women of her kind have a right to put their gifts to their natural use. We must not find fault with what is natural. And in spite of your concern for her, it did not occur to you to escort her home. It is a good thing that you were out of her mind."

Elizabeth went from Josephine's door with rapid feet and upright head, her face betraying her inward rehearsal of a humorous scene. When she reached her lodging, she leaned over the steps and tapped with a sprightly hand on the window.

"Such nice, prompt attendance! Thank you, pretty parlourmaid," she said, as her daughter came to the door. "It is late at night to bring the wretch from below. Such funny things I have witnessed, late though it is! A little refreshment will help me to evoke them. So surprised would Josephine be by my needing it, when so much has been offered me. I could not feel tempted, when it all seemed so valuable and so valued. Now I can't waste my gifts on a lackadaisical audience: let your mother keep what is her heritage, what has stood between us and so many things. The truth defies even my talent for pictures in words. Josephine, looking like a statesman in a woman's dress! Such a sinking of the heart I had, when I remembered we were young together! The funny sight, but sad too, poor Simon! And the end the funniest part of all, that I am to be housekeeper in the school where she is head mistress! Such a contradiction of all memories!" Elizabeth wiped her eyes, as if her tears of mirth had changed their kind. "I wonder if Josephine will think of it. Well, what do you say to your news?"

"I have hardly had my own news yet," said her daughter, in her husky, languid tones, turning to her mother her dark, unusual face, with its absent, indifferent eyes and curved and protruding lips. "What part am I to play in this comedy, tragedy, tragi-comedy? It is the first of the three, I gather, with the hearts of clowns as sad as they are said to be."

"As if that were not the point, that I am to keep you with me! As if I should have yielded to pressure, if they

349

had not pressed that! Ah, they saw your mother and remembered her. And it need not be such a place as some of them have been. I know you have been brought to a dark outlook. Yes, a sad burden to bear, and shoulders tried by bearing it! But young shoulders are supple, and the least harm comes to the bravest. We have spirit to recover, and I think that the time has come for recovery. Keep up your heart, or your mother's heart will fail. There will be enough to make it in this new life based upon the old. But poor Josephine and Simon! I feel so much sorrier for them, than they for me, if only they knew."

"We can hardly expect them to guess it. Is the problem of my clothes to be left to solve itself? I suppose I shall need the outfit of everyone, with everything made a little stronger, to stand an extra strain. The bright side of not being trained to any one thing is that you are qualified for all things."

"No, it is not to be left to solve itself; it is to be left to your mother to solve. I have brains and hands, and the skill and will to use them, and an extra spur this time to urge my gifts to their best. There will be other eyes than mine to be rejoiced by the sight of my daughter. I am not making a mistake in taking you to Josephine's house. It is not for nothing that I have an eye to character. I am not of the meek who inherit the earth. Enough of the earth will do, to make a share for you. Ah, Cinderella in her ashes was a princess. And it is not meet that some should be so light, and others so heavy laden."

CHAPTER V

JOSEPHINE entered the room known as the library, which was the scene of her family life, and coming up to the table, paused with her hand upon it.

"Well, I have welcomed the junior staff. They have gone to their quarters, taking with them a word from me. I have done for them what I did for their seniors yesterday. I cannot bear the thought of these women, coming from some distant place, it may be, not meeting with any respect and understanding in their work and their lives."

"You do not assume that we find the thought bearable?" said Gabriel.

"Can I be of any help to you, Josephine?" said Simon, in a manner of saying what should be said, whether or no with hope of result.

"No. Everything is on its foundation now. The classrooms are arranged and assigned; the one thing was as much of a business as the other. The new basis of the accounts is settled. That took some delving into the deeps of one's mind; but, as it hardly seemed advisable to add a chartered accountant to our staff, I delved until the result commended itself. The time-tables are organised, in so far as it is possible for human capacity to bring them to such a stage. The preliminary steps are behind; it is only the term that is ahead."

The intensity of Josephine's tone caused Simon to lift his eyes, and she continued in a different manner.

"The worst of it is, that another little piece of energy is behind too. Well, we can only go on until our store runs out."

"I am glad you have come in while you have some left," said Gabriel. "We should not expect to make a move towards our own refreshment. And pouring out tea would stress my position as companion."

"As companion you need do no more," said Josephine.

"And I am very used to making any moves that are necessary."

"The best companionship is known to rest upon difference," said Simon, with an indulgent smile. "The impulse that has had its result in the school, as yet hardly repeats itself."

"Impulse!" said his wife. "It takes something more than impulse, to set on foot a large, organic concern; to give it its life, to breath its vitality into it every day, to keep from somewhere at its source, a hand on the pulsing current that looks to you for its force. Not much in that line would be done, if we trusted to mere impulse."

"It would be safer to trust to every human quality we possessed," said Gabriel.

"Yes, that is just about what we have to do. And the more we possess, the better."

"It was not a considered word, Josephine," said her husband.

"Now don't get absorbed in discussion just as the kettle is boiling. I am housewife as well as head mistress, and laxity falls as hard on me in one sphere as in the other."

"And I am master in logic and history," said Simon.

"And be thankful that you have the work to do. What would any of us be, without our work?"

"I should be a leisured man," said Simon.

"I should be what I am," said Gabriel.

"You are a boy, just through your boy's training. But your uncle talks as if he carried the weight of the house, when his work would not keep the wolf from the door."

Simon's face relaxed into a resigned, but settled hopelessness.

"The wolf is always represented as at such close quarters," said Gabriel. "Why may he not lurk at the outer gate?"

"He is not at any distance at all, thanks to the school that you both regard with such bare tolerance."

"I admit he would be too much for me single-handed,"

said Simon. "But I am grateful for myself for my privilege of a day's work."

"It is a foolish theory that a man should not give his life to teaching girls," said Josephine. "A woman would not be ashamed of teaching boys; and the two things are just the same."

"They may be said to be the opposite of each other," said Simon. "But I am of your mind, my dear; I am not above teaching anyone."

"We should be strange people, indeed, to be above that."

"We should, in two ways," said Simon.

"I am above teaching girls in the despicable way," said Gabriel.

"You are a very young man," said Josephine. "It would not be suitable for you or for them. But your opportunities would have been very different, if I had been above teaching them, or below it. The one, as your uncle says, was as likely as the other."

"Don't say it was all done to prepare for my future, the future that does not come to pass."

"Are you at home, madam?" said the maid at the door.

"Well, I think we may say we are, Adela," said Josephine. "I cannot see any reason why we are not."

"Adela means, are we ready for guests?" said Simon, with his faint frown.

"Well, I think we are. Here is a good fire, and a good tea, and everything governed by law and order. It seems to me rather an opportune moment for guests. The more, the merrier, I say for my part."

Simon for his part said nothing, and Felix Bacon entered the room.

"Well, how are you?" said Josephine. "Have you come to see us professionally, or as a friend? I need not say how welcome you are in either character."

"I have come professionally. Perhaps I am not any

longer your friend. I am here because I heard you were seeing your staff to-day. I am the last person to presume on the past."

"Will you have some tea with us, and then come with me to my study? Your colleagues have tea in their room upstairs, but you are rather late to join them. You have the run of that common room, when you are in the house. Some people separate the men and women in a school; I believe it is the usual thing; but I have never seen any reason for doing so myself."

"It would be dreadful if you saw reasons, especially in a school for girls. I am surprised that the men and women have to be separated, and that it is the usual thing. I will do nothing out of my sphere; so I will come with you to your study. Am I the only newcomer this term?"

"There is Miss Keats, the new, young, classical mistress," said Josephine, walking at his side to the door; "a very gifted and accomplished girl. You will be interested to meet her."

"I have always wanted to meet someone really accomplished, to compare myself with. Do you sit alone in this study? I think I am glad I belong to a common room. It seems to be you, who really have to be separated."

"Yes. It works out like that," said Josephine, looking for something in her desk. "Yes, here is your time-table. Your hours and classes are marked. I hope you will enjoy your work here, the more that I knew you as a friend before we came together as colleagues. That has not often happened to me."

"I hope it does not give me an unfair advantage?"

"Now, you will know better than to talk about advantage, when you have known me as a head mistress a little longer."

"I already know better. I am very uncomfortable at fancying that I might be singled out. How many of us are there, equal in the common room?"

"In the senior room, where you belong, Miss Munday, Miss Rosetti, Miss Luke, Mrs. Chattaway and Miss Keats; besides the visiting masters, who are there at times. You know them by sight, except Miss Keats. She is young to belong to that room, but is there by virtue of her work. Mrs. Chattaway is there by virtue of her age; her work is in the junior school. It might be uncongenial for her to be always with younger women."

"Am I there by virtue of my age or my work? It would not be uncongenial to me to be with younger women."

"Now I daresay it would not," said Josephine, pointing at him with her pencil. "But I would have you know that there are other things here to command your attention."

"But it would be more congenial to be with the older ones, though you may not believe it."

"Yes, I believe it; I think I should have guessed it. You are in that room by virtue of your work. When that is the case, the question of age does not arise."

"That is a good thing, as I do not confess to my age. I suppose Mrs. Chattaway does to hers. It shows how untrue it is, that women are less ready to admit their age than men."

"I do not know her exact age. I have found her very kind and charming as a friend, as I have all the members of my staff."

"I did not mean to talk about Mrs. Chattaway's exact age. I hope they none of them presume upon their friendship?"

"I trust that they deal with me fully as a friend. I hardly understand that phrase, 'presume upon friendship.'"

"I quite understand it. Shall we have a gossip about your staff?"

"No!" said Josephine. "When you have known me a little longer, you will know that my mistresses, in their presence and in their absence, are safe with me. I hope I could say that of all my friends."

"I hoped you could not. But it is interesting that they would not be safe, if we had the gossip. They must have treated you fully as a friend. I almost feel we have had it."

"You will find that not much gossip is done here," said Josephine, smiling as if in spite of herself.

"I suppose it hardly could be in a common room."

"Either there or elsewhere."

"And in a community of women! I am glad I am seeing life for myself, as all the theories about it are untrue. Now I see that you are dismissing me with a look. Of course you are one of those people whose glance is obeyed."

Josephine gave him a bow from her desk, and when he had gone, returned to the library.

"Well, there is another person sent on his path with a word! I could hardly be blamed if my stock of apposite words gave out, with the demand upon it. Happily it seems to increase with need. Nothing would do for Felix, but that he should be initiated with due and official ceremony."

"Do you think you will get on with him in his new character?" said Gabriel.

"Well, if I do not, he will be the first person I have not got on with."

"You have never dealt with anyone who has been a friend first."

"Friend first, fellow-worker afterwards; fellow-worker first, friend afterwards! What is the difference?"

"The others may feel there is one."

"Indeed they will not. I can set your mind at rest there."

"Will the mistresses like him about in their common room? He will be there oftener than the other men."

"Well, I should think they will. I find him very charming; and I do not see why they should not do the same. I make it a rule in making arrangements for people, to judge them by myself. It is the best, the simplest, and the friendliest thing."

"Suppose you have to give him notice?" said Gabriel. Simon laughed.

"Well, I have had, of course, to break my relation, professionally, with certain people. That is simply as it has had to be. But I have never terminated it in any other sense; they have always remained my friends. In one case a woman came back to me and was married from my house: I found she regarded it as her home. It was a good thing I did not realise that before, or I should have felt some scruples in parting with her. But now, with my trained judgement, I should not be mistaken."

"It will be difficult to steer between our old and new relations," said Gabriel.

"You will only have the old relation. And for your uncle and me, Felix will do his work in one capacity, and depend upon our friendship in the other. He is a gentleman." Josephine moved her hand. "There should be no difficulty."

"I seem to be a person not versed in the ways of gentlemen."

"What you are, is a jealous boy. You want me to have no other friend but you. But I am very used to having streams of people pass before my eyes. Felix is only one of a group to me. I had to prepare him for that: I did not find him exactly in a state of preparation."

Felix was presenting himself to his future companions. "I have come to introduce myself. I daresay you all know me by sight. I think my face is one that you would remember."

"Do you know us by sight?" said Helen. "Or are our faces less memorable?"

"Perhaps it is a sex difference," said Miss Luke.

"It is men who generally look at women's faces," said Miss Munday.

There was a pause.

"I am a little taken aback," said Felix. "I did not expect that your touch would be so much like my own.
And I don't think you are trying to put me at my ease.
Did you know that I was a person who could not feel
awkward?"

"Yes, I think we sensed it," said Miss Luke.

"I am not surprised by your saying that. Mrs. Napier
told me about your high level of charm."

"That was surely a rash thing to say," said Mrs. Chattaway.

"Perhaps it would not have occurred to Mr. Bacon, if
he had not been warned," said Miss Luke, joining in the
amusement at this possibility.

"I rely simply on being my natural self," said Miss
Munday.

"Have you ever seen a more distinguished plainness
than mine?" said Felix.

"No, certainly not," said Mrs. Chattaway. "I do not
mean that there is any plainness in question."

"It is known to be a thing that is often forgotten,"
said Felix.

"I have seldom heard about plainness, without hearing
too that it was forgotten," said Helen. "There hardly
seems any point in mentioning it."

"Is this the first time you have done regular work,
Mr. Bacon?" said Miss Luke.

"Do you not like to talk about my looks?"

"Yes, very much," said Miss Luke, yielding to the
situation.

"I thought you would. We cannot often agree that a
person is plain, to his face."

"Or that something makes us forget the plainness,"
said Mrs. Chattaway, with a touch of archness.

"Oh, do you really think I am plain?"

"They were your own words, Mr. Bacon."

"I had no idea that they would be anyone else's. They
never have been before."

"You may not have started the idea before."

"I never will again, for fear the same advantage is taken of it."

"You will find it a change to be occupied every day, Mr. Bacon," said Miss Luke, with a touch of firmness.

"I have heard that women are cruel. I cannot expect them to let bygones be bygones."

"Surely there is nothing to be ashamed of in having the opportunity of a leisured life," said Mrs. Chattaway.

"No, I really agree that it is a thing to be proud of."

"So do I," said Miss Rosetti. "But you betray what you think of our position."

"I have always felt very chivalrously about it. But now we are all in it, we will not tolerate pity. I did not know before that pity really could not be tolerated."

"What drove you—what led you to take up the position?" said Mrs. Chattaway.

"Thank you for remembering in time about pity. My father makes me too small an allowance, but only small enough to lead and not drive me. And he could afford to make me a large one."

"I am sure he could," said Mrs. Chattaway.

"Do you expect us to think more of you for that, Mr. Bacon?" said Miss Luke.

"Yes, but not as much more as you fear. I am very sensitive to atmospheres."

"Is this atmosphere different from others?" said Helen.

"No, very nearly the same. No one admires riches as much as he feels it natural to admire them."

"He has always found out that they are not the one thing in the world," said Helen. "What is that bell?"

"Oh, how many years is it since we said that?" said Miss Luke.

"What is the bell?" said Felix. "Not a knell, is it?"

"It is the knell of someone's innocence of a working life," said Miss Luke.

"No wonder you hesitated to talk openly about it."

"It is the dressing-bell for the mistresses' first supper," said Miss Luke, with an atoning manner of full information.

"Then I have stayed to the last moment. I am not embarrassed by doing that. I do not recognise the politeness of leaving early. We ought always to seem as if we could not tear ourselves away. I really hardly can to-day, I have so enjoyed my first hour of work. And I am so sorry that I shall not see you all dressed."

"A most charming man!" said Mrs. Chattaway, as the footsteps died away. "He really seemed as if the society in this room were the one thing he would choose; and that is the essence of good manners."

"It must have been polite fiction?" said Miss Luke.

"Well, he seemed too good to be true," said Helen.

"It is a pity he did not see us dressed," said Miss Munday.

"I believe in some schools the mistresses do not dress at night," said Mrs. Chattaway.

"I know they do not," said Miss Rosetti. "I have lived and not dressed in them."

"It seems odd," said Miss Luke, with a slightly puzzled frown.

"It is only a superficial difference," said Mrs. Chattaway.

"Now is it?" said Miss Luke.

"I will put on my satin one evening early enough for Mr. Bacon to see me in it," said Miss Munday, meeting without flinching the mirth caused by a happy view of her appearance at its best.

As Felix reached the Hall, Gabriel crossed it and went towards Josephine's study.

"I bid you good-night with the respect I owe to a member of my employer's family," said Felix.

"I respond with the respect carefully paid by that member."

"It is not true that people have real esteem for workers.

I thought my view of work as degrading was original, but it is almost universal. People who think it not degrading are too proud of thinking it, for it to be their natural opinion."

"How did you get on with the learned ladies upstairs?"

"I found I had a great deal in common with them; and that rather put me out. I thought I should be so different. I think perhaps I must have found my vocation."

"It is the same as mine, then," said Gabriel. "My elders don't seem to know of another. It is time I departed to pursue it. And I find it is easy to get exhausted without doing any work."

"I am only beginning to know about work. I am glad it is not that, that causes exhaustion. But will you not find it a refreshment to see me flitting through the house about my duties?"

"Oh, don't apply any more emotional pressure. I shall faint beneath the heat and burden of the day." Gabriel broke off as Josephine came from her room.

"Well, you have met your colleagues?" she said, giving a word in passing to Felix.

"Yes. I nearly outstayed my welcome. I left them barely time to dress."

"Well, I daresay they like time for that," said Josephine, and turned to her nephew, as though the attention at her disposal for Felix were spent.

"Well, lazybones, standing dreaming instead of bringing me those books! I haven't the time to waste that you have. Where would you be without your man of the family?"

"I might be a man myself," said Gabriel, using a voice not often heard from his lips.

"Why, what is this? What is it?" said Josephine, with instant grasp of the position, while Felix vanished, as if of previous intention, from the house. "What is this line you take? What have you had from me but kindness?"

"It is time I did something besides take kindness: it becomes a reproach and a burden. People are so conscious of what is taken, and so unconscious of what they take. I can't be anything but a fund of easy companionship. Apart from anything else the life is too exhausting."

"Oh, is it? Exhausting is hardly the word I should apply. You had better find some life that is less exhausting. That is the cure for that sort of mood."

"I had better have found it months ago. I recognise the mistake."

"Ah, your real self was not hidden for long," said Josephine, in a tender, almost shaken tone. "And I saw it through the cloud. You may trust me not to take you at a disadvantage. You have a right to ask that from your best friend."

"I must claim the right to my different moods, as other people have it. I can't be simply an automaton of flattery. It is not a reasonable thing to ask, nor a possible thing to do."

"An automaton of flattery! Well, I don't recognise much sign of your being that in the last few minutes. Have your moods; I will not quarrel with them, as long as they are yours. It is your own self that I want."

Josephine passed into the study, and Gabriel wandered about the hall, wearing a hunted look.

CHAPTER VI

ON the next evening sounds of arrival were heard of a more insistent nature than the many of the previous days, and Josephine came from her study, and hastened to the outer door.

"Welcome!" she said, in a deep, vibrating voice, drawing Elizabeth into the hall, and keeping a hand over her daughter's shoulder in avoidance of premature signs of intimacy. "Welcome home! Come and say a word to the masculine side of my household. The two complete families greet each other at last."

"So we exchange a word of friendship before we go to our own place? We take a breath of affection, and carry away the fragrance, fresh and sweet? So your boy and my girl meet for the first time, Simon, as you and I met so many years ago! There were meetings between the boys and girls in the old days too. The old days pass, and the new days come, and we do our best with all of them. We will, indeed, do it with those that are to come. But we are to linger for a first dear moment?"

"You are to linger for more than a moment, sorry as I am to dispute your first words in this house," said Josephine. "Our family dinner awaits your pleasure. You have come to friends and not to strangers, and at the risk of imposing directions at too early a stage, I would have you remember it."

"Such a happy remembrance! Such a sweet reminder! My Ruth is as glad as I am of the respite before the usefulness. She has been so blithe and busy in helping us to flit; but the spirit of weariness will creep apace in spite of the brave resolves. And the privilege when it is so sweetly offered, is doubly sweet. We will not be so churlish as not to welcome it."

"You will be doing us a kindness in keeping Josephine's attention to her own fireside," said Gabriel. "Her family is never enough by itself. She has been gadding off to-day to some part of the building unknown to us."

"Now, I have been doing nothing of the sort," said Josephine, in a distinct, conscious tone. "I had to have a word with my younger mistresses; and found myself committed to further communion before I knew where I was. They only wanted to make some confidences after the separation of the holidays; there is not so much in that.

So away with your gadding and the rest! I had no anticipation of being detained, when I entered their presence."

"Well, you will be able to prophesy the result of further visits," said Elizabeth, in a bright tone.

"Yes, I think I shall," said Josephine frankly. "I had
not happened to introduce myself to their quarters
before; and when you take an unprecedented course there
is no certainty about the result. I could not be sure if my
effort through the years to observe a simple equality,
toned up rather than deteriorated by the spice of control,
had met with success. In its nature it must be a precarious
effort. But the least element of failure would have been
revealed to me to-day. Why, Simon, have I shaken your
chess-board and baulked your genius? Well, a game is
not of the things that mould the future, and Gabriel is
saved from another signal defeat."

"Gabriel plays for the game and not for victory. These
things do not repeat themselves," murmured Simon,
pressing his fingers to his brow.

"Well, the game is not like Humpty-Dumpty, impossible to put together again," said Elizabeth. "The king's
horses and the king's men can do their work this time."

"Josephine, you distinguish too much between your
own employments and other people's," said Gabriel. "We
see why your being asked to remain upstairs was not so
certain."

"Well, we see that it was certain. And my poor young
mistresses! I wonder what they would say, if they knew
how my lingering in their quarters would be taken hold
of in mine. They would not have had the courage to
press me in their pleasant, spontaneous way. Their eagerness could not have seemed at all such a simple, natural
thing."

"It is strange to think we have people fulfilling their
destinies within our doors, whose lives are all but a sealed
book to us," said Simon, his eyes on his moving fingers.

"That could never be the case with me. It would go too

much against the grain." Josephine smiled at Elizabeth,
as if her words foreshadowed their own relation. "It
would simply be a contradiction in terms. I know what
is to be known about each individual who comes under
my survey. And often what is not to be known as well.
Ah, what they tell me in their eyes and in their very
silences, these women who have poured past me, working out their history! Ah, if we knew everyone's story!
Well, if we are supposed not to know, we do not know;
that is how it has to be."

"I was beginning to hope it had not," said Gabriel.
"How do they have so much in their lives, when the outer
world is so uneventful? Do you suppose Felix will be as
fortunate?"

"Mrs. Napier," said Ruth, "you will let me say how I
appreciate your not treating Mother just as one of the
women who work here? I am the last person to speak;
but it makes such a difference. Her being obliged to work
does not mean that there are not ways and ways of letting her do it."

"My child, your mother and I are old friends. With
others I have not been so fortunate. I have had to build
up the background, that in this case is ready to my
memory. But I never treat anyone 'just as one of the
women who work here.'" Josephine bent to Ruth with a
smile. "You need not fear, stranger though you are in
yourself to me, that you would meet such dealings at my
hands. It is not only as your mother's daughter, that I
shall deal with you to the best that is in me." She ended
on a lighter note. "I find so many of my matter-of-course
actions taken as benevolence, that I get into the way of
making provision accordingly."

"It would not do to make differences for us, dear, that
the others would resent," said Elizabeth.

"I should hardly have the opportunity. We work too
much in our different spheres. The room set aside for
your activities belongs only to you; 'the housekeeper's

room' is the legend on the door, if there is anything in an inscription. Then there are the common rooms for the senior and junior staff: Ruth has the run of the latter in her own right. And I have my room across the hall, and possess it in solitude, as you do yours. I do not move amongst you all, dispensing benefits. I sit and work alone, realising that I am receiving them. That is a far more accurate picture of me."

"Well, we will make the most of the evening of simple friendship."

"Pray let us do so," said Gabriel. "We seem to be using it entirely for professional purposes. Is there anything we ever talk about, apart from the school?"

"I do not want to discuss the school at this end of the day," said Josephine. "Too many problems have arisen by that stage, to be dealt with in a drawing-room spirit. So, if our guests have absorbed enough of its atmosphere to possess their souls in peace, let us choose any subject that is congenial."

"Let us ask them to supply it," said Gabriel, "and give us a glimpse of the outer world."

"It is the inner world they must be thinking of at the moment. Their rooms are waiting for them, and they will dress and eat before they are at your disposal, though their experience of the outer world may well be larger than yours."

"It must be, as mine is non-existent."

"Well, it may not sound such an enviable place, when you hear it described with all the vigour and realism of which Mrs. Giffard is mistress. Perhaps she would not have chosen this world, if the other had made such a great appeal."

"Still, I think I can let you have your glimpse," said Elizabeth, rising and taking her wraps. "I have been in the outer world a good deal, as I daresay you can gather from signs that I betray unconsciously. I must not expect not to bear the marks of the fray; they are honourable

signs of war. My experience shall be at your service. We
will not hide it under a bushel, if it is to be our talent, or
the material for our talent. It is an ill wind that blows
nobody any good. Do we go straight up the staircase,
dear Josephine?"

"Straight up and straight along. I am not giving you
an escort. The sooner you know your way about your
home, the better."

"Shall we come down when we are clothed and in our
right mind?" said Ruth, a drooping figure in the door.

"Come down as soon as you will spare yourselves. I
won't suggest how soon that will be. I do not know your
ways; if you like to be unpacked for, or to unpack for
yourselves, or to superintend the unpacking. The third
and middle course commends itself to me, but I do not
claim the same knowledge of you. I find that I must not
burden my mind with such details about my charges.
Not that they would be a burden, if my mind had room
for them. As it has not, I appoint a deputy, and I recommend the experienced corridor maid in the part."

"Well, shall we unpack for ourselves or not?" said
Ruth, as she followed her mother upstairs. "Can it be
that we are people to be waited upon? I fancy I detected
signs that that was not really the case."

"I think we will superintend the unpacking, the third
and middle course," said Elizabeth, holding her hand to
her lips in silent laughter. "That is the method I shall
adopt with a hundred boxes every term; so it is as well to
get into the way of it. It might have been recommended
with confidence. Well, how do you like my family of
friends?"

"The proof of the pudding is in the eating. I have
taken such a very small bite as yet; though I believe it
was regarded as a large and succulent portion."

"I am sure that one of them is inclined to like
you."

"Oh, people might like me, if I ever happened to

pass before their eyes. They cannot form opinions of a young woman who does not come within their range of vision."

Josephine came to Elizabeth's room before the family dinner-hour.

"Now, I hope you will excuse my prowling about your passage? I prefer people to keep to their own quarters myself. Not that there is any particular point in it; it is just a feeling I happen to have. But I thought, as mine are open to you, that yours would be to me on this occasion. I want to introduce you to my mistresses myself. They are eager to welcome an old friend of mine, and there is no reason to defer the pleasure. Have you any feeling about the manner of your introduction?"

"I will leave it to you, my dear, the head of all matters in this house."

"Then I will do it in the way that seems to me natural." Josephine knocked at the door of the common room. "Here is Mrs. Giffard, my old friend! As I had a natural wish to present her to you myself, you will pardon my breaking in upon your privacy? If you have had too many glimpses of me to-day, you have not of her. And I warn you that she is not accustomed to being a sight to be wearied of."

"Such a lot of clever faces! Such a lot of lore and learning confronting poor me, who am so eager to lap it all in comfort! It gives importance to my so unimportant work. Will you grant it a little importance, and me as well, because I do it? Importance is so much the fashion that I must have my little share."

"Your work is the most fundamental of all," said Miss Luke.

"Now I regard my work as equally fundamental, though I say it as shouldn't," said Josephine playfully. "Because all work is equally so; for that reason and no other."

"I wonder some of this accomplishment does not break

out into the world," said Elizabeth. "We must indeed take care of it, or it will escape."

"Oh, we are content with our narrow sphere," said Miss Luke, laughing.

"And it is not as narrow as you would think," said Mrs. Chattaway.

"Experience is not a matter of doors and walls," said Josephine, glancing round. "Though other things may be a matter of them sometimes."

"The deepest experience always takes place within them," said Miss Rosetti.

"Yes, yes, indeed," said Josephine. "That is profound."

"I have a great deal of knowledge of life," said Miss Munday.

"If I may say so, I have noticed it," said Josephine. "And again if I may say so, I have noticed it increasing."

"You may say so again," said Miss Munday.

"Well, we all have this in common," said Elizabeth, "that we must put our gifts to the purpose of honest self-support."

"Have we?" said Josephine easily. "I happen to have passed that stage."

"So have I, in the last years," said Miss Rosetti.

"I am provided for," said Miss Munday.

"I am partly," said Miss Luke, laughing at the turn of subject. "I am engaged in building upon the rather frail foundation."

"I am dependent upon myself, being just the person who ought not to be," said Mrs. Chattaway.

"I am, too. I feel it is rather a heroic position," said Helen.

"Yes, yes, it has a dignity in a way, that no other position has," said Josephine. "I remember feeling that I was losing something, as I left it. Well, I must return to my family. Thank you very much for your welcome of my old friend."

"Why do they lead this life, if they need not, Josephine?" said Elizabeth, as they went to the stairs.

"Why, we all choose some life, don't we? There would be no explorers or scientists or poets or politicians, according to that view."

"Miss Keats is very much younger than the rest. She has an unusual type of face. Do you find her a magnet for Gabriel's eyes?"

"No, I do not; I can give you a simple answer there," said Josephine, with a little sound of mirth. "The mistresses in that group do not contrive to be that. He is a very one-idea'd young man. It is not the result of any training of mine. Sometimes I get quite borne down by the unvarying direction of his emotions. But they will settle into a steadier current in the end."

"He is very young as yet."

"I think it is not a question of youth. Twenty-three is the romantic age. But some people must deal with romance in their own way, have it in their own form. But the idea of his turning to my staff for his satisfaction in that line"—Josephine's voice broke again—"gives me to smile, I admit."

"My dear, you are more than wonderful in your touch with all of them. I shall get to be in awe of you, if you go on being so wise and great and good. You have left the past so much further behind than I have. We were not so good in the good old days, or the naughty old days, whichever they were. Well, this is the library, the dear home room? Well, Simon and son, I have returned from my venture into the lions' den. Such a feeble, feminine creature I have been brought to feel, such a light, bright, opinionless person, with such a woman's mind! Josephine came to my rescue and coaxed them back into their cage. And I am ready to tell Gabriel the story of my life in the wide, wide world. Such a different thing I see it has been from being in the cage! When he is ready for the feast of words, I will lay it out for him."

"I think the feast we are ready for, is of a more tangible kind," said Josephine, moving to the dinner table. "Quite such an unsubstantial repast is hardly adapted to our immediate needs. Plain living and high thinking are very well; but as our living does not look so very plain, and as the thinking did not sound as if it were to be so very high, we won't concern ourselves just now with the combination. Mrs. Giffard may be too tired to amuse you to-night, Gabriel; and as your path and hers will not often cross, you may have to learn that her energies are not to be dissipated in masculine service."

"No, no; we have dedicated ourselves to feminine service. That is in the inside world, and we must be content to fulfil it there. And content to be there, too." Elizabeth gave a bright glance at Josephine. "We have so much cause for content."

"Is not Miss Giffard to join us this evening?" said Gabriel.

"My poor, weary girl!" cried Elizabeth. "She is wandering companionless in these perplexing corridors!"

"Leave this to me with confidence, Mrs. Giffard," said Gabriel.

"Well, I should hope so," said Josephine, looking up. "I was wondering how far Mrs. Giffard would get, with a young man sitting looking gracefully on. Go and find her daughter and escort her here. This is a difficult house for a stranger, the great rambling, complicated place! I often wonder at myself for having got it added to so often, unawares. You go too far in recognising only one woman in the world. I am ceasing to be flattered by it."

"I am ceasing to flatter you by doing it. I am occupied with the picture of our guest. I know that passage which is the undoing of strangers."

"And when you guessed all about it, too!" said Josephine, with a sigh.

Gabriel came upon Ruth at the expected place.

"I have been blamed for not guessing your predicament, and more blamed for guessing it."

"I am the person to be blamed," said Ruth, hardly hastening her steps. "This is a pretty way to be useful, isn't it?"

"You are not going to be useful to-night. If you knew the atmosphere of this house, you would understand the arrogance of that speech."

"Yes, I will believe it is arrogant. I am learning about the dignity of toil. I would modestly relinquish the distinction."

"I would relinquish my distinction of being the only person in the house without yours."

"We ought to be shaken up together," said Ruth, lifting her large eyes to his face. "Instead of which I suppose we shall live at opposite poles."

"We are reaching the pole at which my life is spent. Poles are known to be chilly places. We will venture sometimes into the warmer climes between. Josephine, I have found the lost sheep, but in a state of exhaustion."

"Well, that is natural, when she forgets her dinner. Come in, my child, and make up for lost time. I hope you will forgive our beginning? We would have waited of course, except for involving your mother. Yes, Simon, you may help yourself; Ruth is safely supplied. Will you allow my husband to use your Christian name in private life? He will not in professional relations."

"I feel so guilty that anyone has waited, Mrs. Napier."

"My dear, we do not serve men before women," said Josephine.

CHAPTER VII

"MAY I come in?" said Josephine, hesitating after her knock at the door of the common room, as though uncertain that the formal command to enter extended to herself. "Or am I intruding?"

"You are intruding, of course," said Miss Luke. "You should hesitate to enter a room in your own house."

"I certainly should," said Josephine, advancing with a still tentative step. "This room is not in my province: it is good of you to make me welcome in it. And I don't know why I should have the easiest chair, unless it is because I am the guest. I should certainly give it to any one of you in my rooms. Well, they did not play me false in the matter of the springs; that is one thing. Miss Munday, I believe I am turning you out of it?"

"Yes," said Miss Munday. "I was sitting in it."

"I am indeed sorry to be displacing you; but there is a matter that I wish to discuss with you all. I hope you will give me your advice?"

"Yes, we will," said Miss Munday.

Josephine joined with some vagueness of thought in the mirth that ensued.

"We will advise you to take any step you have decided on," said Miss Luke. "It must be advisable to take a step. There is more point in a step when it is taken."

"Now it is very nice to see tea coming in," said Josephine, not passing over this item in her companions' lot. "I don't know if you are going to allow me to share it with you?"

"We will not enlighten you," said Miss Luke.

"Are we going to send for another cup?" said Josephine to Miss Munday, somehow attaining a decision, but hesitating to take upon herself the office of hostess in the room.

"Will you bring another cup and saucer, please?" said Miss Munday to the maid.

"Thank you," said Josephine to Miss Munday.

"We have hot scones on the day when our head comes to tea," said Miss Luke.

"You always have hot things brought to you, I hope?"

"I do not know; I do not care for them," said Mrs. Chattaway, looking faintly startled.

"I meant, we did not always have this rare kind," said Miss Luke.

"I hope you send for any kind you prefer," said Josephine, in the tone of what went without saying. "Or more than one kind, if you care for it."

"Oh, surely no one could do that," said Mrs. Chattaway, with a suggestion of shuddering, which she checked with a glance at her friends.

"Oh, thank you; am I to come first?" said Josephine.

"Yes, before me," said Miss Munday.

"Well, I should think so!" said Mrs. Chattaway, replying to Josephine, and running forward with the sugar and tongs, and for the last steps without the tongs.

"Thank you," said Josephine, taking some sugar with her fingers, as if unconscious of another method.

"I am very clumsy," said Mrs. Chattaway. "I never had clever hands."

"Neither had I," said Josephine, with a faint note of surprise. "But as we both live rather by our heads, it is not of any great consequence. Not that I am not an admirer of a delicate hand."

"Our eyes turn to Miss Rosetti's," said Miss Luke.

"Yes," said Josephine. "If I may be very personal, I have seen no one else with hands of that type, unless it is my nephew, Gabriel. I say to him that his ought to be the woman's, and mine the man's, a speech which does not appeal to his sense of fitness."

"You wear such beautiful rings, Mrs. Napier," said Mrs. Chattaway, her tone suggesting full compensation for Josephine.

Josephine gave a perfunctory glance at her hands.

"They were presents," she said in a careless tone. "One naturally puts presents to the use for which they were intended."

"Are you going to begin with a scone, Mrs. Napier?" said Miss Rosetti, sauntering forward with her hands under the dish.

"Yes, I am, please. I think tea should go through all its proper stages. I hope it does that with all of you?"

"Yes," said Miss Munday.

"It is not for lack of temptation if it does not," said Mrs. Chattaway, who had run back for the tongs, and forward again to Josephine, as if the latter also might remedy her omission.

"Yes, I will have a little more sugar. Thank you," said Josephine.

"It is a pity we only have four meals a day," said Miss Munday.

"I should be sorry to have any more," said Mrs. Chattaway. "I can hardly manage those there are."

"Why not miss some of them?" said Miss Rosetti.

"It would be unsocial," said Mrs. Chattaway, just inclining her head.

"It would indeed," said Josephine. "And what is more, it would be very bad for you. I hardly like to hear of it even in jest."

"I like to hear of more than four meals a day even in jest," said Miss Munday.

"Well, I am on the side of Miss Munday, in the sense she means," said Josephine. "Why not have as much as we can of a pleasant and beneficial thing? That is, if the diet merits that description where we happen to be. In some households I should not want to hear of more than four meals a day, even in jest. Jest would be the last word to apply to it."

"It would be wrong to joke about it," said Helen.

"Now I am glad that you concede significance to the material life," said Josephine. "When the health and comfort of many people were about to depend on me, I asked myself: 'Am I prepared to adapt my own instincts to the extent that may be demanded?' And having answered the question, and lived the answer for over twenty years, I feel myself a larger rather than a lesser woman."

"What led you to take up educational work?" said Mrs. Chattaway, sensitively cloaking any harshness in the truth.

"I might put that question to you."

"Oh, well, I had no choice: I was left very badly off," said Mrs. Chattaway, in a parenthetic manner.

"Then our initial reasons were not so different. I was myself too poor"—Josephine gave the last word a full utterance—"to do all that I wished. But the reasons that lay deeper were my love for teaching; my belief that seeds were sown in youth that would bear fruit in the later days; my passionate desire——" She held her expression carefully still—"to sow with my own hand some of those seeds. Do you not think that the resemblance between us goes further than the beginning?"

"Yes, oh yes," said Mrs. Chattaway, her voice hardly in keeping with the extent of her claim. "But in your case the stage will soon be reached when you can leave all such necessity behind."

"Have I not made it clear that I shall never reach that stage?"

"Oh, that is just what you say," said Mrs. Chatttaway, again making rather light of Josephine's meaning.

"How I hate myself for saying a dull, dutiful thing!" said Miss Luke. "But some of us have to be at classes at five."

"Now that brings me to the point of my dilemma. I think you are too much tied to classes, especially to those that make no claim on you as individuals. I have been thinking that an extra junior mistress is indicated. Well, the truth is, that my friend, Mrs. Giffard, was so anxious to have her daughter with her, that I found myself doing what is really against my principles, and creating a post. But do you not think, quite apart from any whim of mine, that you would be the better for a little less routine?"

"Yes," said Miss Munday.

"Most human beings could say that," said Miss Rosetti.

"I am so glad that you agree with me," said Josephine, her voice losing a little in fullness.

"Now, I don't know; I have not said that I agree," said Miss Luke, standing with a considering, honest air. "I don't take to the idea of admitting to too much work. It is one of those little, unsatisfactory things that one somehow does not do."

"You have certainly not done it," said Josephine, her manner sacrificing her own point of view.

"Mrs. Napier may not require a unanimous vote," said Miss Rosetti.

"No, no, that is quite fair," said Miss Luke, sitting down. "I am taking advantage of the rest of you. I can only admit it, and say no more."

"I cannot say that I have too much work, Mrs. Napier," said Mrs. Chattaway.

"Can you not?" said Josephine kindly. "I am very glad to hear it. But we are considering a question of general policy. How the matter works out, is for all of you to settle between you. It is nothing to do with me."

"You are so kind in your manner of doing things, Mrs. Napier. We all ought to be most grateful."

"No," said Josephine, "it is I who should be that, if what you generously say has any truth. It is what we meet with, that brings out what we have in us for help or hindrance."

"You are doing Mrs. Giffard a great kindness," said Miss Rosetti.

"No kindness comes into it. She was my girlhood's friend; and I am not happy in seeing her life go too

377

much awry. I am considering myself, as I believe we all do really."

"I believe we do," said Miss Luke. "I believe that is so; that characters make history."

"It is extraordinary what reversals of position life brings with it," said Mrs. Chattaway.

"Why, what reversal is there here?" said Josephine. "Mrs. Giffard and I were old friends then. We are older friends now. Surely life may be allowed to bring those changes?"

"You are too kind to admit my meaning, Mrs. Napier."

"Yes, I think I am. I shall see no difference in the value of our work, as we do it side by side. You will all do me the service of observing that spirit towards her daughter?"

"We can do nothing else, with your example before us," said Mrs. Chattaway, making no personal claim.

"Well, in a way I resent the young woman," said Miss Luke. "She will be taking on herself what I have a right to feel depends on me."

"Now you are to fall in with my scheme, and realise that I think it best for you," said Josephine. "I cannot have objections raised to a decision for your welfare."

"It must be sad for the girl to give up her youth to routine," said Mrs. Chattaway, attending without delay to Josephine's request.

"It is different for mature and settled spinsters!" said Miss Luke.

"Now, I can tell you that there is no conflict between the two spheres of work and marriage," said Josephine. "If there were, marriage could not be what it is, a different usefulness."

"Indeed there is none, when abilities are up to both," said Mrs. Chattaway.

"I would not claim that abilities have much to do with marriage," said Josephine, bending her head as though to cover a smile, and then raising it frankly. "The forces that unite two personalities, defy definition, though the business is attempted without any beating about the bush in some modern books I could mention. But there would be no meaning in these things, if each case did not work itself out for itself and by itself. Do you not say that that is so of every human experience?" She turned about her to relinquish any claim to an isolated position.

"Now," said Miss Luke, drawing quickly into herself; "let us admit it. When we meet a married woman, do we not feel a certain respect for her?"

"Well, I hope so," said Josephine. "Poor woman, why should you not? I hope you feel a certain respect for me, as I sit here?"

"Now, now, Mrs. Napier, again you are too kind to admit our meaning."

"Well, then, let us be plain," said Josephine. "We feel a certain respect for the woman who attracts and possesses a man? Is that it? My words are what yours would be? Well, and why should we not? We should feel a certain respect for any human ability."

"Ah, but they are the elemental things, the love between man and woman, marriage, motherhood," said Miss Luke in a deep, quick tone, placing herself fully outside her initial heading. "The things untouched by civilisation, primitive, immune from what is called progress."

"Yes," said Josephine gently.

"I was forgetting that Gabriel was not your own son," said Miss Luke, very low.

"In this case it must be exactly the same," said Mrs. Chattaway.

"No," said Josephine; "it is quite different. In early days it could not but have an element of sameness. It fades with every day now."

"You are always conscious of the difference?" said Miss Rosetti.

"He is always conscious of it. He does not let me forget

it. He is my masculine companion, my protector. And that reminds me that you yourselves have a new masculine companion. What is your verdict upon Mr. Bacon's presence in your common room?"

"By no means an open verdict," said Miss Luke.

"I am sure it is not," said Josephine, with a smile of fellow-feeling. "But, seriously, do you not think him a very brilliant and polished man?"

"We could not think it more seriously than we do," said Helen.

"I am glad it is to be such a high quality of companionship," said Josephine, with a touch of earnestness. "He will spend some time here between his hours of work. I should not care for you to be thrown with every man of my acquaintance. By the way"—she spoke with sudden concern—"you do not object to his presence here, do you?"

"No," said Miss Munday.

"It seems a strange profession for him," said Mrs. Chattaway. "I mean, the mere fact of working, when he has been used to a life so different, may put a strain that he does not anticipate."

"I daresay he does not," said Josephine, with a touch of grimness. "I did not myself. We have to make the effort. I made it; and I venture to think that it will not hurt him to do the same."

"I cannot bear to think of it," said Helen. "I feel like the savage women, who do the work while the men sit idle. Perhaps the extra mistress will be a help to him. I feel inclined to let him have my share of her."

"Well, I hope she will be a help to all of you," said Josephine, rising. "That is the purpose of her, after, of course, the fulfilment of her own life. I hope she will give just that little extra easing, which makes so much difference in any arduous lot. And I am not going to sympathise with you over its being arduous: I should envy you that side of it, if I did not share it. Now it remains for me to thank you for your hospitality, and to betake myself to the masculine side of my world. I wonder which side is more dependent on me? Or to which I owe the greater debt? That is the truer question."

"Is there much difference between the sides?" said Helen.

"Well," said Josephine, "there is a difference, and there is not. I see it so plainly, and I see it does not exist, if you know what I mean." Nobody gave any sign of not knowing. "Well, it is my lot, what I have undertaken. I must not complain; I do not. I would not change it, even when I find it much. And I don't know what my men would say, if I made the suggestion."

"Your nephew is making a long stay at home," said Miss Rosetti.

"Well, he has spent his college days apart from me," said Josephine, in a condoning manner. "I must not be surprised if he wants a little of the other thing now. I am not surprised; though I admit I was not prepared for the violence of the reaction. And I find that we must not joke about apron-strings. I have to be very respectful to young manhood, very heedful of a young sensitiveness. It is not a charge in which I would fail, not the least of my duties."

"You will find it a change when he marries," said Miss Rosetti.

"I must recognise that I have no prospect of such a change. His attitude towards me must keep me a prisoner: I don't know what any young woman would say to it. Well, I must remember that the tie of blood between us is not of the deepest kind. Anyhow, it is put aside by my young gentleman, in determining the basis of our intercourse. I am not his aunt any more than any other woman."

Josephine moved to the door, and Mrs. Chattaway was a moment behindhand in running forward to open it. Josephine paused, as her exit was impeded rather than eased, and acknowledged with a bend of her head a courtesy due to a guest.

CHAPTER VIII

"WHAT shall I wear for the school entertainment?" said Gabriel.

"Anything tidy that you have," said Josephine. "You must be properly dressed to show the people to their places."

"What will Miss Munday wear?" said Gabriel. "I should like to be equal to Miss Munday."

"Well, you can't be," said Josephine. "Miss Munday is the senior mistress, and you are a foolish boy. There is no question of equality. You can put on anything fit to wait upon her in."

"Felix will wait on Miss Munday," said Gabriel. "The junior mistresses have fallen to my portion."

"Well, I hope you will attend to them properly. Felix is so very dependable in that way. I feel that his compeers have definitely been better looked after since he has been with us."

"What about the question of all questions, my dealings with the parents?" said Simon.

"Why is it more of a question than the others?" said his wife.

"Ah, we know why," said Simon. "Yes, I fear we know why."

"But I feel that Josephine is right in repudiating the truth," said Gabriel.

Josephine laid her hand on her nephew's head, and hastened from the room. In the hall she came upon Ruth, and paused to speak to her.

"You have done the programmes, my dear? I am afraid you had not much time."

"I had not, Mrs. Napier, and so there are not many programmes. More time would have resulted in a larger number."

"Well, I hope you will enjoy the afternoon after all the preparations."

"Oh, does one ever enjoy a thing when one has been involved in the preliminaries? And it is the people who have not been involved in them, whose enjoyment matters."

"Dear, dear, I should have thought that that was the best foundation for enjoyment," said Josephine, laughing and passing on. "I am quite prepared to find it so myself."

The mistresses came into the concert hall, with their demeanour modified as much as their dress, indeed modified by it. Mrs. Chattaway cast furtive glances from the others to herself; Miss Munday's expression suggested humorous awareness of her own festive aspect; Miss Luke, by moving rapidly amongst her companions, laying her hand on their shoulders and indulging in lively talk, proved that she was without any such awareness.

"I feel a little conscious of my appearance," said Felix, coming up to the group. "Perhaps it is being one of the few people who can wear formal clothes."

His speech was met by incredulous mirth, his hearers keeping their eyes on his face, in case of further entertainment.

"Well, I hope that no one will be conscious of mine," said Josephine. "It is not my habit to be aware of it; but when I am oblivious, it may be hitting other people in the eye. I got into the garment in time, but I admit it does not add to the occasion."

"People always seem to think admission alters things," said Helen, "when it really rather helps to establish them."

"You are right; I have been remiss," said Josephine, catching the words and giving her a smile as she went to her place; while her mistresses regarded her in silent appreciation of the difference that had raised her above themselves.

Josephine listened to the concert with a demeanour that proved her unprepared for its items as they came. When a girl performed especially well, she leant across her neighbour and inquired the name of both pupil and teacher, and gravely nodding her head, sat back in her place. Jonathan heard the performance with his face covered with his hand, and his body swaying to the music. At its conclusion he emerged into the open room, but perceiving his sister mounting the platform, resumed his seat and his expression.

"Now I feel that I am not doing well by my speech in choosing to make it directly after the concert. That had the excuse of honest preparation, one which as a schoolmistress I feel should command indulgence. And this has no excuse at all; hardly even that of being felt a duty; for I should have taken leave to doubt the need of it, if I had been permitted." Josephine smiled at her mistresses, and pausing in what might have passed for a recourse to her memory, if it had not been for her confession, continued with an air of confidence gathering, as she found that words came. "What I am conscious of, as I stand here, is that I am the last and the least of the people present; the least as the head mistress, as the simple means to an end; and that anything about me that is not in some way revealed by my pupils, can have no meaning. So I will ask you to take the simplest word, born of the moment, as fulfilling the moment's need. I find that I would only, that I should only, that I can only say one thing; and that is that I am grateful; to my pupils, to their parents, to my staff; to all who give me of their best in return for mine." Josephine paused, and perceiving that this limit to her words had caused a miscalculation, waited with her eyes down, as if under the influence of her feelings, until a little girl, carrying a bouquet, approached the platform.

"Now, here are two charming things!" she said, standing with the bouquet in one hand and the other on the child's head. "I do not know which gives me more pleasure, but I do know which is the more important; and I think I cannot end better than by saying that there can be no one present, to whom it is more important than it is to me."

There was applause, whether for Josephine's self or her devotion of it to others, was not apparent, and Mrs. Chattaway turned to her friends.

"An extraordinary speech for the spur of the moment! Just the sort that one would think would need the most preparation. One can hardly believe it."

"No," said Miss Munday on a rather high note.

There was a tendency to titter, and Miss Luke set her teeth through her own participation in it.

"Come, come. What we could not do ourselves may be possible for others, for one other, anyhow."

"And we have Mrs. Napier's word," said Mrs. Chattaway.

"I admire the speech more, if it was prepared," said Felix. "Fancy planning to make that kind of speech and not an elaborate one! I had a glimpse into my own soul."

"What is the jest?" said Josephine, as she passed.

There was a pause, and then Miss Luke stepped forward to do to all concerned the justice of truth.

"It was suggested that you had prepared your speech, Mrs. Napier. The idea of your not being above human weakness struck us as ludicrous, you see."

"Oh!" said Josephine. "I had not that temptation. I speak much worse, when I do not speak extempore. I am afraid that your impression that I was doing myself more than justice, had a certain truth."

Jonathan for the second time emerged from his seat.

"Well, that was a pretty sight, a satisfying feast for the ears. A very high standard, Josephine, my dear, both in you and your pupils; my congratulations. Well, Miss Munday, we are both interested in education: I have given much my of life to it. Miss Rosetti, I have promised myself a talk with an old friend. Yes, is there anything more to come?"

"The exhibition of drawings," said Felix. "You need not be afraid of their quality: I entrust the mounting to no one but myself. I should be ashamed to let a pupil take home a drawing that had no merit. The old-world atmosphere is so important, and I pay it strict attention."

Josephine glanced at Miss Munday and Miss Luke, and raised her brows in mock despair.

The father of a pupil came up to Felix.

"So you are the drawing-master of the school?"

"Yes," said Felix in a cordial tone.

"And you are quite settled in the post?"

"Yes. I do not lose my positions."

"Have you had many?"

"No; that would mean that I did lose them."

"You find the work interesting?"

"Yes. I was saying what interesting work I did."

"Why did you choose to teach girls rather than boys?"

"Everyone asks me that. I wonder how girls get educated. I knew people didn't always believe in women's higher education; but I find that they don't believe in any education at all. I wonder why they send their daughters to school. I suppose you have your own reasons?"

The guest smiled and moved on to Josephine.

"He has his own touch, that drawing master of yours. He seems to take his work in a serious spirit."

"I should hardly have thought that that was the phrase to describe his talk with you," said Josephine, with a smile.

"I was speaking of his real attitude, apart from his talk."

"I hope that goes without saying of anyone who teaches

here. And in his case the attitude cannot arise from his background. It is his own."

"Where does he come from? Was he not intended for the life?"

"He is the son of Sir Robert Bacon, whose place is about thirty miles to the west," said Josephine, her easy voice easier as she ended: "The only son."

"Oh yes, of course," said the guest.

"Is there any 'of course' about it? Men whose roots are in the country, generally give their hearts to hunting and such like, don't they, rather than to the furthering of art?"

"Oh yes. No doubt you are fortunate to have him."

"Yes; I think it shows a genuine inclination," said Josephine in an even tone.

"It seems an odd life for him, teaching drawing to girls."

"If I thought teaching girls an odd life, I should not have chosen it. You cannot expect me to agree with you there."

"No, no; but I meant for a man."

"Well, you cannot expect me to agree with you there either, or I should not have men on my staff."

"Well, I must say that I agree," said Fane, pausing with the simple purpose of sharing the talk. "I thank heaven that there were other choices open to me."

"Then I think we all thank heaven for it," said Josephine, smiling.

"Yes, yes, indeed," said the guest. "Do you find that men teach better than women, Mrs. Napier?"

"No, but I find they teach as well; so that there is no reason for debarring them from the work."

"No, no, of course not," said the guest, inwardly confronting the question of human eagerness.

Jonathan left Miss Rosetti and came up to his sister; and the guest gave a glance at this further masculine element as he went his way.

"Well, Gabriel is still domesticated, my dear. Is enough getting to be as good as a feast?"

"I don't think anything is as good as a feast, at tea time after an amateur concert. And Gabriel will certainly not cease being domesticated just now. He will bring refreshment to these kind ladies, who have borne the concert with such fortitude, knowing how unwillingly I inflicted it on them. So allow Miss Rosetti to drink her tea in peace."

"Miss Rosetti and I are old friends. It was I who introduced you to her."

"Well, having done one great thing for the school, come and do another, and talk to some parents. That seems to me a great thing at this moment, distorted though I admit my sense of values to be. We will leave the qualified ones to make merry at the expense of the concert. I'll warrant that will be the better of the two entertainments to-day. Why, what a crash! Has somebody come to grief?"

It was seen that a pupil, who had been carrying tea to the guests, had stumbled with the tray to the ground.

"Dear, dear, what is this, what is this?" said an old gentleman. "All the best cups and saucers! Well, I hope nobody is hurt. The china is hurt quite enough."

"Here is somebody in trouble!" said Fane, as Gabriel and Felix approached in haste. "Now there is no need for a fuss. Accidents are bound to happen."

"Are you shaken, my dear?" said Josephine to the girl. "No, don't trouble to pick up the pieces; my nephew is here. Yes, you must want a chair; thank you, Mr. Bacon. Now they will fetch you some tea for yourself. You have had quite a shock; the state of the china shows that."

"Your pupils expect gallantry while they are at school, Mrs. Napier?" said Fane.

"Surely school should be a preparation for life."

"I hope they will get what they have been taught to expect."

"I hope so," said Josephine, with a touch of gravity.

"You treat school-girls as if they were grown-up women?"

"Always, when it is possible. But perhaps there speaks the educationist." Josephine smiled at Fane, and turned to the mother of a pupil.

"Who was the girl who played the violin, Mrs. Napier?"

"I am afraid I do not remember her name. I know her well by sight."

"Of course you cannot give personal attention to all the girls."

"I can see that they all have personal attention. That is what I do with my time."

"Do you know who teaches her the violin?"

"Yes, I have just asked. I, too, was struck by her playing. And I ought to know the good gentleman: I find I have a talk with him every term."

"Would you recommend my girl to learn the violin?"

Josephine placed her hand on the speaker's shoulder.

"I should not, at the moment. I must find what her talents are, what her health is, in a word, who she is, before I offer an opinion. There are people who will tell me all these things."

"The girls of to-day are fortunate," said the mother, realising the distance between her child and the person in charge of her. "Will you ask someone to write to me?"

"I *hope* to write to you myself," said Josephine, emphasising her second word, and leaving her companion in favour of the state it indicated, as compared with certainty.

"May I have tea with you?" said Felix, joining the mistresses, who were still a group by themselves. "I want to seem a person apart from the other masters."

"Well, that is the way to do it," said Miss Luke. "Their bearing seems to indicate that we are the subordinate half of mankind."

"So many things indicate it, and yet it is never really settled," said Felix. "I hardly think you can be, or it would have been proved by now."

"Do many things show that man is the ruling half?" said Miss Rosetti.

"Yes, a great many," said Helen. "And yet that is never settled either. It may mean that we cannot judge by appearances."

"I believe you are a feminist, Mr. Bacon," said Miss Luke, her tone hardly bearing out her own opinions.

"He is indeed," said Helen. "He said that it was not settled that women were subordinate to men, and he could not be more of a feminist than that."

"Here is an impressive-looking person!" said Mrs. Chattaway. "Whose father is he?"

"Oh, he is mine," said Felix. "And he said he could not come. He must think it his duty to take me by surprise. I hope I have not caused him inconvenience. I must behave to him very carefully. People's manners to their family are such a test."

An upright old man about seventy-eight, of the same height, but of heavier build than Felix, with the latter's features in a more solid and regular form, was advancing across the room, impeded by his fellow guests, one of whom addressed him, as they were compelled to a pause.

"This is a pretty sight. All the young faces."

"Ah, yes, indeed," said Sir Robert, turning his glasses about him.

"You have a daughter, you have a grand-daughter; you have come to visit one of the girls?"

"I have come to visit my son."

"Your son?" said the other.

"Yes," said Sir Robert, with grave simplicity. "He is the drawing master here."

"Oh yes; I have heard people speak of him. I hear that he puts his heart into his work."

"I trust he does, as he has undertaken it."

"My father is the first person to take the right view of my profession," said Felix. "I am glad to see you looking so well, Father. Will you come and see the exhibition of drawings?"

"No, I will take them for granted, thank you," said Sir Robert, shaking hands with his son, with his eyes on his face.

"Then will you come and be introduced to my colleagues?"

"No, I will also take them——ah, I shall be most pleased," said Sir Robert, observing the sex of these persons, and accompanying Felix towards them.

"May I introduce my father?" said Felix, pronouncing the names of the women in turn, and causing each to give a conscious little bow, and Sir Robert a series of salutes that had not merely a numerical advantage.

"Are your son's surroundings what you expected, Sir Robert?" said Miss Luke.

"Ah, yes; a pretty sight," said Sir Robert, giving a general glance about him after his words.

"Confess you would like him to give up his post to-morrow."

"I should be sorry to see him change his mind so soon."

"He says that in your view he might be a woman," said Miss Munday in a plaintive tone.

"A father is disposed to take a hopeful view of his son," said Sir Robert, bowing as he turned away.

"Do you not want to have a talk with your father?" said Mrs. Chattaway to Felix, with an improved opinion of this opportunity.

"No. I look rather undistinguished beside him. And he might try to make me look foolish; and it would not be fair to Mrs. Napier for me to look both. One cannot only consider one's own family."

Sir Robert was approaching Simon.

"You have great doings here to-day."

"Yes, it is our great occasion."

"A pretty sight, the young faces," observed Sir Robert, after a silence.

"Yes, here to-day and gone to-morrow!" said Simon, in a rather drawn-out, dreamy tone. "A world of fleeting generations."

Sir Robert agreed, and moved on to offer a formal hand-shake to Jonathan. Jonathan returned it in a cringing manner, stooping and looking shorter than he was, and vanished into the crowd.

"It is a pity that I have not inherited my father's appearance," said Felix. "I am really almost a trivial figure in comparison. Here is Mrs. Napier, bringing another father to see us! I see how much mine is above the average. I am not at all self-conscious about being the only man."

"Not as self-conscious as Mrs. Napier is about being the only woman with the father," said Helen to Miss Rosetti.

"Now, here are the senior mistresses grouped for your introduction to them!" said Josephine, keeping her eyes averted from Felix, to give full weight to the convention of precedence to woman. "They will be interested to know that you hope to place your daughter with us next term."

"Will you pay extra for drawing?" said Felix, as he was presented.

"Why, I don't know. Is that the thing to do?"

"Yes, quite the thing," said Felix.

"Mr. Bacon is the drawing master, and anxious for the success of his subject," said Josephine.

"Well, it shows that he takes his subject seriously."

"I am shocked by people's attitude to their daughters," said Felix. "They all express open surprise that their education should be taken seriously. It is a good thing that they entrust it to other people: they are evidently not without parental instincts. But they don't seem to give any real thought to their being the mothers of the race."

"Well, but too much education may not result in their being the mothers of the race," said the father, lifting his eyes lightly from the mistresses, as if they had not had this direction, and then hastening his words. "Well, we spend nearly as much on the girls' education as on their brothers' nowadays."

"It is so savage of us to be proud of that. We aim at real equality; and every extra is a step towards it. So as drawing is an extra, I am sure that your daughter will take it."

"But I am not sure she has any talent."

"But I am sure she has. You see the difference between the parent and the teacher. Will you come and see the kind of talent she will have?"

"I would rather see some average drawings, and know what is done by the ordinary girl."

"You shall see any kind you like, though I cannot bear your daughter to be called ordinary. I will show you some drawings that are not yet mounted, and then you will know that she will do much better. You won't come and see how much better she will do?"

"No, I will be content with the average. Though I shouldn't be surprised if my girl is a thought above it."

"I knew it," said Felix. "You see how well I already understand her. You will wait for me while I fetch the drawings?"

"I will send for them," said Josephine, turning to Elizabeth, who was standing near. "Mrs. Giffard, you will do me a kindness, and fetch a portfolio from the left-hand bookcase in my library? You will not mind an odd job to-day? We are all occupied with them."

"An odd job?" said Elizabeth. "If I minded odd jobs, dear Josephine, I don't know what would have happened in this house to-day, or failed to happen. But this odd job doesn't sound as if it called for my peculiar talents."

"It does not, and that is why it is an odd job," said

393

Josephine, coming to her side and lowering her voice. "I think, you know, that I would call me Mrs. Napier, if I were you, on these formal occasions. And I will make a point of calling you Mrs. Giffard. You must trust me to take on myself an equal share of a bargain."

"Now that you break one that has lasted for forty years! But I am yours to command, as we are both aware."

"I am always sorry to be compelled to any such awareness. But if I must recognise that I am, I will request you to do as I asked."

"There are several maids about with nothing on their hands."

"Well, if you are happy as the housekeeper," said Josephine, using an audible tone, "in allowing the maids *carte blanche* on my shelves, I will follow my rule and leave your own work to your own judgement."

"Simon, are you coming to help me to accomplish my duties?" said Elizabeth in ringing tones. "They are branching out in so many directions. Shall we follow the example of our boy and girl, and address ourselves together to usefulness?"

Josephine glanced at Ruth and Gabriel, who were dispensing refreshments together, and summoned an indulgent expression to her face.

"Simon is occupied with his guests," she said, turning back to Elizabeth. "If there were any need for assistance, I should have provided you with it. There is only one portfolio."

"Well, he and I have so often done one thing between us in the past, that we can safely essay another in the present. If practice makes perfect, you will soon have your prize."

"I am sorry to have caused any trouble," said the guest. "We could have seen the drawings another time."

"That would be a pity," said Felix. "It would postpone your recognition of the inferiority of other people's children. The parents of daughters are not so unnatural in that matter as in others."

"You seem to know a good deal about parents. I suppose you have been here a long while?"

"Anyone would suppose that," said Felix.

"I daresay your staff has not much to complain of, Mrs. Napier."

"Hear, hear!" said Miss Luke, stepping impulsively forward from her place.

"Hear, hear!" said her companions, moving forward a shorter distance, and dropping their eyes as they voiced their exclamation, Mrs. Chattaway with emphasis, Miss Rosetti with acquiescence, and Miss Munday in a falsetto tone, which provoked a twitch on her own face. Miss Luke joined in on a lower note, proper to support of her own initiative, and the guest made a movement to tap his stick, as if hardly accepting his own isolation.

"Well, what am I to say?" said Josephine. "I think I will say that I have been told to 'hear,' and that I have heard, and that if it is enough for you, it is indeed enough for me."

The guest fulfilled his impulse and desisted, finding himself without real faith in the method.

"Well, I will go and pursue those drawings," said Josephine. "They seem to be shy about not being passed for exhibition."

She went down the room and crossed the hall to the library, from the open door of which voices came to her, with their meaning blurred by her own emotional mood.

"Yes, I sat here alone, Simon, waiting for you to come in to me with Josephine. I sat and called up the past, until your family came and brought the present. Such a strange present it was for a moment, while it pressed back the memories and took possession! Yes, it has possession now."

"You are a great help to us in it, and it is in the present

that we live. Shall we let the dead past bury its dead, and deal with it in the better way?"

Simon steadied himself on the ladder where he stood and turned towards Elizabeth. A step was heard at the door, Josephine's step; and Elizabeth sprang away from the ladder, unconscious that she held it, unconsciously tightening her hold. Its balance was shaken, and it fell to the hearth, carrying Simon with it, and casting his head against the marble curb.

Josephine entered and started forward to her husband, who lay as he had fallen. The two women bent over him together, stood up together, and faced each other, as the truth was flung upon them; and Elizabeth found herself hastening for help at Josephine's word.

Jonathan and Gabriel came to Josephine, and she turned to them almost with a smile.

"Gabriel, I have to call on you to do your first action as a man."

Simon was lifted and carried to his room. The doctor gave the diagnosis of instantaneous death. The temple had been struck on the fatal spot. The routine of the house went on, and it was known that there was emptiness in Simon's place, and how near to the heart of things that place had been. In spite of the violent incident of his death, he seemed to have died with the evenness with which he had lived. It seemed that nothing sudden had taken place. There was less a blank than a difference.

At first Josephine was calm, alert, alive to every need. Then she drew apart, gave some rapid, final directions in a failing tone, and hastened from her husband's room. She went in search of Gabriel, and found him alone, and drew him into a solemn but sustaining embrace.

Jonathan stayed for the evening, and sat at dinner in Simon's seat, in obedience to his sister's quiet word. The hour was to be marked by no particular observance. Josephine was gravely cheerful, and refused to be relieved of the duties of her place. She talked to Gabriel with reassuring ease, and made no demand on him for grief, assuming simply that the loss was light to his youth.

She went herself with her brother to the door. "My dear sister, my heart is full for you. You are beyond praise. Just take each moment as it comes."

"There is no fear that I shall do more than that; and no fear that anything will go amiss with anyone else, as long as I do it. That at the present must be enough for me. Yes, I must find it enough."

CHAPTER IX

T HE next morning Josephine came downstairs at the usual time. She assured herself that Gabriel had slept, and making no response to the similar question to herself, moved to the breakfast-table.

"You did not sleep, then, Josephine?" said Gabriel.

"Well, no, I did not, naturally, my dear. But I am glad you did; that was just as natural. Now let me see you do the natural thing by your breakfast, and do it justice."

She supplied his needs as usual, moving her hands with energy, and adjusting the things on the table, as though she hardly took into account that they served any purpose for herself.

"Are you going to have absolutely nothing, Josephine?"

"Yes, I am this morning. I shall eat as soon as ever I can, I promise you. I am not a person to take a pride in not being able to eat and sleep. I am proud of things that do more for other people. As soon as Nature can control my foolishly responsive organism, I shall let her and be thankful."

She raised her eyes with courteous interest as Ruth Giffard appeared at the door.

"Dear Mrs. Napier, Mother has arranged for the dressmaker to come to the house. Do you think you could bring yourself to see her? She is in the housekeeper's room. You know certain things have to be done."

"Dear child, how thoughtful of your mother! Of course certain things have to be done. I cannot be seen at all as I am now; and as I have no intention of immuring myself for the rest of my natural life, I will go and submit to the necessary steps to prevent it." Josephine rose with a movement that revealed her unused plate, and, throwing her napkin over it, went to the door. "And will you stay and say a word to this poor Gabriel of mine? I cannot bear that mine should be the only woman's face he sees to-day."

"So brave and good this is, my dear," said Elizabeth, as Josephine opened her door. "You need hardly be conscious of what is happening, if you will put yourself in our hands."

"I must do so indeed. I plead guilty to being a very dull and unresponsive subject, and must simply hope to be borne with. I confess that I had not thought of this necessity, which was parasitic and dependent, and really exacting of me. I will be frank, and ask you to do your best for me, without expecting return; which is frank indeed."

"Which gown shall we take first?" said the dressmaker.

"Good morning, Mrs. Faulkner," said Josephine, roused to observation for the first time. "I hope you will excuse my not seeing you before."

"I thought this for the day," said Elizabeth, showing a material. "That very deep mourning is not worn now."

"Simply the deepest mourning that is made for a widow," said Josephine, in an almost light tone. "That is all I have to say."

"But you will get tired of such heavy black, as the months go by."

"Will you not sit down, Mrs. Faulkner? No, I shall

not get tired of it, dear Elizabeth. I shall not give it a thought. That is where I have to ask you to be patient with me. And the same with the other things." Josephine turned to the woman, and hurried her words, as if anxious to get the matter behind. "Simply the deepest widow's mourning that is made. And of good quality and no definite date. I shall wear such things for a long time."

"Well, you must have your own way," said Elizabeth.

"It is not my way. It is my character, and has nothing to do with me. I have no way in the matter. It is settled for me from within, as it were behind my back."

"Will Mrs. Napier be going to the funeral?" the dress-maker asked Elizabeth, possibly hardly going to meet Josephine's methods of decision. "Because, if so, we must hurry some of her things."

"No, I shall not be going," said Josephine, turning on the speaker quiet, serious eyes. "I have no opinion on the question of women's going to funerals. I simply know what I can do and what I cannot."

"That will make things much easier. What I mean is, we shall not be so pressed."

"I am glad of that," said Josephine.

"I am sure you are wise, dear," said Elizabeth.

"Well, there again it is settled for me. Now, if I have done my part, I will leave you both to do yours. Thank you for coming to the house, Mrs. Faulkner. And, Elizabeth, you will let me give you your dress for the service on Friday, and arrange for Mrs. Faulkner to make it? You will not deny me a small privilege just now?"

"No, dear, no; I shall not be going to the funeral. I will stay behind with you."

"Simon would have liked you to go," said Josephine, bending and looking into her eyes.

"No, I don't think so. I find funerals upsetting. And I shall not need black clothes. I shall have no right to wear them, no use for them afterwards."

"Black is always useful," said Josephine gently. "I

often wear it myself; often did, I mean. But perhaps you are right, that there is no need for us both, for anyone but me to be involved in the sombreness. You will have something else for a gift, some remembrance of Simon. He would have wished you to have one." She turned to the dressmaker and took a kindly leave.

At the funeral luncheon she presided herself, calm, considerate, self-controlled; talked in a normal, if rather absent, manner on matters of the day, and met with kindness rather than solemnity the mourners' farewell.

"Keep your thoughts on one thing," she said to Gabriel, her low, clear tone not approaching a whisper, "that your home and your life are safe. You are too young to be held by sorrow. I will see that the future is fair to you."

On his return she gave him a cheerful welcome, drew him out on the funeral for his own relief, and left him while she went herself on a pilgrimage through her awakening house.

On the mistresses' landing she came upon Mrs. Chattaway, who turned and ran back as she saw her, and then turned again and ran forward, as though reconsidering the question of an encounter.

"Well, how have you been in these last days?" said Josephine, with an open smile for this vacillation. "You have found me but an indifferent head, but I can assure you only in one sense. Has everything gone well with all of you?"

"Yes, indeed, Mrs. Napier; as far as it could, considering the trouble of the house. It is a small matter how things have gone with us; the question is, how they have gone with you. Of course, there is no question; we have been so grieved for you."

"Now, that does not alter the fact that the question exists with you. Believe me, you have been much in my mind. If I had thought that you could doubt it, I would have made the effort, made a point of coming to see you."

"No, of course not, Mrs. Napier. How could we think

of such a thing? I cannot express what we should have felt. We should have sunk through the floor with shame and compunction."

"Well, I hope you will let me do so almost at once, and that you will not sink through the floor, but will all sit comfortably in your chairs. It will be a satisfaction to me to see you. Will you give your companions that message?"

Mrs. Chattaway remained still for a moment, and then openly abandoned her errand and ran back to the common room.

A little while later Josephine knocked at the door.

"May I come in?" she said, entering with hardly a question in her tone, in simple acceptance of the concessions to her situation.

"Indeed you may," said Miss Luke in a low, deep voice.

Josephine sat down, and placing her elbows on her knees, leant forward over folded hands.

"I have not seen any of you for several days. Have you all been well?"

"The point is, how you have been, Mrs. Napier?"

"I have been well," said Josephine, in an incidental, cordial tone, that at once assigned her health to its place and readily bore witness to it.

"You have been constantly in our thoughts," said Miss Luke.

"I have felt it. I assure you it has been a support to me."

"Oh no, Mrs. Napier; if we had known——" Mrs. Chattaway broke off.

"I know," said Josephine, leaning forward to touch her hand. "It was clear to me; I am grateful."

Mrs. Chattaway withdrew her hand and replaced it, withdrew it again, and again set it at Josephine's disposal; and Josephine turned as if unconsciously to Miss Munday.

"I have to thank you for taking prayers for me. I must not impose my duties on you any longer."

"You should not return to them yet, Mrs. Napier," said Miss Rosetti in a friendly tone. "You must spare yourself."

"No," said Josephine, her voice rising; "that is just what I have been doing, and what I must not do. I do not see any of you doing it, and that should make me pause and take myself to task. It has made me do so."

"You must not pretend that it is not quite different," said Miss Luke.

"Yes, it is a little different; well, quite different, as you are so kind as to see it. But I must not yield to the difference. I have faced it; you need not in your kindness fear for me."

"It does not seem to me right," said Mrs. Chattaway.

"Well, you know it does seem right in a way," said Miss Luke, wisely making the move to normal ground. "What did not seem right, was that Miss Munday should take prayers."

"Prayers do seem rather too right a thing for Miss Munday," said Helen.

Josephine gave a ready laugh.

"No, and it is not right," she said. "She has her own duties complete, without mine."

"You will not take prayers in the morning?" said Miss Rosetti. "I hope you will not be down as early as that."

"Now," said Josephine, looking straight at her, "why do you hope it? You will all of you be down, and I should take my place with you."

"Well, it will relieve me of the strain of being in time," said Miss Munday.

"Yes," said Josephine, with an uncritical smile, "I thought of that; of your waiving your personal inclinations in deference to mine. I have not thought little of it."

"Are you eating and sleeping, Mrs. Napier?" said Miss Luke.

"Now," said Josephine, "what an awkward question!

Suppose I asked any of you, if you had taken your proper recreation during these last days! What answer should you make?"

"You are thinner, Mrs. Napier!" accused Mrs. Chattaway.

"Am I?" said Josephine, absently lifting her bodice a distance from her figure. "I daresay I may be."

"Your dress is quite loose," said Mrs. Chattaway.

"Well, we could not expect the dressmaker to foresee the changes of the immediate future. Exacting as we are with dressmakers, we do not expect from them the gift of prophecy."

"No one could have foreseen that anyone could be so affected in so short a time," said Mrs. Chattaway, half under her breath. "It shows how much more sensitive some people are than others."

"Well, in that case, I think they should hide their sensitiveness," said Josephine. "It is a quality that should work both ways."

"How is your nephew, Mrs. Napier?" said Miss Rosetti.

"Keeping up his spirits, thank you. It is a great relief, that he is not letting them get out of hand. Happily youth is resilient."

"It is a great loss for him," said Miss Rosetti.

"Yes," said Josephine; "so great, that I shudder at the thought of a greater. There are some things—well, the heart stands still before the imagination."

"Your courage must have done everything for him," said Miss Luke; "or rather, done the one thing, and held out hope for the future."

"What I have tried to do," said Josephine, "is so to appear to him, that he should not have to counterfeit a maturer than the natural grief. That is often the saddest side of sorrow for the young. That is the principle underlying the course I have been seen to be taking."

"We have thought you so brave," said Mrs. Chattaway, disclaiming misconception of Josephine's demeanour.

There was a knock at the door, and Josephine turned on Miss Munday a look of question.

"Come in," said Miss Munday.

Felix came in, and perceiving Josephine, made as if to withdraw.

"Now, I don't know what is the matter with me," said Josephine, in another tone. "First Mrs. Chattaway runs away from me in the passage, and now Mr. Bacon gives a glance in my direction, and prepares to flee! I had better take myself off, and leave you free of the sight of my sable form. You will become inured to it by degrees."

"I am glad that I am not capable of a real grief," said Felix, as he closed the door behind her.

"Most people would not like to feel that. They are so blind to their own advantage," said Helen.

"I am afraid I should not show the dignity of it."

"You can plan your own death after everyone else's, without a misgiving," said Helen.

"You have a right to, as regards most of us here," said Miss Luke."

"Oh, I shall really have a great deal of real grief," said Felix.

"I have not been marked out for sorrow," said Miss Munday.

"What I cannot understand," said Felix, "is how all of you, who knew Simon Napier, are not in real grief and showing its dignity."

"I thought I was showing it," said Helen. "I am."

"We did not see much of him," said Mrs. Chattaway.

"Well, that is some excuse."

"But not enough," said Helen.

"Did you—you were very much attracted—you liked him very much, Miss Keats?" said Mrs. Chattaway.

"Yes, very much," said Helen.

"So did I," said Felix.

"I had a great respect for him, of course; but I cannot say he was my ideal for a man," said Mrs. Chattaway.

"No—no—perhaps not," said Miss Luke.

"He was mine," said Helen and Felix at once.

"You two seem to think very much alike," said Mrs. Chattaway.

"Exactly alike in this matter," said Helen.

"When people feel that there cannot be two opinions, they have to share one," said Felix. "I am glad I am not alone in feeling an admiration for a fellow creature. I might be thought to be easily pleased, when really my standard is very high."

Josephine had gone downstairs and entered the library, unreminded once again of the scene it had witnessed.

"We have reached the stage when realisation sweeps over us, Josephine," said Gabriel.

"Don't realise more than is necessary, or more than is natural," said Josephine, taking the hand he held out to her. "That kind of realisation tends to become imagination, as the days go by, if we do not put on the curb in time. I am thinking of myself more than of you, as my danger is greater. I shall put myself under a tight rein. Think what it would have been, if we had lost each other."

"You talk of putting curb and rein on imagination, and then allow it to become utterly unbridled."

"Yes, it was going too far, imagining too much. I should not have said it; I do not say it. We shall be nearer than ever to each other. You have a right to demand it. I am under the duty to meet the demand."

"Will you keep on the school?" said Gabriel, after a silence. "Of course you have hardly had time to decide."

"There is nothing to decide. The parents and pupils will wish it; the staff and servants will wish it; and I consider all and each of them before myself. And there is someone, for whom I am putting by money with every year that I keep it, and for his sake I shall hold to it as long as I am able."

"You must not save money for me," said Gabriel, in a new, sharp tone. "You have done enough for me, and must do no more. I shall be going forth to work for myself as soon as I can leave you."

"Well, that won't be soon," said Josephine. "I have done a woman's part by you, and you must do a man's part by me. To leave a lonely widow by herself would hardly be doing it."

"I could not take Uncle Simon's place in the school."

"No, you could not," Josephine gently agreed. "It is not a thing I should care for, that you should make your career in a girls' school. Your uncle had the difference within himself; it was involved in his being as an individual, and for him it was possible. I mean nothing but appreciation of either of you, when I agree that for you it is not possible."

Jonathan and his friends were to come to dinner, to help his family over the funeral night.

Josephine gave them her usual welcome, and showed particular concern for their comfort.

"My dear, you must think of yourself, and not of us," said Jonathan.

"No, that is what I must not do. That is where my danger lies. And it is best to avoid danger. Surely discretion is the better part of valour."

"It is good of you to tolerate the company of a comparative stranger, Mrs. Napier," said Fane.

"I must have ceased to regard you in that light, or I should not have expected you to tolerate my company, even the glimpse of it that I shall give you." Josephine put a cushion behind her brother. "Now, are you all as you like to be?"

"Are you not going to stay, Josephine?" said Gabriel.

"No, not to-night, my dear."

"Then are you not going to have any dinner?"

"Yes," said Josephine, in a light tone. "I am. I am rather faint, rather hungry. It will be brought to my room."

"Why do you not stay and have it with us?"

"Why, you do not want to know my reasons, do you? They are not of a surprising kind."

"You will get into low spirits, if you do not take care."

Josephine gave a low laugh at this account of her situation.

"Of course you are already in low spirits. But there is no point in letting them get lower."

"I am going to let them get a little lower than you have seen them," said Josephine, almost brightly. "That is my object in going away by myself, since you insist on a precise explanation. There is just a little point in it for me, you know; I am not an abnormal woman."

"Ah, your aunt is a courageous creature, Gabriel," said Jonathan, when his sister had left them.

"I am less proud of her at the moment than I have been."

"Ah, the spirit is willing, but the flesh is weak," said his father.

"You will have to fill your uncle's place, Gabriel," said Fane.

"I am far from such an ambition. I shall have all I can do to fill my own place, when I find one to fill."

"Is not your aunt very dependent on you?"

"She is dependent on herself, as you can see. It is I who ought to be dependent on myself. I hope to get a post in my old school, and cast off my reproach."

"I shall not miss you," said Felix. "You have killed my feeling for you. And I find that I like women better than men."

Jonathan looked from Felix to Gabriel, as if rejoicing in his possession of each.

"I suppose all men do, in a way," said Fane.

"I did not mean in a way," said Felix.

As Jonathan and Gabriel laughed, Josephine came into the room, and giving them a smile of sympathy for their mood of mirth, crossed to the bookcase, and taking a packet of letters, left them without a word.

CHAPTER X

"WELL, I am grateful," said Josephine, looking over her desk at Miss Luke and Miss Rosetti, who sat before her. "It is a load lifted, to feel that my husband's work will be done, until I can fill his place, in the ways in which it must be filled." She ended in a manner of forced cheerfulness. "We must be thankful that we can deal in such a healthy way with the gaps in life."

"It is a privilege to do what we can, Mrs. Napier."

"Well, that is another demand of your kindness, that I am afraid I do rather feel it a privilege," said Josephine, with a touch of amusement at herself. "Even if I cannot be blamed for that, you miss your proportionate gratitude. And I fear you will miss it. I am not going to express suitable appreciation even now. You will be lenient towards my inevitable attitude?"

"The largest share of the work is falling on you, Mrs. Napier."

"Well, I should hope so. I should not have much right to expect your help, if that did not go without saying. I am not so muddle-headed about the rights and wrongs of a case."

"We shall have the practical advantage. We are not doing the work for love, not on an intangible basis, in a word, not for nothing," said Miss Luke, amused by the final length to which she went.

"My husband's labour is surely worthy of its hire. Or do you not think, now that you come to experience it, that it is?"

"It seems, in other hands than his," said Miss Rosetti, "hardly worthy of so much hire."

"Well, that is perhaps another point on which I am adapting matters to my own feelings. I hope that you will allow me the indulgence? Believe me, I do not intend any overreaching of my place. If it is a convenience to you, I am glad; though I have not thought of it more than you have. And now you do not want the burden of my society at this particular juncture of my experience. I am under no delusions about it, though I may say that I have appreciated yours, and taken its lesson. As this nephew of mine appears to desire it, we will allow him to take the step over which he properly hesitates, and supplant you. I will not offer more thanks. I told you that you would not get your share. And now, young man, the next time you make your appearance with a lady, you will allow her to precede you, I hope."

The women left the room as Gabriel entered it, leading Ruth by the hand.

"Well, amusing each other, like the good children of old friends? It is kind of Ruth, my boy, to adapt her leisure to yours."

"We wanted to see you about something important, Mrs. Napier, or I should not have left my work."

"I meant simply what I said, my dear. I do not communicate by implication. I am grateful for any happiness that you will give Gabriel just now, when the companion of his life is so little to be recommended."

"In that case you will be grateful to Ruth, Josephine," said Gabriel, coming nearer with a stumble, to avoid lifting his head. "She is giving me a happiness greater than I had conceived."

"Then it must be on a generous scale indeed, indulged boy," said Josephine, her tone out of accordance with the change in her eyes. "Let us hear about it before I resume my labours. Come to the point, and enunciate some demand of youth."

"It is the demand that I was bound to make one day. It is naturally often a demand of youth. This breaking up of our life seemed the best time to make it. The lesser change must count less at the time of the greater. I make the demand with confidence, having been taught, as you will say, to make demands. I have said enough for you to understand me?"

"No," said Josephine, in a quiet, conversational tone; "I don't think so. You have not said anything definite, have you?"

"Mrs. Napier, Gabriel and I find that we belong to each other," said Ruth, standing with clasped hands. "We are waiting to tell the world, until we have your sanction."

"No, come, I don't think so," said Josephine, seeming to suppress a smile. "Quite apart from telling the world, which would never be necessary, what you imply would involve issues of which you have no understanding. I don't want to snub youthful earnestness—you know I am not a person to do that; my life is based upon the significance of youth—but you will forgive me for not taking you very seriously? Silly little people!" She ended on a tender, final note, her hands trembling beneath her desk. "You would be nicely up a tree, if I did."

Gabriel looked as if he had met what he feared, but Ruth shrank back and lifted her eyes to his.

"You must surely understand the feeling between a man and a woman, Josephine?"

"Well, let the feeling help you to do more for each other than it is doing, or it will not be at all the feeling between a man and a woman, that I understand. No, I have had understanding of a very different kind. Even in this break of my last and lasting experience of it, I can look back on the earlier ones"—Josephine raised her eyes and seemed to be counting on her fingers—"and see them unsullied by any simple grasping for self."

"Early love may be the only love, Mrs. Napier."

"No, my dear, it may not."

"We are living our youth, of course, as we are young," said Gabriel. "There must be something in the first love, that anyhow is its own."

"Come, don't be highfalutin. You will be sorry for extravagant speeches soon. You will look back and squirm over them. I remember my own youth."

"Perhaps it would be as well if your own youth had borne more fruit," said Gabriel. "I don't remember any feeling between you and your husband, that can be taken as an example."

"Don't you, my dear, don't you?" said Josephine with almost fervent hopelessness. "You think that that was not much, that daily feeling that you saw; that humdrum, tried affection, that was before your eyes! You think that most married lives hold more; that this that you were trying to imagine, would hold more? Do you, poor boy, poor boy?"

"I am speaking as a man, Josephine."

"Oh, no, you are not. When you refer to the person, whom from your childhood you have known as 'Uncle Simon,' as my husband, you are speaking as the silly boy you are. It is natural: as you said, you are living your youth, and youth has its own ways of dealing with its set-backs, its innocence, its spleen." Josephine spaced the last words, uttering them with quiet philosophy. "Ah, a man would know that there are many claims to be fulfilled, before a boy can take his place. No, be a boy a little longer; and you, my child, be satisfied with your youth; and presently find a partner more advanced to man's estate, than this beardless boy of mine."

"Of course I admit the appearance of ruthless egotism," said Gabriel.

"No. Why should you admit that? There has not been much appearance of it, has there?"

"I mean the leaving you by yourself in your new loneliness."

"Oh, I thought you said 'appearance.' You meant

411

reality, did you? The less said about that, the better. We certainly will not turn our eyes on the figure you cut in any real sense."

"We are pledged to each other," said Ruth. "We are not people who could break our faith."

"Now, now, you know we none of us can take that stand. I, for one, should be ashamed of taking it, of re-solving never to change. If we can never change, we can never learn. And that admission means more for me, than it would for you. Why, you have broken your prom-ise to me, that you would throw yourself heart and soul into your work. You must have had a wandering mind of late, while I have been—well, also breaking my prom-ises, and yielding to the claims of my own life. So I am not going to take you up hardly for it. We have to go back on promises too lightly or confidently made. We know there is a real promise to be made by both of you, by and by, and that this preliminary is better quickly put aside, if it is not to cast its shadow forward over the real thing that is to come. That is a tragedy we do not want for you."

"Would you not like to see Gabriel's children, Mrs. Napier?" said Ruth, in a pleading tone.

"Gabriel's children?" said Josephine, with a little frown. "How do you mean, my dear? Do you—can you mean your children and his? Because it is not for me to refuse to follow you wherever you care to lead."

"Josephine, that is absurd," said Gabriel. "It was a perfectly reasonable speech."

"Yes, it was very reasonable," said Josephine lightly. "As reasonable and tangible and practical as it could very well be. It was I who was not tangible enough, I quite agree."

"You do not try to understand, Mrs. Napier."

"My dear, I understand without trying," said Jose-phine, almost tenderly. "It is a difficult moment for you, a moment that does call for courage. It must be, when we make a mistake in the deeper things, as we do in youth. We need the courage to admit the mistake to ourselves, and to see that what we thought we had attained, is still beyond. But you have it; you are your mother's child. The spirit you show in holding to your purpose proves it. It is only the adjustment that is needed. Gabriel has not been unworthy of himself in his first stumble"—she gave Gabriel an almost radiant look—"of the many that are to come before the final steadying."

"To refuse to accept a simple truth is neither moral nor reasonable," said Gabriel.

"Well, may I ask what you will live on, since I am to be so reasonable? I admit that I was rather trying to be the other thing, by way of covering what needed covering, and saving the faces that required to be saved."

"I shall get a post at my old school. They give a preference to old boys, and my degree is good. We shall be able to manage."

"Well, well, manage then. I am glad you have the grit to face it all together; to meet the grinding daily round of contriving in pence, and cutting off amenities that have come to seem the decencies. For it does need character. I for one have never done it, or thought I could do it. I admit that for me life is dependent on a certain seemliness. If you can do more than I, be it so. Though it has never been so, has it, in our years together? And now you know that my work cannot wait, and that it is necessity and not indifference, that drives me to dismiss you. You can tell me the details presently, of all you have arranged. It must have been a complicated piece of planning; I feel how much you have had on you."

Ruth and Gabriel found themselves in the hall, and breaking at once into talk, forgot where they stood, and before many minutes Josephine emerged and came towards them.

"Now," she said, brushing past them with some letters in her hand, "let me pass, chattering pair. What are you

413

doing, blocking up the hall for people who need it? I suppose you think no one has more to do than you have. If that is your influence over each other, you must see that you do not exert it for too long."

Her manner put them behind her in thought as well as in deed, but in a moment she turned her head and came to a pause. Then, waving her letters to them, she went her way.

CHAPTER XI

THAT evening, when Josephine and Gabriel had dinner as usual alone, Josephine made no mention of what had passed, and appeared in a more than usually genial mood. When the meal was over, she set the places at the hearth, so that the grouping seemed complete.

"Josephine, may I ask Ruth to join us?" said Gabriel, springing to his feet.

"What, my dear? Yes, fetch anyone you please," said Josephine, stooping and making a noise with the fire-irons. "We ought to make our party brighter in the evenings, and remember that you are young, and that neither of us is old. What about bringing Mrs. Giffard as well, asking her if she will kindly join us? I must not forget, in the egotism of trouble, that she is my old friend, and that it is because of her that her daughter is in my house."

Gabriel carried the message, and presently Elizabeth came by herself.

"Why, what is this that happens, or threatens to happen, Josephine? Have the boy and girl confided in you, and not in me, when one of them is all my own? Such a jealous real mother I shall be, if the adopted mother is given the first place! Well, she is used to it, and must not be grudged her dues. But what do our little people say, that shows that they are little and ours no longer?"

"There has been some talk about their being engaged, or being unengaged or something," said Josephine. "I never know what they mean, these dilly-dallyings between the very young. They mean that they need to be thrown together, I think, so that any spurious ebullition of feeling may wear itself out. It almost seems that they are of that mind, and disposed to apply the curative method to themselves."

"But they want to be married, the naughty ones to want to leave us?"

"They are going to be married, if I heard aright before dinner," said Josephine, with a little laugh. "They may not be going to by now, for all I know. Gabriel's wanting to fetch Ruth in this public, family way, rather looks as if there was a settlement of things."

Gabriel and Ruth returned to the room together.

"This is well thought of on your part, Josephine. As I am to be Mrs. Giffard's son-in-law, it is meet that she should know the group that I regard as my family."

"It is only you and I now, dear; hardly a group," said Josephine, in a low voice.

"So sweethearting has been going on, when we none of us suspected it!" said Elizabeth, throwing a bright glance at Gabriel. "It is all settled, is it? Such a lot of being unsettled I had, when I was at this stage! Such a lot of shiftings and shilly-shallyings, naughty one that I was! But my daughter has hidden her lights under a bushel; and this is the first time—well, nearly the first time; I must not tell tales, must I?—that she has let them shine before men; as represented, shall we say, by a certain young man?"

"This is a thing to be told in Gath, and published in the streets of Athens," said Gabriel. "People had better prepare themselves for it."

"They won't want preparation, dear, for such an everyday occurrence," said Josephine, reaching for her knitting. "They are accustomed to its happening amongst their younger friends."

Ruth looked at Josephine, as if the latter might be changing her ground.

"It is everything to us, Mrs. Napier."

"Yes, yes, my child. We were talking of the other people who exist in the world beside you."

"I don't see why we should trouble about the other people in the world," said Gabriel, in his less familiar tone. "It is not the custom in our position."

"Well, you are not troubling about them, are you?" said Josephine, rapidly changing her needles. "You are behaving in completely the customary way in your position. You need not fear that you are affording us a glimpse of anything out of the common. We can set your mind at rest there."

Elizabeth gave a swift glance from face to face.

"People always give up their old life when they marry," said Gabriel.

"All living creatures mate while they are young, if their life is natural," said Ruth.

"Well, I suppose that is the level of the beasts," said Josephine, laughing as if in genuine amusement. "And they mate afresh every year, don't they? I confess I had not thought about them, at any rate in connection with our own life. And if I wanted to live at their level, I don't know that I should put it as plainly as you did, you frank, modern child."

"You seem to be knitting for dear life, Josephine," said Gabriel.

"It rests me, my boy," said Josephine, leaning back and then resuming. "It won't do for me to give up any means of rest, if I am to need them more than ever. I may be knitting for dear life soon; you seem to be planning that I may."

"I wish you would give Ruth a chance to know you, Josephine."

"She has had every chance to know me," said Josephine gravely. "I have been her principal, her adviser—her benefactor; if we are to get down to rock bottom, as she does. In all those capacities she does know me. If she is to know me now as a human woman, with human claims, it will not do her harm. I am giving her the chance to know me, that she has not had."

"My marrying her will make no difference to my feeling for you."

"I wondered when that was coming," said Josephine, with a note of contempt. "It would have made no difference to my feeling for you, would it, if I had abandoned you in your orphanhood?"

"Josephine, I simply don't understand you."

"No," said Josephine gently; "I expect you don't. I have given you no opportunity. You have only had to conceive of the side of me that gives. I see you have actually had no glimpse of any other."

"There must always be give and take in any human relation."

"There must. That is my point. I have done my share of giving. Now is the time—yes, I will say it—for me to take."

"I don't think you understand the nature of giving."

"Well, show me that you understand the nature of giving back. That is all you have to be concerned with. No one is asking you to take any initiative in the matter."

"You would share our happiness, Mrs. Napier," said Ruth.

"My child, happiness must come out of our own lives, not out of other people's. I think you must know that. Indeed, the course you have been taking shows that you know it. I might say that you would share my happiness, if Gabriel remained in his old place. But be assured that I shall not say it." Josephine bent towards Ruth with her old smile. "I have not so little knowledge of human nature, or so little sympathy with it."

"But we must think of our happiness, as you think of yours."

"The time for it is all to come," said Josephine, moving her hand. "When you have earned it, is the time. It will perhaps not be just yet."

"I think I had better take Ruth away," said Gabriel.

"Yes, you take her away," said Josephine, pointing at him with her needle; "and make your peace with her for dragging her into this morass. She wants a man ten years older than you. She has not forgotten, if you have, that a woman is ten years older than a man. It can never be out of the poor child's mind. You overrate your claims quite pitifully, or shall we say youthfully? I hope Ruth will let us say it."

"Well, so it is all to be held up, Josephine?" said Elizabeth, as she and Josephine were left alone. "It is not the romance that must come in the end to my orphan girl?"

"My dear, I hope not much experience of that kind has fallen her way yet?" said Josephine, bending towards her friend with a concern so kindly as to preclude any doubt of her soundness.

"The real experience must come in the end. We shall have to find it in us to give it a welcome."

"We shall find it in us," said Josephine. "Do not fear. I have no fear for you. We shall yield when the moment comes, yield to keep more truly. But this time it has not come; and we must not take the easier path, must not disport ourselves in the broad and flowery way. We must face a little bitterness of spirit; at least I must. And I can face it for Gabriel's sake, and a little for my own as well. I wasn't quite insincere in saying all that I said; it had its elements of truth. I am not a person to rate my own claims at nothing, or to think it well for other people to do the same. I have too much respect for my fellow

creatures and myself, especially when one of the fellow
creatures happens to be my adopted son."

"I wonder if the news is all over the school?"

"Yes, I should think so," said Josephine, in a careless
tone. "A girl, you know, any ordinary girl, would be
eager to record any score along that line. It is under-
standable. I think we must understand it."

"Of course, there is no real objection to the marriage."

"Now, I do hope," said Josephine, "that you do not
feel I have not watched over her, that she has made a
false step, and one which I am afraid is a pity. But I
have been torn aside by personal sorrow, and it may be
that I have been less alive to other people's needs. If it
has been so, then so it must be said."

"We could have expected nothing else from you. She
had her mother to watch over her, and there is no harm
done."

"Yes," said Josephine seriously, "I think you could
have expected something else from me. I hope you will
always expect it. And the harm done is of the kind that
I forgive myself the least, needless suffering for youth."

"They should have enough to manage on, if Gabriel
takes a schoolmaster's post. There is no real obstacle in
their way."

"No obstacle is real to young people, who find their
purpose criticised, and criticised justly." Josephine smiled
into Elizabeth's face. "You have learned your lesson
well. I recognise the arguments of this afternoon."

"They held good this evening."

"Yes," said Josephine, with sympathy in her tone.

"Shall we send for them, and talk it over again?"

"No," said Josephine, more sharply. "I have had
enough of that, all that I can bear of it, if you will
pardon me."

"Of course you must be considered."

"Yes, I begin to see that I must."

"Love never takes heed of other people," said Elizabeth, looking at Josephine.

"No, that is as I said. But when it is as young as this, it soon passes. Yes, that is the sorry side of love between a boy and girl, often in itself a beautiful thing, that it does tend to pass."

"Are you talking about me and my early marriage?"

"There! You see that in every case some truth comes home. No, I was not talking about you; and I am sure you know I was not, and should not, in that veiled way. It is simply that the cap fits you or me or anyone; and so it probably fits your child and mine."

"Did your first love come to an end?"

"Yes," said Josephine, with a look of reminiscence; "and my second and third, since you ask me piercing questions. I see I have perhaps laid myself open to them. I think and hope that they also came to an end on the other side; that I have no harm to look back on. But you see the cap fits me as well."

Elizabeth took a step towards Josephine.

"You will take my daughter's lover, as you took mine?"

Josephine moved a pace apart, her eyelids falling and her head back, seeming to force a contempt through her silence.

"I think it is time for me to go, Josephine," said Elizabeth, beginning to weep. "In my present mood I am a stranger to myself. And in yours you cannot bear with a stranger."

"If I had regarded an old friend as a stranger, I should certainly not have been able to bear with you. And as things are, if I have betrayed myself, I have; so I will not flatter myself that I can contradict what I have not hidden. To be something and then deny it, is not a combination that holds water, is it?"

CHAPTER XII

JOSEPHINE made no mention of Gabriel's marriage during the next weeks. She went through her days in outward calm, holding at bay the danger that seemed too great. The only change to be seen was a general increase of kindliness, an instinctive laying of the foundations of a different life. Gabriel spent his time with Ruth between her hours of work, and in his intercourse with Josephine, showed himself affectionate and filial, as though forbearing to feelings he could not explain. One day he and Ruth came to her study together.

"Josephine, we have another demand to make. Ruth has lost her zeal for professional life, and requests you to release her at the end of the term."

"Well, she can request me then, can't she?" said Josephine, looking up from her work, and resting her eyes on their locked hands. "I am not an ogress."

"Well, you are rather. That is why I feel it my duty to come between the two of you."

"And what are you doing, I should like to know, coming between me and a member of my staff? That is a duty rather off any known line. Now let Ruth—Miss Giffard you ought to call her in this capacity—speak for herself."

"I don't feel it is honest to go on, Mrs. Napier. My heart is not in my work. I find that I can only live in my future with Gabriel."

"Now, that is a nice confession for a mistress of mine to make! How long have you been feeling like that, I should like to ask, you travesty of a professional woman! And will I release you? Indeed, and with all my heart. And glad I am, that I have not had to ask you to release yourself, you awkward daughter of my old friend! And at once, if you please, and no mention of the rest of the term, if you love me, from someone who openly confesses that her heart is not in her work!"

"It is better to be open about what is inevitable, Josephine."

"I should rather prefer a decent veil to be drawn over it, myself."

"You do understand, Mrs. Napier? You don't think that things are going on, except as they are? Mother would be so distressed, if we gave you a wrong impression."

"What, my dear?" said Josephine, in an absent manner, bringing her hands alternately down on her desk.

"You don't think that either of us is deceiving you?"

"No, I do not," said Josephine, turning roundly on her. "Think you are deceiving me, when you boldly state that your mind has not been on your duties! I do not think you are deceiving me at all. I half wish you had deceived me. You give me a sense of compunction for my school, the feeling of all others, that I desire to avoid."

"I wish that so much of yourself had not been given to the school," said Gabriel; "and that there was something over for other purposes."

"Oh, do you?" said Josephine, with suddenly flashing eyes. "Then you wish that I had not sent you to Oxford, do you, and that I would put you now to some grinding toil and moil, instead of leaving you to meander and philander through your days, while I give so much of myself, as you put it, to the school? It is a nice, unselfish wish, but it is rather late."

"I shall soon be working now," said Gabriel.

"And how long would you have been working, if I could go back and take you at your first word? *Soon* be working? Soon! It is an amusing phrase. Still in the future, is it? Well, well, well!"

Josephine made no comment on this scene, and maintained her silence until the morning when there lay on the breakfast table Elizabeth's invitations to her daughter's wedding. Elizabeth had taken rooms for the occa-

sion in the town, and despatched the invitations without
a word to Josephine, taking advantage of her position as
mother of the bride.

Josephine sorted the letters for the household herself,
and added thereby to her knowledge of it; though she
would have scorned to open the letters, and depended
upon as accurate as possible a deduction of their contents.
Gabriel saw her recoil before the significant envelopes,
and brought himself to words.

"You have the invitations to the wedding, have you?
They bring home the fact that I have no wedding garment."

"Invitations? No, I have no invitations, dear. A letter
from my cousin, whom you have never seen; a line from
my lawyer, that you would not understand, and the usual
missives, reasoning and otherwise, from parents, with
which I will not bore you. That is the sum total of my
favours this morning."

"I mean the invitations for the other people in the
house. Mrs. Giffard would hardly send one to you. It is
assumed, of course, that you will be there."

"The invitations for your wedding and Ruth's?" said
Josephine, saying the words clearly and fully. "For her
friends in the house, I suppose? The envelopes with the
oblong shape? I took them for a set of appeals for charity.
Though I should not have escaped one myself, in that
case, I suppose. I should be the first person to be approached. I believe I am approached, on some such
grounds, in some of the others." She laid her hand on
some envelopes.

"They are in a sense a set of appeals for your charity."

"Why did they come through the post? What a needless complication, to send letters to the post from their
eventual goal!"

"But by no means a crime."

"Oh, no, dear. Nothing worse than the outcome of a
lack of training."

"It was to let you know of the wedding."

"Well, then it had a reason. But why could you not tell me of it?"

"You know very well why, Josephine."

"Well, it seems that you too had your reason. But, my dear, when you have not courage to speak of a thing, examine into your own heart. What is the reason why it should not be spoken of? What is there against that thing?"

"Nothing in this case," said Gabriel.

"Then you have nothing to worry about," said Josephine. "By the way, what arrangement are you making about Miss Giffard for the future?"

"She refuses to allow me to support her. I can only hope that she will do so in time."

"You did not insist upon it?" said Josephine, just raising her brows.

"I had not enough to offer, to warrant that. Josephine, you will come to my wedding, won't you?"

"I suppose I naturally shall. Nothing else would be practicable, would it?"

"I meant that you had not much time in these pressed days."

"Why, it won't take long, will it? You can tell me when it is time to start, for the matter of that."

"You will get to care so much for my wife, Josephine. You will come to think me the unworthy member of the partnership."

"My dear, I have many people to care for. Miss Giffard came to me as a member of my school, the school that you have such a dislike to hear mentioned, and that happened to be the solution of her life. For, for home life, as you know, or will know, she is not fitted. It was in that capacity that I saw to it, that I indeed cared for her. I did not undertake a relation with her in any other, or put any other at her disposal."

"Well, you will do your best?" said Gabriel.

"I will, indeed," said Josephine in a cordial tone, that did not hold any confidence of result. "What is that other letter you keep staring at?"

"A letter it is natural to stare at. It is from Fane, in his capacity of lawyer, and states that a client, who must remain anonymous, will pay me two hundred a year through Fane's office, on the condition that I make no attempt to discover the donor! A client! The donor! No clue of any kind! Neither he nor she! I suppose it is Father; unless it is you, Josephine? Of course that question is breaking the condition of acceptance; and I confess my inclination to accept."

"No, my dear, it is not my way to do things anonymously. I should frankly say it, if I were to offer you an allowance. And that reminds me that I was about to offer you one; of lesser munificence; a hundred and fifty a year; openly tendered from myself. Would it be of any good to you? It would have even more point, combined with the other. Yes, no doubt that is from your father, and given anonymously, lest you should fear that he could not spare it. But he must know his own affairs. I think you would be right simply to accept both offers."

"My breath is leaving me at the rosiness of my future. I was wondering how I should manage on a salary not meant for a married man. And now my way is not only smooth, but paved with gold. It is very generous of both of you."

"I was wondering how you would manage, too. But why is it generous of me? Of your father it is much more generous. Money and the material things of life are not what I have had traffic in. My truck has been in different commodities."

"It is I who am having to do with material things," said Gabriel, hastening his words, as Josephine rose and came towards him.

"My son, is it too much to ask, that for your own sake and mine you should give this first fancy a chance to prove itself? That you should spare a few years out of your many, to help the few that are mine?"

"Josephine, you know you ought not to ask it."

"Well, may I ask if you definitely accept my allowance?" said Josephine, moving away. "That is the sort of thing I ought to ask, is it? Would the hundred and fifty a year be of any use?"

"You know it would: I don't know what to say."

"Well, you don't say it is not the sort of thing to talk about, anyhow. You don't give vent to that particularly unhappy little saying. It is all right to make mention of it, I gather. Or ought it to have been anonymous like the other? Oh, never mind, my dear. I have taught you to be as you are. It is more blessed to give than to receive, is it? That is your motto in disposing of me?"

"You make things more than difficult for me, Josephine."

"Make things difficult! 'Make them easy' is the phrase I should use. A hundred and fifty a year is a lubricating kind of obstacle, in my opinion."

"I see how magnanimous it is of you, in the face of this unforeseen help, and of your disapproval of the marriage."

"I can't see that those things make any difference," said Josephine, with a faint irritation, as if at obtuseness. "The unforeseen help makes it more worth while for me to add my quota; and it is your comfort that we are considering, not the means by which you have endangered it. It won't look after itself, because it has a less experienced person to look after it. It is because of my disapproval of the marriage, that I am trying to arrange that things should not be worse than they must be. I don't want hardship for you; I should not have looked after you as I have, for all these years, if I had wanted that. I believe you think me capable of a sort of revenge. I hope you are not like that, yourself, my dear? They say that we judge other people by ourselves. I certainly am not, because I wanted

426

a little support in the days of my loneliness." Her voice shook and then rose on an easy note. "Now take these piles of letters, and put them, including the invitations, on the post table. And then leave me in peace to deal with my own. When I have breakfast without you, I shall have disposed of them by this time."

"I am humiliated to think of your finding letters a substitute for my companionship."

"No, you are not, my dear. It is what you are deliberately planning. It is the thing you ask of life, as far as I can gather. It is I who am humiliated by it. I don't make any secret of that. I have not made a secret of it on purpose. It is well that people should know what they are doing, that they should not go blindfold through their lives."

CHAPTER XIII

FROM this moment Josephine showed herself in another light. She referred to the marriage as to a normal event of the near future, and addressed herself to the preparations in an open, kindly spirit, arranging for her staff to attend the ceremony, and organising a celebration for the school.

"We must celebrate the marriage of the son of the house. I want to feel that you are all rejoicing with us."

When someone observed that it was not entirely an occasion for her to rejoice, she replied with an air of amused admission.

"Well, my nephew and I may stand a little aloof in our hearts. The force of advancing life has been too much for us, and deprived us of our bearings; and we find ourselves clinging to each other as the only rock left. But do not breathe a whisper, and you shall see that we shall not betray ourselves."

On the day of the wedding, at breakfast with Gabriel for the last time, she studied some papers during the meal, looked up to speak as if for the sake of convention, rose prematurely from the table, and returning as though recollecting herself, laid a hand on his shoulder.

"Why, what an absent-minded woman, adopted mother, lifelong friend! Too many capacities to be absent-minded in, at our last breakfast! I ought to suffer a lifetime's remorse."

"Don't think that you will dispose of me at that light cost," said Gabriel. "You will often have my wife and me seated at your board. Your house is the old home to us both."

"Yes. What a way to celebrate our last experience of our real home life! What an unsentimental pair we are!"

Josephine conducted the early luncheon with liveliness and ease, appeared to eat herself with interest and appetite, admonished Gabriel of his duties as host, and talked on topics unconnected with the occasion. She had made no difference in her usual dress, and wore simply her better outfit of widow's weeds. Her bonnet, with its crape and veil, lay ready at the side, indicating that her toilet was complete.

"Try to manage a little more, Mrs. Chattaway. I think we have plenty of time, and anyhow they would hardly begin without so many of us."

"No, thank you, I could not, Mrs. Napier. I have had too much, and we must not delay the hero of the ceremony."

"It is our safeguard, that we have him with us," said Josephine, smiling at Gabriel. "There have been so many preparations unconnected with him, that we forget he has quite a prominent part to play."

"We are hardly in danger of feeling that we are the protagonists," said Miss Luke.

"I am not putting myself in Miss Giffard's place," said Miss Munday. "I do not mind if you cannot believe me."

When the other women went to dress, Josephine moved to the side table, pushed aside the bonnet, and began to turn over her accounts.

"You are surely going to appear in something more festive than that?" said Gabriel.

"No, why should I, my dear? This is what I wear at this time of my life. What else should I wear? What else could I? I can put on my simpler things, if you would prefer them, though I think they are a little soiled. This is my dress for occasions; and I thought you would wish me to appear in it. I can change it, if you would like." Josephine took some steps towards the door, moving with deliberation, as if time were of no account.

"I did not know that people went to weddings, dressed so completely as widows."

"I suppose widows dress as widows, just as bridegrooms dress as bridegrooms."

"It is quite a long time, nearly six months, since Uncle Simon died."

"Five months, twenty-three days and nineteen hours," said Josephine, with her voice dying away and her eyes on space.

"Haven't you anything less funereal? Surely you got something new for the occasion?"

"My dear, it was for you that I got things, not for myself. You are the instigating character of this festival, not I. And I had not personally thought of it as a festival, if you remember."

"I took it for granted that you would dress in a suitable manner. You might be going to a burial in those garments."

"Well, I might have gone to a burial in them. That was their purpose. I should have gone to one in them, if I had been equal to it, if you remember that, too. That is why they are suitable for me at this stage of my life. Not that I want to remind you of it, at this stage of yours. So if you have done advising a middle-aged widow on her apparel, suppose you go and brush your own! It is not too late for that improvement, and it is a distinctly more appropriate one. It is you who are to appear as the bridegroom, not I."

"Well, I should soon be starting," said Gabriel in an aloof tone. "I have to do some confabulation with Felix. And the other carriages will soon be here. You were to arrange with Mrs. Giffard about going up the aisle."

"Yes, I believe something of the sort was planned," said Josephine, moving to the table for her bonnet, and assuming it with simple regard to neatness, and with no attempt to suppress the veil. "You are a practical person to remind your aunt. It is encouraging to see that my training bears fruit, on the day when you are dispensing with it."

Gabriel made a movement to embrace her before he left, but she raised her eyes from arranging her skirts, and parted from him simply with a nod and a smile.

She drove to the church in a carriage by herself, and walked to her place in a manner that somehow drew attention to her widow's garb. She was calm as the ceremony proceeded; followed the words of the service; watched with interest as Elizabeth gave her daughter away; and at the significant moment turned her face to the kneeling figures in natural emotion, and openly wiping her eyes, returned to her book.

At the subsequent gathering she was a benevolent, dignified figure. She looked maternally at Gabriel's wife, made a point of talking to her staff, and on passing Elizabeth in her place as hostess, went up to her with a friendly word.

"It is all so very, very nice. You will let me pay you a compliment? I don't know why we should congratulate other people to-day, and not you."

"Now it is you whom I am going to congratulate, Mrs. Napier," said Fane. "Keeping a stiff upper lip, as you have! Well done!"

As he raised his hand to pat Josephine's back, he found it turned towards him, and for some reason drew back and failed to avail himself of the convenience.

"Ah, we must feel that Gabriel's happiness makes up to us for our loss," said Jonathan.

"When people are happy in leaving me, I do not admit that they are a loss," said Felix.

"And all this business connected with them takes a good afternoon out of a good working day," said Josephine in a hushed and rueful manner.

"Have you filled Ruth's place?" said Jonathan. "It is strange to me that I have a daughter."

"There is no place to fill," said Josephine, in the same conspiratorial tone. "I have tried to make one, tried to keep it, tried to regard it as deserted; but I confess that on all those scores I have ignominiously failed."

"Mrs. Giffard will miss the girl," said Jonathan. "I almost feel that she and I are related. We must make a point of seeing each other."

"Yes, she will miss her for a time," said Josephine; "until the pendulum swings and the girl's lifelong feelings reassert themselves. Gabriel will miss her then, if the same thing has not happened to him."

"My son," said Jonathan, approaching Gabriel, "my token to you has been in my mind. This is a great occasion for a father."

"Then you are not guilty of the Titanic gift?"

"You are no nearer to the truth about that?"

"It is a condition of acceptance that we are never to be nearer to it."

"Well, let us consider the sentimental token. In a way that is the significant thing."

"Ah, you are the guilty one!" said Gabriel.

"Now we will leave impersonal things, if you please, to their proper fate. Anonymous people have a claim; there is a duty we owe to them."

"I suppose I must not utter gratitude?"

"How can you utter gratitude to a person or persons unknown? If you as much as harbour suspicions, you are guilty of a breach of faith. And ought you not to be standing by your bride, instead of trying to shock your father? I don't grudge you to your wife to-day, my son."

"Don't you think that the bride's appearance does us credit?" said Josephine, pausing by her mistresses.

"Indeed, yes; she could not look more charming," said Mrs. Chattaway.

"Ah, youth and happiness and looking forward! the permeating things!" said Miss Luke. "We must not underrate them."

"Are we inclined to underrate them?" said Miss Rosetti.

"I admit that it was clothes I was thinking of," said Josephine, dropping her eyes in mock guilt. "I must be in a very unspiritual mood."

"Ah, but the wedding-day is a great moment," said Miss Luke, adhering to her stand against the natural opposition. "It must be the climax, the coping stone, the peak of youthful experience."

"Oh, don't use the word 'climax,'" said Josephine. "It has such a suggestion of anti-climax. And we hope that things are not over for them yet."

The bridal pair were leaving by an early train, and the intimate group assembled to speed their departure. Josephine quietly stepped into a prominent place, and when Ruth's farewells were accomplished, moved forward to Gabriel, in a manner of approaching the culminating moment of the day. She relinquished him with her eyes held from his face, and waved a perfunctory, cordial hand as the carriage drove away.

An hour later she stood at the door of the common room.

"Have I given you time to change the charming dresses, that have been such an asset to the occasion?

432

Being outside the necessity myself has perhaps made me unimaginative."

"The time has sufficed for those who cared to avail themselves of it," said Miss Luke, looking down at herself with a little laugh.

"You are very wise," said Josephine.

"You are fortunate, Mrs. Napier, in being exempt from these exactions," said Mrs. Chattaway in a rather artificial manner, keeping her eyes from her own dress.

"Fortunate?" said Josephine, looking up amusedly from under her brows. "I am not sure that that is quite the word."

"I was not speaking in jest," said Mrs. Chattaway vaguely.

"It is I who was doing that," said Josephine. "Though the question of dress has been little enough of a jest for me to-day. If I had known the fuss there was going to be, I should have done something else than follow my own instincts. I see it was a selfish line to take, but I honestly had not meant it so. It was more that I had not thought of my appearance at all, than that I was self-indulgent over it."

"Your brother was anxious for you to do him credit?" said Miss Rosetti.

"My brother! It was my nephew! It was he who fussed and fumed, and almost forgot to go to his own wedding, because his adopted mother and best friend— they are his words; I am not originating them; occasions of emotion loosen the tongues of the reticent—had omitted to drape her mature form in a manner he approved. I might have been the bride instead of her imminent aunt-in-law. Well, I am cured of taking the line of least resistance as regards my apparel. And here is Mr. Bacon, come to complete the lesson with an illustration."

"I am proud of being able to enter this room without knocking," said Felix. "I have only just brought myself to do it."

433

"It must be a pleasant privilege," said Josephine. "I happen to be the only person here without it."

"I hope you are not hinting for it."

"I am not indeed; I have no claim."

"We have been talking about the clothes we wore for the wedding, Mr. Bacon," said Miss Luke. "I already speak of them in the past tense."

"I am glad you did not wear those you have on," said Felix. "We should not have liked to say anything about them. I think you carry off changing them. I should feel a little uncomfortable if I had done it."

"Oh, pray let us drop this subject of clothes," said Josephine.

"You will miss your companion, Mrs. Napier," said Mrs. Chattaway.

"Oh, we do not lose the people whose lives take a different turn from ours," said Miss Luke, quickly and slightly averting her eyes.

"Well, I have not lost Gabriel," said Josephine in an almost comfortable tone. "I must take myself to task, and remind myself how much I have in the concentration of his feeling; and not fret about his having had to tear himself away in the flesh. But poor boy! His face at parting does come back to me; it will. I am not one to make a fuss about nothing; but this is not quite nothing."

"A wedding upsets me," said Miss Munday. "I am very sentimental."

"So it does me," said Felix.

"Well, do you know, so it does me," said Josephine. "I cannot explain it, but there it is."

"I can explain it," said Felix; "but I do not think I will."

"I explained it," said Miss Munday.

"We feel that the bride and bridegroom care more for each other, than anyone cares for us," said Helen.

"I do not feel that," said Josephine. "You must find some other explanation for me."

434

"I suppose that Gabriel and Ruth are very devoted?" said Mrs. Chattaway.

"Devoted?" said Josephine, raising her brows. "Ask me another. I am not in a position to give you an account of their feelings. They draw the modern veil over them too successfully."

"Gabriel does not confide in you?" said Miss Rosetti.

"Oh, I have had it all," said Josephine, almost airily. "How hard it is to throw oneself into a new life, when the old is tugging from the past—that was the word, tugging; not elegant, is it?—and how long it will seem before the upheaval is over, and the old peace returns. Oh yes, I have had it."

"It does not sound the deepest devotion," said Mrs. Chattaway.

"Well, I think hardly any modern young people's relation sounds like that," said Josephine leniently. "But I have seen cases that suggest that things may be more often than we think, the same at bottom. We must hope this is one of them; I indeed have reason to hope it."

"Do you find Ruth a confiding daughter-in-law?" said Miss Rosetti.

"No, I do not. She has honoured me so far only with plain, laconic statements about her material future. But I daresay she found me a great rock to come up against; a formidable bulwark, built out of lifelong feelings; offered to her as an allurement, poor child, when she could only see it as a menace. I was obliged to put the question of ways and means too; and that was not a popular measure, until I added an item of my own to one side of the account; when they liked my exposition better; both of them; not only Ruth; and I admit with reason."

"You are a very unselfish aunt, Mrs. Napier," said Mrs. Chattaway.

"Yes, I have been unselfish," said Josephine, without emphasis. "There is not much temptation to be anything else, when you are considered harsh for doing what you may not leave undone. If you can do something to balance things, you find yourself simply doing it. And I have little use for material things. In other words, I have not been unselfish."

"Many people would have a use for them."

"Then they would be unselfish."

"Will you convert your nephew's room into an extra class-room?" said Miss Rosetti.

"No, I shall not. There would be a fine to-do, if I did. I am not courting such a shindy. It is to be left as it is, with the adventure books by the window, and the photograph of myself by the bed. I repudiate that version of myself; I would gladly throw it on the fire; but I am taking no liberties with my instructions. When young master comes home he is to find things as he left them."

"I did not know he was masterful," said Miss Rosetti.

"Oh, well, this is a matter of his private and precious feelings. He is not in a general way. I am the only person who has been shown his masterful side. I am sure he will make a most amenable husband."

Josephine took her leave with a somehow fallen face, as if baffled of something she had looked for. As Felix's step sounded behind her, she turned to meet him.

"I could not stay with women who have no sorrow to hide, and not enough to hide of anything else. I am ill at ease with people whose lives are an open book. There is so much in me, that must at all costs be hidden. Jonathan and I were coming to dinner; so may I stay and not go home to dress? My wedding clothes are nearly as becoming as my evening ones."

"Stay by all means. Your clothes do not matter at all."

"I noticed that you thought that about clothes; and I see that your clothes did not matter; but I don't think mine can be dismissed like that."

"I am sure your clothes are admirable. I cannot imagine you without them—without your own kind of them, I mean."

"I don't think it matters which you meant, as you cannot imagine it."

"I admit I was ashamed of my clothes to-day," said Josephine. "I see I should have thought of Gabriel."

"I am coming into the library to gossip about Gabriel. Do you think that Ruth is worthy of him?"

"We may be pardoned for thinking she is not."

"I don't think we ought to be pardoned. My feelings, when I think it, are quite unpardonable."

"We may surely hold unbiased opinions on occasions."

"I don't think ever on occasions."

"Ruth looked very pretty to-day. You will say that there is an example of the importance of clothes."

"No, I certainly shall not. I cannot consent to be dragged down too far."

"Did you not think that she looked particularly well?"

"Yes, but I did not know it was clothes. I was afraid it was happiness."

"Well, you need not accuse me of dragging you down," said Josephine.

"We are always hard on our own faults in others; we know how inexcusable they are. I have never met any of those faults that are almost lovable. I have been more unlovable on Gabriel's wedding day than ever before."

"I have not been at my best," said Jonathan, coming into the room. "I feel the loss of my son more than I have any right to."

"You have come to his help with great munificence," said Josephine. "But I don't know why an allowance is better for being anonymous."

"I do," said Felix.

"I mean a father's allowance to a son."

"So do I," said Felix.

"It is not for me to say anything about it, one way or the other," said Jonathan.

"There is the reason illustrated," said Felix.

"Well, I did not see any reason for not admitting my

quota," said Josephine. "I simply acknowledged it, as I do most of my actions. It seemed such a natural, inevitable thing."

"Then there was no reason for not admitting it," said Felix.

"An allowance from oneself hardly seems to me a natural thing," said Jonathan, with a laugh. "But we are talking about what has to be a mystery. I have been remembering, Josephine, that you will be alone after tonight. It goes to my heart to think of it."

"Alone? In a house of a hundred and eighty people?"

"Well, well, essentially alone."

"Well, actually alone very little. I hope I shall snatch a few moments to myself sometimes."

"I mean you will be alone at meals. That seems to me the dividing line."

"Well, I must try to get time for those, certainly. The interruptions get more and more continuous."

"I wonder Gabriel put up with it," said Felix.

"He did not put up with it. He guarded our tête-à-tête most jealously. But lately we have had the Giffards with us sometimes, and he seemed to think that a larger party justified intrusions. I shall have to cope with the precedent."

"Will you see much of Mrs. Giffard now?" said Jonathan.

"I shall see her daily. The running of the house depends on my seeing her."

"Can Gabriel love his wife as much as he loves us?" said Felix.

"She fulfils a relation to him that none of us can fulfil," said Josephine, with full concession. "It is not a question of comparative affection. That may be why we feel a faint resentment over people's marriages. Because I think there is no doubt that we do."

"Well, we must become more to each other," said Jonathan.

"We can hardly fail to become so in a way," said Josephine. "Gaps must close up; and any closing up involves a coming together."

"I think we are becoming more to each other already," said Felix.

CHAPTER XIV

"WELL," said Josephine, entering the housekeeper's room, where Miss Rosetti was sitting with Elizabeth, "here is my young gentleman already homesick! Already confessing to it, which is a further step! He wants to come home with Ruth to-morrow; is coming home, for he does not put it as a question. Home is the word that indicates that he is within his rights, I suppose. Is there any objection to it? The matter is more in your province than mine."

"And so sweet it is to have it there! Here is my dear companion letter! Such a funny round-off it is to our friendship, that we share the married pair! I almost feel that my share is the greater, as one of them is really mine. Any objection to their coming home? Ah, that is what we love them to say. Our two old heads are turned by the mere thought."

"It would take more than that to turn my head," said Josephine, smiling at Miss Rosetti, whose eyes were on her face; "or it would be like a planet in a state of continual revolution. But in my life anything has to be reckoned with, to be managed. And it seems that we have to manage this: it is taken so very much as a matter of course."

"Ah, it is better sometimes to be the housekeeper than the head mistress," said Elizabeth, as Josephine left them.

"I would choose to be the head mistress," said her companion.

"Oh, I feel pity for my superior. I would rather welcome my own daughter than somebody else's son."

The next day Josephine listened for the sounds of arrival, held herself in check until they had advanced to the hall, and then came forth with a pleasant, casual welcome.

"Well, my punctual travellers! Home, sweet home to the moment! I hardly expected you quite on the stroke of the clock. A minute earlier, and I should have been engaged."

Gabriel approached to throw himself into her arms, but she held him gently back, and keeping her hand on his, turned to give the first welcome to his wife.

"Why, what a wan and weary-looking bride! I hope you are safe in your husband's charge. You did not look like that when you were in mine, but we must not expect old heads on green shoulders. We knew he was young to have the care of a wife. So, my boy!" She turned to give Gabriel a tranquil greeting. "It seems so natural to have you here, that I catch myself feeling surprised at having to celebrate such a normal condition of things. Now tell me where you both would like to sleep. The spare room is ready for Ruth; her own old room is occupied; but yours is just as it was."

"We are easy people, and only want one room or the other," said Ruth. "We always take our rest side by side."

"Do you, my dear? It is a short 'always,' but it is even simpler to arrange, if you actually prefer it so. You will be able to stay in any kind of house, being easy, as you say. Here there will be a dressing room, to prevent the 'always' from becoming an oppression. We need not be the slaves of a word."

"We have never spent an hour apart," said Ruth.

"Have you not? Then you are not as I was in my early married days. I remember that I used to manœuvre separations, to come upon my husband afresh, and recapture the first fine, careless rapture, emotional young woman that I was!"

"It sounds as if your feelings required a stimulus," said Gabriel.

"Well, I could not have borne the full flood of them always: I should simply have been shattered."

"It would not do for them to be too violent to last."

"I certainly did not discern that possibility," said Josephine, laughing. "It would not have occurred to me. You cynical, disillusioned young man!"

"It was the natural thing to say at the moment."

"It hardly seemed so to me, with my old-fashioned ideas. But we will not bear too hardly on a casual word. What does seem natural, is that Ruth should be impatient to see her mother, and be about to turn upon you for your preoccupation with your own home-coming and oblivion of hers."

"We share our home-coming with other things," said Gabriel.

"Yes, we promised to rush to Mother's room," said Ruth. "We knew you would let us keep the promise."

Josephine walked to the bell and rang it.

"Now that will not do," she said. "The housekeeper's room is as honourable as any room in the house, perhaps the most honourable, as the workings of the house have their source in it; but it is not the recognised background for a welcome; and I think a welcome should be organised fittingly as an important thing."

She waited with her foot on the fender while Elizabeth was summoned, and then averted her eyes from her meeting with her daughter, but restored them as she turned to Gabriel.

"Such a rich woman I feel, with my son and daughter! Why should I mind the funny housekeeper's place? What better position could I wish, than the one that puts them in my care?"

"Well, for all that," said Josephine, "I do not extend the functions of the housekeeper's room beyond a point. It is a time-honoured custom to hasten to the hall to our guests; and if I have taken it upon myself to stage your reunion, I have done it according to my own taste, which is the only sincere method in judgement."

"Such a sweet reunion, such a thoughtfully staged welcome! Such a dear memory it will be, though it yields to the trivial round, the common task!" Elizabeth went to the door kissing her hand. "I will not attend to dear ones with half a mind, who have such a claim on the whole. The long, long talk will wait until the time is ripe —that is to say, free for it."

Josephine did not look after Elizabeth, but turned at once to Ruth, as to a personal charge.

"I do not think Ruth looks well, Gabriel, now she is out of my hands. Was it wise for her to travel to-day?"

"She has had a chill, and the alternative was to stay at home with servants who are foolish virgins. You will judge that she is better here than there."

"I always judged that she was well enough here. The suggestion of her making a change was a surprise to me. I hesitate to make much of her looks, as her mother was not struck by them, but I am going to take advantage of her absence and conduct her daughter to bed. Come, my dear." Josephine held out her hand to Ruth, as if to a child.

"Please let me be ungrateful and cling to the fire, Mrs. Napier."

Josephine resumed her seat.

"Such a peevish, poorly wife you have brought home, poor, dear Gabriel."

"We all keep saying the same thing in different words," said Josephine, laughing a little, and rocking herself without looking at either.

"Josephine, I think your advice was good," said Gabriel.

442

Josephine looked kindly but easily from one to the other.

"I shall have to unpack, I suppose," said Ruth.

"I will show myself a master of the accomplishment," said Gabriel. "You shall choose the better part, and sit at Josephine's feet."

"My dear boy, what are you saying?" said Josephine. "You cannot unpack for yourself, much less for anyone else."

"You have no conception of what I can do in these days. I am a qualified family man."

"I daresay you are," said Josephine, in a faintly commiserating tone. "Well, go to the duties you have become qualified for, poor, toiling, moiling boy."

"Shall I leave your things on the sofa, my wife?"

"There, you see!" said Josephine, laughing and rising. "He has learnt how to unpack, hasn't he, when he does not suspect that putting things in their places is the foundation of it! Keep by the fire, my child, and I will go and superintend this newly learnt accomplishment. I do not expect to recognise the rudiments of it."

"We could not let you wait on us, Mrs. Napier."

"Well, we will go and face the herculean task, the three of us together. Not that there is much reason in that. There is hardly scope for a trio in a piece of work suitable for one." Josephine sat down, and Ruth and Gabriel left her.

"Your aunt wanted a talk with you alone, Gabriel. She gives the impression of a volcano on the verge of becoming active."

"It seems odd to hear Josephine called my aunt; she has always fulfilled such a different character. You know there is room for more than one person in my life."

"Only for one chief person. Mother saw that for herself. You can't put two people into one place."

"Gabriel's taste seems to be for several people in one place," said Josephine's voice at the door. "Three people

443

can unpack, and three people will have to, if it is left to the third to supply the keys. These were in the hall, and there is reason in regarding them as a necessary preliminary to unpacking. The third person's contribution was indispensable."

"None of our things is locked, Mrs. Napier."

"Now, now, the third person really was indispensable. You will never be able to accompany Gabriel on further travels. This is the first time he has made a journey in that way."

"It is the first time he has been married, Mrs. Napier."

"Yes," said Josephine, in a tone of pleasant corroboration. "Both are for the first time."

"I always came down from Oxford with my baggage unlocked. I got quite used to it," said Gabriel.

"Yes, I was as indispensable as ever then. You never went back with it unlocked. I know that."

"No harm seems to have come of either method."

"The large one appears to be locked after all," said Ruth.

"Ah, you see, the keys were necessary," said Josephine. Gabriel laughed.

"Gabriel could have fetched them, Mrs. Napier."

"Did he know where they were?" said Josephine.

Gabriel assumed a humorous expression of unconsciousness.

"Ah, you see, you needed me after all."

"Yes, but I asked you to come," said Gabriel. "I made no secret of my dependence upon you."

"Never make a secret of it," said Josephine, in a voice that suddenly defied his wife's presence; "and I will never fail you." She turned and left the room.

"Well, she is failing you over your marriage, Gabriel."

"Is she? Ah, my dear," said Josephine, looking back, "it is failing over a marriage, is it, to sacrifice both tangible and intangible things, to further it? Well, I think with you that it may be failing, that it is doing ill

by people to deprive them of their sense of human justice."

"She must have known she was not meant to hear,"
said Ruth.

"No, I hardly knew it," said Josephine, causing Ruth
to clench her hands. "I hardly understand this talking
according to whether or no the talk is heard. It makes
no difference in speaking the simple truth, as I speak it."

"Josephine, pray come in or go out," said Gabriel. "We
hardly understand this talking to someone neither here
nor elsewhere. It is an unbearable method of communica-
tion. Do make up your mind."

"It is made up for me, my dear. I have gathered—
overheard, if you like—that there was some harm in my
hearing what was said. Conversation is for me a thing
that everyone within earshot may hear; but of course my
principles may not be those of other people. I am not
saying they should be. Every human being is one by himself in this world." She ended with a bitter lightness and
closed the door.

"This is quite a false augury for the future," said
Gabriel. "You will soon see the side of her that is superhuman. You and I will end by vying for her favour."

"Well, we have not begun by doing that. I cannot
face the next meeting without Mother's protection. I
wonder if she has been asked to dinner. I suppose it goes
without saying that she has."

At dinner, where Elizabeth was not present, Josephine
appeared oblivious of the scene upstairs. When she
caught Ruth's glance, she leaned towards her and laid
her hand on hers.

"Suppose you give up regarding me as if I were a
tigress, because I am not accustomed to having Gabriel
belong to anyone but me! You don't take so very kindly
to the idea that he can belong to anyone but you, do
you? And you let me see it, as is natural. I am not slow
to understand it. I never think it honest or desirable to

hide too much of ourselves. You will find me charitable over the darker glimpses, if they are not too dark. And you and I are not dependent for our mutual feeling on our new relationship, are we?"

"No, Mrs. Napier," said Ruth, in a manner derived from the old relationship.

"It was as much my true self that you saw then, and your true self that I saw, as the selves that we see now; though, of course, my dear, I have my life as a woman, as well as a head mistress. It is because you had your life as a woman, as well as a junior mistress, that all this has come to pass, isn't it? And it is so bad for this boy to feel that two intelligent people are competing for him, that I for one withdraw from the competition; if I ever entered it, which I doubt. And as I am sure you never entered it either, we are neither of us in it, are we?"

"No, Mrs. Napier."

"Are you always going to call Josephine Mrs. Napier?" said Gabriel. "She might as well call you Mrs. Swift."

"Well, hardly quite as well," said Josephine, laughing. "She is a matron as much as you are."

"Well, a good many years less."

"I do not think of myself as Mrs. Swift," said Ruth.

"No, my dear, it is premature," said Josephine in a sympathetic tone. "You are Mrs. Gabriel Swift. My brother and I have several married relations senior to Gabriel. And you and I have known each other by settled names for a long time, haven't we?"

"Yes, we have, Mrs. Napier."

"Well now, your mother will be waiting in the drawing-room. I knew she was too busy to join us at dinner: I did not try to deceive myself about the amount of her work. This is a busy time in a busy house, and I am not one to deny what I have brought about myself. But her free hours have begun; so we will go and take advantage of them."

"It is dreadful that Mother should work, while we are

free," said Ruth, crossing the hall with her arm in her husband's."

"No, why is it dreadful?" said Josephine. "I assure you I do not feel that about myself."

"You are such a powerful person, that it seems to be right that you should use your powers," said Gabriel.

"That is a good thing," said Josephine; "or a good deal would seem to be wrong."

"Well, Mother darling, free at last?" said Ruth.

"Free to take my real look at my boy and girl together. The girl looks as if it were time her mother's eyes were on her. Such a pale, pale face! The place for that head is on the pillow."

"I am giving a sad impression of myself," said Ruth, lifting her arms above her head. "I can't be bright and entertaining when I am drooping with fatigue."

"You are a fortunate person, if you are bright and entertaining whenever you are not in that condition," said Josephine; "or rather other people are fortunate." She changed her tone. "I am sure they are, my dear."

"I feel a most unsatisfactory guest, Mrs. Napier."

"My child, you are in your mother's home. I do not forget that, if you do."

"Then I will betake myself with an easy mind to bed."

"Why not lie up on the sofa," said Josephine kindly, "and watch us all from there?"

"No, I would rather go upstairs and get away from human eyes."

"Be off, before you pay us further compliments," said her mother. "I will come up in an hour to see that you are asleep."

"She is paying me a compliment," said Josephine gravely. "I take it as such, when people in my house are enough at home to do as they like. And the poor child is simply doing what she must. It is easy to see that."

"I will follow you soon," said Gabriel to his wife.

"Now you sit down in your chair, and don't use your

domestic gifts to keep her from her sleep," said Josephine. "We have had enough of those with your unpacking. There is a fire in her room, and a hot-water-bottle in her bed, and a hot drink on the way. I have not had my experience of young people, without becoming qualified to observe that such things would be needed by this young person, as soon as I received her into the house."

"My dear, those duties were not yours," said Elizabeth.

"They were of a kind to be anyone's who chanced to think of them. So as I chanced to do so, they were mine. As I did so, rather; there was not much chance about it."

There was silence for some moments, while Josephine seemed to be listening. At the closing of Ruth's door she turned to her friend.

"Now, as this is the cronies' chance of an evening together, shall we release you from the tedium of their sentimental intercourse? And postpone our general gathering until to-morrow night, when you will be free for dinner, and the child will be able to join us? I think I may say that she will be herself by then."

Elizabeth rose and went with running steps to the door.

"Yes, yes, I will not delay for a moment. A moment is a large proportion of the length of my sojourn. We know that all things are relative."

"They are a difficult pair," said Josephine, with a sigh.

"Do you mind if I smoke in your face?" said Gabriel, ignoring the words.

"I mind nothing you do, my boy."

"Even if the pipe burns your cheek?"

Josephine remained as she was, her eyes meeting the pipe as if in submission to his pleasure. Presently Gabriel started and moved aside, and a minute later his wife appeared in the door.

"I am a hopelessly harassing creature, Mrs. Napier. I am too restless to sleep, and I would fain have my husband sit at my side and soothe me. He need not disturb you by coming down again."

"Need not perhaps; but possibly he would wish to," said Josephine, mildly meeting her eyes. "He knows I should not be disturbed."

"He is as tired as I am; he will be better reposing at my side."

"Well, take him to his repose then, if repose is the word for what you were suggesting. I have yet to learn the effect on him of his new responsibilities; he has never been in need of repose at this hour. But I ought to be up for a while by myself; I have a good deal to get through. I must not forget the new drain on my resources."

"Good night, Josephine," said Gabriel, kissing her.

"Good night, my boy. I will try to make it up another time," said Josephine, patting his shoulder and looking into his face.

Gabriel led the way from the room, and as he disappeared round the door, Josephine came up close to his wife.

"So, my dear, you listened from your room, and heard your mother come upstairs, and knew that Gabriel and I were alone? That was your method of finding it out, was it? Believe me, you were not dependent on it. I would have told you, will aways tell you, when it is so, if it causes you uneasiness."

Ruth looked at her in silence.

"When you are alone with people, it is safe to leave you, is it not?" said Josephine, bending and speaking gently. "I am not so different from you, in that I thought a private conversation permissible. In fact, you tried to teach me that lesson yourself. And think of the number of times that Gabriel and I, or any other woman and her son or adopted son, must have been alone! If that did him harm, he would not be as you find him, would he; would not be the one man in the world to you? I hope that is how you feel to him? Suppose I could not leave him alone with you?"

"I am his wife," said Ruth.

449

"Well, no one will think it, if you go on as you are doing. They will take your marriage for some temporary, passing union. I would not force my worldly wisdom on you, but you must learn to be less afraid, must learn to be sure, or to seem so. Poor little one, you are young for all that. I knew that your time was not yet."

CHAPTER XV

THE next day Ruth was unable to rise, and the doctor forbade her to leave her bed. From her pillow she held to her contest with Josephine, until something in Josephine rebelled against the unequal strife. As the morning went on, the latter came to Gabriel.

"I cannot feel easy about your poor little wife. She will never rest while you are with me, and you cannot live in a sick-room. Would it be wise for you to be called away to your work? She will be easy when you are out of the house, that is, outside my influence. And I shall not have this sense of taking advantage of her. It is a strange feeling to have, for spending an hour with the nephew, whom you have brought up from babyhood; but so things are just now. They will be better when health is better, and we all start again. I am prepared to start again myself; things were unfamiliar to me as well. But do you not think I am wise?"

The relief on Gabriel's face gave Josephine her answer.

"Ah, I know what is best for you. Trust me, and all will be well. Be wise in choosing the woman's hands into which you put your life."

"Mine not to reason why; mine just to do and die. At your word I will be dead to the house."

Josephine gave the word for the afternoon of that day. She sent her nephew for a walk in the morning, and letting his wife know he was out of the house, showed the girl a maternal kindness that conquered any reluctance to be left to her care. Her face was cheerful and her step light.

At the hour for Gabriel to leave, she led him herself to his wife, and stood smiling in the doorway over their farewell. Ruth lifted herself on her pillows and looked from one to the other, and Josephine, warning her back with a gesture, nodded and withdrew. In a few minutes, but not too few, her step was heard again, and her clear, unhurried knock, and Gabriel rose from his kneeling position by the bed. Josephine followed him, shaking out her dress, and exchanging a smile with his wife over some need of repair.

Towards evening Ruth was greatly worse, and the doctor diagnosed inflammation of the lungs, and pronounced her condition to be grave. A nurse was established to attend her by day, and Josephine was to undertake the night, as Elizabeth's hands were full. Miss Rosetti, as Elizabeth's friend, was permitted to give her aid.

"No, I shall not be exhausted in trying to work day and night," said Josephine. "Trying to do it! Really doing it, or it would be less than no good; it would be criminal. No sleepy nursing for me! If I give up my usual work, I give it up. A mother is bound to make a nervous nurse. I can do a simple duty that is plain before me."

Josephine seemed impervious to weariness, and to be buoyed up by some inner strength. As Ruth's sickness drew her down into depths of fear and suffering, she turned to her husband's adopted mother as much as to her own, seeming to recognise a greater force. When the crisis approached, and she cried out for her husband, who, though summoned, seemed to be delayed, Josephine moved as seldom as the mother from her side. It was imperative that she should remain covered in her bed; the slightest exposure might be fatal; and there was need for complete devotion. On the second evening, as Josephine watched in the dying light, her delirious murmurs became distinct, and Josephine's ear was alert.

"I knew he would belong to me when I saw his face, though he did not know. I cannot go to meet him now I am ill; but when I am well, I will go to him; and nobody shall watch us. We will tell her not to watch us. He is coming now!" The sick girl raised herself with all her strength, and seemed to be summoning it again to leave the bed.

Josephine sprang to prevent her, but stopped and stood with an arrested look, that seemed to creep across her face and gather to a purpose. She moved with a soft step to the bed, where Ruth had fallen.

"Do you want to get up, my child? Do you want my help?" Her tone seemed of itself to have become a whisper. "You know you may trust me."

"I think I can trust you in some things," said Ruth, meeting her eyes with a bright, clear gaze. "You are kind when I am ill. I must put on my things and go to Gabriel. He wants to see me by myself. You know we do not want anyone with us?" She turned her eyes again to Josephine. "You will not seem as if you did not know?"

"No, he shall see you by yourself. I have been too much with you: I will see it is never so again. Which dress would you like to wear? Which does he like to see you in? Come to the fire and tell me." Josephine lifted Ruth to her feet, and stood with her arm about her, but did not guide her forward. It was as if she felt some security in nearness to the bed. The girl leant against her, falling but for the support, and made no further movement. Josephine glanced from the open window to the door, and contracted her shoulders in the draught between them. Ruth's voice came again, steadied by the cold.

"I cannot be dressed to-day; Gabriel will know that I can't. He would not like me to be in the cold." She shuddered, and indeed the daught seemed stronger. "I will lie down and go to sleep; I am very tired. You will watch me, and wake me when Gabriel comes? If you listen, you will hear him coming. You know his step."

Josephine felt her body respond from head to foot, as the trust and weakness of the tones pierced something that bound her. Her face was that of another woman. She lifted the girl to the bed and covered her, bending to secure the clothes. As she raised her head, her eyes fell on the door, and set into a stare, while her body seemed to be fixed in its stooping posture. The door stood open; the reason of the draught flashed to her mind; the silent movements of sickness had escaped her ears. Miss Rosetti stood in the doorway, with something for the sick-room in her hand, her feet riveted to the floor, her eyes to Josephine's face.

"Oh, what a moment!" said Josephine, standing up straight. "I shall never forget it. She was out of bed in a second. I should not have thought she had the strength. I was not reckoning with it, and time got wasted. I could not lift her by myself. Oh, I wish someone had been here. I found myself counting the seconds through the horror of it."

The pause that followed seemed as full of effort as Josephine's words.

"It was a strange thing to happen," said Miss Rosetti, her glance going up and down Josephine's frame, as though measuring it against the task that had been beyond it. "One of those things that we cannot explain. Was she long in the cold?"

"It seemed hours to me," said Josephine, letting out her breath. "You must have seen us. I could not get her balanced, to help her forward. And she was hardly a yard from the bed; there seemed such irony in it. And the window was open, as the doctor said it must be. The draught was full on her; I felt it on myself. If only its being on her had mattered as little!"

"Yes," said Miss Rosetti, her eyes again covering Josephine's form. "But it does no good to talk about it. We may be in danger from our memories. And she seems to be sleeping now."

But Gabriel's wife did not sleep long. Her temperature went to a dangerous height, her breathing was ominously shallow and swift, and the doctor, summoned in haste, betrayed that his hope was gone. Josephine tended the girl with intense absorption, let no one but herself and the mother approach the bed, and seemed to feel it the object of her life that she should be saved. But the disease had gained ascendance, and they were losing hours. The crisis came with the expected force, and as it ebbed the life ebbed with it.

Josephine fell on her knees by the bed and broke into weeping. She and Elizabeth clung to each other, and Miss Rosetti went in silence about what had to be done.

Gabriel arrived in the small hours of the morning. The telegram sent to summon him had arrived too late, although Josephine had written and despatched it with her own hand. Josephine met him in open grief and weariness, but as she fell on his neck, her tones rang.

"My boy, you have what you have always had. You are not alone."

But after that moment Josephine herself gave way. She wept for her nephew's wife as she had never wept for her husband. There came no reaction from her despairing grief, and Gabriel, in his rather gentle sorrow, found himself consoling rather than consoled. She lamented her dealings with his wife, and held her own against herself.

"I do not need false comfort. I can face the truth. What are called the little things are the gravest human wrongs. No recognised wrong, even though it were injury or death, takes its place beside them in the scale of human harm."

"It is a good thing that you will never have a real wrong on your mind."

"It would be easier to bear; it would be a better thing. Better a murder than a meanness."

"A murder is the worst meanness. Yours were the least."

Gabriel's mood was readily in tune with a suffering that he saw as sympathy.

"A murder would never be done without an excuse: the things without excuse must remain the inexcusable things."

At last weariness had its way, and Josephine slept; and after the unconscious hours arose in her own strength. It had been assumed that she would not attend the burial, and she met the assumption with gentle surprise.

"I should not let anything keep me away. My place is with Gabriel."

"We thought you would not feel equal to it," said Miss Rosetti.

"I do not know that I do feel equal to it, But that has little to do with the matter."

"You did not go to your husband's funeral," said Miss Rosetti, her voice significant from its very lack of force.

"No," said Josephine, her hands trembling. "And you know that I know that, without your telling me."

"I suppose you see your own difference."

"And do you not see it? Then I will help you. Simon was a man and my husband, and this was an orphan girl. Then I had myself to consider; now I have Gabriel. Then my feelings were of personal loss; now they are of pity. Do you see the difference now? By the way"— Josephine spoke with a haste that precluded words from the other—"if you would find it too much for you, you will not go, will you?"

"I am not going, but not for that reason. I am remaining with Mrs. Giffard."

455

"I should have known if I had thought. It lifts a weight from my mind. I will not say that I am grateful."

Josephine stood with Gabriel at his wife's grave. Gabriel did not weep, but Josephine wept. A wreath inscribed with her name was laid on the coffin by his own.

On their return she parted from him as they entered the house.

"My son, we know what you have in your life. But to-day you must dwell on what you have not. I will leave you for a while alone."

There was a remembrance in both their minds of the day of Simon's burial.

"I have come to say a word of gratitude," said Josephine, as she sought the familiar common room. "I have not been blind to what I have not seen, your loyal carrying on of the school in your own anxiety and sorrow. I know that my feelings have been indulged, and yours conquered. If I could have a pleasure, it would be one to make my acknowledgement."

"We ought to say more than that to you, Mrs. Napier," said Mrs. Chattaway.

"No," said Josephine, her tone rising at this unconscious testimony to Miss Rosetti's silence. "It does not apply to me. I am the first to say it. That does not alter my recognition of a more selfless courage."

"You had a nearer anxiety than any of us," said Miss Luke.

"Nearer in that it was to me, that the child turned of all people at the end?" said Josephine in a voice so low as only just to be heard.

"I meant the anxiety for Gabriel," said Miss Luke, at the same pitch.

"No feeling is nearer to me, than that I have for those who work for and with me. In giving her that I gave her what I could give."

"It is tragic that your nephew was not in time," said Mrs. Chattaway.

456

"No," said Josephine gently; "not tragic. You must not encourage me in making too much of what is in itself indeed enough. The child was, as I have said, content; and he could only be satisfied that it was so. And he was himself, and let himself be satisfied."

"You have to attempt more for him than ever before," said Miss Luke. "And I know that is saying much."

"In trying to comfort him in a trouble that leaves him myself? No, I have attempted that, and succeeded many times. You must not make me feel that I am doing more than I am."

"But never in such a trouble as this," said Mrs. Chattaway.

"Never in this trouble. But all the troubles have been such as this, in, as I say, leaving him myself. And it has already happened in the old way; and I am here with you, feeling it has so happened. If it were not so, I confess I should not be here."

"Then he did not—did not feel even to his wife, as he feels to you?" said Mrs. Chattaway.

"I have meant to say simply that I have left him comforted. I may say that simply, I think, among my friends."

"You may indeed," said Miss Luke.

"You have the anxiety and responsibility of Mrs. Giffard as well," said Mrs. Chattaway.

"The anxiety I have; the responsibility I have allowed to devolve upon Miss Rosetti. I have felt, rightly or wrongly, that a woman of her own will childless was the best comforter. And there must be other things in Miss Rosetti, that qualify her rather than me. Anyhow, it was to her rather than to me, that my old friend turned." Josephine folded her hands and dropped her eyes upon them.

Miss Rosetti did not speak.

"Of course we look back in doubt on our dealings with

the child," said Miss Luke. "We cannot expect to escape that burden."

"If there are burdens for all of us, does it not come to there being no burden for any?" said Josephine. "For some young natures—I say it in all tenderness, seeing in their youth their full excuse—tend to find grounds for unhappiness. It seems to satisfy some young need. The questions we have asked ourselves, for that we all ask them, lay themselves to rest."

"It is a great bond between you and Mrs. Giffard, that Gabriel must feel he is a son to you both," said Mrs. Chattaway.

"He is too much under the weight of things at the moment, to feel he is a son to more than one person. He has come creeping back to me like a little child. He can only feel that what has always supported him, is with him, and turn to it blindly, as the beginning and the end. I have simply to accept it, having no means of combating an instinct so deep and blind."

"It is terrible that he should be crushed on the threshold of life."

"It would be terrible. But he is young and brave. The young do not see courage in yielding. Forth they go on their different ways and in their different worlds!" Josephine moved her hand.

"And always together," said Mrs. Chattaway.

"And always apart. That is where the bravery lies for them. For us it lies in the truth, that the young in their eagerness and bewilderment ask so much, that we feel we have given little. And my own is perhaps the harder, the more humiliating. For I have to feel that Gabriel might have given more as a husband, if he had given less as a son. I have to let the truth close over me. And you with your little load of regret, come to me for comfort! Well, you may have the comfort of knowing that I am in comparison heavy laden."

During the silence that ensued, Josephine rose and

moved to the door, stooping to Miss Rosetti as she passed her.

"May I ask you for a few moments of your time? I have taken so much, that I can claim no scruple in going further."

Miss Rosetti rose and followed, and at a distance along the corridor Josephine came to a pause.

"It is a strange place for setting on foot a discussion. But Gabriel is in the library, and we can hardly talk into youthful ears. And our friends seem to be established behind. I should have thought that this house was large enough for all its purposes, but we seem to be blocked up fore and aft. I wished to ask you if you are still available for me as a partner. If you are not, I must remind myself that I have given you time to change your mind, and not be surprised that you have used it. But now that I am harassed by personal troubles, I should be grateful for support in my working life. At one time it was not so. It is so now. Will you give me your answer, or do you desire me to wait? I need not say that I am in your hands."

Miss Rosetti looked at the ground, something like a smile creeping across her face.

"It is wise of you to make the offer. It is clever as well as wise. I do not say that it is not also kind. I will tell you that I would accept it, if the choice were mine. But the choice is no longer mine. If it were, I would be your partner, surprising though that may be both to you and to me. I will not give you the wrong reason for my refusal: I find that what I say is the truth."

"I am indeed sorry," said Josephine, in simply expressionless tones. "If things are ever different, I may rely on you to tell me?"

"I can tell you now that they will never be different. But I will remember the chance you have given me: I will remember both the sides of you that I have seen, the many facets that go to make up the surface of a soul." Miss Rosetti spoke in her natural voice as she turned from Josephine. "Thank you very much, Mrs. Napier. I will not forget."

Josephine took a deep breath and stood as if bewildered, and then continued her way to the library.

Gabriel was turning the leaves of a book, and looked up and closed it, uneasy at betraying interest in it. Josephine went up to him and passed her hand over his head.

"Not equal to reading as yet, being as you are? Shall we lift the troubles off your mind, that I know are on it? What do you feel about returning to your work? Can you face the return alone? Ah, don't be afraid to break down, my boy; turn to me, and let me comfort you. You have it all left, a home and a woman in it. We will give up your house and make our life in this one, in yours and mine."

"What about my work?" said Gabriel.

"What could there be about it? Some other young man will take it, and be gladder to have it than you can be, because it fulfils his need. You are not a person who thinks himself indispensable in any little place?"

"Of course not. And this was a little place indeed. But there will be the money wasted."

"Not as much as will be saved."

"I shall give up both my allowances, when the bills are paid. My proper pocket-money, as a lad at home, will be five shillings a week."

"Well, have your proper pocket-money then," said Josephine, with easy tenderness, "and let the balance accumulate for the future."

"But you and Father will stop giving me help. Nothing else would be thinkable."

"No, why should I? Why should he? Why should an established plan be changed, when nothing has happened in direct relation to it?"

"Most people would see reasons."

"Well, perhaps I am a little different from most people."

"You certainly are," said Gabriel, a gleam of interest appearing on his face.

Josephine kept her eyes averted from it.

"My dear," she said, still in the manner of easy perplexity, "all that I have is simply yours, of course. You may as well see the stone gathering the moss. Your future is longer than mine, and I am concerned with nobody else's. I shall not leave my hard-earned savings to hospitals, whatever you may expect of me. You have by no means such a charitable aunt."

"A charitable aunt is what I have, if charity begins at home."

"It seems to me a good place for it to begin, if it does not to everyone. I will show you in a moment how our affairs stand." Josephine observed Gabriel's recoil, and sank back as if unconsciously. "I mean some time in the future, but I think in the near future. Nothing so helps to steady nerves and spirits as concentration on material things."

As the gleam of interest again appeared, Josephine left the subject and took up her sewing, her expression showing her own great weariness.

The cloud grew deeper on her face as her fingers worked. She felt no sense of comfort in her restored world. Something had not been returned to it; something was wanting.

A light seemed to dawn at the back of her mind, as she recognised a knock.

"I can hardly apologise for intruding," said Felix; "as I am a person who could not be felt to intrude. And I am not forgetting my position in the house. I simply thought that an outsider's influence might be wholesome."

"Come in, in whatever character you will," said Gabriel. "My present course is where madness lies."

Josephine seemed to herself to experience a familiar pang without feeling it. She sat in silence, her eyes going from one to the other, blinded by a flash of understand-

ing. The pang she actually felt, was not for Gabriel, but
for Felix! She rose and stumbled from the room, her face
dazed and startled, as if from a shock. With her own
power she faced the truth, and grappled with her knowledge of herself. Gabriel's place in her life had been filled
by Felix! Gabriel had been snatched back to a world
that was his no longer. If he had remained away, it would
have been better for him; it would have been better for
her, as it would have left her Felix for her own.

Moving along, hardly knowing where she went, she
came upon Helen, carrying some books.

"You are laden, my dear," she said.

"I am taking some books to the library, that Mr. Bacon
has chosen for Gabriel—for your nephew, Mrs. Napier."

"Call him Gabriel, my child. I am glad for him to have
friends of his own age. He must not lose youth and hope
because one chapter of his life is closed. It is only a reason
for his starting another. I hope you will cultivate a
friendly feeling towards him?"

"We all have it already, Mrs. Napier."

"I meant you yourself, if you will let me say what I
meant. You are of his age, of his tastes, of—may I say it?
—his class and kind. I should be grateful for your companionship for him; and he would be grateful, if you
would allow him the necessary time. May I ask you to
join him sometimes when I have to leave him?"

"It would give me great pleasure, Mrs. Napier."

"It would give you a sense of duty done, of kindness
accomplished, that would be a pleasure, I am sure. You
may rely upon us to grant you the pleasure as often as we
can persuade you to accept it."

CHAPTER XVI

"I WOULD not say anything out of keeping with the circumstances of the house," said Felix, entering Josephine's library. "But this is quite in keeping. My father's health is failing, and he may not have long to live. I feel less ashamed of being alive myself, that I can offer you a death in my own family quite soon."

"That is sad hearing," said Josephine. "I think I am even sorrier for you than for him."

"Why? My health is good. You should be sorrier for my father."

"Well, your father's hold on life is light. He must be an old man."

"He is seventy-nine, and I am afraid his hold on life is confirmed. He is very used to living."

"Will you have to go and see him?" said Gabriel.

"Thank you for making it easy for me to ask for a holiday."

"I cannot refuse one for such a reason," said Josephine, moving in front of Gabriel.

"Would you refuse it for other reasons? I might enjoy a holiday more, if I were not in trouble."

"Are you really in trouble?" said Gabriel.

"The astonishing thing is, that I am. I thought I should have to face the absence of sorrow. And what I am facing, is just the ordinary presence of it. One thing about the sorrow is, that it is known not to be the sadder kind."

"Your mood seems to be one of complete unseemliness," said Gabriel.

"Surely you know what may be covered by a jesting exterior. You speak as if I had not just told you what is covered by mine."

"Is your father's health really failing?" said Gabriel.

"Do you think I would obtain a holiday under pretences?"

463

"Is your father becoming more resigned to your work?" said Josephine.

"He may be: he has always said it would shorten his life; and we must suppose that he is facing his end with resignation. Not that that seems to me a possible thing to do."

"Whom has he living with him?" said Gabriel.

"Some servants who are very attached to him. My father is never rude to a servant."

"Is he rude to you?" said Josephine.

"He has told me that he could not be rude to anyone. So I know he cannot be."

"There must be good in him, for his servants to be attached to him."

"Of course there is good in him. Did you think I would suggest there was no good in my father?"

"Well, you have often referred to his failings," said Josephine, smiling.

"I do not think it is time for remorse yet. It is the dead we do not speak evil of, and I shall treat my father as living for as long as I can. It is treating the old with more sympathy to speak evil of them."

"It is a change for you to feel sympathy with your father," said Gabriel.

"How can you say so? I have always spoken evil of him."

"What is wrong with his health?" said Josephine, in a gentle tone.

"His heart may fail at any moment, or he may live for years. It is very awkward for me. Behaviour is so different for years and for a moment. You have seen what mine has been for years. I think I must pay him a series of short visits."

"Won't he want you to stay?" said Gabriel.

"If I behave as I should for a moment, he can hardly fail to. Unless it is almost too much for him. He would not like me really to shorten his life."

"I don't think your father has any great reason to be dissatisfied with his son," said Josephine.

"I hope you would never think such a thing. My father does not like anyone to criticise me but himself."

"I suppose he will leave you a great inheritance?" said Gabriel.

"Would your plans change, if he died?" said Josephine, almost at the same moment.

"I never talk about plans for after a person's death. And I never talk about inheritance at all. I cannot approve of your treatment of my father."

"You would go to live in your ancestral home," said Gabriel.

"He could not give up the life he has made for himself, for one simply handed down to him," said Josephine.

"That comparison might be made in another spirit," said Gabriel.

"Felix must do the right thing by his own life. That is a serious necessity in itself, apart from any reluctance of mine to make changes in the school."

"Were you reluctant when you changed to me? I did not suspect it. That makes me feel quite foolish."

"Well, I had my moments of anxiety. But while they are having their reward, I see no reason to complain."

"I will tell my father that I have given no cause for complaint. He sometimes asks me if I have, in a manner meant to wound me. I am glad now that I have so much to forgive. It will soothe me very much to forgive it."

"You will return to his house, when it becomes your own," said Gabriel.

"Well, if he returns," said Josephine, swinging her arms, "I shall give up being a slave to the school, that has only to be set on its proper basis, to get upset again. I have been getting tired for a long time of humdrumming along, and this shows that other people are in similar case. I had got so far a week or two ago, as arranging about a partner, but that has fallen through for the time. It will materialise in the end, and I shall be free to come and go with the rest."

"You don't mean that you will give up your work?" said Gabriel. "You have kept all this inner fermentation to yourself."

"People would not allow me to give it up. And I always keep things to myself until they come to pass. But I see that it does not do for me to be pegged down to one place, and make it a jumping-off ground for other people. So you will soon find yourself with a different aunt-sister, with part of her life in the school, and the rest of it elsewhere, wherever it takes its course."

"I hold my breath before coming events," said Gabriel. "And I see my father as the victim of one of them, rather than Felix's. My heart stands still before the thought of his future."

"Mine does not," said Josephine. "He will make his life for himself, as the rest of us do. We cannot check natural progress for people's dislike of it."

"I think my father would like us to in his case," said Felix.

There was a knock at the door, and Helen came into the room.

"My dear, this is kind," said Josephine. "People are not always so ready to confer a favour that is asked for. Gabriel, I have persuaded Miss Keats to spare us an hour sometimes. She is without contemporaries in her own sphere, and you are in the same plight. Shall Felix and I remain with you, or retire?"

"I think we have a touch with young people," said Felix.

"I should be badly off without that in one sense," said Josephine.

"I think I have it in the other sense."

"At what age does one cease to be young?" said Gabriel.

"I shall always be young in heart," said Felix.

"That may be when we cease to be young," said Helen.

"When we are really young, I think our hearts age with the rest of us."

Josephine turned and gave Helen a smile.

"Yes, we are talking about youth in years," said Felix; "I must face it."

"I never think about people's age," said Josephine.

"I often think about it," said Felix; "and hope they show it more than I do, and wonder if they can guess mine."

"I don't think it is a compliment to a man to be taken for less than his age," said Josephine.

"Is it a compliment to a woman?" said Helen.

"I don't think it is, my dear, though I believe I personally suffer from it. I seem never to be accorded the dignities of middle life."

"Surely no one is accorded more dignities than you are," said Gabriel.

"Oh, other dignities. I meant those that definitely pertain to middle age. I hardly take it as a compliment either, though I have not given the matter much thought."

"You and I are so different," said Felix.

"Well, we both seem to have our trend towards youth," said Josephine.

"I think I will go home to Jonathan," said Felix. "I see that Gabriel shrinks from my company, because of my shallow experience. But I shall be able to take him on equal terms when I have lost my father."

"I have lost both father and mother," said Helen.

"Then I think you may take him on equal terms at once," said Josephine. "We will leave you to take advantage of it, leave him to do so rather. I also have lost both father and mother. We all seem to have a bond of that kind between us."

A few hours later Felix was greeting Sir Robert Bacon.

"Well, Felix, you have come to see me die?"

"You told me to come, if I wanted to see you alive,"

said Felix, sitting down by the invalid chair. "So I have come for that."

"Well, I am still breathing."

"I am glad I am in time; I am glad I am not too late. You must see how ill at ease I am in your presence."

"Ah, you may never live to be my age. It is not every man who lasts nine years beyond the three score and ten."

"No, I may miss the years of labour and sorrow. But it is not kind to remind me of it, when everyone wants them so much, and you have just had them. And I think you seem to think less of me for it."

"Ah, people may tell you that you are not equal to your father."

"Well, of course, they will not know that you have told me."

"I daresay you are imagining yourself in my place."

"No, it is you who are doing that. It is not a picture that I should choose to dwell upon."

"You will not escape hearing of the difference between us."

"I don't believe people will be as careless of my feelings as you think. When you came to the concert at the school, nobody let me hear a word of it."

"So it will take my death to get you out of that position?"

"Well, I could not tender my resignation on any trivial ground."

"Well, that will not be trivial."

"No, no, that will do," said Felix.

"My son, we may get to know each other better in my very last days."

"I am sure we shall. I know you better in the very last minute."

"Felix, would you keep a promise to a dying man?"

"Yes. I am one of the very few people who would. Now do you think you know me a little better?"

"Will you promise me to marry and carry on the place?"

"Do you feel that that would be fair to a woman, when your opinion of me is so low?"

"You will be able to offer your wife a good deal."

"I don't think you have a high opinion of my wife, either. As you feel we are so suited, of course we will marry. I am glad that she will accept me, even though it is not for myself."

CHAPTER XVII

"WELL, my only child," said Elizabeth, as Gabriel entered the housekeeper's room, "so you have re-membered again that we are going on with our lives under the same roof? I am not to feel that I am left with nothing of my own?"

"I hope you do not feel that I am nothing. I meant to come to you earlier, but empty lives are always so full. Tell me how you have spent your day."

"I have done my work as usual. Josephine thought it was better for me to do it, or anyhow better for the work that it should be done. And between whiles I sit and call up my courage: I do not let it go. It has held through so much of my life, that it ought not to fail now. But if yours fails, I shall not love you less; I confess that I shall not. No, I know it is Josephine who will take thought that it does not fail."

"Josephine is not the arbiter of my happiness."

"Not, my love?" said Elizabeth, putting back her head in a faint peal of mirth.

"She acquired the habit of doing without me with most unlooked-for ease. We are apart now for hours in the day."

"But those are the hours she takes thought for."

"She disposes of them as a duty. I can give you as many as you like. I am flattered to feel that I am not superfluous in the house."

"Well, of course I should like them, my son. You are all I have; and I gave you all I had. You represent my life to me. And Josephine has had so much that was mine: I feel I must tell you of all she has taken: I cannot carry the burden of bitterness alone."

Elizabeth told the story of herself and Josephine, believing that she knew it to the end.

"Josephine is built on a large scale," said Gabriel. "She is powerful for both good and bad."

"Yes, she is destiny, and we are her sport."

"I should not describe myself as that."

"No, no. It was foolish to use the words. We are only talking of the wind and the way it blows: it must carry the young and tender with it."

"I married in the teeth of it, and it is not such a blast as it used to be. My life is my own."

Gabriel went downstairs at the hour when he expected to be joined by Helen, and Felix overtook him in the hall.

"I have come to keep you company."

"So have I," said Helen. "I hope it will not become more general."

"I don't feel a very fit companion."

"Do you want to feel your loneliness?" said Felix. "Then why not remember that the truest loneliness is amongst numbers? When my father dies, I shall at once seek society."

"Mrs. Napier did not mean us both to be here together," said Helen. "You may do her that justice."

"Which of us would you like to go?" said Felix.

"I will go myself. I am going to sit with my wife's mother, and dispose of loneliness for both of us, now that there is no question of it for either of you."

As Gabriel left the room, Felix came up to Helen.

"Do you feel a faint admiration for Gabriel, for not being embarrassed that his mother-in-law is the housekeeper?"

"Yes, a very faint one."

"Mine is very faint, too. We are much more alike than most people."

"Then we may as well keep each other company."

"I think we had better just keep company. I think my father would wish it. Would you be disconcerted if Mrs. Napier came into the room?"

"Yes, just a little; she would expect Gabriel to be with us."

"That shows I am keeping my promise to my father," said Felix.

CHAPTER XVIII

"I HAVE told your father that we will bring Miss Keats, when we go to dinner," said Josephine to Gabriel.

"She must be tired of being involved in our family life. We have not concerned ourselves with hers."

"She has no family life. You told me yourself that she was an orphan. So do not pretend to be more ignorant than you are; it is a thing that is seldom advisable. Your father wants to give you a companion of your own age, and to set me free for companions of mine. The older men want a word at times with a mature, feminine fellow-creature. And why should I always be the only woman in the company?"

"You must be inured to it by now. I don't know what has come over you of late. You seem to have your being in the clouds."

"Well, we all seem to have our being in some such wise. So I am only in the fashion if I do. And I daresay the clouds will break."

"You are of the wrong age to become unsettled in your life. At once too old and too young."

"Oh, too old and too young, am I? At once too old and too young for a good many things. Other people have noticed it."

Jonathan came into the hall to meet his guests, walking with an old man's step, which had suddenly come upon him, and of which he seemed to be aware.

"My dear sister, my dear son; ah, my dear, you are very kind to us; I should not have ventured to ask you for myself. You are all three doubly welcome. We need a tonic more than you know. You have not heard what has come to us, Josephine? We are at a parting of the ways. You know that Felix's father died last week?"

"Yes, we have heard. May I offer you my sympathy?" said Josephine, giving her hand to Felix. "You must have had a full and exacting time since I saw you."

"Do you not generally feel that my time is that? But it is especially so, when you atone for forty-one years in a few weeks. That is so different from a day's duty for each day."

"You feel you have atoned?" said Josephine in a low tone.

"No; I have found how impossible it is to undo the past. It is odd that people should ever think it is possible."

"Your father was content to die?"

"No. So little content that he could not be told he was really going to."

"Did he not suspect that his end was near?"

"Yes. It made things very difficult for everyone, and of course unbearable for him."

"Content to die?" said Jonathan. "Ah, I must try to be content."

"Well, people are so, under the influence of some re-
ligions," said Fane.

"That is a different content," said Helen. Provision is
made for its being the opposite."

"I suppose your father did not hold any dogma?" said
Fane.

"I should have supposed that he held the dogma of the
Church, as he did."

"His religion was of no help to him?" said Fane

"None at all. He died," said Felix.

"Had he hope for the future?" said Josephine gently.

"No. He had certainty. He told me. But I think he
must have been living in the present."

"People never do live much in the future they are certain of," said Helen. "They live more in the nearer
future, that is known to be uncertain."

"Well, his place will know him no more," said Fane.

"That was just it," said Felix.

"Ah, another place is to know its possessor no more,
Josephine," said Jonathan. "Felix is to succeed his father
in his home. I am an old man to remodel my life."

"That is really your decision?" said Josephine to Felix.

"It was my father's."

"Was it his last wish?"

"That was that he should live to fill it himself. It was
one of his last commands."

"There was an element of real pathos in it," said
Josephine.

"It sounds to me to have been all pathos," said Gabriel;
"to have had no element of anything else."

"Well, he would have been eighty on his next birthday," said Fane.

"Yes, but he was probably not going to have the birthday," said Felix.

"People are often hardly responsible on their death-
beds," said Jonathan.

"I promised not to be influenced by people who said

that. I did not know that I was promising not to be influenced by you."

"No one would try to influence you."

"My father did not know that."

"Of course Felix will spend his life where his forbears lived before him," said Gabriel. "It is what he was born and bred for."

"My father said those very words. He must have been responsible."

"How does it feel to be called 'Sir Felix'?" said Josephine.

"It makes me feel rather inclined to give a faint smile, and inwardly to admire my father for taking it as a matter of course."

"I suppose you will give me a certain amount of notice about your work?" said Josephine in an almost rallying tone.

"He told me to tell you, that I must give it up on his death. But he hoped it would be a good deal of notice. You will do him justice?"

"I was not prepared for quite such arbitrary dealings."

"And I have so often told you things about him, that might have prepared you."

"I thought I was dealing with you, and not with your father."

"It seems extraordinary now, that you should have thought that."

"You are not a man of an independent mind," said Fane.

"I know that people are often taunted for attending to a death-bed wish."

"Now I must have justice as well as your father," said Josephine. "You must allow for my moment of anxiety for my own plans. Your place will have to be filled; but that can be done with all places: I daresay mine could be filled to-morrow. Life has to be a succession of changes. It may be well to recognise that change is good."

"You think that change is good in itself, Mrs. Napier?" said Fane. "Well, I daresay I allow myself to sink somewhat into a groove."

"I sometimes think I have allowed myself to do the same," said Josephine. "It might be salutary to be rooted out."

"How soon shall we come to visit you, Felix?" said Gabriel.

"As soon as it is possible for me to entertain, without disrespect to my father's memory."

"You appear to show more respect for his memory than you showed for himself," said Fane.

"Not more than is always shown to people's memories, compared with themselves. And of course I did not show enough respect for himself. Is not my remorse sacred to you?"

"Yes, yes, we have to be on our guard in our dealings with the dead," said Fane.

"And we may do as we like about the living," said Helen. "It never seems a practical arrangement."

"Well, the dead cannot retaliate," said Fane.

"That is what I was thinking of," said Helen.

"I never feel I have to be on my guard in my dealings with people, alive or dead," said Josephine in a quiet, distinct tone.

"Well, that is a great tribute to you, Mrs. Napier," said Fane.

"You can have us to stay with you, one by one, Felix," said Gabriel.

"Wouldn't that seem like trying to fill my father's place?"

"You will be in your father's place yourself."

"If it will be only trying to fill my place, of course I can have you."

"You are already changed by your position," said Gabriel.

"I do not at all mind your saying it. I promised my father to let it change me at once."

"Most people lose their fathers," said Fane.

"That does seem to me astonishing," said Felix.

"Your pupils will miss you very much," said Josephine to Felix.

"I am so much changed, that I feel it odd that I should have pupils. Of course they will feel it a come-down to be taught by a woman."

"I am sure you do not think that."

"I am talking about what my pupils will think."

"Why do you assume that they will have a woman to teach them?"

"My father told me that no man but me would do it. And what do my personal opinions matter, compared with his?"

"Our personal opinions always matter, if they are honest."

"I don't know that my personal opinion about teaching drawing to girls was honest. It was just in keeping with my whimsical side. It was my father's opinion about it that was honest."

"It is natural that you should feel in that way about him just now," said Josephine.

"You think the feeling will pass? Of course you have had more trouble than I have, and know about it better."

"I know about it only too well."

"You do seem to, rather," said Felix.

Josephine laughed and rose from the table, and stood with her hand on Gabriel's shoulder, courteously waiting for Helen to pass.

"My dear, you are my brother's guest to-night, and hold only that relation towards me. Not that I should not welcome you in any other."

The four men followed the women, Jonathan leading the way, with a gesture of relinquishing on this occasion the talk of his own sex.

"Will you still have a home for me, Swift?" said Fane.

"No, neither for you nor myself, Fane. My evil days have come. But I shall be doing something for my sister's life by joining her; and I have enough for that, without being a burden. And I shall see more of my son. I have little to complain of. No one is less alone."

He went forward into the drawing-room, blinking his eyes.

"This is great news!" said Gabriel. "It atones for the loss of Felix. Have you told Josephine that you do not propose to continue in neglect of your family?"

"No, my boy. You might do that for me, might just say a word," said Jonathan, edging up to him. "I have a hesitation, if you understand me. I have a claim; I know I am claimed. It is enough; and yet I do not deny the feeling. But I will not yield to it. Josephine, you have a place in your home for an old man?"

"For an old man, or a young man, or any kind of man at all. That there is a place for any kind of woman, I have given proof. My house would not be mine, if it could not expand at need. And I welcome a deputy to leave behind, in the event of my visiting pastures new. It will give me a large part of my life for my own, which has been my ambition for some time."

"I hope you will appreciate your post among the ladies, Swift," said Fane.

"He cannot fail to," said Felix. "I know what such a post is like."

"I shall not be among the ladies," said Jonathan. "I shall share my sister's family life."

"I am glad of that," said Felix. "I want my tradition to be something quite by itself. Do you ever have former members of your staff to stay with you, Mrs. Napier?"

"Very often," said Josephine.

"Because if you did not, I could not come. I am going to be more conventional now my father is dead."

"And now it is of no good to him," said Fane.

"I see you cannot understand loyalty to the dead," said Felix. "I should hate to die, if I belonged to you. I begin to understand my father's uneasiness."

"You were never unconventional," said Gabriel.

"No, never: I quite agree. I think it was wonderful how beneath everything I really conformed."

"You have the funeral and everything safely behind you?" said Josephine in a low tone.

"Yes, but I have not used the word, 'safely'."

"You are free to look forward?"

"Yes, but I have not used the word, 'free.'"

"No, no, a funeral is a great landmark in our path."

"Especially in my father's!" said Felix.

"Yes, yes. But your father would not wish you to look back."

"He said he hoped I always should. On our last days together."

"But you will not, I hope?"

"You and he never seem to agree," said Felix.

"I suppose you are really looking forward in your heart?"

"Why do you suppose that, after what I have said? And the heart would be a shocking place to look forward in."

"I mean, you must be making plans for the future."

"No, I am still making plans for the past, and imagining myself my father's comfort and companion."

"That will not have much result, will it?"

"No, but sometimes one likes people better for doing foolish things."

"Are you not indulging in a little self-deception?"

"Yes, and I am finding it an indulgence, and almost feeling that my father is, too."

"Well, you are honest with yourself, anyhow."

"I think you are contradicting yourself."

"Well, that is better than contradicting somebody else," said Fane.

"When the first alternative is Mrs. Napier?" said Felix.

"No, no, well, perhaps not then," said Fane.

"You are both very kind to me," said Josephine.

"Will you walk home or drive, Josephine?" said Jonathan.

"Well, I think we will drive," said Josephine, in a deliberate tone. "Having given up a good many years to economy, I think it is time we adapted ourselves to a different routine. I am a great believer in adaptability."

"It is Felix who will have to show that virtue," said Gabriel.

"Or has he already been showing it?" said Josephine, with an arch expression. "Has his part in the school been the most subtle exercise of it? Ah, there have been times when I have had suspicions. I am not a person whose mind is bounded by the walls of a school."

"Stone walls do not a prison make," said Fane.

"No, I have freedom—in my soul am free," said Josephine.

"Our world is tumbling about our ears," said Gabriel, as they drove home.

"No, it is only building itself up after a shock," said Josephine. "The death of a man in the position of Felix's father was bound to have its reverberations. We must be able to turn our eyes to the future. I am sure Miss Keats is of that mind."

CHAPTER XIX

"WELL, Jonathan," said Josephine, entering her brother's study, "it is a new experience to me to be despatched on errands; but I am too much against becoming set in any one character, to be disturbed by it. The truth is, though I would not say it to anyone; the

479

truth is, Jonathan, that I have got over Simon's death, and
find myself anchorless and rudderless. Well, we must not
be restive under the hand of time. It may have further
changes for the future."

"For those of us who have a future," said Jonathan,
who was rummaging in his desk in a purposeless manner.
"I am glad you are over your trouble; I would not ask to
get over mine. My miss of Felix will be my life."

"You are busy very early," said Josephine, looking at
her brother, who seemed to be restless and uncontrolled.

"Yes, you find me preparing for my last journey. Naked
we come into the world; naked we go out of it. I am not
planning to go with more than I came. I do not feel I
can carry my treasures in my hands; I have not quite so
much in me of the ordinary man. I am preparing for my
last two flittings at the same time. It is the last thing I
have to do for my friend."

"You have not come to the end of things with the end
of one chapter. We must not set ourselves against the
advance of our lives."

"That has to stop some time, or go in the wrong direction. I have no part in the future. You have come to talk
of what has nothing to do with your brother."

"I have come with a message from Gabriel. He insists
on giving up that allowance. You know he found out it
came from you. It has been generous of you, Jonathan;
I have never known how you spared it; and you cannot
spare it in the future. He is right to save you the move
in the matter. Shall I tell him that you make a virtue of
necessity?"

Jonathan stared at his sister, with his hands still, and
suddenly threw himself back in a fit of laughter.

"My dear Josephine, I never gave Gabriel an allowance! I give people nothing. I only take from them. I
thought you knew that."

Why did you say you did, then?" said Josephine in a
bewildered tone.

"I did not say so. He insisted on it. The poor boy wanted to have something from his father; and I wanted, wretched old man, that he should have it. I have not been able to give much to him; it seemed I could give him this; and what was the meaning of it from no one, the good of it from nowhere? The giver would never have made herself known, made himself known—he, she, it—what a silly thing secrets are! They make us solve them somehow. Well, I gave my solution of this." Jonathan went into further laughter, this time it seemed as a cover for his feelings.

"It was an extraordinary thing to do."

"Why was it extraordinary? It served a purpose for two people."

"Did you mean it for a sort of joke?"

"No, it was not a joke; it was a temptation. Why was it a joke to give my son an illusion, that his father had done something for him, one little thing in all his life? You don't understand the pathos of never being able to give."

"Well, what are we to do now? You know who the giver is? It is a woman, did you say?"

"No, I did not; I say nothing," almost shouted her brother. "I do not speak the truth, so of what use to tell you? Of what use to speak at all? You would not be any wiser. When I told Gabriel, he was not any wiser, was he?"

"I am afraid he was not. But what are we to tell him now? He must know that the money does not come from you, as he insists on returning it."

"You would not like me to have it, as it comes in?" said Jonathan, with an openly crafty expression. "To tell him to send it back to me? Was it fair to take me by surprise? To behave as if you did not know me?"

"Come, pull yourself together. Tell me what you wish me to say."

"Oh, say that the money comes from you. Say that I

began to give it and stopped, and that you continued it. That sounds true to life and character. Or say that you always gave it, and did not like to seem to give so much. That saves my face, and ends my concern with the matter."

"We must say something. We can hardly admit either the truth or the mystery. Gabriel might talk about it to Felix and his other friends."

"Well, say that then. Have the credit for yourself, and understand how I felt in trying to get it."

"It is a funny person I have for a brother, to be sure. What are you doing, making that mess and muddle? Are you stirring up your papers or sorting them?"

"Stirring them up, stirring them up!" cried Jonathan, sweeping the pile together, and causing some to flutter to the ground. "Stirring them up for the bonfire! The past may have what is its own. Let my dead things go before me."

"You are not in a mood to make a decision. So we may as well give your account for the moment," said Josephine, picking up a paper and toying with it, her eyes down. "One story is as good as another, when neither can be true. This is a familiar writing, Miss Rosetti's, from a long time ago. A hand does not change any more than a face; or it changes like a face, becomes older and remains the same. Gabriel will have no need to speak of this, Jonathan. I will explain our joint thought of him, and he will be grateful."

"I shall have his gratitude after all, shall I? We shall both have it, you more out of proportion than I." Jonathan spoke in a harsh manner, glancing at the paper.

"Miss Rosetti might have been my partner by now," continued Josephine in the same conversational tone; "but she had some reason against it; some question of money, I suppose. I may offer to give her a partnership; why should we go through life doing nothing for our friends? This note has no beginning or end." Jonathan moved his hand towards it, but withdrew it and gazed at the ground. "The writing is clearer than her writing now. The words stand out apart. 'Gabriel is safe for life, and I will no longer see him as mine. That is best for all of us. This is my very last word. Maria'—Maria! Maria Rosetti! What is this, Jonathan? Had Miss Rosetti anything to do with Gabriel when he was young? Did she know him then? Tell me it all."

"Of course she knew him then. She is my old friend, as you know. She had some thoughts of adopting him, and changed her mind."

"Did she ever adopt him? This sounds as if he had belonged to her. Tell me the truth." Jonathan was sitting with his shoulders hunched, his eyes looking straight before him, his body still. "He was only a few months old when I took him; and she came to me soon afterwards. Is this what it seems to be?"

"I know nothing; I say nothing. As you know my words mean nothing, why ask me?" Jonathan plunged his hands about on his desk, drumming his feet on the ground.

"Your wife never existed?"

"You have never believed she did exist. To pose as knowing less than you do, is not the way to get to know everything."

"You pretended to be a widower for Gabriel's sake?"

"And for my own sake, and your sake, and the sake of your girls' school. You did not want me to do anything else, did you? If you had an alternative, why did you not offer it?"

"I see you could do nothing else," said Josephine, in a quiet, charged tone. "But you could do something else than put Maria Rosetti into my house; to watch me in my life with Gabriel; to spy on my dealings with him; to satisfy herself that he was safe; while I, your sister, went on my way, unwarned, watched, in danger. You could have done something other than this, Jonathan."

"No, I could not, to serve my double purpose. It was the only thing that could serve it. Why should I not put them both in your house for you to look after?" Jonathan laughed and drew with a pencil on his desk. "You have served yourself and Gabriel and her and me. Surely it was a good thing that you should serve us? And if you had made her your partner, it would have been a good finish up. It is a pity that you did not see your way to it, before her position changed, before she changed her mind."

"Oh, that is it!" cried Josephine. "I see it all. Miss Rosetti gave the money to Gabriel! She saw the chance at long last of doing something for his future. And I think it was time. If you want a finish up, this does very well."

"I am glad it satisfies you; I should have preferred the other myself. It would have been better for her, and through her better for me; and Gabriel would have got as much from you in the end." Jonathan's voice fell away again into laughter. "Well, you know all my story now. I can be at ease in your house. If I want a word with Maria, I shan't have to hide it." He moved his fingers as though he were playing the piano, and moved his lips as if in song.

"Tell me about your earlier life with her."

"No, I will not," said Jonathan, shutting his lips. "When have you asked me about my life with Gabriel's mother? I was a widower to you, wasn't I? It is not worth while to change my habits now. I will prepare myself for the long silence."

"Why did you not marry her? I suppose Gabriel is really your son?"

"Oh, know it all, know it all," said Jonathan, banging down his hands. "Gabriel is Maria's son and mine. She did not want to marry me. She wanted to support herself; and I did not want to support her. I put her in your school to work for herself, and, as you have said—it seemed to me a natural thing—to watch over her son.

She has not watched over him. She saw he was safe, as you say, or she saw nothing. If she did not look, she would not see. I don't know why she came to his help over his marriage. When I asked her for money, she did not often give it to me."

"She has lived in my house, as Gabriel's mother, deceiving me, letting me give her my trust, treat her as my friend——"

"She has never lived in your house as Gabriel's mother. You have never treated her as a friend. She has worked in your school and earned your trust."

"I must see her," said Josephine, drawing herself up. "I must tell her simply, that there are some things on which I cannot turn my eyes."

"Yes, tell her that simply. Turn her out and keep her son. I don't mind what you do. She has not cared for Gabriel; we have agreed never to speak of him; I could not bear her words of my son. She can have my money to live on, and I will live on you; I don't mind living on a woman." Jonathan moved his hands and feet together, adding the pedals to his performance.

"What are we to say about the allowance? Gabriel can never know the truth."

"Keep to the account we settled on. Take something else from his mother."

"I have borne that from her, which no woman should bear from another," said Josephine, in slow, recitative tones. "I do not speak of her having a child; I would not speak of her in that matter, except as another woman should speak." Jonathan raised his eyes, with a movement of snapping his fingers. "I have my own understanding. I could sympathise with her there."

"Well, sympathise then; because I could not; she has repelled my sympathy all along the line. Well, who comes here?" Jonathan turned to the door with his pipe set jauntily between his teeth. "So, Felix, it has come on me at last! It has come out at the end. We need never think to escape the end, of life or anything else. This is an end indeed." He made a motion towards the paper, and Felix took it up and turned to Josephine.

"You have had an experience that comes to very few," he said.

"Yes—yes, I have. I have to do my best with it. It is a revelation to me, something new. Well, I must try to do my best." Josephine suddenly spoke to her brother.

"So Felix has always known the truth?"

"Of course he has known. We could not have lived on the terms we have, with our tongues tied on our memories," said Jonathan, with simple testiness. "He has not known what we were talking of before, what you know now." His voice grew loud and hard. "I mean about the boy's money! But he may know. Another thing between us won't make much difference."

Josephine laid her hand on her brother's shoulder.

"He will not want to know. He will leave it between the brother and sister. He knows that that relation goes back to the beginning; that it is the longest, if not the deepest. He will leave it its own silences." She paused and turned to Felix with an uncertain smile. "I find myself in a difficult position, in a hard place. I cannot at the moment see my way."

"I could see mine in your position, the position of knowing something against someone who knew nothing against me. I should enjoy showing a quiet freedom from superiority. That has no point when you are really free from it. I have a great respect for you."

"I must do my best. It is a real experience. I must remember that it is real for someone else. Yes, there must have been much reality. There may be temptations to which I would not yield. I trust I shall not betray any littleness, any inclination to the use of power."

"I trust not: it would kill my respect."

"Well, my brother, I will leave you for to-day. The times of our separations will soon be of the past."

"Until the long separation," said Jonathan in a deep tone, giving his sister his hand without raising his eyes.

"Until death do you part," said Felix. "Those words remind me of something to do with myself. May I come and see you later in the day, Mrs. Napier? People are so much easier to deal with, when their own lives are disturbed. We have to watch for the time and take advantage of it."

Josephine stood as if arrested for a moment, and then rather blindly gave him her hand and left the house.

"Your influence over my sister is good, Felix," said Jonathan, speaking on the instant.

"But it does not seem to have had much effect on you. What is this about Gabriel's money? I don't claim not to be curious: I beg you to tell me."

"Maria gives it," said Jonathan in a nonchalant tone, his lips twitching. "I knew I was safe. If she had heard that it came from me, she would not have betrayed me, or been surprised. But it is a good thing that you are leaving me, Felix; you want a fitter companion."

"We all come round to my father's views in the end. What will Gabriel say when he knows?"

"He is to think that Josephine gives it; that I came to her rescue over her giving too much," said Jonathan, his smile broadening. "We can make quite a useful world out of our imagination. I don't know why falsehood does not do as well as truth."

"It often does better; that is why it is used instead." Felix broke off, and the two friends went into laughter. "I always wondered how you got the money. I like to think I have been the intimate of a bad man."

"Well, you have a future of innocence before you. It is not for me to disparage any kind of future; I have none."

"I wonder if I can be innocent without becoming ordinary. I see you think it is impossible."

"You are bound to become more ordinary. Your father wins in the end. I must not grudge him his victory."

"Indeed you must. I do want to feel that I leave empty hearts behind."

"Well, we will make the most of our last days. I will not cloud your looking forward with my looking back."

"How do you know I have been looking forward? I thought I had concealed it."

Felix locked his arm in Jonathan's and danced across the room. The old man fell out in a moment, stiff and breathless.

"Ah, there is a parable! I have gone far enough at your side. I can go no further."

CHAPTER XX

JOSEPHINE went home, walking rapidly, seeming excited and upheld. She reached the library and remained for a while by herself, and then sent a summons to Miss Rosetti. As she unfastened her bonnet and cast it on a chair, she saw it with a new sense of its significance. She took it in her hand, and perceived Miss Rosetti coming towards her, with her eyes upon it, as though she guessed her train of thought. Something resolute and braced in her bearing revealed her sense that the moment had its meaning.

" My dear," said Josephine, hesitating after the phrase, as though she had hardly brought herself to use it, and moving her hand towards the other woman's shoulder; "I have sent for you to tell you that I know it all; the meaning of your life with me; the meaning of my life with you, under your scrutiny. My poor brother betrayed it; in innocence; do not blame him. I came to understanding in innocence; do not blame me, more than you have had cause to blame me during my twenty-four years before your judgement."

The other met her eyes with an almost humorous expression, that implied that she had not herself rehearsed a speech.

"Will you now tell me your story of your own life?" said Josephine.

"There is nothing left to tell. My early years I have described to you; my later ones you have seen; the few in between have been betrayed in innocence—that is, completely betrayed. Few of us should reveal the whole of our history, and you and I are not of the few. It is not through the fault of either of us that ours has been revealed." There was a pause, and then Miss Rosetti continued in quick, almost careless tones. "I have said that there is nothing to tell of my life, but there is one thing that I will tell. I have not cared for Gabriel; I have cared in my way for the women whom one by one I have tried to care for; and I have come without trying and almost without knowing to care the most for you."

"There is the money you gave to Gabriel," said Josephine, with almost a threat in her tones.

"I hardly know why I gave it. I suppose from some sense of pity, duty—some sense of atonement." Miss Rosetti made a gesture as if perplexed at herself. "It is given: I will not take it back."

"I would not ask you to do that; I would not so far violate your human feeling. I am wondering what else to ask of you, what to ask of myself that some solution may be found for us. Have you enough affection to give to me"—Josephine showed no surprise at the other's admission—"to take the partnership in return for what is given to Gabriel, and so given to me? Because, although he is your son, he is mine. Will you give me your answer? On that matter you must know your mind."

"Yes, I have enough feeling," said Miss Rosetti in a slow tone. "I see that the money is in a way given to you. I refuse to be even a name to Gabriel. And you and I have each looked at the other's hidden side, and looked away; and that is much." She paused, and as Josephine was silent, resumed in her usual manner. "I shall be grateful to have my share of the school, interested to use it. It will satisfy my ambition, satisfy my human side; for I have come to love it. It would seem to some people a small ambition; but I am content with it; it is mine."

"Then you are my partner, and I am yours; and we will live our partnership in our lives, observing it in thought and word and deed." Miss Rosetti knew that on some things there would be silence. "We begin our new life from this moment."

"It will easily cease to be new to me; it is my natural life; my happiness depends on women."

"I think with me it has been the other way round," said Josephine, causing the other to give her low, deep laugh before she knew it.

The two women seemed to be easy with one another, with their permanent ease.

The younger voices were heard in the hall, and Josephine seemed to brace herself to sustain a shock.

"Here are some of our young companions! Well, two of them young, and one approaching our own age. We will say a word to them as the partners that we are. I am glad of this practice in going into partnership; I have seldom met an experience that has not been grist to my mill."

Miss Rosetti stared at Josephine, several expressions succeeding each other on her face; and shrank back as Helen and Gabriel and Felix entered, as though in recoil from the coming scene.

"Let me introduce you to my partner," said Josephine, in an almost triumphant voice. "In every capacity but that, you already know her. It is to her that you should address yourselves; there is no reason to turn your attention to me. Not that I also do not accept congratulation. Both for my partner and for the coming freedom of my life I accept, nay, demand it. I am almost disposed to become a sleeping partner, and establish Miss Rosetti in my place. So you see, it is indeed to her that your words are due."

"Words are due also to my partner," said Felix. "I also accept, nay, demand congratulation. And I also am disposed to become a sleeping partner, and establish her in my place. I am sorry that your satisfaction cannot equal mine; but I am in that foolish state when we think that no one's experience can compare with our own."

Josephine looked from him to Helen, as if she hardly followed his words. Afterwards she seemed to remember hearing her own voice, coming after a crash and through the ensuing din.

"Why, what an interesting piece of news! Did we expect it, or did we not? I can hardly say for myself: I have been too much occupied with my own partner to think about other people's. How egotistic that sounds, when it is the first time I have had an engagement in the school! It quite marks a stage in its development. And I am in a position to give a recommendation to you both. That is one happy side of it for me."

"I am not sure that the development is on the right lines," said Miss Rosetti, with a natural liveliness. "We shall have the school meeting the fate of over-developed things, and neutralising itself."

"What can Felix have been thinking of, when his thoughts should have been on his work?" said Gabriel.

"And what have you been thinking of, to let him get the better of you?" said Josephine in a sudden, startling manner, which she at once controlled. "Well, I am glad I have a partner, who can take a firm line about such proceedings."

"It is too early for Miss Rosetti to take lines," said Felix. "It will be a long time before I behave to Helen as her husband. And I don't think I shall ever behave as my father's son. He said I should not. I can hardly tell you how sensitive and gradual I shall be."

"Well, I can tell you what I shall be, and that is far less idle than I thought, in the future," said Josephine. "With two of the people I depend on deserting me, I shall have to put my energies back into the school. Miss Rosetti will be justified in insisting upon it."

"I don't think Miss Rosetti is behaving well," said Felix.

Josephine turned a smile upon Miss Rosetti, who was regarding her with a look of simple admiration.

"Do you think of being married soon?" Miss Rosetti said to Felix, pushing the truth at once to its extreme for Josephine.

"Well, it is hardly worth while to learn to manage my house, when I shall so soon endow Helen with it."

"You take your marriage vows literally," said Josephine.

"There is no other way of showing that you are keeping them. When people have kept them in other ways, I should never have guessed it."

"Well, tell me the worst about your intentions."

"The worst is that Helen has to wait, until a relative's house is free for her to be married from. She has no settled home."

"I should have remembered that: I blame myself that you have had to tell me. I cannot claim that this house is her home, as she has been here so short a while; but if she will be married from it, I shall appreciate the feeling it will prove. She will not be the first or the second, and I have always appreciated the feeling."

"I should be most grateful, Mrs. Napier," said Helen.

"Grateful? My dear, why?"

"I hope I did not seem to be hinting," said Felix. "Not that I am a person who cannot be under an obligation."

"There is no obligation here. And if there were, I should be too used to it to reckon with it."

"Did your father know of your intentions, Felix?" said Gabriel.

"He told me he wished me to marry, and I am sure he did not think I should disobey him."

"He gets more and more fortunate in his son."

"And I in my father. He simply thought of everything."

"I think we are all fortunate in each other," said Josephine, taking a step away from the group, as if feeling her presence were due elsewhere.

Helen and the men withdrew, and Miss Rosetti came up to Josephine.

"Do you still want me as a partner?" she said in a blunt, rather ruthless voice.

"Why, what a question! I want you more than ever. And you are already my partner; so the question cannot arise. With yet another vacancy on the staff to fill, we shall indeed be dependent on each other. I cannot have you talking so out of the spirit of your place. And you know Miss Keats better than I do, and will be able to tell me her youthful desires. She may hesitate to impart them to me: I make no claim to your gifts with young women." Josephine's tones seemed to fail through some lack in the feeling behind them. She caught the eyes of her companion, and, starting forward, fell into her arms, and the two women stood locked in their first embrace.

Josephine freed herself and hastened from the room, to be met and checked by Gabriel.

"My boy?" she said, with something of her old tone.

"Did you give my message to Father? Have you his message for me?"

"Yes, I gave it: I did not fail you. His answer is, that the money never came from him. I was to tell you that, as his message; and I can tell you myself that I fully sympathise with what he did. You may assume that the money comes whence you will; or you will be wiser and assume nothing."

"Tell me the truth," said Gabriel.

"There has been no change in the arrangement, peremptory young man."

"You always gave it! As well as the other! You did well to be ashamed. So that was the mystery. And Father —Well, poor old Father!"

"Yes, your poor old father, my boy! My poor old brother!"

CHAPTER XXI

"IT is a rule that women should not appear on similar occasions in the same clothes," said Miss Luke, coming downstairs dressed for the wedding. "Well, someone must play the part of the exception that proves it."

"I have a varied wardrobe," said Miss Munday.

"Well, I have been brought nearer to that state than for some time," said Josephine. "I am not forgetting my last *faux pas* in the matter of wedding garments."

"It is a pleasure to see you out of your widow's dress, Mrs. Napier," said Mrs. Chattaway.

"Then I am glad I am out of it on this occasion; though it will be a pleasure to me, or a relief rather, to be back in the habiliments in which I am at peace with myself, in so far as a sense of what I am wearing has any effect upon me."

"You are not going back to them?" said Mrs. Chattaway.

"My poor, suitable, useful garments! What a tone to take! I am living in other people's lives to-day, and not in my own. As I said, I have had a lesson on indifference to the bridal mood of others."

"You are that rare thing, Mrs. Napier, a truly considerate person," said Miss Luke.

"Yes, I am completely considerate, in this one small matter, on this one small occasion; great occasion rather, as it is great to other people. That is not much to do for my friends. And as I am to give the bride away—Sir Felix was clear that that was my prerogative; he seemed to think the position nearly as important as her own—I want to look as fully in sympathy with the moment as I shall be feeling. No doubt I made that demand on others when I was a bride."

"It is something to have been less exacting in one's life," said Miss Luke.

"I think that romance must have passed me over," said Miss Munday.

"It is sad that Miss Keats has no parents," said Mrs. Chattaway.

"Now that was not at all the speech to make at that juncture," said Josephine. "Yes, I have felt it sad; but I think less so on this occasion than on others."

"Do you think that the pair are suited to each other?" said Mrs. Chattaway.

"I trust so; indeed I trust so. I don't know why I should use such vehemence, except that my connection with the occasion hardly requires the enhancement of remorse."

"Ah, it was you who brought about the marriage?" said Miss Luke.

"I wonder if we have prompted things as often as we think we have," said Josephine, almost in soliloquy. "It may be that we are carried with them. Well, these things are as they are."

"They no doubt have the impression that they have been independent agents."

"Yes, yes, surely," said Josephine, putting a touch of anxiety into her tone.

"The wedding will bring back the other wedding to us all."

"Now," said Josephine, "you must not let it. You must

yield yourself to the moment. Believe me, I shall not find that effort harder, that I have friends making it with me."

"Mrs. Giffard and Gabriel are in the heroic place," said Miss Luke; "play the heroic part."

"Mrs. Giffard is not playing any part at all; I thought it better that she should not. Especially when I found that Gabriel was willing to attend the wedding; glad indeed to do his duty by his friend, but glad also, poor boy, of the break for himself. That perception might have given her an heroic part; but I thought of it in time for her."

"Ah, we must not forget the difference between maturity and youth," said Miss Luke.

"Well, I think my friend must, on this occasion. I hope I have contrived that she will. And here is our bride, coming downstairs with Miss Rosetti! I wonder which of them looks nicer in her way, and which way is the better? Sh. does Miss Rosetti great credit! I see I was wise in not offering my own help. I admit I felt rather maternal and interfering, but I controlled my impulses. Well, my dear, this is the first and last time in your life that you will look like that. And I have an odd confession to make, one that will seem to you very odd. You bring back to me my own wedding day and wedding dress, though I was much older than you when I became involved in such things. That must be my excuse for the insistence of the memory."

"I have never imagined myself a bride," said Miss Munday.

"Oh, I have; oh yes," said Miss Luke, looking straight about her. "It took me some time to set into myself. Mrs. Chattaway did not leave the matter to imagination. So, Miss Rosetti, we have only to await your confession."

"I have never imagined myself a bride. I tried to, and found that I could not. Your carriage is waiting, Mrs. Napier."

"Now, my dear," said Josephine to Helen, in an almost regretful voice. "It is time for you to offer yourself up as a sacrifice. Yes, there must be something of that in it for the woman; but we do not regret it; no, we do not. No, you lead the way, and I follow: I am in the man's place, and must not fail in chivalry. And I don't think any feeling is more suitable"—Josephine looked back to the other women—"in an elderly woman toward a young bride."

"No, it is not, it is not," said Miss Luke, looking after Helen. "Well, we must soon be following. We are able for the part of spectators."

"Of course, Mrs. Napier is not elderly," said Mrs. Chattaway; "but she does look older than usual, which is odd, as she is in lighter clothes. No doubt the other wedding is in her mind."

"The other weddings, yes," said Miss Luke.

"The gift from the girls has come after all," said Miss Munday. "Perhaps it can be presented after the service."

In course of the reception in the concert hall, this token was carried by the youngest girl to the bridal pair.

"Is this for my wife and me?" said Felix. "We really feel it is too much, but, of course, we can do nothing but simply accept it. I will make the speech of thanks myself, because I feel I shall make it better, and not because I think the man should take the lead.

"We are the more delighted with the gift and the inscription, that we were beginning to be afraid we should not have them. We knew that you would not offer us wishes by themselves, would not ask us to accept only empty words, would not say that it was feeling that counted, and not material things. It would be absurd to say that a thing like this does not count. We are only sorry that we almost misjudged you; we feel we should have known you better, and now, of course, we do.

"And am I to make the mistresses a separate speech, or have they joined in the same gift? I knew there was some explanation of its being so good; I saw at once that it was no ordinary gift; that is why I was curious about it.

"Now I know that my worldly goods belong to my wife, but surely this does not belong only to her. A thing with this inscription cannot possibly be called worldly; and I will keep my share for myself.

"We have both been very happy amongst you, doing our daily work for the best kind of reward; not that we mean any disparagement of the gift. And I hope that you will never forget your old drawing master, and that when a different one comes, you will never feel he is the same.

"You know you have taken us quite by surprise, and so you have proof that I speak on the spur of the moment; and I feel that is a good thing, as it does need proof."

As applause ensued, and Felix left his place, Miss Luke ran up to him.

"There is a small token coming from us by ourselves, Mr. Bacon. You need not fear we have forgotten you."

"I did not really fear it. I should not be clever at others' expense, especially at yours. I have only been clever at expense to myself."

"We are sorry that our small remembrance is so late."

"I hope it was not an afterthought?"

"No, no. We claim for it all the value that comes from thought and feeling; though not much of any other kind."

"We will try not to mind," said Felix.

"May I congratulate you on a charming speech?" said Josephine.

"I was afraid you were going to congratulate me on my marriage, and opinions differ so much more on speeches. I am sorry for the hint of effort about mine; I had no time to make it spontaneous."

"Do you know, I find it odd to think of you as a family man?"

"I don't think the words quite give me."

"You came to the family state yourself, Mrs. Napier," said Miss Luke.

"Yes, I did. I have admitted to-day that the occasion has stirred my own memories."

"Are you dressed like this in sympathy with them, or with us?" said Felix.

"With you. In sympathy with them, I dress as I generally do. I fear it shows that we live for ourselves more than for other people."

"I don't think that needs showing," said Felix.

"Well, anyhow, you will not see me in these clothes again."

"Why not?" said Gabriel. "They will surely wear for longer than Felix's wedding day."

"They will wear for several years, as the best garments of the woman to whom I propose to send them. At least I am afraid they will."

"What will you wear when you come to visit Helen and me?" said Felix.

"The things you generally see me in, or replicas of them."

"Oh, I am sure they would be replicas. But it is getting out of sympathy with us very soon."

"Well, I cannot live always in other people's lives. I shall not expect you to live in mine, and assume a sable array."

"Well, you are safely married, Miss Keats, I should say Lady Bacon," said Fane. "No one can take that from you now."

"Do you believe in one standard for the man and another for the woman?" said Felix.

"No, no. But it is the lady we think of on these occasions. There are more on which the men have to be reckoned with."

"That is so untrue," said Felix.

"Yes, I think that on the whole women are accorded the human interest," said Josephine.

"Now I wonder if there is a difference," said Miss Luke.

"I have been wondering why people are supposed not to enjoy their wedding day," said Felix.

"I was very happy on mine," said Josephine.

"Yes, yes, I think it would be a happy day," said Miss Luke.

"Well, I daresay you chose your life of your own free will, Miss Luke," said Fane.

"I was helped a little towards it by poverty," said Miss Luke, giving no further account.

"Well, that is not so much of an admission," said Fane.

"I am enjoying my wedding day more than I thought," said Felix.

"Well, Miss Rosetti, we can give you congratulations of your own kind," said Fane. "The partnership is what has come to be important to you. And it is important in itself. Oh, yes, it is."

"Now, if you want to catch your train," said Josephine, in a mellow tone.

"Good-bye; good luck; long life; health, happiness!" said Fane.

"All those things and more," said Miss Luke.

"Good-bye," said Miss Munday.

"We are glad that you are not as sorry to go, as we are to lose you," said Mrs. Chattaway.

"I think they are a little sorry to go," said Josephine, looking gently from Felix to Helen. "I mean in the midst of their other feelings."

"It is not in the midst of them," said Felix. "It has ousted them: I am afraid it will overcome us."

"Then we will not prolong the moment. Good-bye, my dear; I am not going to say anything of all that goes without saying. But as I have been in the position I have, you will treat me accordingly and let me hear."

"We will write to-night, Mrs. Napier."

"Oh, no, you will not: I have no intention of being

such a burden. If you write in a week, that will be about
what I ask. I am not anxious about you in safe hands."

"Well, we have had our vicarious glimpse of romance,"
said Miss Luke.

"Yes, we have lived through it, Josephine," said Jonathan. "Ah, I do many things for my friend. You have
not had to put the force upon yourself that I have. Well,
I shall soon be coming to your house to die."

"No, I have been able to give myself a free rein, certainly. But the pleasant occasion will be spoiled, if you
choose it for talk of that kind. And we have not been so
entirely out of sympathy with you; we have our own
little regrets."

"Yes. Things will never be so amusing again," said
Mrs. Chattaway.

"No, I do not think they will. Not just that," said
Josephine.

"Well, I suppose the next thing will be the christen-
ing," said Mrs. Chattaway.

"Well, I hope not quite the next thing," said Josephine,
with a laugh. "And I am always a little sorry when the
first deflection of feeling comes."

"Poor child, she has all the future before her," said
Miss Luke.

"She would pity us for having so much less of it," said
Miss Rosetti.

"Yes, yes, but I know," said Josephine to Miss Luke.
"The compassion of maturity for youth."

"It is quite nice to hear your cynical view, Miss
Rosetti," said Mrs. Chattaway. "You have been silent to-
day."

"A wedding strikes no chords in my heart."

"Oh, it does in mine. Oh, yes, it does," said Miss
Luke.

"I cannot think of a pair more suited to each other,"
said Mrs. Chattaway.

"No, neither can I," said Josephine, "in the sense of

striking, as it were, the same note. We certainly must not
pin our faith to the attraction of opposites."

"I can just imagine their conversation," said Mrs.
Chattaway.

"Now I don't know," said Miss Luke, with her head
slightly on one side. "Does Mr. Bacon like an audience?"

"He will have the audience he likes best," said Mrs.
Chattaway.

"Now that is too pretty to dispute," said Miss Luke.

"Which of the two do you regard as the more attractive, Mrs. Napier?" said Mrs. Chattaway.

"Well, on a wedding day the bride surely carries all
before her."

"You are looking tired, Mrs. Napier," said Miss
Rosetti. "You have been filling too many characters, even.
for you."

"I am ashamed to say that I have been filling one
character, and that my own. I have already made the
admission that the day's proceedings have raked up my
own past. Well, I will go and divest myself of these trap-
pings, that no doubt do make an odd set-off to my experienced phiz. You are accustomed to seeing me attired
in harmony with it. I promise you that when we next
meet, it will not suffer from the force of the contrast.
Well, it has been my sacrifice to the occasion."

"It had not struck me," said Miss Luke; "had it struck
any of you—that Mrs. Napier is a tragic figure?"

"Yes, it had struck me," said Miss Rosetti, idly.

"She would be, if she were not so strong and masculine," said Mrs. Chattaway.

"I should not call her masculine," said Miss Rosetti.

"No, perhaps she is too maternal," said Mrs. Chattaway. "But the feminine type is often quite as strong."

"Yes," said Miss Rosetti.

"I think we might call you masculine, Miss Rosetti,"
said Mrs. Chattaway.

Miss Rosetti was silent.

"Miss Munday and I can only claim to be neuter," said Miss Luke.

CHAPTER XXII

"WHAT time does our late employer arrive, Helen?" said Felix, entering the drawing-room in his own house. "As I do not keep my least thought from you, I confess that I hope she will be impressed by what she sees. That is really my least thought. I have no other quite so small."

"I have one smaller. I hope she will suffer a personal pang."

"Must you have one as small as that?"

"Yes, I must, because of the thought you do keep from me. You can't pretend that you did not suspect the truth."

"Of course I pretend that I did not suspect it. Would you have me behave in a natural manner?"

"You need not improve on yourself when you are with me."

"I meant that for the height of sensitive chivalry."

"It was anyhow the height of self-esteem."

"The very height. I could only just attain to it. But chivalry rises out of esteem for others, even less than other virtues."

"I almost admired Mrs. Napier, when she proved that the truth did not exist," said Helen.

"I am going on with my chivalry," said Felix. "What could she do more than give us proof? The odd thing is that none of the other women gave us any truth to suspect. Eligible bachelors are not prepared for life as it is. They ought to be trained quite differently."

"Most of them were older than you."

"Yes, but that was not their reason. They did not need

any reasons. Their attitude to me was the same as mine to them; and that was much less natural than it sounds."

"I am not the person to explain it. I showed the natural attitude."

"I should not mind, if they had not been sensible of my charm. But they were sensible of it, and yet they did not want to spend their lives with me. I think they must have thought that charm was not everything. So they were content with their lives as they were, though the neighbours here would never believe it."

"I was not so content."

"It will be wiser to give the impression that you were. Doing something derogatory is better if you enjoy it. It is a mistake to think it would be worse. Of course it would be best to have done nothing at all."

"Neighbours don't seem to hold the Greek view of the nobility of suffering."

"Neighbours are English," said Felix.

"There is no disgrace in honest poverty."

"You can't really think that. There is no point in being too Greek."

"Well, there is none in useful work."

"You can't separate the two things," said Felix.

"No. No one calls wealth honest, though its honesty is above the average. It is like talking about the dignity of grey hairs."

"You put me in mind of Jonathan, though his grey hairs have no dignity. I hope we shall be able to carry off his visit. It is more awkward to meet the person you have lived with for twenty-three years, than it sounds as if it would be."

"He knows your feeling for him will never change."

"He knows it is changing. Things are easier for us, for being put into words. And I daresay they are easier for him than we think. They so often are."

"Did he feel your leaving him less than you expected?"

"Yes; I almost thought it would kill him. I suppose I

was just going to let it. Engaged people are supposed to be selfish, and I think this shows that they are. But he is still looking forward. He has a wonderful hold on life."

"People have. What kills them is their own death, and not the loss of anyone else at all."

"Yes. My desertion never killed my father. What killed him was his own heart at seventy-nine."

"There is the carriage!" said Helen. "We must hasten to the hall. If we let Johnson announce them, it will look as if we were conscious of our new position."

"As if we thought living in a family home with family servants different from teaching Latin and drawing in a school. It would never do to seem to think that. And I really do not think it, as much as many people."

"I wonder what difference we may be conscious of?"

"Of being everything to each other. It does not seem suitable, when we greet our guests; but it is what they will expect of us."

"Well, my bride and bridegroom!" said Josephine, coming up the steps in full and fresh garb of widowhood. "I have managed to get away to pay my visit. It has not the most spontaneous sound, but 'managed' is the word. With this house on your hands, you will understand the demands of mine."

"My boy, we see you in your proper surroundings at last. We do not grudge you to them," said Jonathan.

"That is shallow of you, after only five weeks. My father comes out better and better."

"'Ah, well, your father was your father," said Jonathan, moving forward with a steady, deliberate tread and a roving eye.

"You never used to think that," said Felix. "I used to wonder that you did not see it."

"Ah, blood is thicker than water," said Fane.

"I used to think water was thicker," said Felix. "And I am sure Jonathan did. But if he has changed his mind, so have I."

"Well, you will both have new duties to take the place of the old," said Josephine, allowing herself to glance round for the first time.

"And it won't be all duty, if I can judge by the look of it," said Fane, having already judged by this means.

"You don't any of you understand the value of leisure," said Gabriel.

"Oh, do I not understand it?" said Josephine. "I had been making plans to get a little more of it; but they have met the fate of the majority of human plans. I have been sucked back into the vortex. I need not have thought I could extricate myself."

"Does not Miss Rosetti make a difference?" said Felix.

"Indeed she does. Indeed she must, being as she is, being as you remember her. But the difference seems to be absorbed somehow in the oncoming force of things, in the flood of progress. In a word, the school is growing."

"But it was not put in a word," said Helen to Felix.

"You are getting accustomed to your new form of address, Bacon?" said Fane.

"Yes, but I find it is not true that pleasure is blunted by custom."

"It is after all a superficial difference."

"I seem as if it were no difference at all."

"Well, I should not like to change my appellation," said Josephine. "I have found doing so once quite enough."

"I have no prospect of changing mine, as I happen not to be heir to a title," said Fane.

"Is the temporary drawing mistress as popular as I was, Mrs. Napier?" said Felix.

"No, I think she is not," said Josephine, meeting a question with the simple truth.

"Are the men generally more popular than the women?" said Gabriel.

"I think women in life are more popular," said Felix. "I often hold unusual opinions."

"Do you know, I think they are?" said Josephine.

"It is not an unusual opinion," said Gabriel.

"Well, I still hold it," said Felix. "I do not change it. Mrs. Napier, we are a little hurt that our places have to be filled."

"Your places will not be filled," said Josephine. "No one who makes a place his own, leaves it without leaving also his own void. And you must remember that you neither of you went at my request."

"Oh, of course we were not dismissed," said Felix.

"I did not tell you at the time quite how much I regretted you."

"Ordinary people would have chosen that time to tell it," said Helen.

"I thought it might cloud your going forth," said Josephine simply. "But I am prepared to admit it was unimaginative to fancy you would give a thought to it."

"We always give thought to things," said Helen. "People always do, really."

"Why not leave the wedded pair to their mutual regard, Mrs. Napier?" said Fane.

"I never mind telling people my good opinion of them."

"I have never met another case of it," said Felix. "I don't wonder at Fane's surprise."

"You have not had all the praise you could do with, in your life?" said Fane.

"I did not know people ever had praise, except from Mrs. Napier."

"Well, I have had very kind things said to me on occasions," said Fane.

"I have met great generosity in thought, word and deed," said Josephine.

"I have met it in deed," said Gabriel.

"You have, young man," said Fane, moving towards him and lowering his voice. "I should have offered my congratulations, if I had felt that the matter came within the bounds of comment. In my mind I have done so each time an instalment of your dues has left our office."

"It is a roundabout way for them to come, when their source is in the house."

"Oh, you know it now, do you? The mystery is out?"

"Yes, it is out. And I am betraying no scruple in benefiting by a woman's toil."

"Now I think that is wise. I congratulate you both upon your good sense and your good fortune. A man must have his own views about being the slave of convention. You have come to the decision that gratifies both yourself and your benefactress. Though she is no relation of yours, she is an old friend of your father's, and your aunt's partner. She has not many claims upon her resources. To my mind you have nothing to be sensitive about."

Gabriel was silent, suppressing the words that sprang to his lips.

"Her business affairs are in our hands, in common with those of most of the people in the neighbourhood. Not every woman is as capable of being her own lawyer as your aunt."

"Of course the fact that I am aware of this truth, does not mean it is to be public property."

"My dear young man, you are talking to a partner in a reputable legal firm," said Fane.

"Do you get on well with your household?" said Josephine to Helen. "A new mistress is the object of a critical regard."

"Helen passes every test," said Felix.

"Well, I should find it go rather against the grain to face all the responsibility under the cloak of ease. I would rather have the responsibility naked and unashamed, as I am used to it."

"People despise responsibility less under a cloak of ease," said Felix.

"That seems to me a strange view," said Josephine.

"And yet it is almost universal," said Felix. "How long can you all stay with us?"

"I must go back to-night, as I have told you. I go because I am needed, and for no other reason."

"We did not expect that you would go because you could not bear to be here," said Felix. "You have not made things any better."

"Things are bad, as I have explained. I hoped for more ease and leisure, and see no prospect of them. You, who are more fortunate, ought to pity me."

"Ought we to pity people who have less leisure than we have? I used to be rather annoyed with people who did that. When my father warned me that I should be an object of pity, I think he meant me to be annoyed."

"Well, I am content with my lot in life," said Fane, "though I also am called back to-night by my duties. May I offer you my escort, Mrs. Napier?"

"You are feeling settled in your new surroundings, my dear?" said Josephine to Helen, as she adjusted her cloak. "I should be so glad to feel that, before I leave you."

"I am not feeling so very settled yet."

"It will come, it will come," said Josephine, letting go her cloak to place her hands on Helen's shoulders. "I remember my early restless time. Believe me, it will pass, and the other time will come."

She embraced Helen with simple affection, and took her leave of Felix with almost indifferent friendliness.

"We were too homesick to be at our best, Helen," said Felix.

"Yes. Seeing Mrs. Napier made us feel terribly out of it all."

"We ought to ask the mistresses to visit us."

"But it might bring on the first feelings. It will be braver to settle down into our new life, and remember it is all we have."

509

CHAPTER XXIII

GABRIEL sought his father as soon as the guests had gone.

"The truth is out about Miss Rosetti. I am not going to tell you how. I am tired of being helplessly involved in mystery. But I ask an explanation from the beginning. It is clear that you and Josephine must know."

"My boy, you have had a shock," said Jonathan, looking at his son with simple compassion. "I never meant you to have it. I thought the truth would never come out. At one time I hardly could think it, but when it had been hidden for twenty years I saw it as safe." Gabriel stared at his father, closing his hands. I don't know how it has come to you now."

"It is time it all came to me. Whatever is to be known, I demand to know."

"My son, I owe you complete confidence. But is there anything I need to say? You ask for an explanation from the beginning. But there is only the beginning. Soon after you were born, your mother gave you up to me. There was nothing further between her and me, or between her and you. She offered nothing to either of us, would have taken nothing. I had my friends, and my sister gave you a mother's care. I did, as your father, what it was in me to do. You have seen that that too was almost nothing. But things have worked out as well for us, as for many fathers and sons. I have not lost your affection: I have never deserved it, perhaps never had it: but I have not lost it. And I hope I have had it in a measure; I have had much for you."

"And the allowance comes from my mother, from Miss Rosetti? That is as I have been told?"

"Yes, yes, the allowance. Oh, the allowance! Yes, that came from your mother, my boy; I was at a loss to explain it. Josephine came to my help at last. Ah, well, you have an odd old man for a father."

"Father, I am not going to say or listen to another word of the past. I can hear it all from Josephine. But there is the future to be thought of, both for you and for me. We cannot live, either of us, in Josephine's house. Things would be too much for all of us, when ignorance had given place to silence. There would be too much silence, and too much underneath. The relation between you and me is anyhow open to the world. We will set up a home, and ask Ruth's mother to manage it. I will get some work, and we shall have enough between us. I could not face a life with my adopted mother, and my actual mother, and my mother-in-law, all under the same roof."

"My boy," said Jonathan, in a broken voice, standing with his hand on his son's arm, looking almost childishly into his face, "this is a great release from hopelessness. I could not face it even with courage, the life with the women. I should not have had human happiness enough for self-respect, for human dignity. A man's dignity must have gone beyond hope. I should have lost it; I was losing it. Some of the consequences have fallen on you. And that poor creature, your wife's mother, is sadly placed in Josephine's house, with her daughter dead, and Maria gone over to Josephine. I have known what it is to lose a friend. It is I who should help her; I have not lost my child. I will ask Felix and his wife to keep me until my house is found. I shall not burden them for long. I have my plans for my future."

He seemed to push his way from the room, his head bent forward in eager purpose.

"My dears, I have come to beg a favour, to ask you to shelter me for a time. I know it is what you have looked for, but it is not asked in that spirit. I am at a loose end only for the moment. My plans are made. My son and I are to set up a house together, and I want a roof over my head until I have my own."

"What is your reason for the plan?" said Felix. "Please tell me exactly."

"Oh, there was a reason that started it. But we feel we shall be in our right place in a home together."

"We might have come to the conclusion before," said Gabriel. "The real reason is, that I have stumbled on the truth about my mother. I suppose you have always known it, Felix?"

"Well, you have always known about my parents. I am not a person to avoid the subject of parents. So pray do not let us avoid it now."

"It is less embarrassing to lose a parent than to gain one."

"Yes, I quite agree. I gained my father at the last, and it was much more embarrassing than losing him. Does Mrs. Napier know the truth?"

"She knew just before she made Miss Rosetti a partner," said Jonathan. "Ah, she is a noble creature, my sister."

"It does not trouble me that my parents were not married," said Gabriel.

"Well, I should think not, my boy. That would be a silly thing," said Jonathan. "It might have happened to any one of us."

"Not to me," said Felix. "I must do justice to my father's memory. Will you speak of it to Miss Rosetti, Gabriel? I would not ask that, if I could bear not to know."

"I shall speak of it once, and then never again," said Gabriel.

"I am upset that you are thinking of the future, Jonathan," said Felix, turning quickly from Gabriel. "I took it for granted that you would always think of the past. I thought I should break up your life, and I seem to have done nothing to it at all."

"Ah, healthy lives pull up. They have their resilience, like all healthy things."

"I did not know that your life was healthy; I thought you had a morbid attachment to me."

"Ah, I have been attached to you. But you have filled

my place, and I must even fill yours. And I shall rejoice to fill it with my son. Ah, that is the natural tie."

"Of course it is. But you wanted an unnatural one. And I have kept your place for you, and carefully put Helen in another."

"Ah, well, words of that kind are words."

"But it is kinder to say them. Mrs. Napier said she could never fill my place, though she had filled it even temporarily. She said that Helen and I would leave our voids. And I had kept a void for you. I don't think you ought to neglect voids. My father was always talking about mine. And to think that I gave you the preference!"

"Ah, well, it was your own choice. I did nothing about it."

"You always did everything about it. I wish my father were here to support me. There is a saying that marriage alters friendship, but I never knew its real meaning."

"Mrs. Napier will miss you, Gabriel," said Helen.

"No, not so much. Ours was a case where marriage altered friendship."

Gabriel returned the next day to Josephine's house, and went at once to the library, where she and her partner were together. Miss Rosetti's presence on the scene of so much of his experience seemed suddenly to weld itself into the material of his life. As he stood in the doorway, she lifted her eyes and gave a startled glance from him to Josephine.

"I think my position is unique," said Gabriel, striving for his usual manner. "But I do not find that any assistance in dealing with it."

"It may be unique," said Miss Rosetti, looking at him with a faint smile. "It is certainly an unusual position, both for you and for me."

"I have come to say that I know it all," said Gabriel, his mood broken, and his eyes swerving from Miss Rosetti's face to Josephine's; "the whole story of my life from the beginning. I should have been glad if I had never known;

but as the knowledge has come, I must do my best with it."

"I hardly know what that need be," said Miss Rosetti. "I too wish you had never known, and I too must do my best with your knowledge. That will be to do nothing. It will make no difference to you or to me. You seem as if you had suffered harm, but you have had great kindness in your life. Many people have done their utmost for you. I have done it, and will do it now. My utmost is to tell you that I am glad that you cannot see me as your mother. When I gave you money, it was to your wife that I gave it: I cannot bear the thought of hardship for a girl. When she died, I could not see how to withdraw it; but you need not fear; it is withdrawn. Mrs. Napier discovered the truth, and offered me the partnership in payment. She felt it was given to her, as it was given to you. So it comes from her, as you have understood. You see how matters are between us."

"If you say that my knowing the truth will make no difference, it must make none," said Gabriel.

His mother did not speak.

"I shall give up the money, of course, both for the future and the past."

"Yes, I suppose you will give it up. I shall be glad enough to have it, and put it to my own use; for one thing a share of the school on normal terms. I thought you would never come on the truth: there was no reason why you should come on it. I do not care if you pay back what you have spent; it will not count more with you than with me."

"I stumbled on the truth. No one has betrayed a trust."

"No, no. I am sure the standard of human behaviour has been high. I do not see myself as a person who need doubt it."

"How are we to meet in the future? I have not said what I should have thought it natural to say; but I must just ask that."

"We seem to be quarrelling already," said his mother, with a smile. "But we shall not have much more chance. We shall meet as we have always met. And we have not met, have we?"

"You have done much for me," began Gabriel.

"That is enough," said his mother. "Surely you have understood?"

"It was hard on Josephine," said Gabriel, in tones of forced lightness, "to be compelled to shoulder my peculiar liabilities."

"It may have been hard. She did not seem to find it so."

"Well, curious young man, have you finished your inquisition?" said Josephine. "If so, run away and sort your thoughts, and leave two experienced women to do the same by theirs. We can meet again later, with all the questions to be asked and answered."

"Josephine, I cannot live at home," said Gabriel, looking at Josephine as if Miss Rosetti were not present. "It would be too much on me, with all this underneath. I could not know it, and not know it; I could not live one life, and live another, hidden by it. We should all be defeated by our common effort in the end. We should be enduring the strain of a double life; and we are people who find a single strain enough. And my father cannot live his last years with all the complications of his youth. He and I are going to take a house, and ask Mrs. Giffard to manage it. That will solve another problem that is not solved here."

There was silence, while Josephine faced the alternative future; a future with Gabriel and Gabriel's mother living and knowing each other under her roof.

"My boy, you must do your best for yourself; your best for those whom you have taken into your life. I know from experience that that is a long, long duty. You have not found me fail in it. You may go and follow my example, if it comes to you that that is to be the final form for the bond between us."

515

As Gabriel left the room, Miss Rosetti turned to Josephine.

"Well, you have heard me speak as a mother, and you will understand that I shall never speak as one again."

CHAPTER XXIV

"I HOPE I am not presuming on your friendship in assuming that I am still welcome?" said Josephine, coming with some hesitation round the door of the common room. "I am ashamed of being so tardy in expressing my gratitude for my partner; but between making the partner of one of you, and a bride of another, my time has hardly been my own."

"The rest of us you have left as we were," said Miss Munday.

"Yes, and I am glad I have. I must have some of my friends in their old relation to me: I have not altered mine to them."

"We are proud of supplying the partner," said Miss Luke; "and of supplying the bride, too. Oh, yes, we are proud of that."

"Yes, I have altered it to that extent," agreed Josephine. "My debt is greater."

"Is Miss Rosetti happy in her higher sphere?" said Miss Luke.

"Higher? In what way is it higher?" said Josephine.

"Oh, I only meant in the spiritual sense."

"I should say that teaching is spiritually a higher work than organising. You meant perhaps in a conventional sense?"

"Yes, perhaps I did. Well, that is a very real sense."

"I don't think 'real' is the word," said Josephine, with a slight frown.

516

"But organising is what you do yourself, Mrs. Napier," objected Mrs. Chattaway.

"Yes," said Josephine.

"It is Miss Keats who has moved to a higher sphere," said Mrs. Chattaway.

"And in what sense?" said Josephine.

Mrs. Chattaway did not say.

"You are losing your nephew again, Mrs. Napier?" said Miss Luke. "This time deliberately allowing him out of your care?"

"I could not help it," said Josephine, putting out her hand as if to repudiate criticism. "I had to teach him at last to recognise my brother's claim. I have always had that duty in front of me. They say that things are never as bad as we expect; but I can't say I found it in this case. Well, it is over now."

"Mr. Swift will not join you here?" said Miss Munday.

"Yes, he will, if I am not careful. That is what he will do, unless I provide for him elsewhere. It seems a natural arrangement; but there are reasons why I feel it is not suitable for him, and perhaps for others. My brother is, if you will not misunderstand me, very much of a man."

"We will not misunderstand you," said Miss Munday.

"You saw Sir Felix and Lady Bacon happy and settled in their new home?" said Miss Luke, breaking in rather hurriedly.

"Well, I flashed upon them, and flashed back again. I saw them happy, I think, but hardly settled. You are right that it seems a new home for him as well as for her. They still seem to be looking out of the haze that envelops the newly wed. I remember too well being obscured by it myself, to feel disposed towards criticism."

"It must have been hard for your nephew to see the married happiness."

"Yes—yes, it must have had its element of hardness. I

thought of it for him when I felt the call on my own memories."

There was a silence.

"We miss Mr. Bacon's and Miss Keats' bright retorts," said Mrs. Chattaway, as though explaining some want felt in the atmosphere.

"Yes," said Josephine, "there was a great element of brightness about both. That is what I meant by saying that there was a haze about them just now. The brightness is somehow a little dimmed. Unless it is that their new atmosphere is less fostering to it."

"Do you mean that they are less happy than they were?"

"No, I do not mean that at all. I should not have chosen that way of stating it; if it had struck me, which, I am glad to say, it had not."

"Do you know that someone once said," said Mrs. Chattaway; "of course you do not, it is too foolish a piece of gossip for your ears, but someone said that you—you and Mr. Bacon—that Mr. Bacon and you wanted to marry."

Josephine looked at her with a courteous expression and made no reply.

"You are surprised at my repeating it?"

"Yes, I am a little surprised at that."

"Of course I should not have done so. But it seemed such an idle rumour, so utterly meaningless, that it seemed hardly to matter."

"In short, its sole point was that it could be repeated," said Josephine, smiling. "It does not matter in the least."

"There was nothing to prevent Mr. Bacon's proposing to any or all of us," said Miss Luke.

"Well, there were things to prevent it," said Josephine. "Our ages, our being settled in professions, other things."

"I wonder which it was," said Miss Munday.

"Whichever it was, it did its work," said Mrs. Chattaway, her eyes on Josephine.

"We were talking about Sir Felix and Lady Bacon's surroundings," said Josephine. "They are beautiful, and they struck me as suitable to both. If my personal feeling is for something more tonic, more productive, it may be that I am influenced by my own prosaic history."

"Would you like to marry a man shorter than yourself, Mrs. Napier?" said Mrs. Chattaway.

"I liked to marry a man taller than myself, as you know. I am not polygamous, polyandrous, whatever the word may be."

"Mr. Bacon was very much moulded by his background, considering how long he had lived away from it," said Miss Luke.

"I think the moulding was a little conscious," said Josephine, drawing in her brows. "Did you not think so? That it would have been a freer, a more spontaneous development, if it had come about of itself?"

"I always thought it was wonderful how he adapted himself," said Mrs. Chattaway. "Of course we cannot know how far it went."

"I am in need of your advice," said Josephine, in a detached manner. "Do you think that Sir Felix's post would be better filled by a man or a woman?"

"Would you be able to get another man?" said Mrs. Chattaway at once.

"With the growth of the school, the post would be suitable for anyone suited to it," said Josephine, gravely answering her true meaning.

"Oh, yes, of course; I know. I only meant——"

"You are mistaken in what you meant," said Josephine.

"I suppose you would not consider a man for Miss Keats' post?" said Mrs. Chattaway, attending simply to her own position.

"As it is a resident post, there is hardly a question of that," said Josephine, scarcely accepting the improvement.

"Dear, dear, the days pass, and our places are filled," said Miss Luke; "and we feel that they are particularly ours."

"I feel I have been using words vaguely," said Josephine. "My feelings are the opposite of value. Two different people will take places that will be determined by themselves."

"And you will have Mrs. Giffard's place to fill as well," said Mrs. Chattaway. "I don't mean, of course, that you can fill it. You will have it on your hands, to cope with in whatever way you decide."

"Well, I think I shall fill that place," said Josephine, causing Mrs. Chattaway's face finally to fall. "I don't see anything about the way in which it has been discharged, to preclude the measure. I am not going to claim that I regard all places as equally well filled; I have too much respect for due apportionment of credit."

"Mrs. Giffard has had to meet many demands from her own life," said Miss Luke.

"She has," said Josephine, "and she has met them fully. And I have met the result with the understanding of one who has felt similar temptation, and all but yielded. But I am not going to exalt the yielding; I can only sympathise with it."

"It will be an ideal solution of her life to keep house for your nephew," said Miss Luke. "It will seem in a way to give her daughter back to her."

"Yes, I think it will in a way seem to do that. There was a moment when I think she rather felt he was taking her from her. But he is in the rapid, youthful stage, and would be about on the point when he should yield her back. The experiment should work."

"She will not expect him to have sent down deep roots in so short a time," said Mrs. Chattaway.

"He is too young a plant for deep roots," said Josephine.

"Will his living with his mother-in-law prevent his

marrying again?" said Miss Luke, in a tone of by no
means repudiating life.

"Yes," said Josephine; "I think it may for a time. But
time is plentiful in youth."

"Is it wise for Mrs. Giffard to give up her work, if she
may need it again?" said Mrs. Chattaway.

"She will never need it again: I have seen that she is
not fit for work."

"You are a wonderful friend, Mrs. Napier."

"If I am told that so often, I shall begin to believe it.
And it surely is not good for us to think we are wonderful."

"Ah, it is a great privilege to give," said Miss Luke,
laughing as she ended. "It must be, I mean."

"Is it?" said Josephine. "I believe I have not found
it anything but a rather prosaic matter of course."

"Your life will be lonely in the future, Mrs. Napier,"
said Mrs. Chattaway.

"Yes," said Josephine; "as it has been since my husband died. But I shall be glad to spare the people the
sight of the loneliness, who believed they prevented it,
dear ones that they were. The effort not to show it made
my life something of a strain. It will be a relief to be
free from it."

"Now, we shall resent your stealing Miss Rosetti, if
she does not cure those feelings," said Miss Luke.

"Yes, that is healthy," said Josephine, not missing the
intention. "And, do you know, I believe she may cure
them? I have even felt myself that she may. I assure
you that I have found myself turning my eyes to the
future."

"We have not realised all you have been through, Mrs.
Napier," said Mrs. Chattaway, perhaps feeling more con-
trition than she deserved.

"Well, I hope not. The heart on the sleeve is not
correct, is it? And I am doing my best to convince you
that much of it, that some of it, is behind."

"Have you engaged successors to Miss Keats and Miss Rosetti?" said Mrs. Chattaway.

"I have offered the posts to two women, who have accepted them."

"Oh, that is exciting," said Mrs. Chattaway, receiving the impression of a simple affirmative. "We shall have two new companions. It will almost make up for our loss."

"Yes, I think in a way it will," said Josephine; "I think it should. We should give people every chance in a new life. Those who are leaving us have it, I hope, in theirs. They too are succeeding others."

"Would you say that the newly-married couple are very devoted?" said Mrs. Chattaway.

"Yes, very devoted in their way," said Josephine, rising. "But there seems to me something hard and bright about them, something hard and bright about their relation. I hardly know how to put it. They are like agate, beautiful and bright and hard."

"Agate is a beautiful material," said Mrs. Chattaway, uncertainly.

"You will not use words upon what we have dealt with without words?" said Josephine, in a low, very rapid tone, going to the door.

"No, indeed we will not, Mrs. Napier," said Mrs. Chattaway, hastening after her with politeness as prompt as her comprehension.

Josephine returned to the library, and encountered a maid coming out of it.

"A gentleman waiting to see me in the drawing-room, Adela? I am quite innocent in causing him to wait: I proceed from one claim to another with all the despatch I can."

"Someone come about the post of drawing master," said Miss Rosetti. "Shall I see him for you?"

"No, I must even do my own business. If I fail to keep my drawing master, I must submit myself to the onus of getting a new one. I hope this one will not be frightened by my sombre figure. He can see, anyhow, that I have no husband to protect me; people are hardly prepared for the masculine element when they come to a girls' school. Not that it is reasonable to object to it, when they are masculine themselves. Well, I will go and do my best with this male aspirant to my post."

I. Compton-Burnett's A Family and a Fortune *and* More Women than Men, *published in England many years ago, have never before been published in this country. They are two of the most brilliant and accomplished novels by one of the leading novelists of our time.*